THE UNHAPPENING OF GENESIS LEE

Shallee McArthur

Sky Pony Press
New York

Visit our website at www.skyponypress.com.

10 9 8 7 6 5 4 3 2 1

Manufactured in the United States of America, September 2014
This product conforms to CPSIA 2008

Library of Congress Cataloging-in-Publication Data is available on file.

Cover design by Erin Seaward-Hiatt
Cover photo credit Thinkstock

Paperback ISBN: 978-1-5107-1537-0
Ebook ISBN: 978-1-63220-229-1

Printed in the United States of America

Book group questions, Common Core teacher discussion guides, and behind-the-scenes bonus content can be found at www.shalleemcarthur.com.

To Danny

For giving me the motivation
For providing the inspiration
For encouraging the perspiration
For being my relaxation

Aishiteru

A memory is what is left when something happens and does not completely unhappen.

—Edward de Bono

1

An awful thought, a life removed…

—Alfred, Lord Tennyson, *In Memoriam XIII*

The Low-Gravity Club pulsed with music and memories.
Chinese techno-trad blared from the speakers, the rhythm thrumming inside me like a delicious double heartbeat. I stood just inside the club entrance and swayed my hips, tuning my body to the beat. And trying to tune *out* the other rhythm in the club. Memories. The inaudible buzz of a hundred different lives, like an earthquake in my brain.

Every Mementi in the club bore a perfect recollection of their existence inside their Link beads. Hundreds of Links. Lifetimes of memories within them. The Links wrapped around gloved wrists and bulged under long sleeves and scarves. Always present, always hidden.

Cora stepped out from behind me and wrinkled her nose. "What are we *listening* to?"

"It's Destinations Night," I hollered over the thumping bass. "Welcome to Hong Kong, chica!"

I spun in a gleeful pirouette, taking in the full circle of wallscreens glowing with a city skyline half a world away. Clusters of buildings reached toward murky clouds. Their light cast rainbow streaks on the lapping waters of Victoria Harbor. A wooden boat with dragon-wing sails—a *junk*, my Hong-Kong-born grandpa had called it—sliced through the colored sea. Like a magical kingdom we in the Arizona desert could only dream of.

Cora waved a gloved hand at the packed club. "This is number two on your list? Take earplugs when you go."

I rolled my eyes. "I'll put them on my packing list when I leave in, oh, like, never."

Mementi didn't leave Havendale. This was the only place we belonged.

People around me headed toward the low-grav dance floors, their movements staccatoed by neon strobe lights. So many of us in one place, more than I'd ever seen. The buzz of memories behind my forehead surged and drowned out the music.

And for just a second, I wished I dared to go somewhere the Link buzz *wouldn't* be a constant reminder of who I was—and who I was supposed to be.

"I'm beginning to doubt the brilliance of this brilliant idea," I said. "I swear the whole town is here. I can barely think with the buzz this strong."

I tugged at my long gloves, making sure they hid every inch of skin. One accidental touch with any other Mementi, and we'd glimpse each other's memories. The insistent pounding of music in my head became a shudder.

Cora shimmied her shoulders at me, laughing. "Don't think. Dance!"

I ran my hands over my outfit: gloves, scarf, long sleeves, leggings. Everybody here wore the same touch protection. Nothing to worry about. Technically. But all of China wasn't as crowded as a club full of Mementi, no matter how far apart we danced.

Still. Dancing the night away on the streets of Hong Kong… even enduring this mob was worth that.

I turned to Cora. She stood on her tiptoes, scanning the throng with a hopeful expression. Too hopeful.

My eyes narrowed. "You aren't by chance looking for a particular someone, are you?"

She ignored me.

I groaned. "Kill me now. If this whole plan was just to hook back up with Dom…"

She whirled, a wicked gleam in her eyes. "There will be no re-hook-uppery tonight, my friend. We're on idiot patrol."

"Uh, I'm on dance-to-crazy-Chinese-music patrol."

"Oh, there will be dancing. It just needs to be done in front of Dom. Where he can watch all night, then watch me walk away, and see exactly what he can't have." She flashed a sneaky smile.

I laughed. Now *that* was a plan. "I love you when you're devious. One problem, though. How are we supposed to find him in this horde?"

"I'll text him again. He said he'd meet us at the door, but, well…it's Dom." The hint of a scowl crossed her face.

Great. The couple-storm was brewing already, and he wasn't even here yet. Visions of twirling in a low-gravity Hong Kong gave way to nightmares of playing referee. A memory of my last encounter with the happy couple played in my mind. A double date. A disappearing Dom. An irate Cora when we finally found him watching a life-sized holo-cast of a soccer game instead of ice skating with us.

The Link bracelets spiraling up my forearm kept the memory sharp, and I focused on a specific moment. I could feel the skates pinching my toes, the chill of the ice rink raising goose bumps on my arms. Each word that Cora yelled, each flimsy excuse he'd retorted with, the number of times she'd blinked away the tears when he'd called her a controlling shrew.

Yeah. And then *he'd* broken up with *her*.

I tugged at the short blue skirt over my black leggings and thought up half-a-dozen nasty names I'd never call Dom to his face.

Cora's phone buzzed. "He bought us drinks and saved us a table. We can meet him there," she reported.

I waved at the dozens of occupied tables. "That narrows it down."

She bit her thumb through her glove. "Not in the Mementi section. The only table he could find was at the back. On the Populace side."

"You've got to be kidding me."

My gaze drifted to the left, where the club churned with near-violence. A girl flipped her long hair and pushed the guy next to her, knocking him into a couple locking lips in the middle of the floor. People elbowed others aside and squeezed through too-small spaces.

Short skirts, bare heads, and exposed shoulders. Not a single Link bead gleamed in the strobe lights. Populace. Their memories still lived in their brains. If you could call it living, to have your imperfect memories fade like colors in the sun. Bleed out of you once a moment had passed, leaving you with a sad kind of half-life. I clutched the Links around my wrist—the perfect entirety of my life—gratefully.

Of course, Populace also didn't pass memory through touch. I was safe from them. Despite all that *skin*.

"He is so not worth that," I said to Cora.

"Making him feel like a complete and utter loser is worth anything."

I gave her a dubious look.

"Come on, Gena, please?" She raised clasped hands in mock pleading. "He wouldn't have sat there if it was dangerous."

My opinion of his ability to be smarter than your average goofball was not as high as Cora's. Maybe not every Populace was dangerous, but one of them was a thief.

A Link thief. The person who did what no one in Mementi history had ever done: stole entire lives. One moment, you'd have your entire life at your fingertips—the next, your mind would be empty, grasping at a past you no longer had. Family, friends, private moments that had made you who you were, all taken away. No future, because you had no past. All because of one terrible Populace with a grudge against Mementi, or maybe a mad desire to experiment with our Links, or a sick fetish for taking lives and watching his victims stumble in the dark. No one was quite sure which.

"No way," I said. "Not for Dom."

Cora bit her lip, then raised her eyes to mine. "We held hands, you know," she said softly.

"*What?*"

"Just once, through our gloves," she said quickly. "Not skin to skin. The night before we broke up."

She'd trusted him enough to touch him, and he'd dropped her twenty-four hours later? No wonder she couldn't let him go. Every time she thought about him, that touch had to be the first memory that came up. Feeling that moment of extreme trust even in the midst of his betrayal.

Oh, he was going *down*.

"We could walk back on the Mementi side, then cut over," I said, forcing confidence into my voice. "The Link thief never strikes in crowds. And nobody's seen him in practically two months."

Two months had seemed a lot longer before this conversation started.

I yanked my sleeves over my blue vine-patterned gloves, giving my Links a double layer of protection. "Let's go make your ex-boyfriend feel just how ex he is."

"I knew I loved you!" Cora squealed. She adjusted her bright yellow shirt and patted her new sheer scarf, making sure it covered her head and wrapped her neck. "Am I good?"

Underneath her scarf, Link beads threaded a net woven through her dark hair that trailed down the back of her head, becoming a necklace. A dangerous look, to flaunt her memories that way. Just the kind of thing Dom would like.

"You are a walking psychological kick in the pants." I grinned. "He'll wish he never dumped you."

She sauntered ahead. "I think he already does."

We stepped into the throng. The crowd on our side flowed in smooth precision, everyone passing on the left and nodding to acknowledge each other, a good two feet of space between each person. We reached the back and stopped at the same time, facing the anarchy a few steps away. I teetered on the edge of the invisible divide between the crowds. *Get a grip, Gena.* Just because the Populace hated us for being better than them didn't mean they'd throw us off a cliff or something.

With head held high, I crossed into Populace territory. And actually, my stomach did feel like it was falling.

Cora followed so close behind me I started getting paranoid, but none of the Populace even glanced our way. I noticed a few—a very few—other Mementi in the crowd. Some of the rebel-types liked the appeal of the Populace's inability to see our memories through touch. A Populace boyfriend meant a lot more…physicality, with a lot less commitment.

Finally, I spotted a letterman's jacket draped over a chair. Dom's jacket, but no Dom. Three soda glasses waited for us on the table. Hot and sweaty already, I gulped down half a glass before a bitter aftertaste caught up with me. I gagged. Must be one of his weird "suicide" soda combos.

Cora frowned at the empty table. "Jerk. He said he'd be here."

"Are we surprised?" I said. "He probably never left the floor."

The group at the edge of the dance floors shifted as we picked our way through. I peered down the fifteen feet to the low-g pits. And I'd thought it was crowded up here.

Throngs of people bounced and loped in surreal patterns— slowed by the low gravity and quickened by the colored strobe lights. It was a mass of heads and arms and the occasional full body when somebody flipped in mid-air. Holo-projections flitted among the faceless dancers: a sinuous dragon, hovering Chinese lanterns, an explosion of fireworks. I couldn't wait to get down there.

Cora grinned. "Let's go piss him off."

She threw herself off the ledge, arms flung out to catch the flashing colors. She drifted like a falling leaf. The dancers parted as she touched down, giving her the requisite two feet of distance.

Two dance floors for two kinds of people. On the higher-g floor below me, the Mementi bobbed in place. Definitely more than I'd ever seen here. Not a hint of flesh showed from this angle. Bubbles of space kept the touch risk to a minimum. Still a risk, though. One my parents would kill me for taking.

Which kind of heightened the thrill factor. And the fear factor.

The lower gravity in the pit on the left attracted the Populace. They leaped in crazy patterns across the floor. Two barely dressed people collided in mid-air, their momentum spinning each other around. Dancers thrashed in tight groups, grinding skin on sweaty skin. Oh my yuck.

I edged to the right. The driving pulse of the music welled inside me, finally, finally overpowering the Link buzz. Let Cora piss off Dom. She was good at that. I was going to live a dream the only way I dared. A familiar shiver of anticipation started at my feet, tickling toward my throat. I bounced on my toes to prep for the jump.

Three. Two. One.

I launched myself from the ledge with a spin, a shriek escaping as I dropped. Pinpoints of light whirled into streaks. A time-lapse photo of the stars engulfed me. I tipped my head back and drank in the dizziness.

My spin slowed, then stopped. I touched down and took a bounding step that ended in a wobble. Holographic soap bubbles swam around me as the world continued to twirl, and twirl, and twirl. Weird. Dizziness from a spin never lasted long for me.

I took a flying leap forward, soaring for a moment between magical floating lanterns. I landed, off-beat with the music. Where was the beat? I swayed a little—not on purpose. Step, tilt. Tilt some more. My shoulder brushed dangerously close to someone's back.

Crap. My one chance at number two on my list, and I had to go lurpy.

With a huff of frustration, I bounded to an escalator that led up to the tables, trying not to bump into anyone. Tilt, wobble, sway. Maybe it was the extra strong Link buzz tonight?

Nauseated by my skewed vision, I collapsed into a chair at our table.

"What's wrong?" someone asked over the music.

Dom sank into the chair next to me. His teeth gleamed in the now-orange strobe lights. Like a jack-o-lantern. A sweaty, obnoxious one. Of course he had to show up *now*.

"Not feeling so hot," I yelled back. I took a sip of the half-empty soda in front of me. Still gross.

Dom put his gloved hand over the top of the glass as I set it down. I frowned and pulled it away.

"You, uh, may not want to drink any more of that." He adjusted his usual baseball hat over the shaggy hair that hung over his high collar. "Here, take this one."

He reached across the table and handed me another glass. The cup wavered in front of my eyes. My brain shuddered through memories, trying to make connections. The nasty tang of the drink on my tongue…the world lurching around me…and…

Dom's mouth quirked up on one side.

And that. The half-guilty grin he wore every time he got caught in a prank.

"You spiked the drink!" I slammed my glass onto the table. Soda splashed over the side, seeping through the thin fabric of my gloves. My favorite gloves. I glared, and he began to laugh.

"You *spiked the drink?*" Cora appeared next to my chair, hands on her curvy hips. A glower darkened her tan face, perfect shades of make-up outlining the angry, almond eyes that had entranced half the boys in school. Link beads glimmered in her deep brown hair.

I'd hated Cora, once. When we first met in dance class, for being so pretty. Until I loved her because she was funny and crazy and as needy as a kitten. And flashy—putting Links in her hair to show off.

Maybe if I put Links in my hair, I'd get some attention too. I'd only inherited non-exotic Asian features from my dad—black hair and flat chest. Maybe Cora would help me dye a blue streak in my hair like I'd always wanted. Why had I never asked her before?

Wait. Wasn't I mad about something? I stared in confusion at my drink.

"Look at her," Cora yelled. "What did you put in there?"

"I—well, it's not my fault. It's a new cocktail mix, Sweet and Strong." He tugged at his black gloves. "I guess it's as strong as it says. I thought it'd be funny to leave it here and see which one of you'd have a little extra fun tonight."

"She's never had a drink in her life." Cora crossed her arms over her brilliant yellow shirt. "You idiot, I will punch you in the face."

Dom finally lost his smile. If he'd ever had a chance of winning Cora back, it was gone. Take that, Mr. Clever.

"Relax." Dom rummaged in the pocket of his jacket. "I came prepared."

He tossed a small packet toward me, but I missed the catch. The packet landed on the table.

"I don't feel good," I muttered. Wasn't drinking supposed to make you feel good? "I think I'm broken."

Cora sighed and ripped the packet open, dropping a small pill in front of me. "Take it, Gen. You'll feel better."

The pill skittered in my vision like a tiny cockroach. Ew. "What is it?" I asked.

"Clairtox. A de-intoxicator."

I grabbed the pill. Nope. Missed. I slapped a hand over it, trapping it, and put it in my mouth. My head throbbed as it melted on my tongue. The rhythm in my head didn't match the pounding beat of the music, which didn't match the buzz of Linked memories, which dizzied me like a tumbleweed in a windstorm.

"Still broken," I reported.

"It takes about twenty minutes," Dom said.

I laid my head on the table and closed my eyes. "I hate you."

"Nah, you could never hate anybody."

"I will sic Hades on you."

"Wow, I'm impressed," he said. "I didn't know pet snakes could be trained for attack mode."

I opened one eye, attempting a cyclopsian glare. Ha. Cyclops. If I were a Cyclops, I'd be bigger than him, and I could make his head spin faster than mine. How did he even get alcohol in here? Nobody at the Low-G would sell it to a seventeen-year-old.

My fist clenched. Sticky hand. Sticky, sticky, sticky with soda. I pulled off my glove and twisted my Link bracelets. Sparkles danced, blue and red and green. Pretty. The sparkles sharpened into bright beams that pierced my eyes.

I wanted to kick Dom in the shins. Six times.

"I need to go outside." I stood up.

"Let's go." Cora shot Dom one last glare. "Glove, Gen."

Right. No touchy. I pulled on my wet glove and followed Cora to the door. We pushed through the exit, and the music and the Link buzz cut off.

Breathing. Breathing was not broken. I could do that for a few minutes. A light wind brushed my forehead, and gradually the world settled back to stillness. With a groan, I sank onto a metal bench next to the club doors. Maybe the pill was working.

Yeah, definitely working. I had a whole slew of ideas for punishing Dom, and none of them involved a Cyclops this time.

The overly sweet scent of a flowering cactus turned my stomach while the heat of the Arizona evening soaked into my skin. The sky was a deep lavender, not dark but not day either. An in-between time. *A wishing time*, Grandma had called twilight. Not one thing or another. A time of possibility, where *you* could be one thing or another. Anything you wanted. If you actually knew what you wanted.

Right now, all I wanted was to not be drunk.

Cora plunked herself next to me. "I will punch him in the face. You say the word, and I will."

I slouched on the bench, tipping my head back.

"Hey." The shout from across the garden reverberated in my ears. "What are you sexy ladies doing out here alone?"

Three silhouetted figures waltzed across the garden. Their shadows stretched toward us in the fading sunlight.

"Let's go," Cora whispered. "They don't have a Link buzz."

Silent bodies meant no Link-stored memories—Populace. My nauseated stomach churned.

"Come *on*, what if one of them is the thief?" Cora clutched at her purse and dropped it. "I mean, it's been a while, but they never actually caught him…"

A spike of panic lanced up my stomach, piercing my throat with sudden pain. As if I needed the reminder.

"Hey there." Three boys stopped on the other side of our bench.

One of them noted our clothing and the Links in Cora's hair. A sneer twisted his face.

"Two Mementi girls out alone, so close to dark? I thought you'd all gone into hiding."

He must be the leader. Dark brown eyes, black hair, full lips, curved scar next to his nose. I fixed a picture-perfect image of his face into my Links. I'd need it for evidence.

Except I wouldn't remember his face if he took my Links. I wouldn't remember anything at all. Every moment of my life existed in the bracelets under my gloves. If they vanished, what would be left of me? I would be like the sunset. Not dead, not alive. In between.

Another boy, sporting a shirt with the arms ripped off, snorted. "Had a little much tonight?"

I clapped a hand over my Links.

"We're waiting for our friends." Cora cleared her throat. "The baseball team. All of them."

And, great, Cora. Kill that potential defense with overdramatic flair. I took a shaky breath. Like I was doing any better.

The third boy laughed, loud and a little out of control. He was the youngest of them, and judging by his inability to stand without swaying, a bit more soused than me.

The leader, Scar-nose, licked his lips. "Come on, girls, we can offer you a better time than your own boys."

Oh, gross. I shot to my feet, anger and alcohol stripping away my usual mask of politeness. "Shove off. We're not afraid of Populace weasels like you."

"Gena!" Cora gasped.

I glared at them.

The Drunk glared right back. "Stupid Mementi freaks. At least we're not brain-damaged."

"Hey," Cora cried, jumping up from the bench.

"You think you're so much better than us. What are you going to do now that I can pop down to Happenings and buy a Memo? Use my *normal* brain to remember things like you can?"

Moron. "I doubt you have the neurological capability to remember to zip your fly, Happenings tech or not. Digital copies of memories are crap compared to our 'brain damage.'"

Scar-nose leaned over the back of the bench. Too close. "You want to watch yourself."

I flinched, and Cora backed away. Scar-nose laughed.

"You guys know how to scare a Mementi?" he said. "One touch is all it takes to send 'em screaming.'"

Ripped-Sleeves shoved the Drunk forward. "Do it. Go for the curvy one."

The Drunk ogled Cora, his unfocused eyes glittering.

"Listen, you mind-stunted Neanderthal—" Cora started.

He lunged over the bench. I threw myself to the side. Cora's scream pierced my eardrums. She turned to run, but tripped over her purse and fell among the scattered contents.

Her purse. Cora had mace in her purse.

I scrambled for the bag. *Where is it, where is it?*

My gloves scraped over the concrete, tiny fibers catching and pulling. My fingers closed around a canister. I whipped around.

The canister slipped from my slick-gloved, shaking hand. It clattered into the growing shadows.

Behind the bench, Scar-nose and Ripped-Sleeves were doubled over with laughter. The Drunk had flipped half over the metal back. His legs kicked in mid-air, and he struggled to push himself upright.

Ripped-Sleeves grabbed one of his legs and hauled him over the bench. The boy rubbed his forehead. "Ow."

The mace, where was the freaking mace?

Ripped-Sleeves flung an arm toward me.

I screamed and dropped to the ground, rolling into a ball with my arms—and Links—protected.

"Boo!" he shouted, laughing again.

What?

I risked a peek. He hadn't even gotten close to me.

Scar-nose shoved the other two boys toward the club. "Let's go find some real action." He turned to flip us off. "The only thing you Mementi girls are good for is a laugh."

A burst of music assaulted me, and they disappeared inside.

"Cora?" I whispered. "You okay?"

"Stupid boys, I could *kill* every stupid boy who ever breathed! Which is all of them! Every single one!"

Yeah, she was fine. She crawled around, picking up her fallen things and shoving them into her purse.

"What about you?" She paused and studied me. "Panicking?"

I forced myself up, wishing she didn't have to ask. "Um, yes. But not panic-attacking."

"There's a difference?"

"I guess."

I rubbed my arms, trying to soothe away the shakes. It felt a lot like the many panic attacks I'd had—just not so out of control. And if I did lose control, Cora had years of experience winding me down. Which I loved her and hated myself for.

She stood, her eyes darting from shadow to shadow. "You lost my mace."

We burst into hysterical giggles.

"I'll buy you a new one."

She shouldered her bag. "I've never seen you so…mean. You should get drunk more often."

"Yeah, right." Saying too much and dropping a can of mace didn't make me anything but stupid.

And it didn't make me any less afraid of them. Not just those boys, either. All of them.

The Populace scared us with their own memory research and the possibility of Link theft. We scared them with our superior intellect and control of the city. No-win situation, there.

Cora kicked at my foot. "Let's go. It's getting too dark."

We hurried around the club, taking a shortcut to the tram-stop. Every sway of a tree branch or snap that could be a footstep set my heart pumping again. Cora's words about the Link thief echoed in my head.

They never actually caught him.

Sometimes, a perfect memory was more of a curse than a blessing.

* * *

The next morning, repetitive beeping startled me from a dream. I shook away the last images of being chased by Populace boys who walked on their hands with legs kicking in the air.

A fuzzy, disconnected feeling seeped into my waking brain. Like I was missing some vital component to the world. I groaned and buried my face in the pillow. Dom needed to *die*.

Three more beeps from my phone. I sat up and pulled my Link buds from my ears; I'd fallen asleep listening to music again. My Sidewinder phone lay on my desk across the room. The flexible band was rolled into a ball, the design of brown ovals along its tan back mimicking the snake it was named for.

"Sidewinder, read me all my unread texts." I flopped onto my pillow.

"Accessing text messages," replied the automated voice. I'd set it to sound like Toben Roberts, the drummer from Frankie and the Boy. I grinned into my pillow.

Toben's raspy voice recited the texts, and any lighthearted feelings vanished.

Text from Cora Julieta Medina to Genesis Lee, TDS 07:01:26/5-4-2084
Need to talk ASAP.

Text from Cora Julieta Medina to Genesis Lee, TDS 07:03:04/5-4-2084
Call me. Mom's freakin, so am I.

Text from Cora Julieta Medina to Genesis Lee, TDS 07:03:48/5-4-2084
Please, Gen. I'm missing a Link.

2

Something it is which thou hast lost,
Some pleasure from thine early years…

—Alfred, Lord Tennyson, *In Memoriam* IV

Detective Jackson filled Cora's living room like a looming shadow. His dark blue uniform sucked the brightness from the colorful pillows and paint. I was used to seeing him in jeans at family parties, and the uniform un-familiarized his face.

"Take your time, Gena," he said. Sharp nose, square jaw, straight forehead. I focused on the lines of his dark-skinned face, convincing myself it was the same Jackson I'd always known.

Cora cowered in her chair across the room, drowning in her over-large purple hoody. Her Links tangled in her hair beneath her scarf. I knew Links in the hair had been a bad idea. She glared at Jackson like he was somehow to blame, but she'd been glaring at everyone this morning.

"Let me know when you're ready," Jackson said.

I'd never be ready. But they needed my memory of last night. My evidence.

I was a horrible friend. It wasn't even that meaningful of a memory. Not a deep, personal one. It would help find the psycho who'd stolen two years of Cora's life, but I wanted to hide it so no one could take it from me like they'd taken Cora's.

Self-loathing left a vile taste in my mouth. I took a deep breath and reached for the memory.

Neurons in my brain shot signals through nerves in my arm, accessing my Links. Strobe lights flashed in my mind. The Chinese music beat out last night's rhythm I hadn't gotten to dance to. The heat and the thrill and the irritation and the scent of sweat and alcohol cascaded through me. An echo of my own thoughts sounded in my mind. The wood bead gave me everything—sensation, emotion, thought. Like a moment relived.

I transferred the memory into one of my metal Links, as easy as moving an object from one hand to the other. The metal zapped away all emotion, and the details sharpened. Every person I'd seen or heard in the Low-G shone like the star of their own movie. I knew all their names. My memory could pinpoint every Mementi in the city.

Faces I hadn't noticed at the time popped out of the background. My friend Kinley and her sister. A bunch of college students, some who used to be friends with my older sister. And Populace, everywhere, including the boys who'd nearly attacked us. All faces without names. All of them suspects.

I broke the memory's connection to my conscious mind and wrinkled my nose. Personal memories did not jive with metal Links. The memory practically *tasted* wrong—sharp and tinny, like putting a coin in my mouth. Wisps of emotion from the night lingered. But that was it. The emotional fire was gone, and all I had left was smoke. I'd never get those feelings back, even if I transferred it to wood again.

The worst was still to come.

I gave a curt nod, and Detective Jackson slid back the plastic cover on his small, square Shared Link System. A white-and-black quartz stone glittered. Waiting. The SLS at school let me absorb knowledge memories from top astronomers at the Havendale Observatory. Jackson's was a storage box for evidence memories that would connect to the city's grid. It would take a memory, not give one.

Jackson held the box in stiff hands. Everything was so *still* today. Jackson's hands. Cora in her chair. Even the sunlight just hung in the air. Somebody had hit pause on the world.

"Now," Jackson said. "Most people prefer to let me view their memory, so I can make my own memory of it. Then I'll transfer it immediately to the SLS. Of course, if you'd rather not share the memory with me, you can transfer it yourself."

The frozen sunlight smothered me in a bright cocoon. If I transferred it myself, I'd have to remove the memory from my Links and give it to the SLS's quartz stone. A piece of me would be missing forever. But sharing. It wasn't like the brief, disorienting flash I'd gotten of my sister's first date when I'd accidentally-on-purpose brushed her ungloved hand when I was ten and curious. That was fleeting, a split-second rush of excitement and fear that was gone so fast I couldn't even categorize it as a memory—more a fragment. She'd yelled at me, and I deserved every curse she'd thrown my way. She'd never said what tiny glimpse of memory she'd gotten from me—probably didn't even realize what it was; it came and went so fast.

Sharing a memory wasn't the same rush, the same bewildering glance inside someone else. Jackson would be inside my memory, taking the time to see and experience every moment the way I had. He had to see the whole thing, so he could create his own own memory of my memory and give it away to the SLS. It was the only way we knew how to copy memories, using another Mementi as a conductor, and it terrified me.

"I think…" I tried to breathe the frozen air, and my voice stuck. I couldn't do this.

Argh! Like this was even a big deal. My eyes darted to Cora in shame. She was studying me intensely, staring so hard I shrank back. Who did she see when she looked at me? The Gena of two years ago? Except I wouldn't match the only Gena who existed in her memory. I wasn't the person she remembered.

I would be better than she remembered me. And better than she *didn't* remember me. I swallowed and said to Jackson, "I'll share the memory with you."

I pulled off one of my gloves with shaking hands, exposing my skin to Jackson. He was Dad's best friend. Knowing him—him knowing me—ratcheted up the fear factor. He would see me drunk and ridiculous through my own eyes. Feel my panic and anger. No one should be able to judge someone else from inside their own head.

"I'll be quick," he said. "I'll barely notice the rest of your memories. Think of the one you want to share."

Cora was my best friend. I'd do anything for her. Even this. Every muscle curled in on itself as I held the entire remembrance of the night in my mind.

For the first time since I was a kid, smooth and terrifying skin warmed my forearm. A rush of new memories—his memories—connected through the nerves in our skin. The outline of his life blossomed at the edge of my consciousness. My soul strained under the weight of extra years and sorrow.

He could see my life too. All of me, exposed like I'd been stripped naked. What would he think of me, seeing me as I saw myself?

The crush of his memories lifted. My eyes flew open. I hadn't realized I'd closed them. He placed his finger on the quartz stone of the SLS, storing his memory of my memory. The cover snapped back into place.

He would take the SLS to the station and plug it into the system. My memory would travel through specialized metal wires, every trace of *me* stripped away, pared down to the nitty-gritty details. Software would change the memory into programmable—and searchable—data. Any detective could re-experience it. Only it wasn't an experience anymore, just data to be filed with finger-prints and swabs of spit. Practically not a memory at all.

I clutched my ungloved hand to my chest.

Mementi crime investigation was among the best in the world. Also among the most brutal.

"Thanks, Gen." Jackson packed the SLS into his bag with slow movements. Like if he moved at his more confident pace, he would shatter the frozen world. "It's all confidential, so don't worry about any—ah—reprisals."

Meaning from my parents. Too late for that. There'd been no way to hide that I'd snuck to the Low-G with Cora.

"Even I don't remember a thing, I promise," Jackson said. "It's all in the machine for others to review."

Well. Now I felt loads better. I pulled my glove on.

Cora stood up. "Are you done?"

"Yes," he said, kindly ignoring her tone. "I'm sorry I had to ask so many questions. Most of the attack must have happened in an unmonitored area, but we have some distant streetcam footage. You were running from an unidentified person. We'll see if we can find out why you only had a single Link stolen. Gena's memory will be a huge help. But I can't guarantee anything. It's a complicated case."

Cora scowled at Jackson. "Whatever. You can leave now. I'm sure you need to process your *evidence.*"

I bit back an apology to Jackson on her behalf.

"Someone from the hospital will contact your parents today," he said. "You didn't lose as much as the other victims, but they'll want to monitor you for…side effects."

Cora stared at the carpet as if she could find her lost memories buried in the shag.

"What kind of side effects?" I asked, worried. I hadn't heard why the other victims needed medical attention, but I could guess. A lifetime of no memories. That'd screw you right up. "She won't have to be hospitalized like the others, will she?"

"I don't know."

His voice dripped with uncertainty—Jackson, who was also so sure of himself. What would happen to Cora if she didn't get her memories back?

"Has Ascalon been doing anything to help?" I demanded.

Dad would know better than Jackson. He'd worked for Ascalon BioTech for years. They'd been the ones to create the SLS. Even restrained by the law against human research, Ascalon always had the answers when it came to our unique memories.

Cora leaned forward eagerly. "The memory backups! I remember, Ascalon was working on those! Do they have…anything new?"

She wouldn't know. Anything could've happened in the last two years, for all she knew. We could have finally come up with a machine that copied memories, instead of having to use a human intermediary. My throat closed, and I was grateful, because I didn't have to be the one to murder her hope.

Jackson ran a hand over his thick, black hair. Slow and careful. "Ascalon BioTech has been making progress on memory backups for years. But no. The SLS is still the strongest memory tech they've come up with."

Cora's eyes darted to mine. She looked terrified. Desperate. "There's always…there's always memory sharing. If someone let me see their version of the last two years . . ."

I dug my fingers into my palms so hard, every joint throbbed. No way did she want me to do that for her. Did she?

And I had to wonder—how far *would* I go for Cora, if she asked me?

"You know that's not an option, Cora," Jackson said gently.

Doctors had tried memory sharing as therapy fifty years ago, with Aria Matthews. She went a little nuts, destroyed some of her memories, then wanted them back. Friends and family shared memories with her, thinking her brain could reorient the perspective. Make the memories hers again. But their memories were *their* memories, tainting her with their realities. When her brain had tried to merge memories that held other people's identities, Aria had too many realities in one head. So she blew that one off.

It had been banned as a medical option at the same time as the prohibition of direct study of Mementi memories and Links.

Some people—like my mom—still let close friends or family *observe* their memories. Mom was so proper and polite, you'd never guess she'd allow the world's most massive privacy invasion.

I secretly thought she only did it because she was too stiff to know how to show affection any other way.

Observing was one thing—as bad as sharing a memory—but you never stored someone else's memories in your own Links. It took a conscious effort not to automatically form your own memory while observing someone else's. You could, though. Had to, if you didn't want someone else in your head. Or to land in jail, in the very unlikely event you were caught with someone else's memories in your Links.

Jackson turned to go, but paused. "I'm sorry. I'm so sorry for your loss."

"Sure you are," Cora muttered as he left. "I'm sure you're sorry you had to rape Gena's memory too."

The words punched me in the stomach. It wasn't. It wasn't like that. Not for me, not when I'd offered the memory. But I wanted to vomit, and I didn't know how Cora could even speak or breathe or move. She hadn't been willing.

"It's not his fault," I whispered. "I said I would. If it helps. He said it could help find your Link."

"He practically forced you into it."

She threw herself in the chair next to the window. I waited for the theatrical gestures, for threats of violence she'd never actually commit, for the typical Cora dramatics. I *needed* them. I couldn't release if Cora didn't.

They didn't come. The stillness wound tighter, ready to snap.

Her face twisted. "How can this be happening?"

The Links in her hair caught the bright sun coming through the windows. A kaleidoscope of colors shimmered on the wall.

Three long bracelets—my own Links—wound up my forearm like snakes. Cora had given them to me for my tenth birthday.

She'd even strung the beads herself, using just wood and metal. The magnetized metal Links locked the strands together without a clasp. She'd even picked my favorite colors. Red, blue, and green.

Cora liked her own Links to be as many colors as possible so they would match whatever she wore. Which color was missing? It didn't matter, I guess. But even the color was part of Cora.

"I could hardly tell the memories were gone at first," she said, her voice hoarse with tears she wasn't crying. "I just woke up and thought it was two years ago."

Two years. Two years was *so long*. And she hadn't even known. I tasted blood, and realized I'd chewed a tiny hole into my lip. If you couldn't remember that you'd forgotten, how would you know how horrible it was to forget?

She stood and began pacing. "But there's also this…disconnected feeling. I didn't even know what it meant until I went to brush my teeth and my toothbrush was orange and I didn't remember getting an orange toothbrush." She laughed, a little wild. "My toothbrush. Can you believe it? My toothbrush was the first time in my life I ever thought the words *I don't remember*."

Her pacing was a small relief from the motionless world. I took tiny breaths and waited for her to go on.

"I can feel where they should be." She trailed her fingers down her neck to her chest, like she was searching for a physical hole. "All the days I lost. I can feel things in me that have changed, but I don't understand them. I don't remember who I am."

"What do you remember?" I was almost afraid to ask. "From last night, I mean. How'd you get home?"

"I remember walking up the front steps and going right to bed. I was so tired, and I felt funny, like I'd been drinking. I thought I'd come from Dom's end-of-school party. We were sophomores."

The night he'd first acted interested in Cora. So she remembered nothing of their relationship. Last night, I'd have said that would be a good thing. But good or bad, memories of Dom were part of her. Except now they weren't. I struggled to find what to say next.

"At least you didn't lose everything." Not much of a silver lining, there. "I mean, one of the victims is Mrs. Jacobs—you know, Blaire's mom, my sister Ren's best friend? And she had all of her Links stolen."

"I remember your sister, Gena, and I remember Blaire and her mom," Cora snapped. "And the fact that I didn't lose everything is not exactly comforting."

We fell silent. What now, after all the preliminary how-could-this-happens? She wasn't the Cora from yesterday, she was the Cora from two years ago. Except she wasn't even that. Invisible cracks split the frozen air between us. A chasm of two years I didn't know how to breach. I missed her already.

"I'm sorry," she said, finally standing still. "I'm not mad at you."

"I know," I said. "I'm sorry too."

She tugged a strand of hair. "How can I feel sad about losing something when I don't know what I've lost?"

I wanted to curl into a ball on my chair. "I wish I could do something."

"You can't."

Two words that drove me from aching to agony.

She didn't have the memory she'd told me of just last night, of holding Dom's hand through thin gloves—her first touch. She didn't have our game of truth or dare where she'd swallowed a gold-fish whole. Or her amazing dance performance last summer when she finally decided she wanted to be a choreographer. Everything that had happened to her in the last two years had unhappened.

I nudged her shoe with mine, our best-friends signal we were there for each other. She didn't nudge back. She picked up a rectangle of paper from the end table next to me. Real paper, not micropaper. I loved that she wrote down her songs. She said it made them more real.

"I don't remember writing this," she said.

She lowered the paper, covered in her flowing handwriting. My eyes lingered on the last line. Not even a complete phrase.

"I don't know how I was going to finish it," she said. "The words don't mean anything to me."

A storm built inside her. I saw it in the tension of her shoulders and the shaking of the paper in her fingers. The stillness was about to shatter. I almost welcomed the impending relief of a moving world.

"Cora—"

"No!" She screamed, like a sudden blast of thunder. "Don't you dare tell me it'll be alright, or that I'll find myself again, or any other crap! I'm *broken*. I'll never be the person I was going to be without those memories. Even if I can make myself into someone else, it's not fair that I didn't get to choose that!"

She crumpled the paper and threw it at me. I couldn't squeak out a single word from my swollen throat. Because she was right, and my heart crumpled like the paper she had thrown.

Cora sank to the floor, sobbing. "I'm sorry, I'm sorry…"

I reached toward her, helpless. "Shh."

The world jump-started into motion as her parents rushed in. Mrs. Webber dropped to her knees next to Cora. Her dad hovered on her other side. Air flowed again, alive and breathable.

"What is it, baby, what happened?" Cora's mom wrapped an arm around her shoulder, careful to only touch clothing.

Cora usually had a dramatic kind of sad, full of flowery words and wails of agony over ice cream—but these sobs. She gasped them up from some deep well inside her that hadn't existed before.

Her father hung back. He and Cora hadn't had a great relationship since her parents divorced five years ago. Things had only gotten better between them in the last year. A year she'd forgotten.

Mrs. Webber turned tear-filled eyes to her ex-husband, and he stepped forward. He touched a trembling gloved hand to Cora's shoulder. They stood in the sunlight that streamed into the room, touching lightly, hesitantly. The only way Mementi families touched. If they touched at all.

The last time one of my parents had touched me, I was five years old. My mother put her gloved hands to my back to send my swing soaring. I'd learned to swing by myself that day, the final hurdle of growing up. I could dress myself, bathe myself, swing myself. She'd thought I didn't need her after that.

"I'll go," I whispered to Cora's family.

Mrs. Webber forced a smile. "Thank you."

Four words were all we could manage between us.

Outside, shadows shifted as palm trees swayed in the breeze. I swayed with them as I walked, almost drunk on the dance of a world rolling forward. The midday sun shone on the distant red cliffs of Havendale Canyon. I should have been on my way there for my weekly internship at the Observatory, but I couldn't drum up the usual excitement. They'd understand if I didn't show today.

I could have gone home. Except Mom would be there, and she wasn't exactly happy with me after finding out about last night. I hadn't technically been forbidden to go out, but I had been very technically forbidden to go to the Low-G. And the drinking was a big issue, even though it was completely not my fault. I'd retained the privilege of "supporting" Cora despite my three-month grounding sentence, and it was sort of shocking that's all I'd been slammed with. Dad's grief at such betrayal from his perfect daughter had nearly prompted him to drive me to jail for my underage drinking. Because that was so much more important than the fact that I'd barely escaped an attack from the Link thief.

I stopped in the street. A dry water fountain sat in front of a dark green, gothic-style house. Complete with turrets, arched windows, and secret passages. It was empty now. Blaire, my sister's best friend, had moved out, and her mother had been in the hospital since her Link theft.

The parched fountain squatted ominously in a bed of dead flowers. A reminder. The Link thief was back, and he'd struck closer to home than ever.

Anyone could be next.

3

Does my old friend remember me?

—Alfred, Lord Tennyson, *In Memoriam*, LXIV

I wanted to hop right back off the tram two seconds after the doors hissed shut behind me. The chill in the air wasn't just the air-conditioning. Like the dance floors at the Low-G last night, the tram was divided. Populace at the front of the car, Mementi at the back. Stiff bodies and silent glowers held enough potential energy to spontaneously combust the whole tram car.

The tram pulled forward. Every person, Populace and Mementi, stared at me. Waiting to see what this unknown element would do.

This unknown element was going to park her rear end right where it was safest. I sat next to Mrs. Harward and her youngest daughter Talise. Tendrils of anxiety tickled my stomach. Maybe it wasn't such a bright idea to head to my sanctuary in Havendale

Canyon. It was a long tram ride, and my untrustworthy emotions were already shot after the morning with Cora and Detective Jackson.

Politeness dictated I greet the people next to me, but what would I say? *Hey there. Looks like everyone's ready to bite each other's heads off. Nice weather we're having, too.* Mrs. Harward took the decision out of my hands.

"Good afternoon, Genesis." Forced cheerfulness oozed from the greeting.

"Hello, Mrs. Harward." I turned to her.

Oh. Oh wow.

Her face didn't match my memory from the Christmas party at the Arts Center, the last time I'd seen her. The wrinkles around her eyes were gone, and the way her cheeks shifted when she talked had changed. Her skin looked tighter. Younger.

She gave a tiny smile at my reaction. "That much of a change?"

"I…suppose."

Her eyes drifted to the Populace, then darted to her daughter. Last time I checked, the Populace hadn't developed telepathic murder, but she hovered like the girl could keel over at any second. Tense muscles quivered beneath her mask of calm.

She spoke again, her voice pitched a bit higher than normal. "The people at the spa say you lose ten years in the space of five minutes with this treatment."

"So Ascalon finally released the new Chameleon injections to the public?" I could play along with her attempt to act pleasant and natural.

"Yes. What do you think, ten years gone?" She rubbed her pale cheek.

Mrs. Harward was only in her late thirties, not an old hag. The new smoothness in her features looked unnatural. Almost waxy.

"Ten years for sure," I said. "You look amazing."

The lie flowed easily. Truth was unnecessary when painful. Mementi politeness wasn't just a way of life, it was a means for survival. A way to stay positive—or at least neutral—in each other's memories. I didn't want to exist inside anyone's Links as being cruel.

Mrs. Harward brushed a loose hair under the thin scarf that matched her red linen gloves. "Thanks."

I forced myself to look away from her too-perfect face. The development of SLS devices to share knowledge memories meant Ascalon BioTech could branch into other "life improvement" areas. Easy, when you could absorb someone else's knowledge and become an instant expert on anything. No longer just involved in Mementi memory tech, Ascalon was now the center of a myriad of freaky-cool inventions for the entire world. Biomechanical prosthetics, gravity manipulation, paint that put electronics on your wall.

Nothing to complain about there, especially when every Mementi had a share in Ascalon stock. But Cham treatments weirded me out. In a city where people barely touched, they inserted synthetic DNA into their bodies to mask the effects of aging. That was straight-up violating.

I fingered my Links. Cora's morning outburst flashed in my mind. A rage against the black hole of her missing years.

A child's voice rang out in the silence of the tram. "I changed my mind, I want my new Links like hers."

Talise Harward, her scarf falling off the back of her head, pointed at the beads beneath my transparent blue gloves. The mention of Links turned every head in the tram. A chill brushed my neck as if the sudden movement threw off a wake of animosity.

"Shh, honey, it's rude to point at other people's Links." Mrs. Harward whispered. She unconsciously brushed her own Links peeking out from her collar. She favored large beads that stored more memories, and of course, she had more than me. More years of memory to store. "Please apologize, and keep your voice down."

Talise swung her legs. "Sorry, Miss Genesis. But yours are cool."

Everyone turned away again, but a tingle of anxiety surged under my ribs. "Thanks." The community calendar flashed into my memory. "And happy birthday."

She turned eight today. They'd buy her new, non-child-proofed Links soon. A proud moment.

Dad had bucked Mementi tradition, worried eight was still too young. Ren and I didn't get our adult Links until we were ten. Now, looking at Talise, I thought she was too young. Too young to have no choice but to keep her memories outside her own mind, where they could be so easily taken away.

Talise scowled. "It's not a happy birthday. Mom, *please* can we get my Links today?"

"We were just looking today." Mrs. Harward got that awkward look that said she was about to delve into personal territory. She lowered her voice. "Genesis, I'm so sorry to hear about your friend. Please pass our condolences to Cora."

So the news had gotten out. No wonder everybody was extra tense today. Even when she didn't mean to, Cora caused drama. I would've laughed if a lump hadn't clogged my throat.

Outside, the white cylinder of Mr. and Mrs. Gibbs' lighthouse-inspired home flashed past. Next to it was the Mower's monstrosity of geometric concrete. Not what you'd call aesthetically pleasing, especially compared to the lighthouse and its other neighbor. People referred to the Larson's place as the Dr. Seuss house. The bright yellow home had been designed without a single straight line.

The tram stopped in front of these familiar landmarks, and a guy with curly blond hair stepped aboard. No Link buzz—another Populace. He stood near the door, taking in the separation of sides. His eyes met mine and lingered.

A pleasant female voice came over the speakers. "Passengers are reminded that standing is not permitted on Havendale City Trams. Thank you."

The boy took a few steps and sat on the Mementi side. Right across from me.

The tram buzzed with the jump in heartbeats. My foot tapped a nervous dance on the floor, and I covered my Links with a gloved hand. Trams were video monitored. He couldn't do anything to me here. Besides, he was no more likely to be the Link thief than any other Populace here.

Or maybe he was just as likely to be the Link thief as any of them.

My hands twitched when I found him studying me. His eyebrows gathered, giving an impression of a confused puppy. A very tall one. I'd bet he had a good ten inches on me, and I wasn't short. He wasn't going to do anything to me. He was a harmless, shaggy-haired Populace guy.

He cleared his throat several times before saying, "Um…I'm Kalan?"

My parents' politeness lessons nagged at my tongue. I'd be polite to my own executioner. Licking my dry lips, I replied, "Gena."

He was kind of cute in a boy-next-door way. I leaned forward, then pulled back. Cute didn't mean nice. The scariest ones were always cute.

"Do you, um…" He cleared his throat.

Do you mind handing over your Links so I don't have to shoot you with this gun in my pocket? I pinched myself on the arm. Get a grip, Gena. Before anyone could say another word, Mrs. Harward spoke. Her voice shook, but she held her head high.

"Excuse me. I don't think she's interested in talking to you."

I blinked. I'd never heard any Mementi be so blatantly impolite.

"Hey," a rough voice called out. A Populace guy in a blue workman's shirt leaned into the center aisle. "He wasn't doing anything. He was just being nice. I thought manners had been hardwired into your Mem-tard brains after they got all scrambled from that memory drug."

All conversation died. Even the Mementi couple across from me paused their gooey-eyed staring session. The slur was bad enough, but add that to the mockery of the Memor-X gene therapy, and this guy had just put himself on a few hit lists. Sure, Memor-X gave our grandparents incredible memory capabilities that had passed to us. It had also destroyed nearly as many minds as it had expanded. Including my Grandma Piper's.

Thom Lancaster, an intern at Ascalon, stood and straightened his high collar. "Being nice doesn't mean she has to talk to every Populace cretin who thinks she's got a pretty face."

Talise shrank as close to her mom as she dared.

A smooth voice made me jump. "Passengers are reminded that standing is not permitted on Havendale City Trams. Thank you."

Mr. Blue-shirt planted his feet in the aisle. The two men swayed slightly in a counter-rhythm to each other, a physical banter that teased out the tension. I held my breath.

The Populace boy, Kalan, raised his hands. "Hey guys, ease off, it's fine." He had the most expressive eyebrows I'd ever seen.

They dropped, shading his eyes in a sad look. "I wasn't trying to…I'll just get off at the next stop."

"You don't have to," growled Mr. Blue-shirt.

"I want to," Kalan said sharply. "This isn't worth fighting about."

The tram approached the last in-town stop. His eyes found mine again. "See you later."

I sure hoped not. I slumped in my seat as he left and hugged my arms to my chest. The tram emptied of most passengers, both Populace and Mementi. I didn't say goodbye to the Harwards.

The tram whirred on to its final destination, the Observatory at Havendale Canyon. When it stopped, I descended to the grass and crossed the bridge. The river rushed below my feet and I tasted moisture on my tongue. The dome of the Observatory glistened white at the top of a red cliff, housing the enormous telescope that I occasionally got to use. Day or night, this place gathered knowledge from observatories around the world.

All around me, cliffs carved into the sky. Each rock face had been chipped and chiseled by the shifting hands of nature. Tiny shifts of dust and rock, wearing away each second. Even rocks had a dance. Slow and peaceful.

Unfortunately, the grav-lift to the Observatory was busy and un-peaceful today. Employees poured from the monstrous elevator to eat their lunch under the carved wood pavilion and stroll in the shade by the river.

People nodded to me as I passed the grav-lift and trekked deeper into the canyon. Kicking my way through tufts of sagebrush, I shed my gloves, scarf, and the gauzy long-sleeved shirt I wore over my green tank top. The sun warmed my bare shoulders. One of the benefits out here was not needing that extra layer of touch protection.

As I hiked, frustration rose inside me. I was hiding when I should try to help my best friend. But what was I going to do, hunt the thief on my own and find Cora's Link? My own helplessness squeezed me until I wanted to claw at it.

The inconsistencies of the theft nagged at me. Dad joked that my memories were dominoes. If you tapped one, it would trigger ten others nobody else had realized were connected. But it made no sense why the thief had targeted Cora. No dominoes were falling right now. Something was missing, something I could almost reach, like a word on the tip of my tongue.

A sudden shower of pebbles clacked down the mountain behind me. I spun, clutching my shoulder bag. The empty trail wound down the red cliffs. Must've been a squirrel. Stupid things were everywhere. I scanned the rocks, watching for it to reappear. No squirrel.

A flutter of nerves sparked shivers down my bare arms. I hiked faster until I reached a wide crack in the red rock. I shimmied sideways, scraping my back in the tight spots, and broke into my haven.

Sunlight danced around me. Shades of white and black streaked the orange rock. I trailed my hand along the gritty sandstone walls, tiny particles rolling beneath my fingers. Ripples of shadow and light skipped across the shallow pond that had nestled its way into the rock. A scraggly tree clung to the edge of the pond, its roots dangling over the cliff. Like a living lullaby, the scene soothed me.

I took off my shoes and dropped my bag, then stepped onto the nature-made platform to the right of the pond. It was smaller than a normal stage, but plenty big enough to dance on. My bare feet found the familiar grooves in the rock. Mom and Dad had originally put me in ballet hoping the movement would give me the focus to handle my anxiety attacks. I'd been off meds with no problems for nearly a year, but today was threatening to end that streak. I closed my eyes and settled into third ballet position.

The trickle of water, wearing the rock into patterns. The heat of the stone, weaving up my ankles. The dusty wind, working its piney scent into my hair. I inhaled and they filled me.

I whipped my head around and danced.

My music was the water and the wind and the rhythm of the ache in my heart. I flowed from the smooth, classical ballet steps my teacher Zahra had taught me into the sharper, dramatic movements of jazz. I blended the dances, flowing from one style to the other. Balancing them as they balanced me. My body arched forward and trickled back inch by inch.

My parents would have died to see me dance so "promiscuously." Cora had taught me jazz in secret.

Cora. Her stolen Link. *What was I missing?*

Something moved at the edge of my vision. My concentration shattered, and I stumbled.

In the shadows of the rock tunnel, someone edged toward me. With a gasp, I dropped into a crouch. Like that would help. Blood beat in my ears. The figure emerged from the crack. Tall, with curly blond hair.

The boy from the tram had found me.

4

Thou bring'st…letters unto trembling hands;
And, thy dark freight, a vanish'd life.

—Alfred, Lord Tennyson, *In Memoriam X*

My legs shook as I held my crouch. He shifted his weight from one foot to the other but didn't come any closer.

"How did you get here?" I meant to demand it, but my voice came out hoarse.

"Through there." He gestured to the crack in the rock. "I mean, well, obviously there, but I saw you heading up the canyon. Don't freak out, I just want to talk. I won't come any closer."

He seemed anything but threatening. Except that he'd stalked me into my super-secret space.

"Talk about what?" I asked.

"About last night. You told me to meet you here at the canyon."

My calves were cramping from my crouch. I stood, my bare toes clutching the sandy rock. Last night? Did he know something about Cora?

No hyperventilating. Hyperventilating near stalker-boy equals Very Bad Thing.

"I never said you should meet me here," I said.

"You did. Last night. That's why I was on the tram, to meet you. Then I realized you didn't remember." His ever-expressive eyebrows pulled together. "I'm sorry."

I slapped a hand over my Links. Two words no Mementi knew the meaning of: *didn't remember.*

We remembered everything. My tongue burned from the sharp tang of the thirteen lemon drops I'd eaten at Grandma Piper's when I was four, and I heard her words of scolding and comfort. My cheeks heated with the same thrilled flush when, at nine years old, my father had bowed to me and presented a rose and a box of powdered sugar donuts after my first dance concert.

Which meant this boy was lying.

Breathe. Relax. He had an agenda, and I needed a clear head to figure out what it was. "What, exactly, don't I remember?"

He shrugged, palms out. "Me."

"And you are?"

"Kalan Fox. We met last night…briefly." He frowned, his forehead puckering. "This is so weird. I didn't realize they'd actually caught you."

Caught me?

"I'm not missing a Link." It was the only way I wouldn't remember him. I ran a trembling hand over the beads on my arm. I didn't have to count them. Just feeling them, I could tell they were whole. "I don't remember you, and trust me, if we'd exchanged as much as one word, I could tell you what it was. What are you trying to pull?"

Cora would be proud of me. Maybe I wouldn't be pleasant to my executioner after all.

Kalan took a step forward. "No missing Link?"

He'd said he wouldn't move from that spot.

"No." I pulled my hands to my chest, every exposed inch of skin on my arms and shoulders tingling. My gloves and overshirt sat crumpled on the ground several feet away, too far to reach. It didn't matter. He wasn't Mementi, so he couldn't see my memories. He could only steal them. Steal my Links.

His face hardened. "If you have them all, then why don't you remember me?"

"Maybe because we never met."

"We *did* meet." A sudden intensity pulsed from him like a change in the music. "We practically collided last night. On the corner of Rowley and Tanner Street. Your name is Gena Lee, and you were running from someone, you said they were stealing Mementi Links. You told me to meet you here today."

I sucked in quick breaths. That was flat-out unbelievable. "What do you want? Why are you here?"

"Because I'm trying to help." He tipped his head back and groaned. "Look, I made a detour on my way here. When you didn't remember me on the tram."

He reached into his back pocket and held out a small white box.

"I don't want it," I said.

"Well, you're going to take it anyway." His voice came out almost as a growl. He tossed the box in my direction. It skidded across the rock floor before stopping near my feet.

I flinched, clenching every muscle so I didn't dissolve into a hysterical ball of nerves. How could this guy be so disarming one minute and so intense the next? What was I supposed to do with that?

"Please, I can help." His voice, soft now, brought my head up. Our eyes met and my cheeks tingled with heat. The tremor in my chest faded and breathlessness took its place.

Cora would smack me. *You don't freakin' fall for the loco stalker guy!* Get a grip, Gena. An attractive loco stalker wasn't any better than an unattractive one. Except possibly more dangerous.

Kalan nodded toward the white box. "My number's on there. Call me when you're ready."

His confidence irked me. "What did you mean, you can help me?"

"You're not the only who wants to stop the Link thief. Hopefully we can help you get your memories back." He gave me a funny half-smile that turned his face from intense guard dog to charming puppy. "And I guess I sort of wouldn't mind getting to know you, Gena Lee."

I swallowed, one-quarter charmed and three-quarters freaked out. He stepped into the shadows of the rocky tunnel. The second he was out of sight, I collapsed to the ground so hard I bit my tongue.

I checked each of my three Link bracelets. Red, green, and blue. Metal and wood, all intact. It wouldn't be easy to take one, like it was from Cora's netted hairpiece. Each of mine was strung on a single strand of beading wire. No missing Links, no missing memories. So I'd never met Kalan.

Except. On the tram, I hadn't told him my last name.

I lay down and the red stone heated my bare shoulders. Clouds brushed through the sky, twirling and wisping into thin strands of cottony white. So what, he knew my last name? That didn't make the rest of his story true. It was almost impossible to lose memories without losing my Links.

Except. Except…

Like a punch in the head, memories connected across my brain, knocking into each other to make a story out of random pieces.

The Mementi dancing at the Low-G, careful not to touch, not to see each other's memories.

Tiffani Donald, the only case of a Mementi stealing memories in two decades, serving life in prison for siphoning memories from her husband so he would forget his mistress.

Siphoning. Stealing through touch, rummaging through another person's Links like they were your own. Pulling memories away from their Links and into yours like some kind of memory vampire.

It had only happened a handful of times in the sixty years since Havendale was established. Or maybe it had only been caught a handful of times. If nobody remembered what they had lost, it could be happening every day.

No way. Not possible. I knew them all. Everybody who was Mementi. Friends and family and neighbors and smiling faces glimpsed on the street, all embedded into my Links. I couldn't distrust everyone I knew because of the lies of a Populace boy.

I sat up to be confronted with the glaring white of his mysterious gift lying on red rock. Kalan said he'd gotten it for me after he realized I didn't remember him. What did that mean?

My eyes darted toward the now-empty tunnel. I picked up the cardboard box and turned it around. In big, black letters, the logo of Happenings stood out against the white. Underneath it was a single word: MEMO.

Kalan had used a Happenings Memo to copy one of his memories for me.

5

O sweet and bitter in a breath,
What whispers from thy lying lip?

—Alfred, Lord Tennyson, *In Memoriam III*

I thought of all the ways I could destroy the Memo. Throw it over the edge of the cliff. Stomp on it. Hurl it against the rock wall.

Instead, I hid it at the bottom of my bag like that would make it go away. Because I was stupid like that.

For a while, I threw pebbles into the pond. Big pebbles, little pebbles, it didn't matter. They all made ripples. I could watch the Memo: big pebble. Or I could delve into my own memory to see what was there and what wasn't: little pebble. Ripples in my life either way.

I brushed dirt from my hands. Heavy with dread, I tapped into my memory of leaving the Low-G with Cora. I nearly choked on my desperate desire to find it whole. Each second from the past rolled through my mind, replaying how we hurried home across the dim garden. My feet brushed across grass, and Cora and I walked a few inches closer together than we normally would have.

And with barely a blip, I was huddled under my blanket in bed. With no memory of how I got there.

That wasn't right. I should have had the boringness of a tram ride to skim over. Something I did every day, something I could skip in the recall, but it had to be there to explain how I got from point A to point B. The empty moments yawned at me like a gaping mouth. Somehow these dull moments were just gone. Like a lost puzzle piece. A tiny, insignificant part of the picture gone, just a few leaves missing from the foliage in the corner.

This wasn't possible. I'd just gone through the memory too fast, that was all, I'd skipped past those moments on the tram because that's what I always did. I forced myself through the memory again, took each step until I stumbled. Because there was a stumbling point, a jump from the streets to my bedroom.

A gap. Minutes I had lived that were now nothing but a hole.

I wanted to scream. I hadn't lost those moments, I hadn't *forgotten*.

My pulse jump-started the sudden onslaught of panic triggering a convulsion in every muscle. Someone had touched my Links. Or my neck or head, where nerve connections were strong enough to suck out—siphon—my memory.

Fingers on my skin, in my mind. Someone feasting on my stolen moments. They were tiny moments, ones that shouldn't matter, but they were *mine*. And now they weren't, now someone else had them, had bits of me that I no longer had. Pressure built in my chest, forcing my heart into my throat. I gasped for air. Jitters crawled up my legs, my arms, my back, my face. Like ants swarming inside my skin. I scrambled to my feet.

I needed movement, meds, something. Cora's voice whispered in my head. *Not a big deal, remember?*

My mantra. She'd come up with it.

Not a big deal. *Yes it was.* Not a big deal. I breathed deep, matching the words to my inhales and exhales. Matching the inhales and exhales to my footfalls. Not-a. Big-deal. I slammed out the drum solo from my favorite song, my thighs and hands stinging. Not a. Rat-a-tat-tat. Big deal. Rat-a-tat-tat.

Screw that. This was a very big deal.

Face, tingling. I slapped it. The blur in my vision sharpened. Air. Breathe. Okay. New mantra.

This is a big deal. I can handle it. Big deal, I can handle it. I slapped my thighs, finding a rhythm. Big. Deal. I-can handle-it.

Minutes ticked by until the tingle of ant feet slowed and the panic attack faded. Soon only a flutter in my chest and a mass of frustration remained. Betrayed by my own emotions again. Exhausted, I sank to the ground and lay back. I breathed so deep, I thought I might inhale the sky. That was a nice image. I pulled the sky inside me, open and free.

Slowed by exhaustion, I traipsed down the canyon and rode the tram home. My bag nudged my hip as I left the tram station, the corner of the Memo box poking me through the thin fabric of the purse. A reminder. I couldn't run from this.

* * *

By the time I got home, I was desperate to just watch the Memo and get it over with. I plodded toward the house, trailing my fingers along our white picket fence.

A flash of movement through the trees stopped me. Someone stood on my doorstep.

It was him, it had to be him. Kalan. He'd followed me. He'd found out where I lived, he was waiting for me, he was…

It wasn't him.

Detective Jackson leaned on the doorframe, his back to me. Out of uniform, but still broad-shouldered in a black mock turtleneck. A brief moment of relief died under the screeching wheels of a sudden thought.

Today someone had touched my skin. Jackson had seen the very memory that was fractured.

Ridiculous. I'd only allowed him to watch the memory, not take it. He was my father's best friend. He'd coached my Little League team and tickled my chubby knees all the way back in my incoherent toddler memories. And he was a *cop.* A good guy, the one trying to catch the Link thief.

"What?" His voice rang across the yard.

I jumped. He raised a hand to the Sidewinder wrapped around his ear. Just talking on the phone.

"I'm not in a good location to talk." He snapped a stick from a tree, his back to me.

My skin prickled.

Jackson moved suddenly, prowling around the side of the house with tight, swift steps. I sneaked up the front walk. Our house was round, meaning no corners to hide behind, but I edged along the curved wall until I could see him. His powerful shoulders clenched, pulling his shirt tight across his back. Like a panther ready to pounce.

I ducked back out of sight. I'd never been afraid of Jackson before. But the whole "someone you don't want to meet in a dark alley" idea got a lot more visual.

"Not much." His voice floated around the bend. "Nothing I got today helped explain last night's fiasco. But we don't have to worry about witnesses, the memory was clean."

I willed my pounding heart to slow down so I could hear clearly. He was talking about me. My memory. I sneaked closer again. His hand came into view, still clenching a stick.

"Of course I'm turning it in to the station, I have to." He threw the stick across the yard. "They won't get much from it anyway, the memory was distorted. She was drunk."

I pressed close to the house. He'd stored my memory in the SLS. He shouldn't remember it at all. I stepped forward and squinted as more of his frame came into view. A thin, metallic string glinted in the sun. It led from his pocket to the Link bud in the opposite ear from his Sidewinder.

Link buds weren't just wireless earphones. The quartz crystals and micro-filament cord were giving Jackson hands-free access to my memory stored on the SLS in his pocket.

And whoever he was telling about it was not a cop.

"No. She's not a risk." Jackson whirled around. "We can discuss…"

Jackson and I stared at each other.

Do not freak out.

He'd said *a* risk, not *at* risk.

Do not freak out.

"I'll call you back." He clicked off his Sidewinder and fumbled to unplug his Link buds. "Gena."

If I bolted, he might reconsider me being *a risk*. Lie. I was good at lying; all Mementi were.

"I thought I heard somebody." I forced a smile. "What are you doing here?"

Within seconds, he'd crossed the yard. I spooked away from the house. Panther, indeed. I'd hardly noticed him moving, he was just…there. Close enough to steal a memory.

He smiled. "Your dad invited me for dinner tonight. I just had to wrap a few things up for another case first." He sighed and looked around the yard. "We've had some good times here. Remember when Ren wanted to rent a pet for her birthday party, and that Doberman dug up all your mom's Mexican petunias?"

"Oh." I forced a laugh that came out as more of a squeak. I wouldn't have pegged him as the reminiscent type. "Yeah. That was awesome."

Jackson stepped forward. I backed away. I couldn't let him close enough to touch me, to yank off my scarf and suck away a memory.

Who had been on the phone, and what was I a risk to?

"I'm sorry about earlier, Gen." He wiped sweat from his forehead, his posture the relaxed pose I was used to. Only now I knew what lurked beneath that skin. "That was really selfless of you, sharing your memory to help your friend."

My voice stuck in my throat. I nodded.

"Mind if we get inside?" he asked. "I'm roasting."

I tried to keep my pace steady as I headed back to the porch. I pressed my finger to the DNA lock, then stepped back and gestured into the house. *You first, Mr. Panther.* Jackson breezed inside. I followed, highly conscious of Kalan's Memo nestled in my bag.

It wasn't the only new memory in the area. No one else was home, but my ultra-sensitive Mementi brain picked up an extra electrostatic feedback in the room—Link buzz. Mom had stashed new memories somewhere. Temporary ones to comfort me, probably.

Mom had a weird attachment to every single object she'd ever owned. She stored memories she connected to those objects *in* them, so the whole family could observe them. She added to them when she had something in particular to say to one of us, but didn't know how to say it. It still gave me a why-the-devil kind of bewilderment. She couldn't remember those moments unless she touched that object again.

At least Jackson gave me an excuse to avoid Mom's preferred method of comfort.

He settled himself into a chair in the living room. "How's Cora?"

"Oh. You know." I backed toward the kitchen. "Not great."

"She'll be okay," he said. "The hospital keeps a close eye on all the victims. She'll be admitted if she loses control."

"Loses control?" I blinked. "Control of what?"

A tiny muscle in his cheek twitched, almost a wince. "Just… well, if she can't handle the residual emotion. The other victims have had some, uh, issues. I guess our Links don't actually store emotional memory. They just change how we connect the memory and emotion. It's hard to cope when you have no memories to tell you what your emotions are for."

"They're not going insane, like some of the first generation?"

He hesitated.

Not good.

"They're having trouble adjusting," he said.

A.k.a. they were going insane. The first gens were a whole bouquet of crazy, thanks to the Memor-X screw-up. Some were fine. Others became borderline schizophrenic. Developed multiple personalities. Were committed for violent acts. Killed themselves.

This was not what I bargained for at all with this conversation.

"Cora—"

"She'll be okay." Jackson held his hands up, as if warding off my worry. "She lost very little compared to the others, so she may not notice the emotions. And there are medications, and therapy."

Cora was a highly emotional human being. Even two years' worth of her explosive ups and downs would be a lot to handle. She didn't need meds, she needed her memories.

"Um, I…" I swallowed. "I'm sorry, can I have a minute?"

"Sure. I'm sorry, I didn't mean—"

I slammed my bedroom door, cutting him off. Rude, but I didn't care. Jackson, the one supposed to hunt the enemy, *was* the enemy. Was he even trying to find Cora's Link? Did he care if she ended up mentally ill?

I collapsed on the floor, leaning my forehead on the glass of my snake tank. Hades slept, his yellow and white body coiled under his hollow log. He was oddly calming, especially all curled up and still. When Mom and Dad told me I could get a small pet for my sixteenth birthday, I don't think an albino corn snake made the initial list. I'm not going to lie, that was half the reason I wanted him. Plus he was just cool.

I stood and emptied my bag onto my bed. Kalan's Memo clunked on top of my lip gloss and water bottle. His name and number were scrawled on the box. Frustration welled up. I *needed* to see this memory, especially knowing that Cora was primed to go loony if she didn't get her Link back. But Jackson wasn't the only one who'd be after me if he saw the Memo.

It wouldn't matter if the Dalai Lama gave me a memory of how to achieve world peace, my parents would freak if they knew I had Happenings tech in my room. Liza Woods, CEO, tried to sell the Populace the kind of memories we'd paid for with years of heartache. It made people downright hostile.

She'd sidled in like some kind of parasite after Ascalon's SLS tech had proved the power of Mementi memories. Determined to use us for profit. Not a good way to make friends, especially with a town already profiting from our own company. Ascalon had been around since near the beginning of the Mementi, it was created *for* us. To make our Links, to research ways we could grow, to protect us from threats we might not even know about. We didn't need Happenings.

A sound brought my head up: the chime that announced someone had come through the front door.

"Jackson?" It was my sister's voice. "Hey. Didn't expect you here."

"Good to see you, Ren. I like the hair."

I burst from my room. Ren stood in the granite tiled entry way, arms folded.

"You cut your hair," I said stupidly. It was short, just-brushing-her-ears short. A thick streak in front was dyed deep purple, almost blending into the black of the rest of her hair. It sort of sharpened her Asian features.

I'd told her I wanted to dye streaks into my hair. Why did she have to go and do it first?

"What are you doing here?" I asked.

Ren had moved out last year and promptly done everything she could to violate our parents' strict sense of propriety. She lived on the Populace side of town. She'd dyed her hair purple.

And she'd taken a job with Happenings.

I hadn't seen her since Dad nearly had an aneurysm about the job. He'd banned Ren from the house for contributing her Mementi knowledge to the "enemy's" work. But I'd caught him sneakily sending her texts, like he was half-ashamed he was still worried about her.

"Cora's theft…I saw it on the news." Ren's gaze dropped to the floor. "You shouldn't have gone out last night."

My nostrils flared.

"Cora didn't ask to lose two years of her life," I said. "We shouldn't be afraid to walk outside."

"Gena," Jackson said gently. "I don't think she was saying Cora deserved it."

Our security system beeped again as the front door opened. "…this new data opens up some more options with the SLS," Dad said, walking in with Mom.

"Absolutely," another voice said. To my surprise, a thin man followed my parents into the house—Drake Matthews, head scientist of Ascalon's memory research. "This is the first time we've had a witness to a theft. Well, not a witness, exactly, but someone there just before it happened. The SLS can do all sorts of things with the info in that memory. Cross-checking other memories, maybe even hooking into streetcam footage to find any connections. I wonder how I could do that…"

Me. They were talking about *me*, my memory I'd given to Jackson. It would help the investigation after all. A sickly, panicked kind of hope rose inside me.

"That's why I invited Gunner tonight," Dad replied. "He's the investigative mind, knows what methods—oh, you're here already."

Dad and Matthews looked old-fashioned in their respective bowler and fedora hats. Jackson, who chose to trust his hair alone to protect his head, looked oddly uncivilized next to them. The hats didn't do much to protect their necks, but an accidental brush wasn't likely there, anyway. And it's not like the scarves most women wore protected us if someone wanted access to our memories. Really, we were exposed no matter what we wore. I suppressed a shiver and tugged on my own useless scarf. It hadn't done me any good.

"Gena let me in." Jackson stood. Every muscle expanded and contracted precisely, even with such a casual movement. Precision. Speed. Power.

Helpful skills for a cop. And for a criminal.

"Ren," Mom said. Her mouth pinched, and she glanced at Dad. "I…didn't know you were coming over."

Dad's face reddened, and he turned to hang his hat next to the door. Of all the nights for Ren to show up, it had to be when he was forced to be polite.

"I wanted to talk to Gena," Ren said after a moment.

Mom's face gentled with an almost-smile. "That's…well, that's sweet of you." They eyed each other awkwardly until Mom shifted her attention to me. "You okay, Gen? You get my memories?"

"I'm fine," I said. "Thanks."

"Drake," Dad said, his neutral tone a bit forced, "this is my daughter Genesis, and her sister Serenity."

Ouch. Ren didn't react, but the sting of his words pierced me too. For Dad, fear showed up as anger. I wasn't sure how much of his mad was pure mad, and how much was scared-for-Ren mad.

Matthews nodded hello to me and my sister, taking off his hat. I'd only seen him from a distance at company parties, and he looked old, though he wasn't much older than my parents. Tiny wrinkles canyoned his thin, frail skin. His hair was a mottled gray-and-black example of a dye job gone bad. It contrasted with the sharp cut of his brown suit coat. A cream turtleneck rose above the suit's collar.

"Gena's also the source of our witness memory from last night's Link theft," Dad said quietly.

"Oh! Oh dear. Oh my." His face drooped in exaggerated sadness. It gave him a weird, unbalanced look. His cheekbones were freakishly uneven.

I wanted to squirm under his overly sorrowful gaze. He'd better not get direct access to my memory. Jackson had said only cops would see it. But then, he'd already broken that rule himself.

"So sorry about your friend, dear," Matthews said. "What a brave, brave girl you are."

"Thank you, Mr. Matthews." I gave him a proper deep nod and gritted my teeth behind my smile.

"So polite. You've raised a fine pair here, Mr. and Mrs. Lee." He winked at me.

My smile curdled. A *wink*. Yuck. Jackson lifted a hand to his face to cover a smile.

Mom set out some wine and glasses on the cherry-wood coffee table, then went back to the kitchen to stick a lamb chop Fast Feast in the rehydrator oven. Politeness dictated that I stay, at least until they decided to really talk shop and banish me to my room.

Sometimes, I really hated Mementi politeness.

Everyone settled onto the square lounge chairs ringing the coffee table. I hesitated. Our giant circle of a house, with bedrooms like slices of pie and the living area an open half-circle, left no corners. Nowhere to retreat. Wall-to-wall windows let in warm evening light. Wherever I sat, I would be exposed.

With no other options, I sat at the opposite end of the room from Jackson and tried to squish myself into the crook of the chair. It was futile. The beige furniture was meant more for looks than for lounging, with stiff cushions designed to force decent posture.

"So, Gunner, things must be tense for the department right now." Dad poured four glasses of wine and set them out on the table. As the server, he took the first glass, then sat back. "I've heard rumors of curfew and police watches being put into effect."

Jackson, to Dad's left, took his wine now that there was no danger of touching my father. "We're on higher alert than ever. The most recent theft really shook people up. Everybody had started thinking that it was over."

"We had over a hundred calls to my department today asking for updates on memory backups." Matthews took his wine glass now, handling it daintily. "It's inching forward, but it's not there yet. But people are getting more desperate with each Link theft."

"And angry," Dad added.

Mom rejoined the party, nodding to each person, who nodded back. She sat next to Dad. "The real question is," she said, "where are they going to direct that anger?"

Jackson nodded slowly. "Right now, it's at the Populace. You've probably already heard about the protest planned on their side of town tomorrow."

"I can't say I'm surprised," Mom said, frowning. "I know the Link thief is just one person, but it's more than that. They outnumber us now—in our own town. We built this place for us and they marched in with their lesser capabilities...no wonder people are scared."

"Yes, it's exactly like living next to dangerous Neanderthals," Ren said sarcastically.

"I'm not saying they're not human, Ren." Mom pinched the embroidery on her dress, the only sign she was agitated. "But they don't have the ability to grow the way we do. They complain about being left out of things, forgetting this is *our city*, made for Mementi minds. Not for people who still have to send their kids to school eight hours every day just to grasp the basics. Add that to all these Link thefts…" She waved her hand vaguely, like she was encompassing the upside-downing of our whole little world.

Last year, all 15,000 Mementi in Havendale had watched the online population records like obsessed sports fans. The number ticked higher and higher, eventually showing a Populace majority. Now they could elect a different mayor. Change laws that were meant to protect us. Set up a branch of police that didn't use Mementi tech so they could finally have a presence on the force. They were taking our town away from us. It shouldn't scare me, but it did.

Dad spoke again. "It's up to us to give people a little more hope. The people trust the police, and Ascalon has never let them down. If they know we're working together with new methods to track the thief, maybe it will calm things down. Though probably not in time for tomorrow's demonstration."

Matthews crossed his legs, sipping his red wine. "I don't think the protest at Happenings—"

"Happenings?" Ren asked, sitting up straighter.

"Serenity." Dad had the Warning Tone.

"It's fine." Matthews smiled sweetly. "I understand you work there."

Ren narrowed her eyes. "Why are they protesting Happenings?"

"Well, people are blaming the Populace, and Happenings brought in a lot more of them. Not to mention a…different class of Populace."

Ren snorted. "Because Populace belong in their proper place as peons, not getting good jobs at Happenings. We wouldn't want to do anything—say, let them buy stock from Ascalon—to jeopardize their status."

Dad stiffened again at Ren's blunt tone. "That's got nothing to do with it. There are rumors that Happenings is behind the Link thefts."

Ren rolled her eyes. "Like that's a surprise."

Dad pinched his lips. "I wouldn't put it past Liza Woods to steal Links and pry them apart so she can make money selling our gifts to people on the street."

"That's ridiculous," Ren snapped.

My eyes widened. What had her so on edge? She'd defended herself when she took the job at Happenings, but she was picking a fight here.

She continued, calmer. "Links are just beads unless they're connected to a Mementi brain. Liza's smart enough to know stealing Links would be scientifically useless."

"I doubt that," Matthews said, glaring at his wine like it had poisoned him.

"If she thought it had a benefit at all, she'd do it," Dad said. "No one expects Happenings to be ethical, merely innovative without restraint."

Ren's face darkened. "Maybe we need some innovation. If Happenings did break that stupid no-direct-research law, we'd have memory backups already."

My hand flew to my mouth.

"Serenity!" Dad half-rose from his chair, nearly slopping wine onto the pale carpet.

Ascalon's restrictions on no direct human research was one of the founding principles of the entire *city*. No testing of Links. No prying into Mementi brains. Observational study only. The law was hammered into the books as a condition of Ascalon's founding, only a few years after Havendale was formed. How could we trust them if they were doing the exact kind of dangerous research that had created the Mementi in the first place?

Fuming, Ren continued. "Some direct research could actually help without harming us. If people would just accept that, we wouldn't have to—"

"*Stop it.*" To my surprise, Matthews stood up. He leaned toward Ren. "You, young lady, are one who would benefit learning the value of *silence*."

Dad glowered, and I had a sneaking suspicion his face was red as much from mortification as anger. I, on the other hand, had a strange sudden urge to tell Matthews to back off my sister. I wrapped my arms around myself, afraid of where things were going.

Ren opened her mouth, but Matthews cut her off again. "We don't always know what will be helpful and what will be harmful. Perhaps you remember the story of my mother? Aria Matthews?"

Aria. The biggest horror story in our history. I swallowed. Ren's impassive expression looked forced.

"I was three when she tried to merge memories with others. Trying to help herself heal. I heard the gunshot that killed her." Matthews fixed Ren with a piercing stare. "Her death sparked the no-human-research law. I'm well aware of its limitations. And its necessity."

"I'm not saying it's entirely a bad thing," Ren grumbled. Matthews sat again.

Ren smoldered, and I knew she'd be tossing out more words any minute. Time to try to appease both sides. Timidly, I said, "And Happenings…I mean, if they want to stay in business, they can't really do anything dangerous. So, nothing to worry about."

Dad snapped. He slammed his wine glass onto the coffee table, and a crack splintered across the stem. I jumped, sudden panic surging inside me. A tremor crept up my legs, and I shrunk back in my chair. As if Dad would ever do anything violent. My own fear of him felt shameful.

"Whether Happenings is breaking the law or not, their research is not focused on the *good of the people*." With each word,

Dad stabbed a finger into the air. "Ascalon was founded on principles of protection and progression for the Mementi. That's why Ascalon is community-owned. It's why we work so closely with all the Mementi in making decisions of what to research—and how. We can't protect anyone if we're doing the same kind of research that created the Mementi in the first place."

Ren leaned forward, her cheeks heating. "The Memor-X trials were done on people—too many people—whose brains were already broken by Post-Traumatic Stress Disorder," she said. "For all we know, that was a factor in the neurological changes. If Ascalon can't research exactly how the gene therapy screwed up, we'll never even figure out how our brains connected to the peripheral nervous system. Isn't *that* worth studying?"

"No," Dad said flatly. "Nobody's willing to risk another Memor-X. You're too young to realize the damage it did to your own grandparents."

Ren pinched her mouth shut—there wasn't much she could say to that. Matthews gave my father a strange kind of smile.

But Dad's words weren't totally true. In all the times I'd snuck to Grandma Piper's house, I'd seen an awful lot of damage. Once, she'd collapsed in tears when I accidentally broke a china plate, though she couldn't remember why it had been important to her.

I glanced toward my bedroom, thinking of the Happenings logo there. An itch rose inside me, a desperation to get to the Memo and learn what I'd lost. If Grandma had had something like that, would things have been different for her? Maybe Happenings tech had some value of its own.

Jackson, I noticed, had settled back in his chair, watching the room calmly. Almost like he found the entire thing amusing. He would.

Matthews' face hardened as Ren leaned forward, hands out like she was begging. "It's dangerous for us right now. We don't really understand what we can do, or what can be done to us. The Link thefts prove it."

"Ren," Mom said loudly. *"Enough."*

"I'm not the only one who feels this way." Ren turned to me. "Even Gena agrees with me, right?"

Dad spun on me, rage in every clenched muscle of his body.

"I—" My eyes darted between my angry parents and my proud sister. Mom and Dad expected a proper and conservative denial. Ren dared me to join her, to agree with her logic.

Ren was right, we barely knew how our own memories worked. We couldn't protect ourselves. We were vulnerable to something as simple as a brush of skin. How would we change if we could be secure in our memories?

Still, Dad had a point. This wasn't testing some new computer chip. Even the rumors of Happenings stealing Links proved how scary that kind of research could get. Finding our limits meant playing with our brains. That hadn't turned out so well last time.

I pressed against the dense cushions, but they forced me forward. "I don't know," I said in a small voice.

Ren let out a disgusted sound. "You're never going to grow a backbone, are you?"

She jerked to her feet and stomped to the front door, slamming it behind her.

"I'm so sorry," Dad said to Matthews and Jackson, trembling as he sat. "She's at that age, thinks she knows everything…"

Matthews' smile seemed forced. He waved his hand in dismissal. "Of course. She's stubborn. But this one's as pleasant and polite as anyone could wish for." He winked at me again.

I bowed my head, thinking very non-pleasant and impolite things about men who smiled too much and winked at teenage girls.

The adults returned to a more civilized conversation, discussing strategies for using *my memory* as a key to searching the SLS database for more Link thief clues. You'd think they could at least wait until I was out of the room. My nerves were officially shot, skinned, and stir-fried.

I stood and went to my room, locking the door and resting against it.

A perfect image of Ren's disgusted face floated in my memory until I wanted to punch it. She saw me as a coward. All Mom and Dad had ever seen was their perfect, proper reflection. Because that's all I'd ever dared to be.

My fingertips pressed into my skull. I hated my family for what they thought of me, and I hated myself because I might be what they thought of me. A copy and a coward.

A knock on the door made me jump.

"Gena? Food's ready," Mom called.

"Okay, be there in a sec." I gave the Memo on my bed a longing glance. The delay was a frustrating sort of relief. Then the relief poofed into smoke.

I had to eat dinner sitting across the table from Gunner Jackson.

6

To bear thro' heaven a tale of woe…

—Alfred, Lord Tennyson, *In Memoriam XII*

I didn't dare watch the Memo until Dad went to bed. Mom left for her night shift at the Observatory around nine. Dad holed up in his study. It was the only room on the second floor, accessible by the winding staircase in the center of our circular house. Nobody was allowed to disturb him there. As if I wanted to.

Hades coiled around my arm, his warmth comforting. The clock ticked ten, then eleven, the minutes rolling past. I wanted to cling to each one I was sure I could remember.

The staircase creaked. I flashed my palm at the wallscreen, pausing the hologram manipulation I'd been playing with. Ria Watanabe, my favorite dancer, froze on a bridge in Tokyo's Shinjuku Gyoen Gardens—number three on my list. The sky above her glowed with the cloud of the Rosette nebula. Dad's bedroom door closed with a soft click.

I unwound Hades from my arm and tore open the forbidden Memo box. Out fell a smart-plastic square I could hide by closing my fist. I slipped a fingernail between the edges and unfolded it into a large screen.

Memories were organic to me, though I stored them in inorganic things. They were fluid, living moments of my past. This memory was a movie screen. No sense of emotion. No thoughts. No aura of reality that seeped through my own Links. How could I trust that kind of memory?

I synced my Link buds with the Share port and put them in my ears. With a shaking finger, I grazed the play button on the touchscreen.

In faded colors and muffled sound, I watched a dark street through Kalan's eyes. The recording was distorted—most of the background was fuzzy. The buildings were unrecognizable. It could have been any street in any town in the world. Faulty, normal human memories. Kalan would only remember certain details, and those might be wrong. A sign on the corner was lit. Rowley Street.

There was a distant, hollow shout, and the view whipped to the left. He started to run. I pulled the Memo closer, willing him to move faster, to turn that corner and race down an empty road.

He rounded the corner.

With a grunt, he collided with a black-haired girl. The force pushed him back the way he'd come.

"Are you okay?" he asked.

"Let me go!" The girl's eyes went wide. She backed against the wall of a building.

It was me.

The Memo shook in my hands. The distortion from his flawed memory was obvious. I wore the outfit from when we met on the tram, not what I'd worn to the Low-G. I was also a lot prettier than I looked in a mirror. Which was sort of flattering.

Kalan cocked his head in concern. "What's wrong? Are you in trouble?"

The girl's breath—my breath—came in quick gasps. "It's the Link thief, it's her. Where's Cora? Do you see anybody?"

I nearly dropped the Memo. Her? The Link thief was a girl?

On the screen, Kalan peered around the corner. "There's no one there. Are you hurt? Did she take anything from you?"

"No, but there's nowhere I can hide it." Memo-me brushed tangled hair from my face. My scarf and gloves were gone.

Kalan focused on me, his hand reaching for my shoulder. I flinched—both in the Memo, and in real life—and the hand withdrew.

"Look, I'm with a group that's trying to stop the thief," he said. "Who did you see?"

Distant footsteps slapped against pavement.

Memo-me jerked away from the wall, studying the boy. "Meet me tomorrow afternoon at Havendale Canyon."

He hesitated. "If you saw her, maybe we can catch her."

"No!" My hand reached out. It clenched for a moment before I gripped his arm. He was Populace. Touch could be used to persuade him, and I'd been brave enough to use it. Go me.

"Please," I said to him. "Meet me there tomorrow."

He took in my wide eyes and pale face. "All right."

My face cleared of tension. I dropped my hand and turned away.

"Wait," he said. "What's your name?"

"Gena. Gena Lee."

"I'm Kalan."

I ran, fading into the darkness.

The Memo flashed to the play button.

I brushed my hair back and leaned into the curve of the outer wall of the house. The memory, now embedded in my Links, zipped through my mind again. I hadn't just run into him, I had touched him. My fingers tingled, and I raised a hand to my face. This hand had touched a boy. I knew he was Populace and couldn't see my memories, but still.

I'd never experienced a memory that way. I hadn't been me, I'd *watched* me from someone else's perspective. Without my own memory of the moments on screen. If I couldn't remember it, how could that girl be me? She wasn't, because that moment had never happened for me.

Populace memories faded every day, every minute. Did that make them different people each day? Did it really make me someone else, because I'd forgotten a few minutes?

Maybe it depended on what you forgot.

I leaped up, startling Hades, who slithered toward the end of my bed. My clenched fists ached to hit something. Someone had taken the girl I had been twenty-four hours ago. Maybe the loss of some memories didn't matter, but losing those few moments changed decisions I had made. Gave me new decisions to make now.

How would Cora change, with two whole years gone? She could make herself into someone completely different in the next two years than she had in the past two. I didn't know if that was good or bad. And the victims who had lost everything, what could they make of their lives with nothing behind them? The Link thief killed our futures by stealing our pasts.

I had to stop her.

In my head, my parents' voices rattled off reasons I should hide and leave things to the proper authority. I was too young, I had no experience, I could have more memories siphoned away.

But Mr. Proper Authority himself was Detective Jackson. What better accomplice than the lead detective who could manipulate evidence? If I left this alone, the thief could steal more lives, including mine. The lives that had already been taken, like Cora's, would never be returned. The sound of her sobs from this morning, the sound of her soul peeling away one memory at a time, rang in my ears.

Hours ago, I'd known the identity of the Link thief. I might be the only person in this town who could find her again.

My brain jumped into action, rifling through everything I'd learned today. It took only moments for the dominos in my head to fall, connecting a few important ideas.

There had been streetcam footage of Cora being chased into a non-monitored area.

Non-monitored areas around where Cora and I had been: an alcove way over on Walnut Street and a wooded area behind the Low-G.

The corner of Rowley and Tanner was a straight shot from the woods behind the club.

I had a location now. Something had happened as Cora and I took the shortcut from the Low-G, so the thief—a female, Mementi thief—had to have been nearby that night. My memory flicked through faces I'd seen at the club, but there were faces I hadn't seen. The thief might not have been in the club itself.

I put Hades in his tank, then jumped on my bed and folded my legs under me. With a quick swipe of Share ports, I synced my Sidewinder phone with my wallscreen. The cops may not have checked the GPS locators of people at the club if they thought the thief was Populace. Only Mementi registered for the GPS locator program. The city map glowed on my wall, covered with GPS dots labeled with ID numbers. I frowned. I needed names for those numbers.

Kinley. She was the only one who could help. I just had to be careful what I said.

"Call Kinley," I whispered, syncing my Link buds to the phone and putting them in. The buds were more comfortable than wearing the Sidewinder itself for a long conversation—and conversations with Kinley often went long.

A few seconds later, her voice sounded in my ear. "Genalee!" she cried. "Oh my holy cow, I can't believe you're psychologically capable of speech right now. How's Cora? I tried to call her all day but her phone is off, and I heard you saw her and the cops took an evidence memory from you—"

"Kins," I interrupted, irritated that her gossip chain already knew this. "You're totally sweet for being concerned. I need a favor, actually."

Kinley was always willing to help. Partly because, despite her motor mouth, she really did care. Partly because she wanted details, details, details, and helping was a good way to get them.

"Anything," she said eagerly.

"You know that hack you wrote ages ago to find out people's GPS ID numbers? I know you don't like to give out a lot of your hack codes, but I need it."

I'd been livid with Kinley when she rolled out that hack. Mostly because it involved sending me and Cora anonymous, stalker-ish texts that pinpointed our location. We'd had some fun with it, though.

"What do you need it for?" she asked.

"I, uh, want to keep an eye on Cora. See who comes around, make sure nobody's bugging her too much." I really needed to think up my lies ahead of time.

"Aren't you a sweet little watch dog. I don't think the hack will do you much good, though. Not since I gave out my GPS-location-changing hack to a couple guys at school. It sort of went viral. Nobody's going to be where the system says they are."

I groaned. That was the same hack I'd used on my Sidewinder so my parents wouldn't know I was at the Low-G last night. If half the town had that, the GPS maps would be useless. The cops would find out and shut it down soon. *Why* had Kinley given that away? She usually guarded her hacks with triple-encrypted ferocity.

"I could give you my newest hack, though," she said. "Since it's an emergency and all. I got into the Sidewinder routing station for texts, and you can do all sorts of things with it that could help you watch out for Cora. Set up alerts when people text keywords, or intercept texts people are sending if you're in Share port distance—"

"Sure," I said to keep up the charade. "Send it over."

My Sidewinder beeped that it had received a new download. It would be useless. Just like her other hack was now useless. I wanted to scream. Five minutes in, and my so-called investigation was at a standstill.

"Just sent the whole package," she said. "So you sure you're okay? You can talk to me about anything. Cora too."

Kinley actually was a surprisingly good listener. She was also a surprisingly good talker. "You're the best, Kins. Thanks."

I hung up before she could dig for more.

There was no way to know who'd been at or near the Low-G last night. It might not have worked anyway, if the thief hadn't brought their Sidewinder. Which was highly possible.

I threw my pillow across the room. I was going to need help, and someone had already offered his.

A Populace boy. I flopped down face-first and burrowed into my blankets. Even if he had more information and a posse of Link thief hunters, I didn't know anything about him. But I couldn't trust the police, not with Jackson in charge. I had nothing to go on. Kalan was my only other lead.

A Mementi was the Link thief. A Populace wanted to help me stop her. My world was a scrambled mess of spaghetti tossed with a heap of angry sauce. If Kalan was the only one who could help, I'd find out how. I turned on my Sidewinder.

Text from Genesis Lee to Kalan Daniel Fox, TDS 16:12:32/5-5-2084
When can we meet again?

7

…howsoe'er I know thee, [I]
Could hardly tell what name were thine.

—Alfred, Lord Tennyson, *In Memoriam LIX*

Funny, how some things stayed exactly the same when the whole world changed.

I raised the holoscreen of my school computer to hide from my classmates. I'd been fielding their condolences for Cora all morning, like she'd died. The four-hour school day had never felt so long.

I'd already absorbed the next informational memory in my personal curriculum from the school SLS. I should have been calculating star masses on my sim. Instead, I huddled in my favorite comfy armchair and peeked over the top of my holoscreen. Jef Normandy drooled onto his chest, slouched in his own armchair with his holoscreen on his lap. Mr. Soto didn't notice; he was helping Kloe Carpenter. Her current focus was differential equations, which weren't Mr. Soto's forte. He'd probably absorbed her daily memory so he could help.

A chorus of *dings* rang out from the holoscreens around the room—the official end of the school day. The standard message popped up on my screen. *You have completed the required school hours. Continue studying?* Normally, I'd have tapped yes like everyone else, but not today. I shut down the holoscreens and rushed around the haphazard assortment of recliners and armchairs, out the door before anyone said a word. My body hummed with a desperate energy. Desperate for Kalan's information. Desperate to get this over with.

I nibbled an apple on a tram that was mercifully almost empty, ignoring constant repetitions of "Passengers are reminded there is no eating or drinking on Havendale city trams. Thank you." The other two passengers gave me mildly disapproving looks.

I felt rebellious, ignoring the rules. Then I felt stupid for thinking eating an apple on public transportation counted as rebellious.

My knees began bouncing nervously as the tram crossed the invisible boundary of Main Street, and familiar anxiety threaded through my body. I patted out a drum rhythm, a new song from Frankie and the Boy, on my thighs. Populace territory. Not nearly as far as Hong Kong or Tokyo, but the farthest from home I'd ever been. The tram pulled to a stop a few miles later. I lurched out of my seat, forcing myself forward. I'd already crossed the line.

I counted the tramstop steps as I descended. My feet hit crumbly pavement and I blinked in surprise at the world that faced me. I might as well have been in Africa for all the similarities to my side of town.

Mementi neighborhoods were peppered with dramatic representations of our dreams. The Wilsons' Neuschwanstein castle replica built for their little girls. The Garcias' imitation of the Sydney Opera House that sounded of music every time the door opened. The Laytons' half-treehouse that attracted all the kids in the neighborhood. Even the more "common" houses like mine featured unique designs. Dad had always thought our perfectly circular home with its perfectly circular garden lent an "elegant" air to the neighborhood.

Houses apparently weren't the thing here. Apartment buildings lined the street, bicycles and barbecues chained to ugly black railings and toys littering cracked pavement. Windows stacked up the building sides like children's blocks, some lined with foil or stuffed with flattened boxes. Maybe to keep the sun out? I mean, self-tinting windows might be pricey, but there had to be another option besides cardboard. How could you even enjoy your home, with cardboard and tinfoil blocking out the world?

Granted, they didn't get much of a view. An empty street limped ahead of me. Instead of rolling away in welcome, it sported hazards. Potholes, crumbly gravel, oil stains—they actually used the roads for something more than footpaths. A half-empty parking lot replaced what could have been a little garden or courtyard for an apartment complex. A rusty white car, an actual manual drive, was parked across the street. Couldn't they see the nice, public trams rumbling overhead?

I headed north to the meeting place Kalan had designated and double-checked my Sidewinder. My GPS told anybody checking—like my parents—that I was at Cora's. Thank you, Kinley.

I touched my Links through my shirt. I'd worn them as necklaces today, looping the magnetic Links long enough to hang under my clothes. Moving Links around was nerve-wracking. I'd dropped one of my bracelets once, and the momentary loss was so disorienting I threw up. But they felt safer around my neck. Harder to get to.

Kalan worked in the tram garage, so I was meeting him at "the end of the line." Irony at its finest. Enormous garage doors yawned in front of me as I approached. A single tram car lay on its side in the yard like it had crawled there to die. Sounds of screeching and clanging came from the building itself.

I couldn't help but think this place was nothing more than a torture chamber—trams shrieking in metallic pain as sadistic mechanics cut into them with blowtorches and laser saws.

Turned out facing my fears made me morbid.

Forcing myself to at least pretend I knew what I was doing, I marched through the chain-linked gate to the door marked OFFICE. My soft knock went unanswered. I pushed the door open. Empty.

I backed away, eyeing the open gate to the tram yard and garages. Option A: enter the jaws of tram yard hell. Option B: wait for Kalan to find me.

Like I'd pick Option A. Standing under the shade of the overhanging roof, I stirred the red dirt with the toe of my tennis shoe. The circles and swirls wove a soothing pattern.

"Hey!" an angry voice called.

Blue coveralls. Angry march. That was all I got before the guy accosted me.

"What are *you* doing here?" he demanded.

Hostile eyes raked over me. They lingered on the scarf draped over my head and wound around my neck. I heard the unspoken antecedent of his "you:" Mementi.

"I'm waiting for someone." I pressed my back to the wall.

He grabbed my arm, sending a shudder of shock down my spine. *Please, please, please let go!* He hauled me away from the building in painful jerks.

"Go stake out some other place to vandalize," he said. "Or better yet, go join your friends at the protest."

Get away, let go let go. I yanked, but his grip only tightened. My fingers tingled. "I'm not—I don't want—he works here, I'm meeting someone who works here, Kalan!"

His fingers clenched tighter. "You're the girl he's meeting?"

I tugged my arm again. A gasp escaped when he released me. I squeezed my shaking hands so tight I could feel the raised embroidery of flowers on my gloves.

"Go find him, then." He nodded toward the tram garage, glowering.

My eyes darted toward the enormous open doors that harbored more potentially unfriendly workers. "Could you, maybe, tell him I'm here, please?"

His laugh came out as a bark. "You want him, go find him."

I darted away from him and into the yard. Potentially unfriendly beat confirmed scary any day. A wave of silence rolled behind me. Work equipment inside the garages went still. Heat waves rippled out from stilled blowtorches and bodies turned in haunting unison to follow my progress. I ran all the way to the garage on the end. So far, the Populace were living up to their reputation for unfriendliness. Finally, in the last garage, there he was. Cuter than a one-time stalker in blue coveralls had a right to be.

Get a grip, Gena. He was a stalker, I knew nothing about him, and he was Populace.

He looked up. The pounding of hammer on metal stopped. He held the hammer high, like he wasn't sure what to do with it now that someone was watching him.

"Give me a few minutes," he said. "I've got to finish this."

He returned to work. The hammer clanged on sheet metal, a rhythm so tight I could almost dance to it. His long arms circled in smooth strokes. An image from the canyon flashed in my mind. Under those long-sleeved coveralls, his arms were toned and strong. Those arms could do some damage.

I pinched myself as punishment for stupid thoughts. He hadn't lied or attempted to hurt me so far. I'd give him a chance to tell me what he knew about the Link thief and then I could scram.

The hammering stopped a minute later. He pulled off thick work gloves and riffled his light curls. "That's as good as I'm going to get it with you watching every move I make."

"Oh. Sorry. I was just waiting." Why did I feel like I had to apologize for *watching* him?

"Nothing to be sorry for." He gave me a lopsided grin, then hollered toward the back, "Jem, I'm taking lunch."

A grunt indicated someone had heard him and approved.

I followed him to a row of lockers where he took off the coveralls, revealing a simple t-shirt and shorts—and those tanned, toned arms.

"So." I focused on the ground. Grease stains dotted the concrete. "You, uh, work here full time? No school?"

He hung the coveralls on a hook inside a locker. "Nope. I traveled a lot growing up, so I homeschooled and graduated early." He faced me. "And you? Ditching?"

I crossed my arms. "Of course not. We only have four-hour school days. We don't exactly need tests or worksheets."

"Guess not." His lips twitched, like he found me amusing.

We turned to the door, and the man who'd grabbed me stalked past. He fixed me with a glare. I shrank back.

Kalan noticed. "You met Luke?"

I rubbed my sore arm.

His jaw set. "What did he do to you?"

"Nothing," I said quickly. "He…uh…asked me to leave. He didn't know I was meeting you."

"Stay here. I'll be right back."

He marched toward where Luke had disappeared. I hurried after him. "No, please, it's okay, you don't have to fight him or anything."

"I'm not going to fight him. Just ask him to apologize."

I didn't have time for this. "I need to find out what's going on. Please, Kalan, I have to talk to you about the Memo."

He stopped at the sound of his name. "So you watched it."

I squeezed the strap on my bag. The Memo was inside.

"Probably kinda trippy."

I wanted to snap at him. "It was rather disturbing."

Turning away, I saw that work around the tram yard had paused again. Wary shifting was the only movement as half a dozen workers stared at me. *Come one, come all, see the magical, terrifying Mementi! Only a quarter, but watch out or she'll chomp your limbs off!* I wanted to growl at every one of them to get back to their manual labor.

"Let's go," Kalan said. "Nobody here is really happy with the Mementi right now."

"Right now?" I asked. "Since when are you ever happy with us?"

My feet hit the ground in a staccato rhythm as we hurried away from the tram garage. Once we reached the street, my joints eased and I felt a little less like a marionette on display.

"The protest has people spooked," Kalan said as we walked. "And there was some vandalism last night, some store windows got smashed."

"Was anybody hurt?"

"Not that I heard." He kicked a rock and it clattered down the street. "But it's only a matter of time. People on both sides need someone to talk some sense into them."

He sounded like he wanted to be that someone.

"Where are we going?" I asked, nervous with him in the lead. Apartment buildings had given way to shoddy storefronts and hole-in-the-wall restaurants.

"I wasn't lying when I said I was taking lunch." He grinned. "My favorite place is up the road here, and there shouldn't be a wait since it's past regular lunch hour. You hungry?"

My apple on the tram hadn't been much more than a snack, and I was starved. I bit my lip.

He paused on the sidewalk. "Or we could talk somewhere else. If you want."

"Well…my parents watch my charge account." I winced thinking of the fallout—the yells, the charge account taken away, and very possibly getting locked in my room with only bread and water to eat.

Okay. Maybe that last one was the anxiety talking.

"Ah," Kalan said. "The folks wouldn't be happy to see a charge on this side of town, would they?" He shrugged. "No worries, I'm paying."

And that turned it into a date. Which was safer from the parent interference standpoint, but a little more risky on the what-to-do-with-this-cute-Populace-boy side.

I needed to get in control, pronto. He had me on his side of town, waiting for his information, and I needed to balance the scales.

"A restaurant would be fine," I said. "But I can pay for myself." I could pretend my charge account number had been hacked.

"If you want." We continued walking. "Did you find what Link was missing?"

"I told you, there isn't one missing."

"Huh." He scanned my face, making me acutely uncomfortable. "I thought you just didn't notice or something."

"Of course I'd notice if a whole Link was missing!" The question hit too close to home. I took a deep breath. "Sorry."

"You keep saying that. What do you have to be sorry about?"

"I shouldn't have yelled at you," I said. "I don't know you."

He grinned, sporting the shaggy puppy-dog look. "Yeah, yelling should be saved for those we love most."

"That's not what I meant. I—" The word came automatically. "Sorry."

He shook his head. "Sorry. Please. Excuse me. You Mementi are always so polite, even when you're looking down your nose at us."

His tone said he was half-joking, but I wasn't laughing. "I am not looking down my nose at you. All I want are answers. What were you doing out that night? You said you're trying to stop the Link thief?"

"Yup. Me and a few other people."

"Why?" I asked. "You're Populace. It doesn't affect you."

He snorted. "Watch the news. All that pent-up anger behind your Mementi politeness is coming out against people over here."

"So you don't want to be blamed. That's why you're trying to stop him. Her. The thief."

"Yeah. And well, it's just wrong, isn't it? Someone stealing lives."

"And you care about that." I couldn't help the suspicion in my voice. "Why?"

He stuck his hands in the pockets of his cargo shorts. "Because of my grandma."

My head snapped around. "What?"

"She got Alzheimer's before she died." He focused on the sidewalk. "It was awful, walking into her house and not being recognized. It's not fair that other people have to go through that because of some psycho."

For a brief moment, I felt connected to this boy through our departed, memory-tormented grandmothers. "I'm sorry."

We walked in silence for half a block.

"So, what about the other people you mentioned? Why are they into this?" I asked finally. My suspicions might be softening toward him, but that didn't extend to his little detective force.

"My dad has a thing about helping people." Kalan grinned. "And his sermons have a way of convincing others to help him do that."

"Sermons?"

"He's a minister."

So. A vigilante church congregation. How frustratingly unhelpful. I eyed Kalan. He wasn't what I'd expect from a churchy boy. "You're a preacher's son."

"Yeah."

"You believe in God?"

"With all my heart." The laugh lines in his face smoothed, and his expression sort of…deepened.

I tilted my head, studying him as we walked. He'd flipped that switch again, from charming to intense. I hated how that fascinated me. "Oh."

"Here we are," he said, nodding to a squat building tucked between an arcade and a bowling alley.

I looked warily at the neon sign. It flickered briefly. *Sushi Ya?* We're eating sushi?"

"Yeah. You a fan?"

"Never had it," I said. Mom and Dad worked so much—and such odd hours—that food at my house usually consisted of Fast Feast meals. Or Dad's favorite Chinese restaurant on the rare occasion we went out.

"Never had sushi? You?"

Tension made me easily irritated, but I bit back another outburst. "Being Asian does not a sushi-eater make. I'm a quarter Chinese. Sushi is Japanese."

"What? No, I didn't even think…" He shrugged. "It's just, you're Mementi, and sushi can get sort of expensive. So I guess I thought you'd eat it a lot."

"Right." Because that was much less stereotypical.

He turned red beneath his tan and paused next to the door. "Look, we can eat somewhere else if you want."

Raw fish. The thought made my nose wrinkle. But I was breaking all kinds of comfort-levels lately. "I'll try it, I guess."

Kalan swept the door open, giving me a deep bow. "My Lady. The feast awaits."

He had just enough nerdiness to not destroy his cuteness. Either that or he was a stellar nerd impersonator who used his charm to lure people into his clutches. An almost-smile dropped from my face and I gave my girly side a stern shake.

A koi pond sat inside the entrance, and the hypnotic weaving of the giant fish mesmerized me. Kalan led me away from it, past a dirty golden Buddha with pennies stacked on his belly.

Low-hanging paper lanterns swayed in the wake of rushing servers, tossing yellow light in arcs over dingy booths. Dishes clattered, and someone yelled from the kitchen. A busser wiped down a table in the center of the room. His rag circled around and around as his eyes fixed on me. Conversations faltered at each table Kalan and I passed.

They knew I was an imposter. I stuck as close to Kalan as I dared, anxiety kicking up a notch.

A frowning waiter slapped two paper menus on the table and slunk off to get our requested waters. To avoid the whispers and shifting of bodies around the room, I studied the menu. Unfamiliar words stuck out: *unagi, yamagobo, nori, tobiko*. The exotic feel gave me a brief thrill.

"I don't even know what half this stuff is," I said.

"It's all good, I promise," Kalan said over the top of his own menu. "I can order for both of us if you want. I've got a few favorites."

I should say no. Stay in charge. But I really wanted my food to be as un-nasty as possible. "Thank you for the offer. I would like to try one with shrimp."

His lips twitched again in a suppressed smile. He picked up a pencil, marked a few boxes next to his choices, and set his menu at the edge of the table.

The waiter dropped off our drinks and snatched the menu. He glared at me, making sure I noticed before he sulked back to the kitchen. I fiddled with the Links at my neck, then reached for my cup.

Seconds later, a passing customer bumped my elbow. Water slopped over the side of the glass, dripping into my lap. I jerked away from the edge of the table and set my glass down, rubbing the assaulted elbow. Kalan scowled at the backs of a couple headed for the exit.

He leaned closer. "You know, you might want to take off your scarf and gloves. They're a dead giveaway you're Mementi."

I clasped my hands under the table. "I can't, I can't do that."

He raised his thick eyebrows. "Why?"

"It's protection," I said. "We can only access memories through touch. It's a chain reaction. When we touch someone, we can see any memory on any Link they're touching, and on any Link *that* Link is touching. Certain fabrics are non-conductive, though. We can't access memories through them. It's not like we want to see each other's whole lives."

Most of us didn't. Apparently some of us wanted to steal everybody's lives. Another good reason for protective clothing.

"Huh." He rubbed his lips. "So you can't store a memory in anything you want?"

I shook my head. "Our neural impulses send charges through the molecules—"

Kalan's eyebrow shot up.

I sighed. "We change stuff so it can store memories. But only some materials. Mostly it's just natural or biological stuff like wood and rock. Different stuff does different things to the memory. Like, we use quartz storage ports and steel transfer cables for the Shared Link System. They have long-term storage and enhance detail."

"Doesn't the SLS grid run under the whole city?"

"Yeah."

"But couldn't you…I don't know, touch the concrete and access all the memories on the grid?" he asked.

"No. The transfer cables are coated in plastic, which is—"

"A non-conductive material." He grinned. "Awesome."

Our testy waiter dumped a plate of colorful, rice-wrapped circles on the table. I stared at the plate, very conscious that I was in a shady restaurant about to eat raw fish.

"What did you order?"

"Your house special shrimp roll, the classic happy roll, and the unagi special. Very basic stuff." He ripped the paper off a pair of chopsticks and clicked them together. "You know how to use these?"

"Yes." Dad was a little over-exuberant about going chopsticks-only when it came to any kind of Oriental food.

"That's the shrimp one you wanted. There's nothing raw in it." He poured some soy sauce into a dish, deftly dipped a sushi roll, and stuffed it in his mouth.

I prodded one of the rolls he'd gestured to with my chopsticks. It wasn't going to squirm around. *Raw* didn't mean *live*. Besides, he said this one wasn't raw. So maybe I wouldn't die of food poisoning after all. I followed his lead, dipping a roll in soy sauce and putting the whole thing in my mouth.

The flavors and textures danced on my tongue, salty and chewy and fresh with a slight crunch. My eyes widened.

Kalan grinned. "Good?"

I grabbed another piece. "Good."

Kalan handled the chopsticks like a pro. I found myself watching his hands. Other than faces, I didn't often see skin or the muscles that rippled beneath it. The urge to run a finger over the back of his hand made my arm twitch.

Stop it. Focus.

"Alright." I laid down my chopsticks and lowered my voice. "So what do you know about the Link thief?"

"To business, huh?" he said. "Basically all I've got is from the news, and what you told me that night. Some of us from the church go out and patrol the streets at night, trying to spot the Link thief and catch her. Nobody's found anything so far."

"You mean you've got nothing?" I'd come all the way out here. Crossed the forbidden line, been accosted by a nasty man, and risked food poisoning. My cheeks heated with anger. "You just wander the streets and pray you'll stumble across the thief in action?"

"Hey, at least we're doing something." He crossed his arms. "Even the cops don't do that much."

My politeness was taking a permanent vacation around him. "Because that tactic is useless."

"Well, what would *you* do?" His eyebrows hung dangerously low.

"I—" There wasn't much I could do. Or Kalan. Or the cops.

I should get up right now. This was pointless. All of it. How could you catch a thief who stole the memories of her crimes? Left no witnesses?

"Why did you even want to meet me?" I asked, slumping against the back of the booth.

"Because thanks to you, we've actually got something to go on," Kalan said, his eyebrows in a more neutral position again. "We know the thief is a girl. We know exactly where she was the night of the last theft. She caught you and erased your memory of her, but didn't follow her typical MO and take all your Links. We've got *clues*."

I leaned forward, my face pinching. "Wait, what do you mean, 'we' know? You told your group about me?"

"Not the group, just my dad. He thinks if we work with you, we'll actually make some progress. And he hears a lot of things at work, too. He's got a theory."

"What theory?"

Kalan hesitated. "One I'm sure you won't like."

I held back a growl. "I like not knowing even less."

He laughed. "I knew I'd like you." He took a sip of water, stalling. "It's not a popular idea on your side. He thinks the thief is actually Mementi."

I pressed my palms onto the table. Having it said by someone else, by a Populace, made it worse.

"Why does he think that?" I said. "What does he do, that he'd hear information to make him think that?"

"He's a bartender at the casino."

"A *bartender*? I thought he was a minister."

Kalan shook his hair off his forehead. "Yup. But everybody loves to gamble, and everybody loves to drink, and my dad loves spreading the gospel to everybody. Not to mention all the rumors he hears. He's got the best seat in the house."

I could tell him that I was proof. That only a Mementi could have stolen my memories. The words felt like a betrayal.

Kalan gave me an earnest look. "We're not trying to blame you. We just want it to stop. The town's already divided about…well, everything. But now people are in some kind of a feeding frenzy."

Divided on everything. That about summed it up. Rich versus poor, perfect memory versus imperfect memory, Ascalon versus Happenings. Our sole uniting factor was our hatred for each other.

Not that you could really blame us. Only a few months ago, my high school tennis team finally beat the Populace team in the finals round. That night, Populace players had vandalized the houses of our team. They killed a few pets, including Dom's puppy, which really put people in an uproar. A couple of Populace students were suspended. Because getting a free week out of school was fitting punishment for animal cruelty.

Mementi didn't forget things like that—we didn't forget anything. No wonder the town was coming apart with the Link thefts.

"It's only a theory," Kalan said, breaking the silence. "But we can't count anybody out at this point. If we work together, we can find the actual facts. Hopefully even find your memories."

I'd hoped for information from him, not a partnership. I hadn't gotten the first, and I didn't want the other.

But I had no idea if the thief might catch up with me. Erase everything I'd learned, and would learn, about the Link thief. I should share everything with someone whose memories *couldn't* be stolen. A Populace sidekick might come in handy. Could I trust that Kalan was who he seemed to be? Could I afford not to?

I bent a chopstick so far it snapped in half. "Your dad is right."

Kalan laid his own chopsticks down and leaned across the table. "What makes you say that?"

"The way I lost my memory proves it. We can *see* each other's memories when we touch skin. But we can also *transfer* memories away from someone else from certain points on the body."

I drummed my fingers against my thighs and told Kalan everything, from the overheard conversation of Detective Jackson to the long list of suspects that included pretty much any female Mementi in town.

"Well. That's mega-creepy." Kalan spun a chopstick on the table. "But why are Links going missing, if the thief could touch people and take any memories she wanted?"

"Maybe she's covering her tracks. If she siphoned something big, people would notice they were missing years of memory. Then it'd be obvious the thief is Mementi. By taking full Links, people still notice, but she can gear the blame toward the Populace."

"So that's why she used siphoning with you. She only had to take a few minutes, which you wouldn't have noticed if it hadn't been for me." Kalan sounded disgusted.

I felt desperate not to vilify my entire town. "We're not bad people. I mean, I know them all. Every single Mementi has a place in my memories. We're…nice."

He raised an eyebrow. "You're all very polite to us, but you still don't like us. Nice doesn't mean a thing."

I didn't respond.

"Why don't you like us, anyway?" he asked—curious, not aggressive.

I wanted to hug him for not being accusatory. I tucked my hands under my arms. Since when did I want to hug people?

"We don't think you're all evil or anything," I said. "You're just so different than us. I mean, petty theft and small-crime rates have gone up by over 75 percent with the rise of Populace in town."

Kalan frowned. "You realize the non-Mementi population of the city more than doubled over the last five years. Rising crime rates are sort of inevitable, especially when most of those people are—"

Poor. Like Kalan, in his cheap t-shirt and his dead-end job and his "splurge" on cheap sushi. He wasn't a criminal, but then he wasn't desperate either. It wasn't exactly the Populace's fault they didn't have the skills for Mementi-tailored jobs, and didn't inherit Ascalon stock.

But nobody said they had to live here. Havendale had been built *for* the Mementi. For our security and prosperity, modified by our unique skills before any of them showed up. It wasn't our fault, either, that they couldn't biologically qualify for positions as doctors, cops, teachers, or anything else that required Mementi memories to function in our town. I pinched my mouth shut.

Kalan leaned back. "You know, you can counter me if you want."

"Counter you?"

"Express your own opinion. You don't have to sit there. I can tell you want to say more."

"There's no point in fighting about it."

"Who said anything about fighting?" he asked.

"What I have to say contradicts what you said. We'd fight."

"There's a difference between a debate and a fight," he said. "Tell me why I'm dead wrong."

That sounded like a sure-fire way to end this possible partnership with a bang. Except he really seemed interested, the way he crossed his hands on the table and waited for me to speak. I chewed my lip.

His eyes twinkled. "I dare you."

Twerp. "It's about what's behind the crime rates. It's the biological fact of how you are. You just don't…*work* in Havendale society, with all the Mementi-specific tech. And…"

I hesitated, but he looked thoughtful. "And well, our brains have adapted to process our memories more quickly. We're more logical. You guys don't make the same connections as fast, so your hearts jump in and make decisions before your brains understand what's going on. It makes you more dangerous, and less…" I searched for a word, but nothing came.

"Less." Kalan fiddled with the fake flower in a vase that decorated the table. "That pretty much sums it up. You think we're less than you."

"No." *Yes.* "Well, maybe some people do."

Confusion wrinkled my forehead. I *had* always thought of them as less—less smart, less caring, less able. Kalan wasn't that way at all. He was everything I never expected in a Populace boy, actually.

"Maybe," I said slowly, "maybe we're more like…Links. We have different strengths and weaknesses, but we're all good for something."

Kalan's eyebrows puckered.

"What?"

"That's not what I expected you to say, I guess. Do you really think that?"

I studied my fingertips through the thin webbing of my gloves. Who decided the Populace were less than us, anyway, basing their level of humanity on a single biological characteristic?

"Yeah. I guess I do."

He smiled. "Then I'm glad we're partners, Gena Lee."

Partners. With a Populace. Mom and Dad would bury him in the backyard if they found out.

"So what next?" he asked.

The question spurred my brain into action. "We have to learn what the thief wants people to forget. If we find the connection between the victims, we can narrow down who has a motivation to steal Links."

"Could you talk to your friend, the one who lost her Link?" Kalan dipped a finger in leftover sushi sauce and sucked it dry. "Or maybe the other victims?"

"There's nothing they would know," I said. "We don't know what questions to ask, even if there was something they could tell us."

The faces of the victims flashed through my mind, and one was more familiar than the rest. Blaire's mom, Miranda Jacobs.

"We can't ask the victims," I said, "but I think I've got someone else we could talk to."

8

But over all things brooding slept
The quiet sense of something lost.

—Alfred, Lord Tennyson, *In Memoriam LXXVIII*

"You'll be late for work if you come with me," I said.
Our feet clanged up the metal of the tramstop steps, and Kalan shrugged. "My boss won't care, as long as I get my hours in. I'm not about to leave a Mementi girl alone on this side of town."

It would be good to have his un-stealable memories there. Though I could do without the male chauvinism.

The tram approached, and we boarded. This one was nearly full, and I faced more stares, some hostile and some curious. Somehow the glares didn't bother me now. A glare was distant. Unthreatening. I'd take that over the menace of a tram full of Mementi pressed too close for comfort.

Kalan let me have a seat at the end of the row and plopped next to me. "Who's this girl we're going to talk to, anyway?"

"Blaire Jacobs. Her mom is one of the theft victims." Miranda Jacobs seemed too sweet to be involved in anything someone would steal her memories for.

"And you know Blaire how?"

"She's my sister's best friend. She helped get Ren a job at Happenings."

Blaire was always the nice one, who'd let me play Barbies or go out for ice cream even when Ren didn't want me there. I hadn't seen her in nearly a year. That time, she'd held tightly to the hand of her Populace boyfriend and hadn't noticed me.

"She works at Happenings?" Kalan said in surprise. "Not Ascalon?"

I nodded stiffly. Blaire had told Ren—and Ren had given the same reasoning to Dad—that working at Happenings would give her an "alternative viewpoint" before she went to college to study neurology. That it was actually an act of devotion to the Mementi, because they were willing to go into enemy territory to learn new things. Do actual research, and take that knowledge with them to Ascalon someday.

Obviously, Dad didn't go for that kind of reasoning.

Both Blaire and Ren had been more or less shunned by the entire community. Hadn't they stopped to think what Happenings might learn from *them*? I knew Ren really was trying to help. But that didn't stop the vague betrayal in my heart.

Now, here I was, crossing lines, too. Walking right into "enemy territory" to learn new things for the benefit of the Mementi. For the first time in years, I felt like I actually understood my sister. I quivered inside at my own necessary betrayal.

"Blaire's not going to know much about her mom's theft," Kalan said. "I mean, if the thief is stealing memories so people forget something specific, Blaire would've had *her* Links stolen too."

I tried to shake off my dread. "Yeah. But she could at least give us some ideas. Maybe her mom had been acting strange, or seeing certain people a lot."

The tram slowed as we approached the stop closest to Happenings. When the door opened, the chants of a crowd sounded in the distance.

I paused on the tramstop platform. The white X-shaped Happenings building loomed over a throng of several hundred Mementi. It looked like an ant hill—disorganized at first, until you picked out the patterns of their march. Back and forth, circling around, bouncing their little signs and chanting phrases I couldn't hear. A huge section of the building painted with tech-paint played Happenings ads. The perma-smile of Liza Woods, CEO, beamed down on the crowd, mocking them.

"I forgot about the protest," I said.

Kalan frowned. "I didn't think it was this big. What do they think they're going to do, close Happenings? Make all the rest of us move out?"

Not my problem right now. Focus on the task. "Happenings won't let us in with that crowd out there."

"Could you call her?" Kalan suggested. "Or call Happenings and say you want to talk to her? Maybe she could meet us somewhere."

Like Happenings would be fielding calls today. *Thanks for calling our protest hotline. You are caller number 3,000,001. Your call will be taken in the order it was received.*

"Let me try my sister," I said. "I don't have Blaire's new number, but she will."

I unwound my Sidewinder from my wrist and wrapped it around my ear. "Call Ren."

It rang for a moment before she picked up. "What?"

"Ren? It's me."

"I know it's you, dummy. I'm at work. What do you want?"

I stifled an impulse to growl at her. "Is Blaire around? I need to talk to her, but she changed her number."

There was a pause. "I haven't seen her in a while. She moved in with her boyfriend two months back, and got some job closer to where they are."

"She left Happenings?" I stared at the distant building. "But Ren, it was like her dream. She's the one who got you—"

"I *know*. Sorry, Gen, but she's all weird lately. Why do you need her?" Ren sounded agitated. I heard voices in the background. Would she get in trouble for being on the phone at work?

"Do you at least have her number?"

"She changed it again."

I glared at Happenings.

On Ren's end of the line, someone called to her. "Look, I've got to go," she said. "Don't bother with Blaire. Her boyfriend is really the only thing she cares about now."

"What's wrong?" Kalan asked as I clicked off. He leaned against the metal railing, strong arms bracing him. His eyebrows knit in concern.

"Blaire left Happenings and moved in with some boyfriend," I said. "My sister hasn't seen her in two months, and she changed her number again."

"So dead end."

"Maybe. It doesn't make sense, though. She lost everything when she went to Happenings, all her friends, everything. And it was worth it to her. She wouldn't just leave that, not after she'd sacrificed so much."

"So, what? You think something happened to her?" Kalan asked. "Two months ago is around the same time the Link thefts happened. Could she have been a victim, too, and…I don't know, gotten lost?"

The possibility made me shiver despite the sun beating down on me. I unwound my Sidewinder from my wrist and twisted the flexible band over the neck of my shirt. I aimed the small projector lens at my hand to see it better in the sunlight, turning on the holo screen.

"Let me see if I can find her," I said.

My hand flickered into a colored map littered with numbered GPS locator dots. I dragged a finger across my gloved palm, moving the map around.

"You know, it's kinda creepy you guys can track each other with these phones," Kalan said.

"It's totally voluntary," I replied. "And the only people who can see your name are ones you've granted access. See the numbers by the dots? Those are codes for emergency services, and each one is tied to a person. The code stays constant if you change phones or numbers. Only on-duty cops are labeled with names, for emergencies."

"Has Blaire cleared you to see her?"

"No. But a friend of mine hacked the system ages ago, and we all found out our numbers. We used them as code names, as a joke." Blaire and Ren had thought Kinley was a genius. Which she basically was.

I entered Blaire's number into the search box. CODE NOT FOUND, blinked the words on my screen.

"She's not here," I whispered. A tremor went through me. It took me a minute to realize it was an approaching tram. It whooshed past us, swirling the ends of my hair out from under my scarf.

"She probably turned off her phone or something." Kalan's voice had an extra-soft tone that said he was trying to comfort me. "Or maybe she skipped town altogether."

Mementi didn't "skip town." This was the only place we belonged. The only place we weren't feared and hated and bullied. Though I couldn't be the only one who dreamed of the rest of the world. Maybe Blaire really had gone somewhere.

My fingers tapped over my laser screen, and I rewound the timing on the GPS map. Her number didn't pop onto the map until nearly two months ago. She spent a lot of time around a certain apartment.

"There," I said, stabbing at my palm. "That's where she lives. Or used to live."

I rushed down the tramstop steps.

"Gena," Kalan called.

"It's not far," I said.

He jogged up next to me. "She's obviously not there."

I shook my head. "I want to see what we can find. It's too convenient. Her mom is a theft victim, and Blaire didn't show up on the map for the last two months. Around the time the thefts started."

I couldn't let Blaire go. Not without at least looking into this.

We soon found a crumbly four-plex with Blaire's name on the mailbox. No answer when I knocked. I tried to peer in the windows, but they were all dark. I jiggled the doorknob.

I paused. "It's not a DNA lock."

Kalan shrugged. "Not many of us have those. Lots more expensive than keys or keypads."

Private DNA locks were another tech Ascalon had perfected and rolled out to the world. They were only about seven years old. Before that, when we still used a key, my parents hid a spare…

A potted cactus squatted next to Blaire's door. I rotated the pot and grinned. She'd stolen Mom and Dad's hiding trick. Nobody wanted to stick their hand into a potted cactus, but if you cut the needles off the back, you could bury a key without getting mauled.

I rooted in the dirt and came up with Blaire's key.

"Wow." Kalan's eyebrows shot up. "I don't even want to ask how you knew about that. So now you're breaking into her house?"

"I'm not breaking in." I stuck the key in the lock. "I have a key. And she's a friend, *and* she could be in trouble."

"This might not be her place anymore. We could ask the neighbors…"

The door opened. As I stepped over the threshold, Kalan said, "Wait."

I froze.

"If she's really missing, they'll search the apartment. They'll pick up your DNA traces."

I looked down at my red leggings, jean shorts, and gloves. "They're not going to find much DNA from me. Besides, she's my friend. It won't be weird to find my DNA here. You, though…"

He crossed his arms. "I'm supposed to stay here while you investigate?"

"Look-out duty is important, too."

He scowled, but turned to watch the street.

I stepped into the apartment and shut the door. With the outside world closed off, the place hummed with silence. Dust motes drifted in lines of light shining through closed blinds, a lazy, eerie dance. Vague shapes of furniture were all I could make out as my eyes adjusted to the dim light. I coughed softly to dispel the emptiness.

I didn't know what to look for. No way was I pawing through Blaire's stuff. Personal space was sacred. Somewhere you could be yourself without worrying what other Mementi would remember about you.

General observations. I could do that.

The place was one big room. A bed to my right, an ancient flat-panel TV and a tattered armchair across from it, a small table and two chairs in the kitchen straight ahead. A few doors—closet and bathroom, probably.

No signs of a struggle. No overturned chairs or drawers emptied onto the floor. A holo-picture of little-girl Blaire with her parents glowed dimly in the corner, still plugged in and undisturbed. The place was immaculate. Just like her. She'd always had a neat line of stuffed animals on her bed, and tried to clean up dishes before anyone finished eating lunch.

I walked to the bed and hit the comforter with my hand. A plume of dust puffed into the air like a mushroom cloud. Way too much for having been gone a few days. Not a good sign.

I turned and something crackled under my feet. I picked up a piece of paper, squinting to read it in the dim light.

Blaire,

I thought you'd be back by now. I tried to call. My place is ready if you still want to move in when you get back. If you don't…please call me.

Love, Tucker

The note set off a domino of connections in my head.

Love, Tucker. The boyfriend, the one Blaire had told Ren she was moving in with.

Thought you'd be back by now. Ren had said Blaire was with the boyfriend. Blaire seemed to have told him she was going elsewhere.

The tidy room. Wherever Blaire had gone, she'd been prepared to leave. It wasn't a last minute dash.

The note drifted to the floor. Even her boyfriend was searching for her, and he had expected her by now. I opened the door to find Kalan pacing.

"You didn't find anything…bad, did you?" he asked.

"Not bad exactly. But not good either." I locked the door and buried the key, then shared my conclusions.

"I don't know what to do next." I tried not to let the fear inside spill over into my words.

"I hate to say it," Kalan said, "but we've got to call the cops. They've got the resources to find out if she ditched town, or if something bad happened."

My body seized up. "We can't, if Jackson is connected to the Link thief and I'm the one to report this…"

Kalan pulled out his phone and wiggled it. "Nice thing about the cheap ones? Easier to stay at least semi-anonymous."

He punched a number into the old-fashioned keypad.

"Yeah, hi," he said into the phone. "I'd like to report a missing person."

9

Strange friend, past, present, and to be;
Loved deeplier, darklier understood…

—Alfred, Lord Tennyson, *In Memoriam CXXIX*

It was all over the news that night. By the next afternoon, the crowd in front of Happenings had swelled. No ordered, busy ants this time. People swarmed like angry bees.

I sat cross-legged on my bed after dance, watching it on my wallscreen while waiting for Cora to call after her doctor visit.

Happenings' pristine X-shaped building always seemed sort of snooty to me. *Behold! We can be just as architecturally creative as you.* Not so much now. The pretentious façade loomed over hundreds of fists stabbing the air and feet trampling flower beds. The scene was a jarring, disjointed rave of chaos. A woman—Mrs. Harward—waved a homemade sign wildly. Mr. Linney yelled at the building, his face red with the strength of his shouts.

These were my neighbors, but they *weren't* my neighbors. Together, they made someone new. A single person in the form of a crowd on the edge of violence. I felt strangled by the sight, and realized I was clutching my Links tight against my throat.

And I realized for the first time that a perfect recollection of all our memories and emotions could be dangerous. All they had were negative memories of the Populace, and so all the anger they had built up could never fade. Mementi were perfect in their hate.

On the wallscreen, Jorge Thomas narrated the scene at Happenings. He was a local caster whose independent newsfeeds occasionally got picked up by the professional news corps.

"...nearly two hundred people have gathered in front of Happenings today to protest this most recent crime. Citizens of Havendale are outraged that a missing person could have gone unnoticed for weeks, and blame it on Miranda Jacobs' recent Link theft. I'm here with a neighbor of Mrs. Jacobs. What can you tell us?"

Another voice came on—Joiya Lind.

"Well, Miranda was the only one who had contact with her daughter anymore," she said. "After Blaire started working at Happenings, she didn't talk to her old friends anymore. And of course her dad was gone. Miranda called Blaire every week, though, until her Links were stolen. After Miranda was admitted to the hospital, the doctors left messages for Blair, but her auto-response said she was out of the country on business. The doctors didn't want to tell Miranda she had a daughter until Blaire could actually stand in front of her, and we all thought Blaire was just being insensitive not to come home...really, I just feel terrible about it all."

That wasn't true. Blaire had told people—her boyfriend, Ren—she was going somewhere. Different stories told to different people, like she'd orchestrated her own disappearance. Like she'd had to go into hiding.

Jorge came on again. "We're going to cut now to an earlier interview with Ascalon BioTech's Drake Matthews."

The screen switched to a view of Drake Matthews outside Ascalon. The glass building bubbled behind him, steel supports criss-crossing over the structure like a tangled ball of yarn. Sweat beaded his pasty face, and his hair looked gray beneath his fedora, now adorned with a small feather. Had anyone ever hinted that that hat was a crime against humanity?

"Mr. Matthews, this recent turn of events has raised a whole new set of questions about the Link thefts," Jorge said, his voice arrogant. "We're left with fewer answers and more dangers than ever. I'm sure the researchers at Ascalon have considered new strategies to help with the investigation."

Matthews cleared his throat. "Yes, we've found ways to use the SLS to aid the police."

"Such as?"

"I'm afraid I can't elaborate."

"Is that why your colleagues say you've been spending less time at your lab? Are you working with the police?"

"Again, I can't say much." Matthews rolled his shoulders, glancing away from the camera.

"There have been rumors Ascalon might, shall we say, 'hack in' to the victims' emotional memories for clues. What's your response to that?"

Whoa. What the devil kind of question was that? Did he really think Ascalon would ravage the tortured minds of those who'd already lost everything?

Matthews, red-faced, had recovered from his own shock. "Even if that were a possibility, it violates every tenet Ascalon holds in trust. I can't even… I *won't* answer that question. It doesn't need an answer."

"In that case, what approaches *has* Ascalon taken?" Jorge's tone was biting. "Continued promises of memory backups have led to nothing. It seems we'd have much more to go on in this investigation if Blaire and Miranda Jacobs had their memories backed up."

Matthews rammed his hat further down on his head. A muscle in his cheek twitched. "Ascalon's researchers are committed—passionate—about developing backups. We've never stopped that research. Not since day one. But science takes its own time. We can't hand out a da—a schedule with delivery dates."

"Can you give us anything other than empty promises and false hope?"

He was trying to impress the press. Get a syndicated spot on the pro press corps. Or was he instead spouting the frustration of the entire town about the lack of protection we had over our own lives?

On screen, Matthews' jaw worked in silent fury. Jorge cut off the interview and said, "We're going to cut now to a live feed from the case's lead investigator."

The view shifted to City Hall, where Jackson stood at a podium in full uniform.

"…though there is much speculation," he said, "we've discovered no evidence that Blaire's disappearance is connected to the Link thefts."

I squinted at the screen. No evidence my foot. There'd be no evidence after Jackson had been on the scene.

"There also don't appear to be any disappearances connected with the other Link theft victims. Liza Woods, former employer of Blaire, has shown Blaire left employment with Happenings. The staff at Happenings is fully cooperating to help locate her."

My phone rang—Cora. I flicked my hand at the wallscreen to silence it and wrapped my Sidewinder around my ear.

"We must have the stupidest police force in the country," she said in greeting. She continued in a high-pitched voice. "How could they not know for weeks Blaire was gone?"

I collapsed back on my bed. "I don't know. How was the doctor? How are you feeling?"

She bulldozed right ahead. "This is so loco. I mean, it's Blaire. We knew her."

Knew. Past tense.

"She might not be dead," I said. "She might be…"

"She might be the Link thief," Cora said.

"Cora!"

"The report said the thefts started like a week after she went missing. What if she went into hiding and started stealing Links from people who saw her around?"

"Blaire isn't the thief," I said, crossing my arms behind my head.

There had to be a connection between Blaire and the Link thefts, but I knew Blaire. This wasn't the right connection, no matter what Cora—or Kalan—said. Just because Kalan was my partner now didn't mean I had to agree with his conclusions.

"Whatever. Are you coming over tonight?" Cora asked.

I wanted to. And I also never wanted to leave my room again. Just riding the tram to school this morning, I'd found myself scanning the faces of my neighbors, searching for suspects. Suspects. Neighbors. Same thing now.

Funny how *anyone* could become *everyone*.

Before I could answer, my Sidewinder buzzed in my ear.

"Hang on," I said, sitting up and hitting the button on my Sidewinder to project a holo. "Just got a text."

Text from Kalan Daniel Fox to Genesis Lee, TDS 19:16:06/5-6-2084
Telegram: Detective Kalan calling Detective Gena. STOP. Can you meet me at tramstop 22? STOP. Important meeting scheduled for 20:00 hours. Over and out.

A smile twitched on my lips. Kalan really was a nerd. Which was kind of endearing, for a Populace guy who jumped to the wrong conclusions.

"A text from who?" Cora asked, curiosity overtaking her former panic.

"No one," I said quickly. "Just, uh, someone I met the other day."

I could almost hear the wheels in her head turning. "A random someone?" And then, the hint of a smile sounded in her voice. "You are totally crushing on someone."

My cheeks heated. "I'm not either, he's just a boy."

"Spill."

"I—" I hadn't planned on telling anyone about Kalan, even Cora. But Cora had a right to know. I was doing it for her, after all. "He's part of a group investigating the thefts."

"A cop?" Cora asked.

"No. A guy I'm sort of working with to find the thief. And your Link." She gave a tiny gasp. "For real?"

"Yeah."

"Who is it?" she asked.

She expected it to be someone she knew. She expected him to be Mementi.

"I can't say. His group doesn't want people to know who they are. For their own safety." True enough.

"Thank you," Cora whispered. "I didn't know you were doing that."

I traced the flowers on my bedspread. "You're my best friend. I want to find the thief as much as you."

"How'd you meet him?" Cora asked. Hope filled her voice.

"It was kind of an accident," I said. "We just…ran into each other."

"Is he hot?"

I couldn't stop a little grin. Okay. Maybe I was crushing a tiny bit, Populace boy or not.

She laughed, a real Cora laugh. "He's totally hot. You're sweet on the secret agent man. You can't tell me his name?"

"Well, he has a—a code name." He'd get a kick out of that. "Kalan. Don't tell anyone, though."

"Not a soul." She giggled.

"Um…" I bit my lip. "He wants me to meet him tonight."

"Oh." Her tone dropped again. "So you can't come over?"

I should. Just for a little bit. I was the rational side Cora didn't have. After a day at the doctor, plus the craziness of Blaire's disappearance, she needed me. Maybe I could be late for the meeting.

"I don't know." I traced bedspread flowers again. "His group is having a meeting about the Link thief. I should go…"

"Yeah. You definitely should." She tried to sound excited about it. "I mean, I want to see you, but you have to go."

I glanced at my bedroom door. "If I go…could you cover for me? Mom and Dad will only let me go out if I'm going to see you."

"No problem. As far as they're concerned, you're here all night."

I stood and grabbed my messenger bag from the floor by my closet. "You sure you'll be okay? What are you going to do tonight?"

"Oh. You know. Watch a movie with lots of kissing. Snuggle with Monkey Brains."

My bag slipped from my fingers. Monkey Brains was her tattered stuffed monkey that had once belonged to my Grandma Piper. Grandma had given it to me when my mom's old dog died. *It has lots of experience comforting sad little girls*, she'd said. The day Cora's dad moved the last box out of their house, I'd passed Monkey Brains to her.

Cora had hardly touched the thing in over a year.

We didn't have her Links back yet. I had to do more for her than offer a shoulder to cry on.

"I'm going to find your Link," I said fiercely. "I swear, Cora. I'm going to bring back your memories, no matter what."

10

Day, mark'd as with some hideous crime…

—Alfred, Lord Tennyson, *In Memoriam LXXII*

It didn't take long to get to Tramstop 22. I was in Populace territory again, but I held my head a little higher stepping off the tram this time. Kalan lounged on a metal bench at the bottom of the stairs. He'd kicked his long legs out in front of him and tossed a small ball into the air.

"Hey," I said, feeling a little awkward.

"Hey. Long time no see." He caught the ball, stuffed it in his pocket, and jumped up. "Ready to meet some people?"

No. "I guess. Who exactly is going to be at this meeting?"

"Some people from my dad's congregation," he said.

"You're bringing me to church?"

He laughed. "No. It's the people from church who are helping with the street patrols. For the Link thief. We're meeting down the street."

This was a good idea, I reminded myself as we headed toward the meeting. The more people searching for the thief, the higher the likelihood of finding her.

"How much did you tell them about me?" Please say not much.

"Hm? Oh. Nothing, yet. Except to my dad." Kalan's eyes scoured the shops that lined both sides of the street.

"Are you looking for something?" I asked. I unwound the ends of my blue scarf from my neck and stuffed it in my bag. Nobody over here would be able to siphon memories. The scarf really did make me stick out.

I couldn't make myself take my gloves off, though.

"I'm nervous after what happened this afternoon." Kalan's eyes darted toward a family exiting a secondhand store with paint peeling from its sign. "You're with me, so you'll be fine."

The father leaving the store glared at me, then hurried his wife along. She picked up her toddler and they crossed the street. Most shops on this road were closed. Some had signs posted that declared earlier-than-usual closing times until further notice.

"What happened this afternoon?" I asked.

"You didn't hear about the guy who was attacked?"

"Attacked?" My voice rang in the almost-empty street.

"I thought everybody'd heard. A Mementi on his way home from the protest got beat up pretty bad. He's okay, but I don't want anybody who sees you to think you're here to retaliate."

I tugged the scarf in my hands. So much for feeling more confident on the Populace side of town. Everywhere I went, I was a target for something.

"No worries." Kalan sliced an imaginary sword through the air. "I'm here to be your knight in shining armor."

I stuffed my scarf in my shoulder bag. "Sweet. But I prefer you as a nerd, not a knight."

"A nerd?" He put his hand to his heart. "My lady doth greatly dishonor me."

I let out a small smile. "My lady doth not wish to be a damsel in distress."

Though to be honest, my lady was a little distressed. Across the street, a girl in ratty jeans grabbed her boyfriend's arm and pointed at me. He lowered his head, like a bull ready to charge. I counted my steps as I walked, trying to slow my heart.

"Ah, behold!" Kalan gestured toward the corner ahead of us. "We've reached the safety of the castle."

"It's the sushi place," I said, relieved as we passed the bull and his girl without incident. "Why aren't we meeting at the church?"

Kalan grinned. "Welcome to the chapel of the United Church of Christ. We outgrew our apartment a while ago, so the restaurant owner rents us his front room for services."

Learning about God in a sushi restaurant. That seemed to be the kind of church Kalan would attend.

Eyes leapt to me the moment we walked through the door. An angry hiss of "Mementa!" sliced through the sudden quiet. I shied away from the waiting customers and wondered how the people in Kalan's church group would be. They were trying to find the Link thief so people would stop blaming the Populace. That didn't mean they'd welcome a Mementi to their meeting.

Kalan led me to a room off the waiting area. A picture window looked out over an orange-tinted view of the street—just over an hour till sunset and the new curfew. This better be a quick meeting.

Tables had been shoved into a corner and wooden chairs lined the room in a semicircle. The smell of fish and rice wafted in, the hum of distant conversations spilling through an archway from the rest of the restaurant. A dozen or so people mingled in front of me. They had a whole room. Why cluster? I couldn't take my eyes off them. They never stopped *moving*. Shaking hands, slapping backs, nudging elbows.

It looked like a lot more fun than a Mementi gathering.

Kalan and I sat down near the window. No one in this room had noticed me yet, or at least they hadn't noticed I was Mementi. For now, invisible was good. I wrapped the strap of my bag around my hand, criss-crossing it and winding it in patterns.

Kalan tugged on the strap and leaned closer. "It's okay," he said. "They're not going to lynch you or anything."

His breath tickled my neck, and a wave of tingles shivered down my arm. I flinched, startled at the reaction. Then kind of wanted to feel it again.

"Kal!" A teenage girl a bit younger than us ran across the room. She tripped on the carpet and stumbled.

He laughed. "Hey Grace."

She stuck her tongue out at him before turning to me. "My name's Rachelle, in case my brother tries to tell you otherwise. What's yours?"

"Uh, Gena."

"Oh, Kal told us about you. Freaky-weird stuff going on, yeah?"

I frowned. Kalan had said he'd only mentioned me to his dad. "Yeah."

She threw herself into the chair next to Kalan, then leaned over him to talk to me. "So you remember, like, everything?"

I cleared my throat. "Um, yeah."

Her eyes widened. "So what was it like when you were born? Was it a really spiritual kind of experience?"

"Rachelle!" Kalan pushed her back. "You don't ask things like that!"

I'd never thought about that. Populace wouldn't remember anything before… "How old is your oldest memory?" I asked. "I mean, how old were you?"

Rachelle grinned at Kalan. "See, *she* asks things like that. I don't know how old. Maybe three or four? Hard to say."

Three or four? I sat back in my chair. No babyhood, toddlerhood, nothing. "Hard to say for me, too. We get our Links immediately after birth, but memories that old are mostly sensation—noise, light." And fear and pain and cold…

"Where's Dad?" Kalan interrupted. "It looks like we're waiting on him."

I bit my lip. Did he think it was weird I could remember back that far?

"Called to say he stayed late talking to a customer." Rachelle sighed and leaned down to rub her calves. "Are we ever going to get more tramstops? I ended up walking all the way here."

"How tragic," Kalan said dryly. "Nearly a full mile."

"It was tragic. My shoes look awful." She lifted two feet clad in white flats with bows on the side. Red dirt stains tinged the edges. Her innocent drama reminded me of Cora.

"You can stick those in the washing machine," I said. "Fabric flats wash out pretty well, and you can use bleach since they're white."

Rachelle brightened. "Ooh, thanks for the tip."

The rise and fall of murmured conversation dropped off as a skinny man in a white shirt bounced into the room. Bald on top, he'd gathered the rest of his graying hair in a ponytail. Not how I'd pictured Kalan's preacher dad.

"Sorry folks," he said, rubbing his balding head sheepishly. "Got a little delayed."

"We're used to it, Elijah," someone called, and a few people chuckled while taking seats around the room.

A birdlike blonde with way too much eyeliner sat next to me. She didn't look much older than me. She turned soft, wide eyes to me and gave me a dreamy smile. "Welcome," she whispered.

Then she nudged me with her elbow.

With a little jerk, I shifted my chair away from her. I rubbed my arm where she'd poked it, banishing the tingles. She was only being friendly, Populace-style. Still. She wouldn't be so thrilled if she knew who I was. Or maybe she was just stoned. It could be that kind of church.

A guy with a beard so scroungy I'd have pegged him for homeless stood up. "Let's sing a praise to the Lord, all!"

Sing? I shifted in my chair. Beard-man hummed a note, and the group began to sing. Hands rose in the air. The girl next to me swayed. I tried to shrink down as small as possible, away from the music and the touchy-feely hands waving around me.

Unity, unity,
Christ will unite you and me.
Unity, unity,
He will unite Him and me.
And when He needs me to fight,
I will fight for the right.
When His will says be still,
Like the waves I'll grow still.
Every person I see
Is His child, just like me.
Unity, Unity,
Christ will bring us unity.

I stifled a giggle and glanced at Kalan.

"Dad wrote it," he whispered. "If you can get past its cheesiness, it's actually kind of beautiful."

A song about being one with God. Doing what's right. Loving your neighbors. Coming from a group trying to help people they didn't even know. I looked around the room again, and my cheeks heated. They were an odd group, but they deserved a little respect.

Elijah noticed me sitting with Kalan and Rachelle. "Give me a moment, folks," he called.

He walked straight toward me. "Gena, glad you could be here. I'm truly sorry for your loss."

I was used to politeness, not sincerity. The tone in his voice felt too warm for a stranger. I cleared my throat. "Um, thank you."

He turned to the group, and to my horror, pointed at me. "We have an exciting addition to our group today! Everybody, let's welcome Gena. She's joining us from the Mementi side of town."

The remains of background chatter died. I shrank beneath the weight of open stares, uncomfortable shifting, and mutters. I pressed my knees together. They were going to yell. They were going to riot. They were going to hurt me.

"It's okay, Gena." Kalan's whisper sent tingles down the side of my neck.

Eyeliner-girl next to me held out her hand, beaming. "Welcome!" she said again.

I stared at her hand. Touching her was the last thing I wanted to do. Would she get offended if I didn't shake hands?

"Thanks, Anabel," Kalan said. "Gena's a little shy about shaking hands, though. Mementi thing."

"Oh, sorry!" She laughed and dropped her hand.

I gave her another smile, this one full of relief. "Thanks."

A few other "welcomes" drifted through the room. Some actually sounded sincere.

Several seats down, a guy about Ren's age stood up. His head had been shaved, but dark stubble showed a widow's peak so sharp he could've been a vampire. "Elijah, are you out of your mind? We can't have her here!"

Somebody wasn't listening to the song. Or maybe unity didn't extend to Mementi. I squeezed the strap of my shoulder bag.

A man sporting an earring, a neck tattoo, and a gray business suit leaned forward. "Stuff it, Joss. We all said we'd welcome any Mementi to join the church."

Whoa, who said anything about joining the church? Kalan shrugged, giving me a half-smile.

"And who said she's joining?" Joss said. I half-expected him to bare pointy teeth. "She's only here for the thief meeting."

"Why shouldn't she be here?" said Mr. Business Punk. "I've been saying we should pull in sympathetic Mementi for weeks."

A woman across the room spoke. "Corben, it's not like we can just walk up and ask someone—"

"Oh, stop," Rachelle groaned. "How many times are we going to rehash this?"

Joss gestured to me. "We don't know anything about this girl."

"Hey," Kalan said. "*I* know her."

"Okay, stop," Elijah said sternly. "You all park your buttocks back in the chair and welcome her all the same. The Lord received everyone, Joss. Sinners and Samaritans and rich and poor were welcome at His table. Gena's the reason we're doing this. She's who we're trying to help."

Next to me, Anabel sang softly, "Every person I see, is His child just like me…"

Joss whirled on her. "You want to say something to me?"

Anabel smiled. "Didn't I just?"

Joss glowered, then gave a bark that vaguely resembled a laugh. He still looked stiff, but he sat. And tossed a lingering glance in Anabel's direction.

Hm. So he was human, after all.

Elijah frowned at his bickering group. "I'll only say this once, people: *shape up.*"

A few faces looked contrite.

"We are disciples of the Lord!" Elijah flung his arms out. "We leave our petty judgments and blaming outside where the Devil can choke on them! Unity, people, unity and love with Christ and with our family of fellow humans—His family. This is His work! And His work is our work."

"Amen!"

"Yeah, Elijah!"

"Praise the Lord!"

Boy, these people were volatile. Possibly not the best trait in a rogue group hunting down a criminal. Kalan shook his head, then winked at me. Infinitely preferable to Drake Matthews winking at me. A grin tugged at the corners of my mouth.

"Let's get this work rolling, then," Elijah said. I squirmed in my chair while he related what I'd told Kalan about my memory loss coming from a Mementi. I'd barely been comfortable with Kalan knowing that info, and now an entire group of Populace would feel they'd been right about the evil Mementi.

Joss crossed his arms with a satisfied smirk. "So it's the Mementi after all."

Prove me right, buddy. My nose twitched in frustration.

"It's probably that missing Mementi girl behind the Link thefts," he added.

Anabel said, "We don't know if that girl was involved. She could be another victim or something."

Thank you. Exactly.

But Kalan had said the same thing, earlier. Was he going to back me, or agree with Joss?

"Why are we even helping these people?" A man threw his cigarette to the tile and stomped on it.

"They've always hated us, anyway."

"People hate Jesus, but does He turn on them?"

"*They're* turning on their own people—"

"We should take the good Lord's fight to them!"

"That's not the kind of fight—"

"We're losing faith, God's still guiding us as long as we—"

"You all just shut up. You're inviting the Devil's spirit!"

Shouts spun through the room until I felt dizzy. A woman with her pockets hanging below the tattered edge of her short shorts had her eyes closed, hands in the air and lips moving like she was praying. Joss and Corben were right in each other's faces. Rachelle stood with hands on her hips, and Kalan glowered.

Threads of anxiety trailed out from my chest. These people were going to kick off a panic attack if I didn't do something.

Shaking a little, I lurched to my feet. "Hey."

My voice disappeared into the din.

Pale little Anabel stood up. "HEY!"

Her shout hushed the uproar. A fork clinked to the floor elsewhere in the restaurant.

"I believe our guest has something to say?" Anabel's voice was mild, but her eyes were sharp.

I swallowed. If I could go a week holed up in my room with no one staring at me, it still wouldn't be enough. So many eyes, watching me, judging me, ready to dismiss me. A surge of anxiety dried my mouth.

"I know you don't know me." I cleared my throat. Had to speak louder. My hands clenched automatically to stop the shaking. "And you don't know Blaire. But I came here because the only way to stop the Link thief is to work together. *I* know Blaire, and she isn't the thief. Her own mom is one of the victims. Right now, though, Blaire's the only lead we've got. We need to find out what happened to her."

Joss piped in again. "How do you propose that, since we can't exactly chat with her?"

Kalan and I had worked out a strategy after finding the note in Blaire's apartment. "Her Populace boyfriend, Tucker. Blaire had planned to move in with him, and he might be the last one who saw her. I've got no clue how to find him, though."

"Ideas, folks," Elijah said. "Who's got 'em?"

Corben tapped a tiny metal implant behind his ear—a Cortex. He'd just turned his brain into an Internet-connected computer. Where'd he get the money for that? Maybe he worked one of the higher-end jobs at Happenings.

"Tucker, right?" he said. "Let's see what I can dig up on Tuckers in Havendale."

His eyes unfocused and shifted. Seeing something the rest of us couldn't. Moments later, a chorus of beeps sounded around the room and several people pulled out phones.

"Okay," the man said. "Only three Tuckers listed. I sent the addresses to everybody."

He'd searched the Internet and sent text messages from his *brain*. Fast, sure. Secure, so they said. But kind of freaky to see in motion. The Cortex was the scary kind of biotech you weren't sure was a good idea. The tech had been banned for decades, until Happenings finally created a secure enough firewall to prevent brain-hacking. Ascalon could've come up with something sooner, but they'd never touch something like that.

"Excellent." Elijah rubbed the stubble on his face. "We'll split into three groups. Don't be ashamed if you feel it's your role to stay behind and pray for God to help us find the right Mr. Tucker. Who's going out on this one?"

Several people raised their hands.

My eyes darted around frantically. When did this become the plan? It was just a souped-up version of their wander-the-streets tactic. We couldn't just go knock on random doors of guys named Tucker.

Well, I couldn't, as a Mementi. I blew a frustrated breath through my nose. We didn't have a lot of options here. I trusted Kalan. Could I trust his judgment of the people around me?

Kalan raised his voice. "Dad, are you sure? It's dangerous out there tonight. Plus the mayor announced that curfew at nine. If we get caught, we're in big trouble."

"Well, I'm in," Joss said. "It's the first lead we've had in a while."

"Let's bring the Lord's justice!" someone shouted.

A few people whooped.

Around me, everyone divided into groups. They knew how to get things done, that was for sure. I stood and shouldered my bag. Bumble around the Populace side of town, or stay in the semi-safe, air-conditioned restaurant?

Kalan's eyebrows lowered into a worried position. "I don't think you should go, Gena. You could be attacked, and then the backlash from that..."

Thanks for the reminder. "Other people will be there. I'll be okay."

And when it came down to it, I *didn't* trust his friends. They were still Populace, and I was still Mementi. I wasn't handing over this investigation.

"You and I can stay here and act as a base," Kalan said. "Have everybody relay info to us."

My nostrils flared. "And where will we go when the restaurant closes? Hang out in the parking lot, alone, and wait for someone to call the cops on me? I'll be safer with a group of you. No one will look at me twice."

"Yeah, but a Mementi, knocking on their doors while everyone's worried about a retaliation attack?"

I pulled out my scarf and wrapped the ends securely around my neck, too nervous to leave it off any longer. "You knock, then. But Blaire's my friend, and it's *my* people at risk. *My* memories. Thank you for your concern, but I'm going."

To my surprise, Kalan laughed.

"What?"

"You're so Mementi. Your mouth says 'thanks for your concern,' but your eyes say 'stop me and I'll deck you.'"

My lips pinched.

He sighed. "Fine. Then I'm going too. As your bodyguard."

* * *

Our group consisted of me, Kalan, Joss, and Anabel. One big happy family.

With the help of my phone's GPS system, we headed south to Cutler Street. Crammed shops in a row gave way to small houses—actual houses. A tiny dog yipped excitedly as we passed, jerking at the end of its chain. Yards sprouted with weeds. Were there any *nice* areas on this side of town? Soon, we found ourselves back in the realm of boxy, boring apartments.

Not a lot of people were out and about. A man left the building across the street, and two women jogged past us. None of them noticed me, but Kalan prowled next to me like a tiger ready to pounce. I reviewed the situation: Mementi girl. Populace side of town. Violence imminent. *All hail Gena, the queen of bad decisions. Bow down before her impressive displays of stupidity.*

I jumped when Joss leaned in, peering at the map I'd projected on my hand. "Zoom closer," he said.

"This is as close as it gets," I said. "But the Tucker we're after lives somewhere in there."

I pointed to two blocky buildings set close to each other. Between them lay a patch of dirt that might have once made a pitiful attempt to grow grass.

"We need to spread out," Joss said. "Go door to door. There's no apartment number on this one."

Dozens of doors on three levels stretched the length of both buildings. This could be a long night. I studied the map again, like Tucker's exact location might magically appear. A glowing dot on the screen caught my eye, and I tapped it. A label appeared—not an anonymous number, but a name. An on-duty cop.

DETECTIVE JACKSON, GUNNER.

My hand convulsed. "Kalan."

He studied the map over my shoulder. "Well. I guess that confirms this is the right Tucker."

The map shuddered on my hand. It took me two tries to click the Sidewinder off. "He can't see me, if he's working with the thief they'll know I'm trying to find her, and Jackson knows where I live, I don't want to lose any more memories—"

Kalan hovered a little closer. "Okay. Relax, we're a step ahead of him."

Right. My GPS gave my location at Cora's. I wanted to slam my hands against my leg in a powerful drum beat. I settled for tapping my fingers behind my back. Anxiety still slithered in my gut, but it wasn't approaching panic-attack levels. Yet.

Kalan turned to Anabel and Joss, who eyed me with concern and contempt, respectively. "We've got to hide Gena from this guy. You two keep an eye on the building. When you see a cop come out, that's where Tucker lives."

Joss rolled his eyes. "Gee, thanks. Never would have thought of that."

"Someday," said Anabel to Joss with a lazy, doe-eyed smile, "you will say nice things. Because you're actually a good guy who's still learning how to be nice."

Joss coughed and turned away. I had some doubts about her assessment of him.

"I'll text you when we see him," said Joss. "You scamper off, now."

His tone boiled my blood. Which seemed to prove useful in banishing fear. "So we just hide until Jackson leaves?"

"Look-out duty is important too," Kalan quipped.

Smart aleck. I followed him around the building and plopped down on a peeling wooden bench. He pulled a small ball from his pocket, rolling it around and around in his fingers. I felt myself shift in subtle circles with it. Spiraling, circling, whirlpooling the tension down some internal drain.

"What is that, anyway?"

He held it up. It was a bouncy ball, swirled with white and black.

"When I was a kid," he said, "I'd get one every time I saw one of those toy machines at gas stations and restaurants. I've got a ball for every place I've ever lived or visited. So I have a lot."

I wanted to ask about all the places he'd been, but the bitterness in his voice surprised me. "It sounds like an adventure."

"I'd have preferred a house and friends and a mom who stuck around." He gripped the ball in his fist.

Maybe adventures only became adventures in the telling of them. "I'm sorry."

He shrugged.

Personal questions weren't my thing, but curiosity was more powerful than etiquette. "What happened?"

"Dad found God."

"Is that…not a good thing?"

Kalan smiled. "It is. I wouldn't have found God without him. I love Dad, but he was always trying to find his 'calling.' Even changed his name. He used to be Henry."

"Well. At least you ended up here." I blushed. "I mean, if here is a good thing. For you. And not because—I mean…"

Crap.

Kalan grinned at the dirt. "Yeah. Here is a really great place to be."

We settled into embarrassed silence.

He rested his elbows on his knees. "It's getting dark."

I checked my phone. "9:03. We're officially breaking city curfew." I could practically hear Dad yelling from across town already.

"We should get you home," Kalan said.

I wanted to say yes—but I wanted to say no more. I couldn't leave this close to seeing if Tucker had answers about Blaire. Before I could answer, Kalan's phone beeped.

"Jackson's leaving." He jumped up. "Stay here, I'm going to take a look."

I gripped the bench, splinters poking into my gloves. It was getting dark. Jackson wouldn't see me peeking around a corner.

Though if I stepped past the barrier of the brick wall, he might feel my Link buzz.

I snuck up behind Kalan, checking my GPS map. Jackson was marked on my hand, walking away from the apartment block. "Do you see him?"

"Gena," Kalan hissed as I hovered behind the safety of the brick building.

"What do you see?"

"Just a cop."

"No partner?" That should be standard procedure if he was interrogating Tucker.

"No. He looks like he's in a hurry, though. He just turned the corner."

"Come on," I said.

We found Anabel and Joss leaning against a twisted tree in the dirt-filled courtyard.

"He's up on the second floor," Joss said. "Let's go talk to this guy."

We climbed the concrete steps and knocked. Kalan stepped in front of me, like he was shielding me. Okay, this was getting a little much. Tucker had had a Mementi girlfriend, so the odds he'd attack me were pretty slim. I stepped out of Kalan's shadow.

The door opened a crack and an angry face peered at us. "What?"

"Tucker James?" Joss asked.

"I don't know you." He noticed my Mementi gloves and scarf. In the sliver of his door, a strange twisting warped his face. "This is about Blaire again."

Kalan shifted closer to me.

"I'm a friend of hers." Could he at least open the door all the way?

"A friend?" The door didn't budge.

"My sister was her best friend growing up. They worked at Happenings together."

"Ren. You look like her." He spat her name like it tasted horrible. Uh oh.

"I, um, was hoping you could tell me more about…well, about anything Blaire said or did before she disappeared."

Tucker snorted. "Don't you watch the news? I don't know squat. The cops still won't leave me alone."

Kalan spoke up. "The cop who just came—what did he want?"

"To ride my butt? I don't know. He won't be back." Tucker sounded bitter, and his head dropped.

"Why won't he be back?" Joss demanded. "You gave him something, didn't you? Some information so he'd leave you alone."

Tucker stiffened. "Get out of here," he snarled.

He slammed the door.

"Brilliant people skills, Joss." Kalan sighed. "Now we've got nothing."

I spun to Joss, infuriated. My mouth overrode my politeness programming. "What is wrong with you? You just killed our only shot with him."

He smirked. "So the Memental does have some heat to her."

Oh, I was going to *slap* him. I clenched my hands.

Kalan whirled. "Don't you dare call her that!"

"They call us 'Populace.'" Joss glared. "Like we're nothing but a collection of stupid losers."

I blinked. It wasn't a slur, it was just…what we called them. "That's not what it—"

"Contention is of the devil," Anabel sang out.

Joss didn't matter. None of this mattered right now. I pulled up my GPS map again and headed down the stairs. Jackson had rushed away from here like he had a goal. What had Tucker told him? Where was he going?

Kalan hurried up beside me, trailed by the others.

"Jackson's headed toward the city center." I crossed the dirt courtyard. "He's not far, I don't think he can take a tram."

"They're all shut down for curfew," Anabel said, coming up too close behind me. A streetlight melded our shadows on the second apartment block as we passed it. "Let's see what he's—"

A shattering of glass erupted next to me.

Shouts and the tinkling of glass shards filled my ears. Something thudded to the ground: my knees hitting hard concrete. A yell from Joss, fading into the distance as he chased someone. My arms wrapped around my head. Something pressed down on my back. The pressure shifted.

"Gena? You okay?" Kalan.

"Yeah." My voice sounded hoarse, like falling glass had stuck in my throat. Arms; head; legs; no pain. I was okay. I was okay.

The pressure on my back shifted again. Kalan's arm. A boy, a boy I liked, was touching me. I sat up with a gasp and the arm fell away.

"What…" Shards of glass glittered in the light of street lamps. The window to my left gaped at us with jagged glass teeth. Inside the empty room lay a rough red rock.

I fell forward on my hands, and they slipped in something wet.

Blood. A growing puddle on the sidewalk, seeping into the blue fabric of my gloves. I followed the trail of red to Anabel. She was sprawled on the ground, her pale hair matted with blood that bubbled from a wide wound above her ear.

"Kalan!" I shrieked, jerking away.

He swore and leaped over me, ripping his shirt over his head. He pressed it against Anabel's open gash.

Footsteps came running. I cringed low to the ground, expecting more rock-slinging assailants. It was Joss, half a block away and headed toward us.

Kalan pulled out his phone, holding his shirt to Anabel's head with one hand.

"Emergency services." He paused while the voice-automated call went through. "There's been an accident, we need an ambulance right away—"

"Kalan." I tried not to gag as blood seeped out from under his shirt. "She's still bleeding, you have to hold it tighter."

He pushed harder on her skull. Cradling the phone against his shoulder, he yelled down the road. "Joss, who was it, did you see anyone?"

Anabel bled harder again. Kalan was trying to do too much at once. "Let me help, Kalan, what should I do?"

He spoke into the phone again. "I don't know where we are."

"Cutler Street," I said.

"Cutler Street, someone threw a rock at my friend—"

Joss jogged up, breathing hard. "I couldn't catch them. Had too much of a head start."

"Joss," Kalan said, "you *have* to get everyone else home, the cops are coming and our people are a few streets over."

"But Anabel—"

"Those Mementi cops won't go easy on anyone out here. I'll stay with Anabel, go—yeah, I'm here. The paramedics, how long?"

Joss glared at me. "This was Mementi. Retaliating from that beating today."

I glared right back. "It wasn't. I would have felt their Link buzz. They were from *your* side, probably aiming…" For me.

My eyes fell on Anabel with renewed horror.

Joss knelt and touched Anabel's hair gently. "She's tough. She'll make out okay."

He knelt a moment longer before taking off down the street.

Anabel's head was beginning to swell. Someone innocent. Someone *nice*. Victim of a stupid hate crime. Victims piled up around me, smothering me, victims of memory loss and disappearances and rocks being thrown in the street. A rock. Such a small thing. It was so easy to hurt people.

I clutched my arms to my chest, trying to stop the tremors rolling through my body. "Kalan, let me help, what can I do?"

"I've got this."

Frustration burned my eyes. "You don't have to be the lone hero for everyone, I can *help*."

"You've got to get out of here too," he said. "Find out where Jackson's headed."

"No, Jackson's close, they'll send him to the scene."

Send him back here.

Kalan whipped around like Jackson would pop out from the darkness. His hand slipped on Anabel's head, and blood gushed over the side of her face.

Kalan swore, immediately adjusting the shirt and stopping the blood flow.

I needed to run, to pretend I'd never been here. Tiny rainbows of streetlight reflected off the shattered glass. Anabel moaned.

"It's okay," I whispered, unable to leave her. "You're going to be fine."

I murmured the words over and over and hoped they weren't a lie. Sirens wailed in the distance.

"Gena, you have to *go*. Now!"

Panic. Sirens screamed in the night, closer than ever. Jackson could be here any second. He'd send word to the Link thief that I needed more memories wiped.

Kalan's hand rested on my arm, and I snatched it away in shock. Touch. Three times now, we had touched. Touch meant something. Something good, for most people. I wished I was most people.

"I'm sorry, I'm sorry." I pressed my palms to the rough concrete.

"No more sorries." Kalan's voice was soft.

"They'll arrest you."

"They'll do worse to you." Kalan's eyes pleaded with me. I couldn't breathe. For a strange second, I wanted to hold this bare-chested, self-sacrificing, imaginary-sword-waving boy in my arms.

Tires raced over gravel and whirls of blue and red lit the street two blocks down. I leaped up. My eyes darted, searching for an out. There—two buildings crammed together, a narrow alley between them leaking darkness.

I raced across the street and prayed the sudden crowd of Mementi would hide my Link buzz. Shadows engulfed me and I pressed against the brick wall. Out on the street, flashing police lights bloomed. I backed farther into the alley.

In the glare of the lights, Jackson stomped into view.

11

And in my thoughts with scarce a sigh
I take the pressure of thine hand.

—Alfred, Lord Tennyson, *In Memoriam CXIX*

Gurney wheels crunched over glass, wheeling Anabel away. A real bandage covered her head. Mementi-invented artificial coagulants and synthetic blood pumped into her veins.

I hoped they'd be nice to her at the hospital.

Jackson grilled Kalan. No shouting, just intense questions. He had no reason to associate Kalan with me, but the granite quality to his stance set me on edge. Finally, Jackson waved Kalan away. I thought they might give him a warning and send him home, but a cop clapped handcuffs on his wrists. Kalan winked in my direction before ducking into the police car. Cheeky.

Jackson began arguing with another cop, jabbing a finger toward Tucker's apartment. I strained to hear. Something about why Jackson was out here alone when he was on duty, and paper-work, and reporting at the station. His jaw set with frustration, Jackson climbed in the car and they sped away.

Silence fell. I took a single step out of the alley. A faint buzz from an overhead light tickled my ears.

I wanted to run straight home and hide under my blanket. Just in case the universe had any more fun in store for me to-night. I rested my forehead against the rough brick wall.

Once he filled out his paperwork, Jackson would go back on his hunt. I still didn't have a clue what he was looking for, or where. But if I got to the city center before he left the police station, I might be able to tail him. Cora's hopeful face flitted across my memory.

My date with the universe's crap wasn't over yet.

I snuck through the streets that cut toward the center of town. Shadows draped the city outside the well-lit path cast by street lights. Non-moving trams hulked above me. Stupid curfew. I shook out my clenched hands.

My hands. I spread my fingers in horror. Blood mottled my blue gloves into an ugly reddish-purple. Like a bruise. So much *blood*. It dripped and puddled and stained my perfect memory. I ripped off the gloves and threw them in a trashcan.

Blood still streaked my skin.

I ran the rest of the way to Central Gardens. Once there, I veered toward a large fountain. Soft lights below the surface gave it a strange glow. I leaned over the marble edge and scrubbed away blood until the cold numbed my fingers. Dark streaks tainted the water, curling away in the wake of my splashing. My hands were pale when I pulled them out. I shoved them under my arms.

And now I had no gloves. Perfect.

My phone buzzed, announcing a text. The fourth in the last hour, I noted when I clicked my Sidewinder on.

Text from Kierce Jameson Lee to Genesis Lee, TDS 21:56:02/5-6-2084
Home NOW.

I sighed. I'd have to postpone that potential panic attack a little longer.

No sign of Jackson yet. My GPS still fixed him inside the police station at City Hall. I left the dim light of the fountain, favoring the cover of darkness. A shadowy obelisk offered a convenient hiding spot. My eyes darted between the police station exit and the GPS displayed dimly on my hand.

The name label on Jackson's dot flashed to a string of numbers the same moment he emerged from the building.

Excellent. Now I could find him when he wasn't on duty.

With a pace too quick for his casual expression, he strode across the Gardens. Toward the tallest building in Havendale. The Memoriam reached into the sky, its spiraling mirrored surface reflecting the dim light of the stars. It was our cemetery, our memorial for the dead.

A realization hit me hard enough to knock the wind out of me.

"Oh, Blaire," I breathed. "You hid a memory."

Link buzz throbbed behind my eyes. The sacred memories of our dead inside the building gave this entire area a constant hum. No one would notice a small addition Blaire had made of her own.

Tucker might have known enough to tell Jackson Blaire *had* made an addition. But he was Populace. He wouldn't know where to find it, or what the memory was.

Evidence. Clues. Confessions?

I sneaked across the grass, trusting the Memoriam Link buzz to keep me hidden from Jackson. I had to find that memory before he did.

Jackson stopped on the cobblestones surrounding the building. His feet set wide, he studied the Memoriam. I hid behind a palm tree. Blaire would've stored it somewhere no one was likely to touch. Somewhere it could hide in plain sight. Not the metal benches. Not the decorative stone urns overflowing with desert flowers. Not the glass of the Memoriam itself.

The cobblestones. Stone was almost as good as wood for preserving memories. Long-term storage, most emotional content intact. Images could get fuzzy with time, though. If she counted on Mementi horror of going barefoot, she could hide a memory easily.

Jackson moved, his shadow leaping ahead of him. I hit the ground flat on my stomach. His smooth, swift stride took him to the quaint stone bridge that crossed the pond near the Memoriam entrance. Actually, that wasn't a bad idea either. He splashed into the shallow pond and brushed his fingers over stone. No time to wonder who was right.

I dashed forward in a crouch, out of sight around the back of the building. Then I pulled off my sneakers and socks. My feet slid from cobblestone to cobblestone. How long would it take Jackson to check the bridge?

My toe caught an uneven stone, and I winced but didn't stop. A breeze brushed a strand of loose hair that fell from my scarf.

It carried a whisper of *hurry, hurry, hurry*. Halfway around the building, and nothing.

A shuffle and a scrape sounded from around the curve of the Memoriam.

My fingers convulsed around my shoes. I ran for the grass. The slap of my feet on the cobblestones thundered in my ears. Shelter, a hiding place, I needed something. A wide shadow hunkered low ahead of me. I dove behind it and caught the rank smell of a garbage can someone hadn't emptied today.

I peered around my smelly haven. My elbows shook so hard they barely supported me. Jackson crawled along the base of the building. The glass walls ended a foot above the ground, like the Memoriam stood on a small pedestal. Stones lined the recessed bottom.

I bit my knuckles to hold back a moan. It was the perfect hiding place.

Let him miss it, let it not be there, let his knees get too sore to keep crawling…

Jackson paused and let out a soft exclamation. I bit my knuckles again, harder. He held his crouch a moment longer, probably siphoning whatever he'd found into his own Links. He sat up and a dim glow appeared on his hand. His Sidewinder. He was texting someone.

If I could find out who, that might give me the Link thief.

I whipped out my own Sidewinder and dialed down the brightness until I could barely see it. Oh, how I loved Kinley right now. I activated the hack she'd sent me, the one that could intercept text messages.

I peeked around my pungent hiding place and eased my Sidewinder out. My Share port had to be aimed at Jackson's when he sent the text. He typed another moment on his glowing hand, then turned off the laser screen.

Seconds later, the Sidewinder in my hand buzzed.

I whipped behind my garbage can and opened the captured message.

Text from BLOCKED to BLOCKED, TDS 22:12:33/5-6-2084
She did hide evidence memories. I've taken them all out.

Since when could you block sender and receiver names? Fail. Again.

I peered around the garbage can. Jackson still knelt next to the Memoriam, hands on the ground, head bowed. He rose and rubbed his knees. Then he paused. He crouched and touched one of the base stones again, then nodded to the Memoriam as if in respect. Like a predator, he padded away until he blended with the dark.

I pulled back behind my garbage can. Nothing. After everything tonight, I would leave with nothing. The scream I couldn't let out vibrated in my teeth.

Except, what had Jackson done at the end? He'd touched the stones again, almost like…he was putting something there of his own. Checking to make sure he was really out of sight, I ran to the Memoriam.

I knelt in the spot where he'd stopped. The stone was rough under my fingers. To my surprise, memories blossomed before me.

They held the tang of another consciousness. Blaire's. Why would Jackson return any of her memories? Blaire's thoughts accompanied blurry images and words, and the emotion was subtle. More like the memory triggered my own emotions that were similar. Happy, sad, in love…I knew what the feelings should be, and had my own approximations. What would Blaire feel if she relived these moments?

That's all they were, small moments. A late-night ice cream feast with her dad when he was alive. A surprise shopping trip during high school with her mom. Kissing Tucker for the first time. Laughing with Ren while Cora and I tagged along on our long bicycle ride toward rumored cave paintings we never found. It was like Blaire reached across space and time to hold my hand for a moment.

She'd left a personal Memoriam. A collection of everything she wanted to share after she was gone. Jackson had taken anything important to the case, but he must have returned these out of respect.

Was Blaire dead, then? A Memoriam implied she didn't expect to return from her disappearance. Using my fingernails, I pried at the stone, but it wouldn't come loose. A lump rose in my throat. I should leave it, anyway. She deserved a place here.

I pulled on my shoes and socks and crossed the lawn of the Central Gardens. My thoughts swirled like Anabel's blood in the water. I had lost to Jackson. There was no way to get the memories he'd taken from Blaire's stone. But at least I hadn't left with nothing.

Taking out my Sidewinder, I dictated a long message to Kalan about the night and said I'd text him tomorrow. I set it on a time-delay so he wouldn't get it until morning. Just in case he was still in jail.

Soft grass gave way to pavement beneath my feet. I was on the street, after dark, and after curfew. Alone with no gloves.

I tucked my hands under my arms and rushed toward home.

12

Treasuring the look it cannot find,
The words that are not heard again.

—Alfred, Lord Tennyson, *In Memoriam XVIII*

My Sidewinder jarred me awake with an early-morning text. I reached for it, knocking my Link buds to the floor with sleep-clumsy fingers.

Text from Cora Julieta Medina to Genesis Lee, TDS 07:17:12/5-7-2084
Early morning wake-up call. Zahra wants to do a mini dress rehersal at 8.

I groaned. Why did Zahra insist we dance on Sunday just because she didn't teach on Fridays? We'd already had two full dress rehearsals.

I buried my face in my pillow. My head felt oddly disconnected from the rest of me. A strange ache settled into my chest.
Sort of a homesickness.

A feeling of missing someone.

My brain fogged over, confused by the feeling that had no
reference. I pushed myself up and combed black strands of hair
out of my face.

Dad was scanning the news holo projected from his Sidewinder on the kitchen table when I walked in, his Link buds in
his ears. I popped a bagel in the toaster, and he glanced at me. Or
glowered, really. Great. Now what had I done?

Mom stomped into the kitchen wearing her grumpy face.
"Morning."

"Hey." My bagel popped up. I slathered it with cream cheese
and poured a thermos of coffee from the pot Dad had left.

Mom rustled her sleep-wild hair. "That's a lot of carbs, Gen."

"Zahra called us in for extra practice before the recital." I
ripped a bite out of my bagel. "I'll be working it all off soon."

"Don't talk with your mouth full, hon," she said.

She poured a glass of orange juice. There was something different about her face. It looked tighter, younger. I choked on
my bagel bite. Mom had had a Chameleon treatment, like Mrs.
Harward on the tram. Ascalon-created fake DNA had firmed
up her face.

I hated it.

Mom turned to Dad. She cleared her throat. Dad finally pulled
out his Link buds.

"Yes?" he said.

"Gena's leaving for dance," she said.

"Oh!" His stern expression cracked with a smile. "Work hard today, hon. I'm looking forward to this recital. I hated having to work through your last one."

"It's okay." It was the only recital he'd ever missed. Mom had still brought the traditional donuts and flower, but I'd missed the dramatic bow Dad always gave when he presented them.

An urge to hurry gripped me. Like I was supposed to do something more urgent than a simple dance practice. For some reason, that brought a wave of sadness. Weird.

I stuffed the last bite of bagel in my mouth. "Gotta run."

"Itinerary?" Mom asked.

I shoved my thermos in my bag next to my pointe shoes. Like they didn't check my GPS twelve times a day anyway. Technology meant parents didn't have to be present to interfere.

"Dance all morning," I recited, "Cora's house after that. If my plans change, I will text you. I will not go anywhere else, and I will be home before it gets dark."

My voice was terse, and Mom's eyes pierced me. "Watch your attitude."

"Sorry," I replied automatically.

"And I don't want to have to tell you again," Dad added with a dangerous overtone, "don't you dare miss curfew. I don't care how bad Cora needs you. Eight o'clock tonight."

Eight o'clock! I turned to ask what the devil I'd done to deserve a sixth-grade curfew. He'd already buried himself in the news again while Mom rummaged for her bran cereal in the cupboard.

I wouldn't dare miss that curfew. Somehow I'd really pissed him off.

As I left, Dad called out, "Love you, Gen."

Winding my Sidewinder around my wrist, I boarded the tram. The engines hummed a melancholy tune and the unexplainable ache in my heart sang along. What was I sad *about*? Eight o'clock curfew was nothing to cry over. My legs began to bounce. I needed to dance this away. The tram couldn't move fast enough.

The familiar taps and thumps of varying dances greeted me when I entered the air-conditioned sanctuary of the dance studio. Teachers counted rhythms behind closed doors, and music clashed in the hallway. I made my way to the main practice room. The smell of floor wax and lingering sweat was oddly calming. My dance teacher, Zahra, stood at the far end of the room fiddling with the wallscreen, wearing a bright pink hijab and her black unitard.

Maybe it was growing up away from Havendale, or maybe it was just her, but she was sort of a techno-phobe trapped in a city of techno-mania. She'd only had the wall painted with tech-paint to turn it into a wallscreen because her ancient stereo system died.

Zahra turned, "Eh, *ma chouchoute!*"

She rushed toward me, the dance mirrors reflecting a dozen images of her reaching out to me.

Her gentle French accent warmed me and she touched my shoulder. Since Grandma Piper died, Zahra was the only person I had physical contact with. The only person I could rely on.

"I hate it when you call me that." I smiled.

"Why? It is an endearment, yes? It means you are dear to me."

"It also means cabbage."

She laughed. "It does not! Not when said this way."

Her laugh dropped off, and lines of worry etched her dark face. Too many lines for someone under thirty. I knew life had been rough before she moved here. A scar slashed her cheek next to her ear, but she'd never gone into detail about how she'd gotten it.

She had lots of good stories about beautiful Paris, though. It was number four on my list.

Zahra studied me. "It is a difficult time for you and Cora, *non*? Do you want to talk about it?"

I hesitated. "No. Not yet."

She touched my shoulder again. "Remember, *ma petite soeur*. You are a dancer. You are strength and grace and stubbornness, and many other things. You will be alright. So will Cora. Now, go stretch."

The other girls trooped in, Darena and Marine laughing. Leigh, the only Populace in our age group, trailed behind them. Ignored. I hadn't had a real conversation with Leigh in years, but still. She'd been in our dance class forever. Zahra noticed the snub too, and frowned. The only time she ever got mad was when her Populace students got harassed.

Cora came last, slinking through the door like a shadow. She hugged her arms close to her chest. When she sat on the floor next to me, her muscles unclenched a little. She reached for her toes.

"Hey," she said. The shadows under her eyes and fly-aways in her hair caught me by surprise. "How was last night?"

"Huh? It was fine." But her words set off alarms in me again. Like last night was supposed to be more.

Zahra called us to the barre to start practice, inspecting each of us through our routine. "Come on, ladies, bellies in, necks straight! Nice clean lines. Gena, this is not proper turnout. Better!"

We moved to center floor to run through our group numbers for the recital, dancing adagios and practicing pirouettes. The cadence of the French terms rolled in the mouth like something decadent. Zahra's accented voice called out the dancing words, and we moved in beautiful unison.

But something was *missing*. An emptiness inside my dance wasn't filling. My movements became uncontrolled as I lashed out with my limbs. Where was this feeling coming from? My brain shuddered, trying to find a reason, to connect the dots. All the dots weren't there.

Zahra called for us to stop, and we went for our water bottles. I gulped down half the bottle, like filling my stomach could fill the rest of me. A blue light blinked in my bag. New text.

Text from Kalan Daniel Fox to Genesis Lee, TDS 09:10:09/5-7-2084
They let me out this morning. I'm really sorry about last night, Gena.

My fingers stiffened around my water bottle. Wrong number. It had to be.

Except it had my name in it.

Kalan Daniel Fox. The name brought nothing to mind, but it sure brought some tingles to the rest of me. I scratched my arms as the tingles turned to jitters, then to shakes. Don't freak out. Not a big deal, not a big deal...

Cora sidled up next to me. "So did you and this Kalan guy find out anything at that meeting last night?"

Not good. Very much un-good. Acid scorched my throat. The sad, hollow place inside me began to ring, a gong in the emptiness. My breath shuddered with each inhale. What was wrong with me?

"I don't feel right." I shook out my hands. "Something's wrong, I don't feel right."

Cora wound her towel around her hands. "Are you sick? What's wrong?"

I needed to not feel anymore. Needed someone to tell me why a strange boy knew my name. "I don't know, I can't think straight and I feel...*wrong*, I don't know. And then I got this text..."

"Was it Kalan? He didn't, like, call things off did he?" Her face pinched tight, like she was afraid to hear the answer.

I was afraid to give it.

"I—I don't know a Kalan. He texted me, but I've never met him, I don't..." My voice echoed like it came from some cavern inside me.

"What are you talking about?" Cora demanded. "You said you were helping him find who took my Link."

"Finding the Link thief?" My breath left in a whoosh. "I'm not…I didn't…when did I say that?"

"Yesterday." Cora pressed her hands to her stomach. "He texted you. You went to meet him."

"No." I skimmed my memory of last night, and it was patchy. Like an audio feed that hadn't loaded all the way.

"Zahra." Cora's voice, laced with an edge of panic, reverberated in my ears.

Zahra turned, looking concerned, and nodded toward the door. Cora nudged my shoe and headed out. I followed, and she led me upstairs and onto the empty stage, hiding us in the maroon curtains.

"Show me your Links." The folds of thick velvet muffled her voice.

I fumbled with the sleeve of my leotard. My fingers ran over and over and over my bracelets. "They're all here. They're all here, how do you know this guy and I don't?"

Cora trembled, her eyes unfocused. She sank to the floor, resting on her heels. I couldn't have forgotten. Not an entire *person*. My brain ran circles around blank spaces. Nada. Empty. Like my lungs that couldn't inhale, like my heart that couldn't beat. If this was forgetting, it was a hollow kind of hell.

I shook my head until it felt like it detached from my shoulders. Proof. I could prove it wasn't true. My fingers fumbled with my Sidewinder, searching my texts from yesterday. And there he was.

Kalan Daniel Fox.

I'd never heard that name. *I didn't remember this boy.* My mind raced through my Links, searching for a face, a gesture, a shirt color. Anything to connect a boy named Kalan to me.

Nothing. I felt myself rolling to a stop while the world spun faster. I fell to the floor and yanked off my gloves. With shaking hands, I felt the grain of the wood floor. Solid and smooth. Tiny particles of dirt pressed into my skin.

Real. It was real. It couldn't be real. Because this was a nightmare.

"This is impossible." Cora's shoulders hunched. They rose and fell slowly, like she had to work to breathe. "But of course it isn't. I'll never get my memories back. They'll never catch him, not a memory thief."

Scream, Cora. Go nuclear. Scream and rant and stomp out all the fear and anger so I can release it too. You're never defeated, you always rage.

The dusty curtains thickened the air. I took shallow breaths, hoping for vicarious relief through a Cora outburst. It didn't come. And it scared me almost as much as the hole in my memory. She was losing herself. Like…someone had said. Who had said? I blinked, sensing another scene that had been chopped into bits.

Not real, not real, not real.

"Someone is stealing my memories." I clapped a hand to my mouth. No vomiting. I swallowed, twice.

Cora didn't answer.

"It doesn't make sense, it can't happen, my Links are all here."

"Siphoning," she whispered.

Another Mementi. Not possible.

A lot of not possible things were happening today.

"I was really looking for the thief?"

"I guess." The curtains absorbed her words. "You probably got too close. The thief must have a Mementi working with him."

So. They were stealing memories so I couldn't find the person stealing memories. A wild laugh escaped my lips. The idea of me hunting the Link thief was as insane as me hunting dinosaurs.

"We should call the cops." Cora toyed with the Sidewinder around her wrist.

"No!" The coppery tang of fear filled my mouth. An unexpected reaction. Why was I afraid to go to the cops?

Cora's head came up, her face pale. "Uh, *yes*."

"They'll…they'll lock me in the house, they'll want to go through all my Links to find out what's happening." I clutched my Links. Of all the idiotic excuses. But the police. I couldn't. I *couldn't*.

"Gena," Cora said slowly, "why are you freaking about the cops?"

I rubbed a finger across the shiny wood floor.

"It could be anybody. *Anybody*. Do you suspect—"

"I don't…remember." The words scraped my tongue like sandpaper.

Cora shrank into the curtains behind her, nearly disappearing into the thick folds. "Who do we trust now?"

No one. I couldn't trust Mom or the cops or crazy Mrs. Bent with her weird love of tomato soup cake. I couldn't even trust my own memory. But…

"What about this guy?" I said. "Kalan?"

"No way. Suspect number one."

But he couldn't have siphoned from me. He was Populace—his name wasn't tagged on my text with a Sidewinder GPS indicator.

Cora apparently didn't know that. Now was probably not a great time to tell her. "Why would he steal my memories about him, then text me?"

She pressed her lips together.

"He's safe, he wouldn't have contacted me otherwise. He could help me."

The thought of meeting a Populace boy I didn't remember terrified me only slightly less than meeting with the cops.

"I guess." Cora tapped on her fingernails through her gloves.

Her agreement filled me with relief. This was a good plan. "I'll text him. Have him meet me somewhere."

I pulled up his text and hit "reply."

Text from Genesis Lee to Kalan Daniel Fox, TDS 9:31:13/5-7-2084
Can you meet me at the Memoriam?

Text from Kalan Daniel Fox to Genesis Lee, TDS 9:32:57/5-7-2084
Church just started. How about 12:00?

"He's churchy," I said, surprised.

Cora snorted. "Zahrad like him."

Maybe. She might also want to tape him to the floor and tap dance on his face for involving me in a Link thief hunt.

"So now what?"

That tiny, frightened voice of hers was going to send me back into panic attack territory. A wave of shivers threatened to reduce me to a quivering mass on the floor. "I don't want to think about it for a little while."

"But when—"

"Please," I begged. "I'm going to go crazy."

Cora nodded. "Dance?"

I could have hugged her. She always knew what I needed. "Dance."

"I'll help you with your solo piece." She sat forward with a lurch, like she was forcing herself back into a world she was drifting away from.

"What about you?"

"I'm not dancing in this recital. Some of the steps come to me a little at a time, but I can't call them to mind on purpose. I'd be dancing worse than in the last three performances."

"But…" I couldn't think of an argument in the world.

"It's okay," she said.

No it wasn't. Cora had become a stellar dancer in the last year. She'd even been granted a full scholarship to Havendale U. All that was gone. Stolen away.

Our memories. Our selves. Ripped away like pages of a book, parts of our story missing. A ragged pain tore into my chest.

Stop. Focus on the distraction. "My dance needs more… something."

"It needs more of you," Cora said. "You're boring when you dance classical. You know, we could change it."

"Change it?" The performance was in a few days.

"Sure. Zahra's been helping me choreograph a new lyrical routine." She paused. "You know. To try to be myself again."

Ballet and jazz met in lyrical dance like some kind of cosmic perfection. This was my last performance before I graduated. I wanted it to be the sum of everything I'd learned. An expression of who I was and who I was becoming. That seemed extra important now that I was losing myself bit by bit. And since it was my last performance, my parents couldn't dictate my dancing anymore.

I'd have the steps memorized by the end of today. "Let's do it."

We danced.

It didn't help.

My thoughts kept sucking me into the hole inside where a person named Kalan Fox once existed. Finding him—and the thief—was more vital than ever.

Because if I didn't, I had no idea how much more of myself I might lose.

13

But thou art turn'd to something strange,
And I have lost the links that bound…

—Alfred, Lord Tennyson, *In Memoriam XLI*

Sundays were popular for visiting the Memoriam. The crowd was thinner today, but I still had to dodge picnickers, strolling couples, and children racing on the lawn. Sometimes Populace mingled here too. Tourists, mostly. I didn't notice any now. The Link buzz reached an almost audible fever-pitch inside my head.

Revulsion nearly made me pause to vomit in a patch of yellow wooly daisies. Someone had reached inside me. Fingered pieces of my soul and ripped them away. Somewhere in this town, parts of me existed inside another set of Links.

People lounged on the benches scattered around the Memoriam. Faces blurred; it was their Links that drew my gaze. Most were hidden beneath gloves or high collars, but they shined under sheer fabrics or made bumps under clothing. Who was it? Who had violated me? I wiped a drop of sweat that trickled down my cheek from under my scarf.

Someone behind me called my name.

The unfamiliar voice reminded me who I'd come to find. My feet grew roots. I'd been all worried about what he looked like and how I'd find him. Now I wanted to un-find him. What do you say to the guy you don't remember? *Long time, no see. FYI, you never existed for me.*

It wasn't just memory I'd lost. It was a relationship. A little world made up of us. How much world had that been, after a few days?

I turned. He was tall and lanky, almost a little gangly. Loose blond curls flattened under a black cadet cap. Bushy eyebrows and a big grin. Cute. Not gorgeous, but cute.

I didn't recognize him at all.

"You walked right past me." He smiled. "I didn't think I blended in that much."

The warmth in his tone heated my cheeks. I rubbed my face, self-conscious about the automatic reaction. The feeling of missingness in my heart burrowed a little deeper. My mind had lost him, and my heart mourned.

For half a second, I wanted to bolt. Hide. Except there was nowhere to hide from my own feelings. That didn't mean I had to trust them, though. Just because I needed his help—just because my heart missed him—didn't mean I had to stick around.

"Hi," I said.

"You okay?" he asked. "Last night was rough. But no permanent record for me, only a night in jail. And the doctors said Anabel's going to be fine. The rock just grazed her before shattering the window. She still had a nasty concussion, but they're sending her home tonight."

Okay. Tally for last night: hospital and jail. What kind of crazy had I jumped into?

"That's good," I said vaguely.

I felt like I needed to memorize him. My brain wanted to catalogue all the details I'd lost. He wore a simple green t-shirt, and wiry muscles stood out on his long arms. Must work out. He twisted something in his fingers, a ball. A nervous habit, maybe, needing something to play with. His smile was wide and goofy, but he had a strong jaw. Like once he latched on to something, he wouldn't let go.

"So you've got to explain more about last night…" His eyebrows gathered. "Okay, what? You're looking at me like you've never seen me before."

His smile dropped, his eyebrows sank low, and he knew.

"Gena." His lips softened my name. "Do you know who I am?"

I closed my eyes and shook my head.

The shouts of happy children grew louder.

"You don't remember me. You don't remember. I should have…No, Gena!"

The anguish in his voice pierced me. I opened my eyes. "I'm sorry."

"Always sorry for things that aren't your fault." His jaw clenched, but the rest of his face was soft and vulnerable. "But you were fine, you sent me that long message."

He dug a cheap phone from his pocket. People walked past us, laughing, and splashed each other in the pond, laughing, and rode their bikes over the bridge, laughing. Secure in a public place in the sunlight. Somewhere their Links weren't in danger.

What would they do if I told them I still had my Links, but my memories were vanishing?

I held my breath against a moan. I was afraid of the boy in front of me. If I abandoned Kalan after today, then later found my memories of him, would I regret leaving? Or regret taking the memories back?

"Right here." Kalan lifted his head. "The message didn't get delivered until today, but you sent it to me last night just after ten. You must have sent it while you were walking home."

And someone had caught me, still on the street. "I'm sorry."

"Please don't say that," he groaned. "Do you remember anything? Anything about the two of us?"

I shook my head.

More silence. He stepped toward me. I stepped back.

"I'll help you remember me." He stepped forward again, ferocity ready to lash out of him. "And if I can't do that, I'll help you know me again."

"I don't want—" I gripped my elbow with my other hand.

His eyebrows contracted, releasing his fierce expression. "You don't want to know me again?"

I didn't answer.

"You don't have to. If it's too hard." His voice was steady, but his shoulders drooped. "What *do* you want?"

"The Link thief." To stop him. To get him arrested. To pummel his face into the dirt.

"I can help you with that."

That was the reason I came. Wasn't it? To get information from this boy, not for the boy himself. I nodded.

"Okay. Okay. I guess we go back to the beginning." His Adam's apple bobbed. "I'm Kalan."

And although he already knew, I said, "I'm Gena. Gena Lee."

* * *

We sat on the shaded concrete, our backs against the Memoriam. Kalan had explained everything while staring at the sky. He said it was easier to pretend he was telling someone else so he didn't leave anything out based on the assumption I should know it all.

Details of our "case" mixed in my mind with less important reveals—Kalan's preacher-father, Elijah; the woman Anabel who'd had a rock thrown at her; meetings at a sushi dive. It sounded like someone else's story.

I ran a finger over my lip. It helped me not to look at him, too. I could pretend I was thinking out loud and not talking to an unfamiliar boy. One I might leave behind.

"Okay, so the thief is a girl. And a Mementi." I swallowed. I'd found the Memo he'd given me of our first meeting tucked in my bag, and I still couldn't shake the shivers of seeing myself in a moment I didn't remember. "We don't know why she's stealing Links. Or why she's siphoning from me, or why she stole only one Link from Cora."

"Right."

"We know from Jackson's text that Blaire had some kind of evidence. Either she or her evidence is likely the connection between the theft victims—the thing they needed to forget."

Blaire. I couldn't think about what it meant that she'd left her own Memorial Link. I hadn't seen her in ages, but her not being there at all? My insides twisted.

"We know something else, too," Kalan said. "The thief would be somebody you talked to recently, someone who knew you were looking for her."

Someone who knew I needed memories wiped again.

"Or not." I squinted at the clouds. "If Jackson saw me here last night, he could have called the thief. Even siphoned from me himself."

"In other words…the thief could still be anybody?"

I sighed. "It could be my own freakin' mother for all we know."

I banged my head on the mirrored glass behind me. Pain shot down my skull and I winced.

"So," Kalan said, "we need to find out more about this connection between Blaire, her mysterious evidence, and the theft victims. See if that gives us an idea of who has a motive to steal Links."

The frustration of forgetting overwhelmed me. "We don't even have witnesses. Anything the theft victims knew, they don't anymore."

I turned to him. And, whoa. Right. Stranger sitting next to me. I'd started talking to him like we were partners. Like it was natural to talk to him this way. Like hunting the Link thief was something I had decided to do when I didn't remember deciding to do it.

There was Option A: Team up with crazy/cute jailbird who scared the socks off me. And Option B: Hide under my covers. Kind of a fan of that option.

I had a sudden frantic wish to talk to Grandma Piper. Sometimes a girl just needed a lemon drop and a bear hug. And someone to tell her to cowboy up. I rested my head against the Memoriam.

The Memoriam. Grandma Piper was inside. She'd died when I was nine, and I hadn't seen her for a full year before that. Mom and Dad had cut off all communication with her for some reason after my eighth birthday. When I'd tried to sneak to her house anyway, she'd actually yelled at me to leave, crying the whole time. The memory tasted as sour as her lemon drops.

I couldn't talk to her, but maybe I didn't have to.

"I need to think," I said. "Can I have a minute?"

"Sure," Kalan said.

I circled the Memoriam, found the glass door, and went inside. Kalan followed me. I suppressed a growl. I'd meant a minute *alone*.

He craned his head back and took off the cadet cap. "Wow. What is this place?"

I stared into the hollow spiral of the tower. Hundreds of memories buzzed inside me like strange music. Patterns of pale pine, deep walnut, and rich cherry wood blocks played on the walls. Stairs wound upward on three sides, stopping at curving balconies. Sunlight streamed through strategically placed windows that shot beams of light in artistic weaves. In tiny increments, the weaves rotated with the path of the sun. Inside the Memoriam, even death had a dance.

"This is our cemetery," I said, my words echoing. "The memories of those we love are stored here with their ashes after they die."

"You're kidding."

I spiraled up the stairs with Kalan close behind. Where was the awkward? There should be a little bit of awkward with this stranger in a personal place. I couldn't dredge up even a hint of it. My own comfort made me climb faster to get away from him.

We reached the third balcony and I turned left. Though it had been a while since I'd visited Grandma Piper and Grandpa Scott's Memoriams, I knew the exact spot where their bricks were placed.

"So everyone's cremated?" Kalan asked. Carved names gleamed on the wooden blocks we passed.

"Yes. The ashes, and usually their Links, are sealed in a plastic box inside the wood. Before they die, they leave behind a few memories they want to share, and those get stored in the wooden block itself. Some people leave all their Links and relatives pick their favorites."

Like Grandma. Dad had never visited her before she died, but he had at least gone through her Links to make her a Memoriam. He'd stayed in his room for two days, and Mom had looked haunted the whole time. I shivered at the memory. I still didn't know why my parents stopped talking to my grandmother.

"You can relive their lives here?" Kalan asked. "That's a little creepy."

"It's not all their memories, just special ones." I lifted my chin and sniffed. It was a wonderful tribute to the people we loved.

Kind of odd, though, when you considered how closely we guarded our private memories. But these people had passed on. It didn't feel violating to glimpse the memories they'd offered us. Come to think of it, some people—a.k.a. my own mother—didn't mind giving others a peek while they were alive.

Not that everybody agreed. Cora's mom hadn't made a Memoriam for Cora's grandpa, saying it was a desecration of his life. She kept his Links in a lockbox in her home. And my own father hadn't been inside the Memoriam since the day of Grandma's funeral.

"Wait," Kalan said. "Your memories still exist *after you're dead*?" The squeak of his steps paused behind me.

"Yeah," I said. "It's actually caused a bit of debate about the meaning of death. You know, if Mementi are in some ways still alive because their memories still exist."

"There's no debate on that," he said flatly. "Your memories aren't your soul."

That's right—churchy guy. And rather opinionated, too. I didn't respond. We'd reached what I was searching for.

PIPER JANE LEE, read the inscription on one deep brown block. Next to it was SCOTT CHI KEUNG LEE. There were no dates or epitaphs. Everything was in the memories inside the wood.

"Do you know how the Mementi started?" I trailed a gloved finger across the carved letters. "How we came to be the way we are?"

"Some kind of drug trial for PTSD patients that went bad." Kalan studied the names.

"Memor-X," I said. "It was actually a form of gene therapy on a specific gene that releases a protein that influences people's ability to store memory. The brain-derived neurotrophic—"

Kalan turned, his eyebrows shooting up.

I sighed. "Basically, they played around with this gene so it directed the brain to store certain memories in a biochip implanted in the head. That way patients with Post Traumatic Stress Disorder could displace their memories for a while. Deal with them a little at a time. But something went wrong. The gene and the protein kept changing the brain until it literally couldn't store memories anymore."

"So it really is a biological thing," Kalan said.

"Yeah. It wasn't like things are now, though. The first generation couldn't store memories in things they touched, not immediately. They had to use those biochips. Some of them lost parts of their memories but still retained the emotional damage. It caused a lot more trauma than it solved."

"So how come you guys can store your memories through touch?"

"Don't know," I said. "It was a gradual process for the first generation, and even their reproductive cells mutated so all their kids were born with it. Somehow the brain rewired itself so it connects to the peripheral nervous system. Nobody's sure how it works."

Kalan ran his fingers over the edges of my grandmother's block. My fingers clenched, though he couldn't access her memories.

"So the Mementi came together to help each other heal," Kalan said, as if rehearsing the end of a bedtime story. "And they sued the company and bought the land for Havendale, where they could live in peace, and started their own biotech company to make the world a better place with their memories."

"Not everyone stayed in Havendale," I said. "Lots of the subjects were military people, and some of them had families and kids so they stayed where they were. And some of the subjects *were* kids. Their parents took them back where they were from."

Like Zahra's grandparents had done to their daughter, Zahra's mother. That's why Zahra grew up in France.

Kalan stepped away from Grandma Piper's memoriam. PIPER JANE LEE. My grandmother had known the horror of forgetting what you didn't want to—and the terror of remembering what you'd rather forget. I removed my gloves. When my fingers graced her name, an array of memories splintered across my mind.

My father's tiny newborn body was both heavy and light in her arms. Her mind filled with wonder and euphoria, and the lingering birth pains faded.

My grandfather beamed at her across a living room strewn with Chinese New Year decorations. Two small granddaughters played on the floor near their parents. I felt my own chubby cheek beneath my hand—her hand. She radiated joy. This was the family she'd always dreamed of having.

And one more. Stored in emotionless metal embedded inside the block, a memory most first generations had. Their reason for signing up for Memor-X. She was seventeen, arms wrapped around the bloody body of her brother. Her father pressed a warm shotgun to her temple and screamed that he would shoot her too, that beatings weren't enough anymore, that she would learn.

I could feel the warm circle of the gun on my head, and the slick weight of the boy in my arms. But not the fear, or horror, or whatever else she may have felt. My eyes stung. That fractured moment was all she had ever remembered of a lifetime of abuse. Memor-X had robbed her of the rest of them, leaving her like the Link theft victims. Struggling with emotions she didn't under-stand, and so couldn't resolve.

I dropped my hand to my side. The images and sounds cut from my mind, forgotten. I called up my own memories of Grandma Piper. She was more than a shattered victim. My memory held the pieces that were really her. The rise and fall of her voice as she acted out hilarious bedtime stories. The purple tanzanite ring Grandpa Scott had given her that she never took off. The piles of Agatha Christie novels that filled the corners of her bedroom. Her temper that would rise at the slightest provocation, like Dad's, but was always followed with a tearful apology, unlike his.

Unchained emotions. Just like Cora and the other theft victims. Oh. Oh, oh, oh.

I brought my fingers to my lips. I thought of Jorge Thomas and his horrid suggestion Ascalon could hack into the victims' emotional memories and take them away as evidence.

But we didn't have to go that far. "I've got an idea."

Kalan stopped tracing names on the blocks. "Yeah?"

"We need to go to the hospital. Talk to the Link theft victims."

"I thought you said that was a dead end."

"I know." How did I explain this? "But with the first gener-ation, they had all these post-traumatic emotions that hung on after the memories were gone. So they still kind of held on to their experiences through the emotions. The victims are the same way, that's why they're in the hospital. Their emotions are going crazy because they don't have memories to tell them what they're for."

Kalan lounged against the carved balcony rail. "So if we talk to them about Blaire, we might get an idea from their emotions how they're all connected to her."

It wasn't that much nicer than Jorge's idea. I'd have to confront the people who had lost more than me. Bring up painful things they wouldn't remember. Look impending insanity in the face. Sounded like a party.

"I'm not close to anyone at the hospital," I said. "The doctors might not let me in."

"Especially with me," Kalan said grimly.

With him. I'd told him everything, like I'd planned on him coming all along. Our eyes met across the balcony.

"Or, I could…not go." He shifted against the balcony rail. "If you don't want. It shouldn't be dangerous. But if you want backup, emotional support…"

Emotional support. A paranoid giggle stalled in my throat. Yes, I needed emotional support. Though seeing as he was half the reason my emotions were acting like a dust devil, I didn't need it from him. But backup. My memory needed that.

"Yeah. Okay," I said.

His entire body seemed to lift, his expression lightening. "Okay. Okay, good. Do you know anyone who could get us into the hospital?"

"I've got a better idea."

14

I cannot see the features right,
When on the gloom I strive to paint
The face I know; the hues are faint
And mix with hollow masks of night...

—Alfred, Lord Tennyson, *In Memoriam LXX*

The afternoon sun slanted through the glass of the hospital atrium, illuminating the sparkling patterns etched into the floor. Wallscreens played silent ads for new healthcare advances from Ascalon BioTech. Flowering plants in elaborate stone pots were the only sign of life. No patients were being admitted, no visitors waited in overstuffed chairs, no staff typed behind the desks. Most of the administrative people were Populace—they hadn't fired them all, had they?

Good thing I'd made Kalan wait by a side exit. Technically, I had permission to be here; Cora had been preregistered at the hospital a few days ago, and I was on the visitor's list. That didn't mean I couldn't get asked to leave, but Kalan…he'd probably be hung by his thumbs in the bowels of the hospital if they caught him sneaking into the psychiatric wing.

Okay. Maybe that was going too far.

I headed down a short hall that was barricaded by a large automatic door. I laid a trembling hand on the DNA lock. *Click.* The door unlatched, swinging slowly open on its hydraulic hinges. A beep sounded from my Sidewinder. I'd been logged as a visitor on the hospital system.

Soothing music played, and a three dimensional holocast unfurled across the floor and walls. Ahead of me, the hospital hallway had transformed into a peaceful beach dotted with palm trees. Beautiful and too bright to be real. If it was supposed to make you happy to be here, it failed.

I strolled past rolling waves, trying to look like I belonged. Nobody would think to ask why I was visiting when Cora hadn't been admitted. I hoped.

Ahead of me, a doctor approached, Larissa Jonas. I fixed a smile to my face, but she rushed by with a hurried nod. My shoulders sagged once she'd passed. Almost there.

I went right past the elevator and pushed open the door to a stairwell. The sudden reintroduction of steel and concrete jarred me. An external exit—locked from the outside—waited across the landing. It really wasn't necessary for Kalan to come. He was coming in through the back, sure, but he could still be spotted. And arrested. And hung by his thumbs while I was interrogated and had my memory wiped.

Get a grip, Gena.

Feeling like a coward, I called Kalan even though he was right outside the door.

"So." Kalan answered on the first ring. "I forgot your real name is Genesis. That's how your calls and texts are labeled."

I tucked a loose hair behind my ear. "Is this relevant?"

"It's the first book in the Bible."

"Oh." Some of my friends were Christian, but the Bible had always been at the bottom of my 'Classics to Read' list. Now I was curious. "It means 'beginning,' right?"

I heard the smile in his voice. "Yup. It's the story of how God created the world."

"You'll have to tell me about that some time." Or not. *Memo to mouth: stop saying words before the brain can process them.*

"Yup. You're not going to open the door, are you?"

A light above me blinked out; they needed to redo the techpaint on this section of ceiling. The light fritzed back on. My neck prickled.

"Maybe my memories aren't as good as yours," he said, "but I should be there. I can put my memories on a Memo right away to prevent degradation. It only takes a few seconds to upload them."

That was his purpose, I reminded myself. My personal external backup. I disconnected the call and opened the door.

Kalan sauntered in and nodded at the stairs. "Up?"

I nodded. "Up."

We climbed all the way to the roof. The inpatient rooms in the psych ward all had private access to the rooftop cactus garden. The hospital schedule Cora had received said "outdoor free time" took place in the afternoons. Hopefully we weren't too late.

Kalan opened the door and we stepped onto a gravel path, the sky wide and blue above us. Small gazebos lined the edges of the roof, each with an elevator to a patient's room. A shimmer at the edge of the building indicated the safety barricade was on. Like they'd ever turn it off.

The path wove through a forest of cacti. Tall saguaros pointed at the sky. Bulbous golden barrel cacti bubbled from the dirt. Blue chalk sticks spread long fingers, making a pale carpet. Several odd-shaped cacti sported red, orange, and purple flowers. Much better than the fake beach.

Our footsteps crunched over gravel. The path turned sharply, and I heard voices around the corner.

"Maybe you should hide here," I said softly. "I don't want any of them to immediately freak out about a Populace up here. It could make things…unpredictable."

"You're not facing them alone if they're unpredictable."

His overly authoritative tone grated on my nerves. "Well, I can predict they'll get unpredictable real quick if you walk up with no Link buzz."

"No."

"This will be pointless if they scream before we can say hi. You can rush in to save the day if I need it." Wow. Sarcasm. How impolite of me. I hid a grin.

"Fine," he growled.

We peeked around the corner, careful to avoid the spines of the saguaro cactus next to us. A simulated fire snapped cheerily in a clay-rimmed fire pit, surrounded by people. Cash Hernandez and Miranda Jacobs lounged on padded chairs, talking. Leeli Hanowitz circled the edges of the shaded area, weaving around the wooden pillars that held up a trellis laced with vines. Her lips moved, though no one stood near her. Valeria Willis sat in a lounge chair she'd dragged away from the fire, turned away from the rest of the group. There should be one more. Jacie Moran, just a little younger than me. I didn't see her anywhere.

"How can they still…I don't know, walk and talk if they lost all their memories?" Kalan whispered.

"Those are procedural memories," I said absently. "We still store those in the brain. It's only episodic and semantic memories that go in our Links."

"I'll take your word that that makes sense," he said.

"Stay here." Clenching my fists, I stepped around the corner.

A clod of dirt smacked the cactus next to me. I jumped, nearly skewering myself on hundreds of needles.

Valeria Willis stood next to her chair. Her loose hair danced around her head in a frizzy red halo. Hospital-issue white gloves covered her arms up to her shoulders. Over the gloves, a diamond-studded gold band wrapped her left ring finger.

"We don't want any more medicine," she said calmly.

I stepped forward, trying to ignore Kalan shifting behind me. "I'm not a doctor."

"Who did you know before?" Valeria asked. Her flat tone contrasted with her wild hair.

"All of you," I said. "But only a little bit."

"Why did they let you in? It's mostly family."

Leeli started walking again, muttering the six times tables to herself and pulling her thick scarf over the dozens of braids in her black hair. Miranda picked at the new Links under her gloves.

I took a deep breath. "I'm here because of my friend. Cora. She—"

"She's the one who lost a single Link." Cash's face reddened. "Stupid girl. Only one."

"You shut up," Valeria ordered. "Any memory lost is life lost. She's one of us."

One of them. Like memory theft was a sacred and horrific hazing ritual for a club. Maybe they'd accept me if I told them about my own memory loss.

But one of them was missing. "Is Jacie here too? Jacinta Moran?"

Valeria gripped her wrist with one hand and looked away. "No. She's not anywhere, really. They used to haul her out here, try to make her talk or move or just look at things. Now they leave her alone." Her eyes darted to an empty chair in the shade. "She was the first victim. At least the rest of us know what we've got ahead of us."

My body went rigid. The bright cushions on the empty chair dented in where a small person might have sat. How many hours had they made her sit, staring vacantly, trying to bring her back to life? How could they bring her back to life when she had no life to come back to?

Cora. Oh, Cora. She wouldn't get that bad. She still had the other fifteen years of life for context. But how empty would she become, if she were never filled back up?

It wouldn't happen. I'd find her Link before she was too far gone.

Which meant I had to ask these people about Blaire. There wasn't a crueler question in the universe than one about the people you couldn't remember. I had to start with Miranda.

I'd tried not to look at her. Hers was the most familiar face. It sparked memories of peanut butter sandwich picnics and calls for Blaire to come home when the sun faded over neighborhood night games.

"Mrs. Jacobs?" I said. "Can I talk to you?"

She eyed me. "Okay."

I approached and sat on a chair to her left. "I'd like to ask you about someone you were close to. Do you mind?"

"No," Cash interrupted. "Absolutely not."

I ignored him. "Mrs. Jacobs?"

She darted a look at Cash.

"You listen to me," Cash growled. "You think you can just walk in and treat us like zoo animals?"

"What?"

"We're not here for you to gawk at."

"I'm not here for that—"

"You shouldn't be here at all!" He stood, waving his arms in the air. "Asking about the pasts we don't have? Nobody asks that, not even our families. What do you want, some sad and pathetic tale to take back to school?"

I shrank away, my automatic anxiety reaction hunching my shoulders. "I'm trying to help."

"You don't—"

"Cash." Miranda held up a hand. "She's just a kid. She's not after you. Or me."

His hands dropped. He opened his mouth again.

"Shush," she said firmly.

I almost smiled. That was a familiar tone. The I'm-the-mom voice I'd heard her use on Blaire.

The tremble of her lips contradicted the strength in her voice. "You…have a question."

"Yes," I whispered.

"I won't be able to answer it." She said it matter-of-factly, but her hands clenched in her lap.

"I know. I'd like to ask anyway."

"Okay," she said. She brushed hair under her scarf.

Exhale. "What do you know about your daughter, Blaire?"

Her hand froze halfway to her face. "Blaire."

"Yes. Your daughter."

The frozen hand shook. The tremor spread to her shoulder. Her breath came in shallow gulps.

"A daughter. A daughter. I'm a mother."

I clapped a hand over my mouth. Even after Blaire's disappearance, no one had told her? Her head shook in a distorted rhythm while her mouth opened and closed. Like she wanted to say something, but couldn't remember what.

"A daughter. I forgot my daughter."

Cash leaped up. "Get out! Get out of here, what kind of person are you?"

Miranda's tremors became a rocking. "What does she look like?" Desperation tinged her words. "Does she look like me?"

"She…" I swallowed. "She's tall like you, and she has your hair. Your brains, too. She graduated top of her class."

Miranda's hands flew to her face, covering her eyes. "Graduated. Of course. Graduated. She wouldn't be a baby anymore…"

The entire rooftop held its breath.

A horrible wail split from Miranda's lips. She yanked her own hair in gloved hands. I drew back, clutching my stomach against the pain eating me inside. If there was a God, he'd send me to hell for causing pain like this.

Miranda tumbled from the chair, sobbing Blaire's name. Her fingers grasped at my leggings, and I backed away.

"Why hasn't she come?" Her fingers dug into the dirt. "Why hasn't she come for me?"

Before I could blink, Cash rushed from his chair. Toward Kalan, who had darted around the saguaro in the corner.

"Populace!" Cash yelled.

"No, Cash, stop, he's a friend!" I yelled.

"Why hasn't she come? Blaire. My daughter…"

Kalan wrestled with Cash, struggling to fend off the older man's blows. I tugged Miranda's hands from my shoulders. She crumpled to the ground. I ran toward the men, but Valeria got there first.

She slapped Cash on the back of the head, knocking off his cap. The unexpected touch stopped him mid-swing.

"Leave him alone," Valeria demanded. "Move, let me see him."

Cowed by Valeria, Cash snatched his hat and backed away. My eyes darted between Kalan and Valeria. Now what? He stood straight, breathing hard.

"Is it you?" she asked. Her body had softened, her face lifted toward his.

"Is what me?"

"Did you come for me?"

He looked away. "I'm so sorry. No."

Valeria's shoulders drooped. Memories and facts connected in a horrible, perfect clicking of domino pieces across my mind.

Blaire, going missing around the time Miranda lost her memory.

Victims losing all their Links instead of having a few memories siphoned. Because they had to forget something—or someone—important in their lives.

Valeria, looking for someone she felt should have been there.

"Valeria," I said, "are you missing someone? Someone who's never come to visit?"

After a moment, Valeria whispered, "Names. Faces. Moments. I almost remember them. And almost is torture."

Her wild hair glowed in the sun. A trace of hollowness crossed her eyes. Like a shattered angel, her wings were broken. I could almost hear the brush of feathers falling to the dirt.

Over the sound of Miranda's piercing sobs, a strange voice called out. "Hey, folks! Who's ready for group therapy?"

Crap. "Kalan, go!" I hissed.

We dashed away, the crunch of gravel leaving a trail of sound for someone to follow. Kalan yanked at the door to the stairwell, but it was locked. I skidded up and slapped my hand on the DNA scanner. The door opened, and we rushed through.

"Think they'll rat on us?" Kalan asked.

"No idea. Run."

Down the stairs, out the back door, and across the lawn. We stopped under the shade of the hospital's solar panel array to catch our breath.

"That was awful," Kalan said.

"That's the connection. It's not just Blaire. Someone wanted to make people disappear, and made sure their relatives never noticed they're gone." I paused. "There's one more thing I want to try. Keep an eye out for anybody coming."

Cash would totally tell on us. At least he didn't know who we were. I unwrapped the Sidewinder from my wrist and tapped through menu options. The visitor check-in list popped up on my screen. I glanced at it, then turned off my Sidewinder.

"Did you even have time to read that?" Kalan asked.

"Shh." I skimmed my memory for names and mentally compared them to the check-in list I'd just memorized. "So check this out. Cash Hernandez's only direct relation is his son, Rory, 24. He hasn't visited once. He's been employed at Happenings for the last year."

Kalan shrugged.

"Miranda Jacobs, mother to Blaire, Happenings employee, never visited, missing. Leeli has a brother and two sisters who visit a couple times a week. She's single, but she's been a friend of the Hernandez family for ages—there are even rumors Cash and Leeli were cheating long before Cash's wife died. His son Rory works at Happenings too. Jacie Moran…hm. She has parents and two brothers who visit her every day. Maybe a friend?"

"And Valeria?" Kalan asked.

"She's engaged," I said quietly, remembering the ring on her finger. I wondered if she woke up and was terrified that she didn't know who gave it to her. "Only her family is listed as visiting. But she thought you—a Populace guy—had come for her. If her fiancé is Populace, it's not too far a stretch that he worked at Happenings."

"Populace fiancé," Kalan said. "Wonder how *that* happened."

I thrilled at the discovery at the same time I hurt for the names on this list. "Almost everyone who lost their Links has someone who's never visited and who works at Happenings. That's why the victims had their Links stolen. They had to forget a whole *person* who'd been in their lives for ages."

Looked like maybe the rumors about Happenings were true after all.

"What about Cora?" Kalan asked.

Good point. Cora had a huge extended family, but none of them had connections to Happenings.

"Ren." A lightning bolt of shock rooted me to the ground. "The thief wasn't after Cora that night, she was after *me*."

My hands shook as Kalan's eyes met mine.

"Why would someone want to make me forget Ren? Mom and Dad would still remember her, it's not like she could vanish without them noticing." She hadn't vanished already, had she? "I have to go see my sister."

"Come on."

I typed out a text to Ren as we left. Kalan's long legs kept up with my stride and we rushed up the tramstop stairs.

"I can't buy that three people could go missing and *nobody* had a clue," Kalan said. "They have friends, right? And what about the doctors, and the cops, and nosy reporters, for crying out loud?"

"Maybe no one's seen the connection to Happenings. Lee-li's is speculative, Jacie doesn't have an obvious one, and no one would have looked at Valeria's Populace fiancé." I paused. "And I wouldn't put it past Jackson to wipe any evidence that came out."

My Sidewinder stayed silent and still. I wrapped the phone around my ear. "Call Ren."

The line went immediately to voicemail. My foot drummed out a metallic rhythm.

"If the thief wanted you to forget Ren, you would have already," Kalan said gently. "She'll be okay, Gena." His hair hung low over his eyes, the combination of brown and blond like a swirl of honey. "So will you."

I couldn't help it. I loved that he wanted to comfort me. For a minute, I let myself fantasize about touching him. To not worry about sharing memories, to just feel his skin. My mind rebelled, spitting the thought right back out. I didn't want that from him. No matter what I may have wanted just a day ago.

The tram pulled up. The worry inside me drowned out thoughts of boys and what I did or didn't want from them. My mind chanted to the hum of the engines as we rushed over the city. Ren would be fine, she was fine, she would be fine. She would text me any minute, any minute, any minute.

My Sidewinder stayed silent.

15

A web is woven across the sky…

—Alfred, Lord Tennyson, *In Memoriam III*

Ren answered the door in her pajamas, her short hair standing on end. I grabbed hold of her doorframe. She was fine. She was fine.

"Gena?" She rubbed red eyes. "What are you doing here?"

"Wow," Kalan said. "Digging the purple hair. And the frogs." He gestured to Ren's cotton pants.

Was he flirting with her? I glared at him.

So did Ren. "Who are *you*?"

"Kalan Fox," he said cheerfully. "I can see where Gena doesn't get her politeness."

I had to stifle a laugh, still a little giddy from finding her safe. Ren turned from him in disgust.

"What do you want?" she snapped. "I was sleeping."

"It's three in the afternoon," I said. "I didn't think I'd be disturbing your beauty rest. I need to talk to you."

"Go talk to your Populace boyfriend. I'm sleeping."

"Hold on!"

The door slammed.

"Ren!" I banged a fist on her door. No response. I hissed into the door crack as loud as I dared, "I'm losing my memories."

The door flew open. Ren had paled beneath her messy hair. "There haven't been any thefts reported."

"All my Links are here." My words echoed in the stairwell. "I'm losing memories anyway."

"Get in here."

Kalan followed me into the tiny studio apartment. Mom and Dad would have been horrified at the clothes on the floor and the unmade bed. I didn't mind. It wasn't a disaster, just... lived in.

Ren sat on her bed. I took the single chair from her desk, leaving Kalan to park himself on the floor. Served him right after checking out my sister.

The place was sparse, almost utilitarian. No pictures, holo or otherwise. No sign of her once-beloved ceramic frog collection. Only the bed, desk, and an old TV. She didn't even have another chair for her rickety kitchen table. I'd thought Happenings paid better than this.

"What's going on?" Ren demanded.

I told her about losing my memories—twice.

"I don't get it." Ren crossed her socked feet on the bed. "What's the point of siphoning from you? What would they want you to forget?"

"The Link thief, probably," Kalan said. "It's like someone's trying to make her forget we're investigating the thief."

"Whoa, hold it." Ren threw her arms up, palms out. "You're *looking* for the thief? Gen, are you nuts?"

Do not yell back, do not yell back. "Cora's my best friend. And I'm losing memories too, even before I started searching for the thief. What else am I supposed to do?"

"Let the freakin' *police* handle it." She ran a hand through her hair, standing it further on end. "You've never so much as picked your own clothes in the morning, and now you decide to hunt a memory thief. What's wrong with you?"

Not true. I shopped for all my own stuff. "You're the one who wanted me to grow a backbone."

She frowned.

"Look, Ren, I need a little help with this. What can you tell me about Happenings?" I asked.

"What about Happenings?"

Kalan reclined on his elbows. "Any chance they might kidnap you?"

Only the deeply driven habit of not touching people kept me from smacking Kalan upside the head.

Ren pursed her lips.

"It's just…well, with Blaire missing and Miranda in the hospital…it can't be coincidence." I kept quiet about the other possible missing people, seeing as Ren was freaking out enough already. "And she left some kind of evidence in a memory, but we aren't sure what. Do you know what Blaire was working on? Was she keeping secrets or anything?"

Ren rested her elbows on her knees. Her head drooped. "Of course she was keeping secrets. I should've known."

Her sudden vulnerability pierced me. I wished I dared put an arm around her. She'd done that for me once. A hesitant, sideways hug when she found me crying in the backyard gazebo after Grandma died. We felt too far apart now for me to return the favor.

"It wasn't your fault, Ren," I said. I cleared my throat. "So… she never said anything about what she was really doing? Maybe she was working with someone higher up—this could go all the way to Liza Woods herself."

"No." Ren lifted her head. "And I think you're being stupid."

"Excuse me?" Trust Ren to resort to insults.

"Those lame rumors about Happenings are bad enough." Ren threw herself on her pillow. "This is completely idiotic. The CEO? Liza's been on sick leave for months, she doesn't even come in to the office anymore. I highly doubt she's sneaking around town kidnapping people and stealing Links."

Liza Woods sick? How convenient. I had no idea how it could connect, but I filed it away for later.

"She's not Mementi, though," Kalan pointed out. "She couldn't have siphoned your memories."

My lips pinched. "All I said was she could be *involved*. There's a lot we don't know, but you have to admit, there's too much weirdness going on to ignore Happenings."

"It's just as likely that Ascalon is involved," Ren said. "If anything, it's *more* likely. All they have to do is point at Happenings, and this whole town goes crazy."

"Huh," said Kalan. "That's actually a decent point. We ought to look into that."

Stupid boy. Was he going to agree with Ren on everything?

"You shouldn't be looking into anything." Ren sat up and clasped her hands in her lap. "Gen, you need to leave the Link thief alone. You're losing memories too."

"You were the one who said we had to take chances with our own memories." The memory from that night was fragmented, but I did remember Dad and Ren fighting.

"This isn't what I meant," she said. "There are acceptable risks, things we can calculate to help ourselves, to reach our real potential. This isn't one of them."

Acceptable risks. What was an acceptable risk for getting Cora's memories back? And my own, and the rest of the victims'? My heart shriveled, and I wanted Dad to be right, that the best approach to memories was to stay hands-off.

I stood. Ren scooted off the bed.

"You're leaving?" she asked.

"Yeah."

"Thanks, Ren," Kalan said. "I'm glad you weren't kidnapped."

I snorted, then sighed. I was glad she wasn't kidnapped too.

"Just—think about what you might lose," she said. "Please."

I met her eyes and saw a hint of fear. For me. No matter how much we irritated each other, my sister still loved me. Even if she completely ticked me off most of the time.

"Thanks, Ren."

Kalan and I walked into the desert heat, headed for the nearest tramstop. The sun scorched through my scarf, and my frustration bubbled over. "I don't care what Ren says, I still think Happenings has something to do with this. Blaire had evidence of *something*. Plus the whole Liza-is-sick thing sounds way too suspicious."

Kalan rubbed the back of his neck. "Maybe. Or we could be totally off-base. Maybe it really is Ascalon, and they're placing the blame on Happenings. Or it could be neither of them. Maybe Blaire just saw the thief, and that was the evidence she hid, and the thief has totally different motives."

Too many coulds and maybes. We were trapped by all the questions we couldn't answer. I twisted a loose strand of hair around my gloved finger, tugging it in frustration.

"You should dye it." Kalan nodded to the hair in my fingers. "Ren's looked cool."

I yanked extra hard on the strand of hair. "You liked that."

"Yeah. The color is fun with the black."

Well, if my hair wasn't fun enough for him, he could hang out with Ren. "I don't want to."

"Why not?"

I paused. "It was my idea."

"What was?"

"The hair dye. Ren knew that I've been wanting to dye blue streaks into my hair for forever. Just a few, near the front." I tugged at my gloves, my hands hot and sweaty.

"So now you don't want to do it because she stole the idea."

"Told you it was stupid," I said.

He kicked a rock and it clattered down the road. "Do you still want blue hair?"

"It'd be cool."

"So do it anyway. Don't let her decisions ruin yours."

We came up on the rock he had kicked. This time I kicked it. "You know, sometimes you sound very much like a preacher's son."

He ran a hand through his curls. "Sorry. I'm not trying to lecture."

"At least you didn't tell me God would smite me for dying my hair an unnatural color."

He laughed. "If that were true, I'd have lost God's favor a while ago. I dipped my hair in blue Kool-aid when I was nine."

I smiled, picturing a mini-Kalan with a mop of blue hair. "I love it."

"So did Dad, actually. I made a good object lesson for his sermon on repentance washing away the stains of sin."

My smile widened. "I think I'd like your dad."

"You do like him. At least, you seemed to the other day."

The sentence came out lightly, but it struck me like a smack in the face, killing my momentary happy buzz. I stopped in the middle of the empty road and stared at the small red rock I'd been kicking. I'd lost so much. Maybe Ren was right. I should savor what I still had. I didn't have to risk bleeding out more memories.

"You okay?" Kalan asked.

"How do we know we're doing the right thing, chasing the Link thief?"

He cocked his head. "Does it feel right to you?"

"That doesn't matter."

Kalan raised an eyebrow.

"I can't trust feelings to tell me what's right."

"Then what do you trust?"

"I—" He didn't get it. "Feelings lie. They come out of nowhere and half the time don't make sense." And occasionally turned you into a hyperventilating freak show.

Kalan reached out, his hand stopping before it brushed my arm. My heart swelled until I thought the beats would take me over. A whisper that he was a stranger fought against the rhythm. I looked away, confused.

He dropped his hand. "Maybe feelings don't seem to make sense because they know more than your brain. Just because you ignore your heart doesn't mean it's not still talking to you. If you listen, you'll know what to do."

That had the ring of recitation to it. "Did you just quote your dad?"

Kalan grinned sheepishly. "Well, he usually uses it in reference to God, not your heart. But I figure in a lot of cases, it's the same thing."

Whether it was God or my heart talking to me, that still didn't mean they were saying the right things.

"Do *you* still want to do this?" I asked.

"Yes." He stepped closer to me. "Do you?"

I'd promised Cora. And to be honest, I wasn't ready to let go of this strange partnership with Kalan. The more I got to know him the more I wanted to get to know him.

"Yes. But we need a plan." Go big or go home—that's what they always said, right? "Let's nail the Link thief. Tomorrow."

"Okay. Um. I'd very much like to know how you plan on doing that."

I crossed my arms. "We're going to break into Happenings."

16

Do we indeed desire the dead
Should still be near us at our side?

—Alfred, Lord Tennyson, *In Memoriam LI*

My parents were plugged into their Link buds when I got to the kitchen the next morning. Newscasts of violent protesters lit up the table, projected from their Sidewinders. Neither noticed I'd joined them. I crunched my cereal extra loud for the annoyance factor.

It's not like I wanted to tell them all about the lovely time I'd had with Kalan yesterday. But couldn't they ask? They scheduled my school and dance, they set my curfew, they demanded my itinerary, but heaven forbid they actually ask how it went.

I wanted to break the silence, loudly. No words, just a scream. Could I get it just right, with the perfect pitch of frustration, the high volume of anger, the hint of a desperate rasp, so they would finally hear me? Because I *wanted* to tell them about Kalan. His goofiness and tenderness and cute curly hair. I wanted to cry to them about what I'd done to Miranda at the hospital. I wanted to confess my mission to Happenings today so they could tell me I was brave or tell me I was stupid or tell me anything at all that they saw in me.

My spoon clattered in my cereal bowl. Loud. As loud as I dared. Mom glanced up, but didn't say a word. And I found that maybe I didn't want to talk to them after all.

I marched to my room and dug out my "I prefer the drummer" tank top. Mom hated it and had forbidden me to wear it outside. I pulled on a cob-webby black shrug over it and finished the ensemble with a thin red scarf. I gave Hades a quick stroke.

"Wish me luck," I whispered to him. "I'm breaking all the rules today."

The house alarm dinged as I left without a goodbye.

I didn't head for the south-bound tram for school. I needed the west-bound. The one aimed at the Populace side. Broken rule number one: cutting class.

I edged down the aisle to find an empty seat. No one nodded to me. No one smiled. No one even looked up from the floor. I sucked on my lip, anxiety beginning to eat away at my protective anger. Why the sudden abandonment of politeness? I'd never missed it, but I almost didn't recognize these silent people headed to work. Or maybe to protest.

Or maybe to siphon memories from unsuspecting victims.

I found a seat in the corner and scrunched in tight, then pulled out my Sidewinder.

Text from Genesis Lee to Kalan Daniel Fox, TDS 9:52:31/5-9-2084
You working today? Can we meet earlier than we planned?

Text from Kalan Daniel Fox to Genesis Lee, TDS 9:53:45/5-9-2084
Work's closed because of the protest. No school?

Text from Genesis Lee to Kalan Daniel Fox, TDS 9:54:02/5-9-2084
Not for me.

Text from Kalan Daniel Fox to Genesis Lee, TDS 9:54:31/5-9-2084
Rebel. We'll get you a motorcycle and blue hair dye. See you there.

I laughed and had the weirdest desire to hug my phone.

The tram pulled to a stop near Happenings. Nearly everyone got off, their determined steps sounding like a march into battle.

Get a grip, Gena. Dramatics were Cora's domain.

I found Kalan in a grove of trees outside Happenings. The midday heat pierced the shade of scrubby pines overhead. A roar of shouting wafted on the wind.

"Did you bring my motorcycle?" I walked up next to him.

He gave me a tight smile. "No time. I've been here all morning."

"Why?"

Kalan kicked up a puff of red dirt. "Trying to stop my dad."

"He's part of the protests?" I didn't remember Elijah, but that didn't jive with my impression of him.

"Not exactly." Kalan scowled. "Some of the church folks are trying to 'promote peace.' I told Dad all he's going to promote is a few people to heaven. He says God wouldn't want them to sit home and watch people hurt each other."

I smiled a little. I needed to meet Elijah. Again. "You don't always agree with your dad on church stuff, do you?"

Kalan crossed his arms, glancing behind him, towards Happenings. "Dad's a good guy. But he's so busy caring about people in general, sometimes he forgets to care about people in particular."

I stepped around the tree and got my first live view of the protest. My arms squeezed to my side, like the press of the crowd reached me even here. Hundreds, maybe thousands, of fists pounded the sky, beating out a rhythm to their chants. Words drowned in the noise. Bodies pressed close, people pushing past each other toward the front lines. Mementi, rubbing shoulders for the first time. Eaten up by fear until they'd forgotten who they were.

What was worse, to lose your memories or to lose your humanity?

They faced off with a writhing swarm of Populace, a square pond creating a sort of no-man's-land between them. Above the chaos, Happenings' giant wallscreen played a newscast of the protest itself. It focused on an uneven line of black-clad police brandishing riot shields, batons, and pepper spray. A Populace man charged a cop, yelling. The cop thrust with his shield, sending the man sprawling to the ground. A roar of outrage swelled. Populace surged into the no-man's-land, only to be beaten back.

I was losing my nerve to invade Happenings, fast. I took a deep breath. Ignore the nutso people in the mob. Focus on the goal: the x-shaped building, ringed by rent-a-cops.

"It's mostly the front doors that are guarded. If we can get around the corner of that wing—" I pointed to one of the arms of the X—"we can find the employee entrances. My friend Kinley had a DNA lock-picking algorithm that actually worked..."

Sort of. She'd only gotten it to work once. On me, actually. She and Cora snuck into my house and plastered my walls with maxi pads as a prank.

"If that fails," I finished, "we wait for people to leave for lunch and sneak in to find out what Blaire was working on."

Her mysterious evidence.

Kalan kicked at the dirt. "We're never going to get through this crowd, let alone into the building."

"So what's *your* brilliant plan?" I demanded. "We have to find the Link thief now, before these people kill each other. Before I lose more memories." Before Cora melted away, life dripping out of her like a damp watercolor painting.

Kalan didn't reply for a moment. "You Mementi have to be right about everything, don't you?"

I glared.

"I'm kidding. You people are smarter than I gave you credit for."

"I'm the only Mementi you know. Even if I am pretty smart."

"Fine. You, Genesis Lee, are the smartest and only Mementi I know. So be smart, and come up with a new idea. Because I *will* stop you from killing yourself with this scatterbrained plan."

Okay, the arrogant tone? Not the way to win me over. "You're the one who said I needed to 'trust my heart.'"

Kalan rested against a tree and crossed his legs. "So your heart is telling you to break into a locked-down building in the middle of a riot to find information we aren't sure exists? Trusting yourself doesn't mean letting your emotions overrule common sense."

I leaned on the tree next to him, looking away. "You sound like a preacher again."

"Maybe you need a little religion."

I pressed my head back and a stubby branch pricked my scalp. Stupid boy—who happened to be right. About the common sense thing, at least.

"Fine." I sighed. "It's a bad idea, Mr. Preachy-Pants."

He bowed. "I am quite intelligent myself, even if I don't have the entire Internet memorized."

I snapped a twig from the tree and threw it at him. "I don't have the Internet memorized. Just the encyclopedia."

"Ah. Then perhaps I might someday approach your level of brilliantness."

A branch cracked behind us.

We whipped around. Crap. Why had we stayed here? We were right in the path of someone coming to the protest from the tramstop.

"Gena? What are you doing?"

Oh no. It was Dom.

He weaved through the trees. Cora trailed him, her arms wrapped around her chest. What the devil was Cora doing out, let alone *here*? And what the devil was I going to say to them?

I drummed my fingers on my legs. "Um, hi guys."

Cora's eyes flickered away from the mob. Her gaze darted between Kalan and me. His unfamiliar face. His lack of Link buzz. Nobody was going to miss it.

It took Dom another two seconds. He dropped to a crouch, his muscles flexing. Kalan was strong, too, but Dom was stockier and had several years of tae kwon do to back him up.

"Who is this?" Dom demanded. "Did he drag you out here?"

"No! Do I look like I'm being dragged?" I edged forward, getting between them. Knowing Dom, he'd rush Kalan without warning.

"Gena, this isn't…is it him?" Cora sounded aghast.

"I'm Kalan." He put his palms up in front of him. "I'm her friend, I'm not going to hurt her."

Stupid boy! Shut your big mouth!

Cora shied away, like his voice could strike more memories from her Links. "He's Populace," she whispered. "You trusted… *him* to find my Link?"

My stomach tightened. "He's a good guy, he really wants to help—"

"Help?" Dom snorted. "They're the ones who stole Links in the first place!"

"*He* isn't!"

"You lied to me." Cora's eyes widened. "I was just your cover, wasn't I? You told me you were hunting the Link thief so I'd cover your tracks. And all you were doing was…" Her face twisted in anger. "*Him.*"

"What? Cora, that's insane—"

She laughed, a harsh, ugly sound. "That's me, crazy all around. All you had to do to get away from me was lie, and lie, and LIE."

"That's not true, you're my best friend!" I stepped toward her.

"You're not. You're not my friend." She clenched her fists. "Don't ever talk to me again. You've never been my friend at all. You're a traitor to all of us, every single Mementi."

"You're wrong, Cora, I swear I'm—"

"You're working with the enemy!" Cora cried, pointing at Kalan. "You're nothing but a nasty, traitorous little *slut*!"

The words pierced my heart like a bee sting. She should know I'd never betray her. But she didn't, not anymore. Two years of our friendship was a lot to lose—maybe too much for her to trust me.

Cora shook, and Dom stepped in front of her. "How could you do this?"

His shout rang loud through the trees. My eyes darted to the crowd that seemed a little too near. If they learned a Populace was on their side of the lawn, they'd rush us. My foot tapped out a rhythm in the grass. Cora's angry, twisted face tore at me.

Dom lowered his head, ready to charge. "He's POPULACE!"

Several people in the crowd squinted our way, lifting hands against the glare of the sun. Time to bolt.

Except I couldn't leave Cora like this. Not thinking I'd betrayed her.

"Cora—"

Kalan swore. "Gena, we've gotta move it!"

A group from the mob ran toward us, faces red from the sun and their anger. Dom lunged. His arm swung toward me in an arc, and I barely managed to duck. He stumbled.

"Here," he yelled, gathering himself for another attack. "Populace hiding in the trees."

I scrambled away. The riot group rushed forward and Kalan swore. He grabbed my gloved hand, yanking me into a run. My heart beat too fast to protest the touch. Running, panting, I clutched at him. We ran. Toward the building. Toward the people coming to pound us.

What in the name of all holiness was he doing?

We flew past them. They skidded to a stop, losing their momentum in the confusion.

Smart boy.

The rest of the mob loomed ahead. Bodies shifted, turned. A sea of faces glared. *Notgoodnotgoodnotgood*, my feet pounded out.

"Kalan!" I screamed.

The bigger mob surged like a giant arm reaching for us. Kalan swerved and wrenched my arm. We dashed toward the line of guards surrounding the building. Black batons waved in the sunlight. Cops brandished cans of mace.

The crowd engulfed us as we reached the guard line. Gloved hands tore at my clothes and hair. The Link buzz swelled in my head, spinning my already shaky world. Batons rained down. Fabric and bodies crushed around my face. All I knew was running and clawing and pushing and my hand in Kalan's.

Then the crushing was gone. Air, free of sweat and fear, whistled as I sucked it into my lungs. Screams and the thump of batons drove my feet across the grass. Kalan held onto me.

The comfort of shade overwhelmed me as we rounded one of the wings of the building. I tripped on a tree root, falling to the ground. Kalan fell beside me. We knelt on the grass, gasping.

"Gena."

His arms brushed my shoulders, wound around me. My head collapsed on his chest. The rough rhythm of his breathing matched mine, an intimate kind of *pas de deux* that bound us together.

Touch. I jolted back. The move unbalanced me, and I fell to my butt. My adrenaline-soaked body shook.

"I'm sorry," I gasped. "I'm sorry."

"I forgot," Kalan said, leaning forward on hands and knees. "The no-touching thing, I forgot, are you okay?"

"Yeah. You?"

He nodded.

We sat against the wall of the building, catching our breath. I drummed the grass in a syncopated rhythm, counting out the beats. This *was* a big deal. But the drumming still helped soothe the panic from our mad dance of escape. The noise of the crowd rumbled around the corner. No one had followed us. Maybe the guards hadn't noticed we'd gotten past them.

The sound of voices made us both jump. Not again, I couldn't run like that again…

"It's not the mob," Kalan whispered. "It's coming from over there."

The grass sloped down to our left, ending at a short concrete wall. We crawled to it and peered over. Below and to the right, more security guarded a cement ramp that descended from the street into a parking garage. An olive-green car idled on the ramp below us. Voices echoed from the garage.

"Shipping guys, maybe?" Kalan whispered. "I applied for a job as one, but Dad didn't want me doing deliveries so far out."

"Out where?" I asked.

"Everywhere. They have stores around the country. They donate to places like Alzheimer's care facilities, too."

Dozens of patients whose minds were wasting away, still able to enjoy and share dim memories on Happenings Memos. I frowned. I didn't want evil Liza Woods to do good things.

The voices grew louder. Someone stepped from the garage into the sunlight. My breath caught.

It was Liza Woods herself.

I leaned over the cement barrier. She really did look sick. Her short black hair was wispy, her bronze face thin. Not as pretty as her pictures. The crisp business suit hung off her in some places while clinging oddly in others. She half-marched, half-shuffled to the car like an aging general, not the forty-something queen of business she was.

"It wasn't smart to come," said a voice from the shadows. A familiar voice. "I shouldn't be seen here, and there are too many people around who can recognize you now. You still haven't perfected—"

"I know," she snapped in a low, gravelly voice. "I don't need reminders. Let's go. I can't be late for this meeting, and I still need to change."

"You've got to cut back. It's starting to show."

My fingernails scraped the concrete through my gloves. That was his voice, all right. Detective Jackson.

Liza climbed in the car. "Shut up and set the driving parameters."

Jackson glided from the shadows like a phantom. He took the driver's seat and they sped off.

Jackson. Working clandestinely with Liza Woods *and* the Link thief. And what hadn't Liza "perfected"?

Maybe something Blaire had had evidence of.

I was right. The rumors were right. Liza was involved in the Link thefts. And if we ran to the cops or the news or anyone at all, the entire Mementi side of town would tear Happenings down granite stone by granite stone.

Suddenly, the murmur of the mob behind us roared into a frenzy. Kalan and I ducked below the wall. Out on the street, past Happenings' grounds, hordes of people rushed toward the Mementi side of town.

"What's going on?" I said.

"Come on."

We ran for the front of the building. I squeezed my sweaty hands into fists.

The police line had fractured. Only a few remained, and the Populace milled around in confusion. Papers swirled in the hot wind and abandoned signs littered the crushed and muddied grass. It looked like the aftermath of a war.

A group stood near the steps to the front entrance, and Kalan ran toward them. His church people. Every face focused on the newscast on the screen. My ears caught the audio feed that had been drowned out by the protesters.

"…largest attack launched from either side," declared a newscaster. "First reports are coming in from reporters and local casters, and we expect to have grassroots footage any moment. Though some have suggested this could be an accident, the state-of-the-art fire controls seem to have been hacked and disabled. After earlier reports of police brutality focused on the non-Mementi citizens, an attack of this size is unsurprising. But this assault launched at the heart of Havendale's Mementi people is truly tragic."

Assault launched at our heart? I craned my head back, trying to get a better view. The screen behind the reporter lit up with a jarring video feed.

Lit up like a burning effigy, the Memoriam was engulfed in flames.

"No." I lurched forward and fell to my knees. "No!"

The tall spiral blazed, its external mirrors shattered or blackened. The wooden blocks of our dead. Feeding the fire. Metal Links melting, wooden ones turning to smoke. Ashes of my family whirling, touching the ashes of other Mementi families. Perhaps we'd never been so close as now, when ashes mixed and burned to more ash.

I ripped my eyes from the screen. Thick smoke billowed into the clear eastern sky.

Grandma Piper. Scott, my grandfather. Jerod and Sophie, my mother's parents who I only knew through their Memoriams and Mom's stories. We'd had what no one ever did—a fragment of them, alive even after death.

And now they burned, my history and my family and my soul blackened and shriveled. Hot bile scalded my throat. Grandma. Gone again. The word echoed, a shriek that couldn't escape my mouth. *Gone forever.*

If there was a God, this must be hell.

Kalan's hand brushed my shoulder, a touch that scorched through my shirt.

"Gena."

My chest shuddered.

"My dad's taking everybody home. We need to get you somewhere safe."

"They..." I could barely speak. "How could they..."

"I'm so sorry."

I wished tears would fall onto my scalding cheeks. Water to cool the heat that seared me. My eyes stayed dry.

Kalan's fingers took my gloved ones, and I clung to him. I barely noticed that he led me to the tramstop. We rode north, alone on the tram. Outside, the black smoke of my past wafted skyward, vanishing in the clouds.

17

And in my heart, if calm at all,
If any calm, a calm despair…

—Alfred, Lord Tennyson, *In Memoriam XI*

My vending machine sandwich from the Observatory at Havendale Canyon tasted like stale ham and cheese, but ash filled my mind. Flakes that fell from the sky, staining concrete and grass and upturned faces with the twice-burned bodies of my grandparents.

I turned on my Sidewinder and projected the holo from the metal picnic table. I didn't want to know. I had to know anyway. A blinking number eleven in the corner made me pause. Eleven missed texts and calls from my parents. I sent them a text saying I was safe but wouldn't be home for a while.

Boy, was I going to pay for that one.

My hands shook when I tapped over to a national newsfeed. No social network updates. I couldn't face the pain of personal right now. In the top corner, a video played. Drake Matthews faced the camera, displaying a hologram of two sets of glowing Links. With his fingers, he drew out tiny balls of light—memories— from each one and tried to force them together. They resisted each other, like opposite ends of a magnet. I was glad I couldn't hear his explanation of why memories didn't merge well.

I scrolled to the impersonal headlines. MEMENTI LANDMARK BURNS AMID PROTESTS; MEMENTI MAUSOLEUM COLLAPSES DURING FIRE; THREE DEAD IN HAVENDALE RIOTS.

Three people *dead?* I'd been focused on the Memoriam, on the ones who were already dead. Now others had joined them. My finger trembled, and I tapped the headline. I couldn't read the story. I scanned only for names.

Jansen Foster.

Lachlan Sandoval.

Trix Fairfax.

Kalan squeezed my shoulder, and I welcomed the distraction of his touch. I knew two of those names. The two who were Mementi. I turned off my Sidewinder and delved into memories of dead.

Lachlan. He did physics research at Ascalon. He was the brains behind the Low-G Club, actually. He had a four-year-old son, and his wife had had twins last year, girls with Lachlan's red hair.

Trix. I'd seen her at the Beach a few times. She did some kind of work with music therapy and liked wearing scarves and gloves with butterflies on them.

I'd never spoken to either of them. We smiled and nodded, like everyone in Havendale smiled and nodded. Content that we knew enough about each other that it wasn't necessary to actually know each other.

Facts made for lonely friends.

I had a real friend, though. Cora's bitter face haunted me.

Text from Genesis Lee to Cora Julieta Medina, TDS 16:41:23/5-9-2084
Are you okay? I'm sorry I didn't tell you about Kalan. I swear we're looking for the Link thief. Love you.

The reply came almost immediately.

Automated text, TDS 16:41:35/5-9-2084
CORA JULIETA MEDINA has rejected the following text: *Are you okay? I'm sorry I didn't tell you about Kalan. I swear we're looking for the Link thief. Love you.*

I dropped my head to the table.

Kalan touched my arm. "To the canyon?"

We hiked through the heat of the dying afternoon. When the cool of my rocky tunnel closed over me, I didn't feel the usual peace. Not even this place could heal me today. I passed the pool and the stunted tree. My toes edged right up to the cliff. The canyon wound into the distance, rocky cliffs waltzing with blue sky on a floor of green.

"What are you doing?" Kalan asked warily.

"Have you ever stood somewhere high and felt that urge to jump?" I said. The wind rushed up the side of the cliff, lifting loose strands of my hair in a tangled dance.

"It's going to be okay, Gena. Look at me."

"My dance teacher calls it *l'appelle du vide*. The call of the void. It's the voice inside us that wants us to fall, to give up. I used to think it was something different. Something calling me to do all the things I wanted. To take a leap of faith. Now I think she's right."

The emptiness inside me yawned wide open.

"Genesis, I'm going to put my hands on your shoulders and pull you back, okay?" His strong hands cupped my shoulders. I stepped back.

"Tell me about the things you want," he whispered in my ear.

He thought I was going to jump. That wasn't what I wanted.

"I want…" I breathed in air that had swirled over the world and touched all the places I could go. It filled me, building me up again, calling to my favorite memories of far-off places I'd absorbed over the years. "I want everything."

"Everything?"

"I want to dye my hair blue and play drums in a rock band. I want to be an astronaut and dance in the stars. I want to go to all the places in the world I'm not supposed to want to go, like Hong Kong and Paris and Tokyo and Tennessee."

Kalan turned me around. Red rock framed the quirky smile on his face. "Tennessee?"

"My grandma was born in Nashville," I said. "It's number one on my list."

"Well. I guess you don't want much, do you?"

"Just the world." I sighed. "And the Link thief."

"I can still help you with that one." His head moved closer to mine.

I nearly whispered the last thing I wanted—him.

"Tell me a story," I whispered instead. "A nice one, without anything being destroyed."

He smiled a little shyly and told me the story of Genesis.

* * *

We talked until the sky faded from blue to purple, sitting against the canyon wall. We should have talked about Liza and Jackson and what that meant. Instead, we tried to forget the entire awfulness of the day. Kalan told me about God creating the world in six days and resting on the seventh, and about Adam and Eve in the Garden of Eden, and about the snake that was really the devil that got them kicked out.

"Do you actually believe that stuff?" I asked.

He laughed and nudged me with his arm. I loved those little touches. The thrill of what had once been forbidden.

"You think I'm nuts," he said.

Only a little. My thoughts drifted to the Memoriam. "Do you believe in heaven?"

His fingers felt for mine in the almost dark, and I took them. "And hell. But especially heaven."

He sounded like he'd looked through the veil of stars and saw God waving at us. "Do you think the people who burned the Memoriam, and the ones who killed those people, will go to hell?"

He hesitated. "I don't know. Maybe. I have a hunch hell's not going to be as populated as we think it should be. I'm glad it's God making those decisions."

"What if he makes the wrong ones?"

"He's God. He won't make mistakes."

"I wonder what he had to do to become a god and make executive decisions about saving and damning everybody."

Kalan laughed. "I don't know. Maybe you can ask him when we get there."

I loved that he took his faith seriously. And I loved that he wasn't afraid to laugh about it. My fingers tightened around his. I drank in the feeling, letting it fill my void. It helped me do the one thing I couldn't do on my own—forget. Just for a second.

"What are you thinking?" Kalan asked.

"About forgetting."

A chorus of crickets sang.

"Not forgetting you. Just that…maybe perfect memories aren't all they're cracked up to be." The image of smoke rising above the trees of Havendale shot me full of pain.

"Are all your memories that way?" he asked. "Perfect?"

"Depends on what they're stored in. Some materials kind of squash certain parts of a memory. Which can actually be a good thing for memories with strong emotions. Some things make memory decay faster, but we don't use those much. Nothing's as porous as a normal human brain, though."

Kalan rubbed his thumb across mine, sending tingles up my arm. I wished I dared to take off my glove. Touch his skin.

He lifted his face to the sky. "You said you want to be an astronaut. Tell me what you have stored in those Links. About the stars you want to dance in."

I tilted my face up too. The band of the Milky Way splashed across the sky like a handful of confetti.

"There are over 100 billion stars in the Milky Way," I said. "Proxima Centauri is the nearest one, 4.2 light years away. It would take over 46 million years to reach it."

He craned his neck. "Which one is it?"

"It's part of the Alpha Centauri system, which you can only see from the southern hemisphere. But you can't actually see Proxima at all without a telescope. It's a red dwarf, so it's too dim."

"What's a red dwarf?" he asked.

"It's a main sequence star, but they're cooler than other stars. Only about 4,000 degrees Kelvin."

"A mere few thousand Calvins, huh? Barely warmer than my toaster."

I smiled. "*Kelvins*. It's a temperature measurement. And it's a lot hotter than your toaster."

"So we can't see this Proxima red dwarf because it's too cold to shine much?"

"Basically. They have a slow nuclear reaction process using a proton-to-proton chain mechanism, so they don't emit much energy, which in stars is seen in their luminosity."

"Eureka," Kalan said. "It's all so clear now."

My cheeks warmed. Sounding like a textbook? How romantic. "It's cool, okay?"

"4,000 degrees Calvin kind of cool?"

I laughed. "Exactly that kind of cool."

"I love that you're this nerdy." His hand shifted in mine, his fingers stroking my gloved palm. Pinpricks of pleasure spread out from my hand.

"Why do you like stars so much?" Kalan asked.

"I guess…stars are always *moving*, twinkling and rotating around the Earth. And their light moves across both space and time. We're watching them dance the way they did millions of years ago."

Kalan tilted his head toward mine. "I have the perfect bouncy ball for you."

"A bouncy ball?"

"I have this theory that every person in the world could be represented by a bouncy ball. And I know exactly which one is yours. I'll give it to you tomorrow."

"I can't wait."

His face angled close to mine. Moonlight caught his eyes only inches away. My body warmed, and the warmth made me brave. I leaned forward. His hand trailed up my gloves to my shoulder. Slid down my back. Our faces drew together until I closed my eyes. His lips brushed mine—

I threw my head back, gasping at a sudden shock of powerful emotion. Grief, betrayal, fury, anguish, terror. Images flickered. Fragments, chewed up by emotion. Blinding me, smothering me. Screaming only in my mind because I can't

breathe

make it stop, make it

I can't

Feel. Cold wind on my cheeks. Warm arms supporting me.

"Gena? What's wrong?" Kalan's fingers clutched at my back.

"Oh no." An image from Kalan's Memo burst into my mind. The night we met. My bare hand touching his forearm in the dark.

"Are you sick? What happened?" His hand came toward my face in the darkness. I grabbed it, my glove a barrier between our skin.

"Don't touch me," I whispered.

His hand withdrew. "I'm sorry. I thought…I'm sorry."

I wanted to cry and scream, but I was too exhausted to do either. I struggled to sit up. "It's not you. It's not that I don't want… it's my fault. I can't believe I did that."

"Did what, Gen?" Frustration filled his voice.

How could I tell him? I'd violated him. I'd used him.

"The night we met," I said. "I touched you."

"Yeah."

I was grateful for the dark, so I couldn't see his face. "I stored a memory in you. In your skin."

18

From whence clear memory may begin…

—Alfred, Lord Tennyson, *In Memoriam XLV*

I counted twelve quick heartbeats before he replied. "What do you mean?"

"We never do it," I said. "*Never*. It's violating, using a person to store a memory. And skin does something no other material does. It enhances the emotions. I couldn't even see the memory through all that emotion."

I counted seven breaths.

"Why would you do that?" In the dim moonlight, his expression was hard to read. He had to be pissed. I would be.

"I'm sorry, Kalan. It was a memory I didn't want anyone else to find." I rubbed my arms, cold with my own past actions. "Memory stored in skin doesn't give off a buzz. With everything else, a

Mementi can sense when a memory is stored in it. Like a tingle in your head. But not with skin."

"That was the night you saw the Link thief."

"Yes."

"So you stored the memory of her in my skin so she couldn't take it away from you."

"Yes." I closed my eyes.

"That was kind of brilliant."

My eyes popped open. "What?"

He chuckled and leaned against the shadow of the rock. "That was why you wanted to meet me the next day. So you could get your memory back. You're amazing."

"I guess." I bit my lip, confused. "You're not mad?"

"No. It's kind of cool. I've been carrying a part of you with me." He brushed my gloved hand with a single finger. Like he wasn't sure if he was supposed to touch me even with gloves on.

I pressed his fingers into mine, yearning to feel him again. "I guess it doesn't matter to you, but I knew what it meant when I did it. It's degrading."

I'd treated Kalan like an object. A convenient getaway car for my memory, one who would never be suspected because he was Populace. One I wouldn't have to feel guilty about. I'd probably never intended to tell him, just get my memory and send him packing.

"I'm so sorry, Kalan," I whispered.

"It doesn't bug me. Okay?" He reached both hands toward my face, then stopped. "It kind of changes things, though. Does this mean you've been hiding your other lost memories?"

"No," I said. "I wouldn't remember the memory I gave you, but I *should* remember the act of giving you the memory. Someone else took away *that* memory, and all the other ones I'm missing too."

He rubbed his eyes. "If the thief took your memory of giving me a memory, wouldn't she know I had the original memory? And she could come get it from me?"

I slumped against the rock, which had finally cooled enough to give me shivers. "It would make sense. So why do you still have it?"

He sighed. "Every time I think we understand what's going on, I realize we don't know anything."

"Yeah."

He took my hand again. "We need that memory."

"Yeah." That drowning emotion waited. I'd have to wade through it again. Swim in it this time, if I wanted to get to the actual memory.

This was the last kind of fight I wanted to have. A battle with my own emotions amplified times a thousand. I'd started the day pretending like skipping school and infiltrating Happenings was something other than cowardice masquerading as bravado. Now I had to do something real. I looked skyward and the stars winked at me.

I might not be brave, but I could learn how to be.

I slipped my hand from Kalan's and, one finger at a time, removed my thin glove. Kalan leaned in. His breath moved across my forehead like a caress.

"This is going to be hard for you, isn't it?" he said.

"Yes." I hesitated, but I couldn't do it alone. "I might…need you . . ."

His hands circled my waist, smoothing across me in a trail of fire. Wild and hungry, warm and comforting. In the moonlight, all I could see were his eyes staring into mine.

With deliberate slowness, I pressed my palm to his cold cheek.

The crush of fear, the tang of annoyance; hurrying past the Low-G with Cora. A muffled groan behind the club; stumbling and knowing someone heard me. Panic raking me like fingernails. Then fury howling in my veins. The tearing anguish of betrayal. Ren's purple stripe flashed in the shadows, a man at her feet, his Links in her gloved hands…

With the gasp of the drowning, I wrenched away from Kalan. My hand scraped the cliff wall. I held the memory in my mind, battling it. *Claw at it*. Like I wanted to claw Ren. *Scream at it.* Like I wanted to scream at her. *Rage, cry, fight*. I rocked, emotion tossing me like waves on a rough sea.

Store it. Get it out of my head. It demanded to stay alive inside me. I wrestled it, forcing it behind the cool bars of a metal Link.

The memory faded, and with it the emotion. But that did nothing for the current emotions. Blood drained from my face, pooling in my feet like my heart had given up trying to channel that much sensation. Kalan pulled me against him. I choked on words I didn't know how to say.

After a few minutes, he asked, "Can you talk about it?"

No. But I had to. "In your Memo," I whispered, "I said it was *her*. A girl. The Link thief."

He stroked my hair, his hands blissfully free of memories. Strong and soft.

"It was Ren."

His fingers froze against my head.

"I saw her taking someone's Links that night, that's why she came after me and Cora. My sister. Ren. She can't be the Link thief."

Ren wouldn't do this. She was a rebel, but she was Mementi. She was my sister. The one who quit dancing because she grumbled I was better than her, but still came to my recitals. The one who taught me about boys, about building trust step by step until we could touch without fear.

I wanted to scratch her eyes out. And I wanted to sneak into her room like when I'd had nightmares as a child, so I could curl up on the floor by her bed and cry.

I pushed away from Kalan. "I have to talk to her. I can't believe it until I talk to her."

"Gena, wait, if she's the thief—" He grabbed my hand, but I yanked it away.

"No!" I scrambled to my feet.

I snatched my loose glove and squeezed through the rock cavern. Kalan followed with a curse. I broke out of the mountain and hit the trail. I blew past dark rock walls, sliding on loose dirt, my momentum carrying me almost faster than my legs could manage.

I pounded across the bridge and up the tramstop stairs. No tram, no tram, where was the tram?

"Gena." Kalan panted up the stairs behind me.

"She has to explain. I have to know why, I have to know, where is the *tram*?"

My yells echoed over the distant gurgle of the river. Kalan wrapped his arms around me. I couldn't feel it. I felt nothing but a sucking whirlwind in my gut.

"We will talk to her," he said. "Together. Tomorrow. We can't barge in there now."

"The tram," I whispered into his shoulder.

"It's after curfew. We've got a long walk to town."

He guided me down the steps again. We traipsed through the desert dust below the tramline. The city glowed, four miles distant. A single thought cycled through my mind like a song on repeat.

My sister. The Link thief. The stealer of memories.

19

Like strangers' voices here they sound,
In lands where not a memory strays...

—Alfred, Lord Tennyson, *In Memoriam CIV*

The next morning, I stared out the window, trying to ignore Mom's yells. I found it hard to care that she was shouting at all. Outside, the sky looked blue but felt gray.

Or maybe it was me that felt gray. Thick and foggy. Like I was lost even though I sat at my own kitchen table. An unexplainable fissure split my heart and bled my soul out of me. It ached, a peculiar homesick feeling.

Like I was missing something. Or someone.

* * *

At the pre-recital dance practice, Zahra smoothed her hijab every minute and a half. She kept walking past me at the barre to ask if I was okay. I told her I was fine, but I'm pretty sure she knew I was lying.

Tears lurked behind my eyelids. Fog still warped my brain, and I kind of wanted it to hang around. It blurred a confusing mix of loss and betrayal that battled inside me.

Leigh and the rest of the Populace students hadn't shown up at all. Neither had Cora. We were on track for a recital of pathetic proportions. Zahra kept yelling at us about lines and turnout and form until Darena burst into tears, which got Marine crying, which made Zahra cry. She pulled the two of them to the side and told me to take a break.

I turned away from the barre in time to see a boy sneak into the practice room.

Populace, which made me nervous. Kind of cute in a boy-next-door way, with curls hanging across his forehead. Tall, nice tan. He caught my eye and smiled.

I didn't want to smile back, but I couldn't help it. His smile demanded a response. He crossed the floor toward me. *Uh, back it up, buddy. That smile was not an invitation.* I swallowed. Maybe he was one of the Populace dance students.

"Do you have a sec?" he asked.

Yeah, but not for you. Curse my inability to be impolite. "Sure."

The gold of his hair mixing with the brown of his eyes brought out a familiar image. Honey. It seemed to fit him, though I wasn't sure why.

"You seem okay," he said. "I'm glad we waited for today."

I blinked. "I'm sorry?"

"Ren. I think it was a good idea to wait. You seem less... distraught."

My pulse throbbed at my temples. "How do you know my sister?"

A long pause. His mouth opened a little, a sharp sound escaping.

"No," he whispered. His eyebrows contracted like he was in pain. "Not again, Gena."

He knew my name. My eyes darted toward Zahra, and I almost called to her. But the boy looked so crushed. For the first time all day, I let emotion slip past my fog. Pain for his pain. Much stronger than it should have been for a strange Populace boy. It drew me toward him, and I felt a need to actually touch him, to soothe him.

I stumbled back.

"It's Ren." His face was so sad I almost couldn't stand it. "You went to her last night, you said you *wouldn't*."

"What are you talking about?"

"I…you…we've been together for days. Trying to find the Link thief."

"That's…" I didn't know what that was. Crazy. "I don't know you."

He smoothed a hand over his face. "You don't remember me. This is the third time. Someone's stealing your memories."

A thrill of terror tickled my ribs. I forced a laugh. "Nice try. I've still got all my Links."

Didn't I? I glanced down. They were all in place.

He shook his head. "Someone's taking your memories without your Links. It's Ren, you must have gone to her last night after you got home. But, hang on, you texted me."

"I texted you."

He pulled out his phone and frantically stabbed buttons.

I fished my Sidewinder from my bag, ready to prove him wrong. This boy was loco. And scaring the crap out of me.

"Here, see?" He thrust his phone into my face.

Text from Genesis Lee to Kalan Daniel Fox, TDS 01:55:18/5-10-2084

Mom and Dad have me on house arrest. Meet me at Zahra's Dance Studio tomorrow, next to the Mementi Arts Center. My concert's at six but I can sneak away from practice before then to get to Ren's.

The same message appeared on my phone. In my sent messages.

I tapped my screen off, like if I didn't look at it, it would go away. "I didn't send that."

"You did, Genesis Lee. Ren must have come to you last night."

The grief in his voice brought a lump to my throat that made it hard to breathe. I turned away from him. "You're lying."

"Ren stole your memories, Gena, that's why you don't know me."

My head snapped around. My protective fog was fading, threatening to let loose a torrent of panic and pain. "My sister would never do that."

"She's been doing it for weeks." He sounded tired. "She's the Link thief. We found out last night."

My head spun; I was hyperventilating. "Get out."

"Listen to me. Last night, we were in Havendale Canyon—"

"Get out!" My scream bounced between mirrored walls. The three people in the corner spun to stare at me.

"Okay. But I'm going to fix this. I'm going to help you remember me." He closed his eyes in a long blink. "Again."

He held out his hand.

"This is for you. To show you who I think you are."

I pulled my hands to my chest. He dropped the object and it bounced into a corner. The door clicked shut. When I looked up, he was gone.

I rushed to the corner, snatching what he'd left me.

It was a bouncy ball.

* * *

Clutching the bouncy ball, I hid in the costume closet for ages. Zahra would want to talk, and what would I tell her?

Oh, that random boy I yelled at? Yeah, he said he and I are trying to stop the Link thief, who happens to be my sister. She stole my memories too, so I don't remember him. And I had the weirdest desire to hug him despite the fact that he's obviously crazy. I seem to be a bit cracked myself.

I pressed myself to the wall. The stiff tulle from a skirt scratched my face. He'd said someone was stealing my memories but leaving my Links. I couldn't possibly believe that.

My fingers opened, revealing the bouncy ball. The dim light of the closet's single bulb caught a shimmer inside. The ball was clear and hollow, filled with blue-tinted water and silver sparkles. When I shifted or shook it, the sparkles swirled, tossing light. Like stars. Dancing stars.

It was like this stupid little ball had captured me completely.

How could he know me like that? There was only one place to look—but sinking into my memories was a scary prospect at the moment. The glitter in the ball settled, calm and shimmering. I took a deep breath. I could be brave.

Start easy, with memories of yesterday. Only one day ago, and stored on one of my hardwood Links, but the memories were as dull as though I'd stored them on a piece of onion paper. I'd woken up and my parents were there. I hadn't gone to school. Why not?

I couldn't remember.

I'd gone somewhere with trees and noise. I'd felt nervous, but happy because…wasn't someone there? Someone who made me happy?

I couldn't remember.

The rest of the day zipped past in a vague blur of crowds and running and panic and bliss and agony and something else that

I just couldn't remember.

Panicked, I scanned my memories of the days before. Moments stood out in sharp color. Waking up, dancing, school. In between, blurred splotches of nothing nagged at me. I only knew those moments existed because I could feel that something had happened.

I batted the scratchy tulle away from my face and scrambled for the door. It was too hot, I was suffocating under the pressure of all that nothing. The door gave way. I tumbled into the hallway and footsteps came running.

"Gena." Zahra's soft accent sounded relieved. She knelt next to me on the floor as I pushed myself up. "Why were you hiding? What's wrong? Who was that boy?"

My elbows weakened. I collapsed to the floor. Kalan Fox, his text had said. Kalan.

"I can't remember," I gasped.

"What?"

"I can't remember." I rolled onto my side. "I can't remember yesterday, or that boy, or anything. Zahra, how can I not remember?"

"*Na uzo billah,*" Zahra whispered.

She only spoke Arabic when something bad happened. A sound like a kitten being strangled escaped my mouth.

The world blurred. A wild tremor rattled me, an earthquake in my soul. "I can't…I can't…"

Zahra's hands reached for me, slow and fuzzy. I slapped at the air. Don't touch me, don't touch me. Someone had sucked away my life. My heart banged against my ribs. Eager to beat away the remaining days and minutes and moments of my life. A weight pressed on my chest. Pushed me down. Down to the ground. Like a grave. Parts of me were dead. Killed. Shaking and shaking, I couldn't stop the shaking.

"Gena!" Zahra's voice beat into my head. "Stop, you can stop this. Focus. Move."

I can't move. I can't I can't I can't.

"One finger, Gena. Move it."

One finger. Tap. My fingernail hit the floor. A tiny vibration in my hand. Different from the shudders. A new rhythm. Tap. Tap. Tap tap tap. The pattern seeped into my body. I lifted my palm, slapping the floor in the rhythm of my typical song. Not a. Rat-a-tat-tat. Big deal. Rat-a-tat-tat.

No. This was a big deal. New mantra.

Don't think. Rat-a-tat-tat. Don't think. Rat-a-tat-tat.

The weight gradually eased off my chest, bringing back air. The world sharpened. Minutes ticked past to the beat of my drumming. Gradually, the panic attack faded. I lay on the floor, clutching at its comforting stillness. Screw a bed, I could sleep right here. Zahra's face, her expressions always so clear with her hair hidden under the hijab, contracted in worry.

"You are okay now?" she asked.

"Yes."

She sat on her heels. "Come with me. We are calling the police."

I jerked up. It made sense, going to the cops. Except the thought had me practically hyperventilating again.

I had no idea why.

She headed toward her office. I scrambled up and chased after her. "No, Zahra, no."

She snatched her phone from her desk. "What do you mean, no? Someone has taken your memories, Gena!"

Ren. He'd said it was Ren. That couldn't be true. There'd be no point for her to steal my memories. I crumpled into a chair as Zahra called the police. I thought of Kalan, of his bushy eyebrows and strong arms. Of how I'd wanted to comfort him. Of the bouncy ball I still clutched in my hand. A deep sense inside told me to trust him.

No way. Not about my sister.

Zahra slammed her phone to the desk, making me jump. "*Ils sont idiots!*"

Something about idiots. I assumed that meant the cops.

"They are patrolling the streets." She smoothed her hand across her hijab. Her shoes beat staccato clicks across the tile. "Almost all of them, he says, the entire force. Too much violence, and you must wait until someone can come for you."

My head dropped into my hands, either from exhaustion or relief. Or both.

Zahra turned sharply and shoved her chair under her desk. I'd never seen her so jumpy. "I will call your parents. They can take you home."

My head jerked up. "But the concert. I'll miss it."

"You are joking. A performance, after all this? You haven't even practiced your solo piece, and you had a panic attack. The recital is in an hour."

"No, please, Zahra. I need this, I need to dance."

"Gena—"

"Please. I need to move, I need to dance." I needed to feel the universe in balance again. I needed my heart to pound because of exercise, not fear.

Zahra put her hands on her desk. "And when did you become so obstinate? Fine. But only your solo, not your group dances. And I am telling your parents the minute they arrive, and the police are still coming. *Bien?*"

"Okay."

My parents would yank me home the second they heard about this. I wasn't worried, though. More than likely, they'd be late, and Zahra'd be swamped getting everyone ready backstage. The younger classes were a handful.

"Now go stretch and at least visualize your dance," she said. "And get in your costume."

I rushed to the costume closet. My solo outfit was near the front of the rack. I ran my fingers over the smooth material, trying to focus on anything but Kalan and lost memories. I loved my costume for this dance. Silver and shimmery, with ruching across the bodice and simple spaghetti straps. Sheer silvery ribbons curled down from the hips. A faux-skirt of starlight twirled when I did.

I changed in the locker room where some of the other girls had already gathered, and pulled on my warm-ups to cover my skin. Barely an echo sounded in the nearly empty room. No hint of the usual giggles and nervous jokes. The Populace students weren't the only ones who'd stayed home.

Still no Cora. I tugged my jacket cuffs over my Links. I didn't remember the last time I'd talked to her. I tried to ignore the dread that thought dropped into my stomach. She had to be okay.

I snuck to one of the main floor practice rooms for a little privacy, leaving the lights off. I synced my Sidewinder with the wallscreen and cued up my song.

Lay down. Close your eyes. Ignore everything about stolen memories and boys you should know and cops coming to get you. The choreography I'd practiced for weeks spun through my head.

It didn't feel right.

The steps were familiar, but they were wrong, somehow. My visualizations faded with the song, and in the silence, a tiny noise registered.

There it was again. A sniff. I raised my head, and in the far corner, wedged between the mirrors, was Cora.

I sat up. "You are here! I was worried."

"You really aren't my friend anymore, are you?" Her voice was small and raw, like a wounded creature.

"What? Cora, why…are you okay?" I scooted toward her.

She pulled her knees to her chest and hung her head. "You're not using my song. The one for the new dance we planned. All you care about is that Populace guy."

I bit my lip. "What did I do? What's wrong?"

She sniffed again. "Like you don't rem—" Her head snapped up so fast, it hit the mirror with a soft thud. "You don't remember. Again."

Prickles coursed up my arms. I shook my head.

"Oh no," she whispered. Her eyes widened. "It's him, Gena, I told you it's him! He's the thief, or working with the thief, or something!"

I crawled closer to her. A note of hysteria had invaded her whispers. "Cora, cool it. Zahra called the cops, okay? They're going to figure this out."

"The cops?" She wrapped her arms around herself. "And Kalan? You're not going to see him again?"

A strange longing tugged my heart at the sound of his name. But I didn't know him. I had to be careful.

"No, I'm not going to see him again."

Her chest rose and fell with slow, heavy breaths. She tugged at her gloves. "I should punch you in the face."

My lips twitched. "Would the shoulder give you the same satisfaction? I'd like to stay conscious for the recital."

Her head lolled back against the mirror. "I'll save it for later. I guess…we can pretend yesterday never happened."

For me, yesterday never *had* happened. My smile collapsed, and my heart fell into a sinkhole. "I guess so."

"That's why you're using the old song," she said. "You don't remember the new dance. The one we've been working on since Sunday."

I shook my head.

With what seemed a great effort, Cora nudged my foot. "Your other dance will be perfect."

I nudged her foot back half-heartedly. My original dance was beautiful. But I had a feeling the new one had been better.

What a horrible reflection of my life.

20

A sphere of stars about my soul,
In all her motion one with law…

—Alfred, Lord Tennyson, *In Memoriam CXXII*

I wound the laces of my pointe shoes around my ankles and tucked in the ends. The stiff, waddling feel of walking in pointe shoes was a typical precursor to performing. The audience applause beyond the curtain faded, and Darena swept off the stage, rushing for her warm-up sweats.

My turn. I lifted my chin and stepped past the curtains and into position.

The heat of the lights on my bare skin. The gentle shuffling in the audience. The twin hums inside me of nervousness and Link buzz. All familiar. But also not right. Like I played a cartoon of myself on this stage.

Classical music poured from the speakers, and I moved into the dance mechanically. With perfect control, my arms swept up. I rose on my toes. Straight lines, hard muscles. Perfection. The strain of it clashed with the chaos inside me.

I couldn't dance this way. I stopped before my first pirouette.

Murmurs and uncomfortable turning of program pages came from the audience. My music cut out. The lights blinded me. The yearning to dance overwhelmed me. Music started again. I didn't move.

"Gena," Zahra whispered loudly from off-stage. "It's all right. You can come off if you need to."

I didn't need to. I needed to dance, but I'd forgotten how when I'd forgotten who I was. Had I ever known who I was? Or allowed myself to be that person?

Maybe forgetting who you used to be was the first step to finding who you really were.

My shoulders straightened, and my spine lengthened. Cora was in the sound booth behind the audience, hiding from the crowd but watching me. I lifted my face to her. She knew what I needed. Cora always knew.

Strains of music wafted across the stage. A different song. It paused, like it was asking me a question. I smiled, then unwound the straps of my pointe shoes and tossed them off stage. They thumped at Zahra's feet. Cora started the music, and I counted out the beats. Five, six, seven, eight.

Energy coursed through me, and I danced. A sharp kick. The ribbons of my costume scattered. I rippled, my body flowing forward and back, neck curving forward and back. A leap, with ribbons fluttering over my thighs. A spin. Tight and strong and controlled and unbound. I heaved my shoulders back. My arms flung out and swept forward.

A strange heat filled me as I continued to dance. I was movement. I was freedom.

I was Genesis Lee.

The music slowed. I dropped to my knees, my cheek sweeping the floor. Sweat trickled down my face and fell to the stage. The last strains of music faded.

Applause roared in my ears. I climbed to my feet. With a dramatic sweep of my arm, I bowed to the dark forms of the audience. To Mom and Dad, who never knew that part of me. To myself, for finally letting that part of me free.

The moment I stepped off-stage, Zahra swirled me into her arms. I stiffened for a moment. But what the heck? I hugged her back, squeezing her ribs until she laughed.

"What was that, *eh,* you crazy girl? That was not the dance you practiced! Maybe it was better."

My heart swelled and filled the holes inside me.

"I need to stretch," I said.

Zahra touched my shoulder. "I'm proud of you, Gena."

"Thanks."

Music blared and a troupe of eight-year-olds started a peppy tap number. I headed for the hallway. The stage door closed off a thunder of clackity-clacking shoes. Light from the stairwells at the opposite ends of the hall illuminated the smiling pictures of Zahra's former students. Hidden in the shadow of an alcove, another face waited for me.

"You were brilliant." Kalan's fervent words echoed down the dim hall.

My heart hammered. He came back. He actually came back for me, when I'd gone ballistic on him barely two hours ago. Did I want that to mean something?

"I don't want to freak you out again." He lifted his hand into the light. "I just wanted you to have this."

A smartplastic square rested on his palm, stamped with the word MEMO.

His memories. Ones of us, I was sure. And oh, boy did I want it. It would tell me what we had learned about the Link thief. Who Kalan had been to me. Who I had been. I was terrified to know everything I'd forgotten.

"I won't touch you," he said. "I can drop it in your hand."

My fingers opened one by one. I stretched out my hand.

"*Genesis Lee.*"

I yanked my hand back. I knew that tone: two steps past the warning tone, one step shy of yelling. I faced him.

"What was that?" Dad's bowler hat shadowed his face. He was nearly crushing the box of powdered donuts in his hands.

Mom frowned at me over a whole bouquet of roses. "That was very inappropriate, Gena. We're disappointed in you."

Right. Not unexpected. But still, a painful lump swelled in my throat. Why would I have hoped, even for a second, they might be anything but disappointed? I stepped into the stairwell light, my dance costume shimmering.

"You want to know what that was?" I asked in a level voice. "That was me."

Kalan shifted in the shadows of his alcove. The donut box crinkled and Dad opened his mouth. I cut him off.

"That was the me you never wanted to see. The me that can't be forced into whatever stupid mold you think I should be. That was the me I'm going to be from now on whether you like it or not."

"Gena!" Tiny muscles in Mom's face convulsed in shock.

"You have no *idea* what you're talking about." The tension in Dad's voice crackled. "We've never forced you into anything."

I grabbed a dangling silver strip from my skirt. "Every time I expressed a preference for something, you shut me down. It always had to be what you wanted. Why does something like dance matter to you?"

"It's not about dance, it's about perception," Dad growled. "It's about how people see you as a graceful young woman instead of some kind of provocative…some kind of slutty…"

He clamped his mouth shut, but it was too late. I recoiled at the slap of his words. Since when was grace and passion slutty? "Dad, nobody cares, that's not what—"

"I care." Dad's breath whistled through his nose. "It makes me look like I raised a daughter as crass as any other girl in town."

Because it was always about how *he* looked to everybody else. Dad and I glared at each other. Kalan stepped out of the shadows, and Dad's gaze shifted. His face seemed to swell, his eyes practically popping out. The box of donuts dropped to the floor.

"YOU!"

Kalan jumped, his eyebrows drawing together in confusion.

"Get away from my daughter."

A white powdered donut rolled to a stop at Kalan's feet. Footsteps sounded on the stairs behind my parents. Detective Jackson's voice drifted up. Crap. Crap crap crap. Why was that crap? No idea, but panic poured down my throat like heavy syrup.

"…said a student was losing memories. If it's another Link theft this town's going to explode."

They couldn't catch Kalan, they'd arrest him for sure—Dad would demand it. And Jackson. Every nerve ending in my body screamed at the thought of him.

"Kalan, go," I hissed. "Down the hall behind you to the other stairs. It's the cops."

He hesitated, eyeing my father. He moved.

And I did the unthinkable: I grabbed his hand. My bare fingers linked with his, our palms separated by the small square of the Memo. Sparks popped across my skin. Familiar sparks.

I'd touched him before. My body knew him, even if my mind didn't.

"Gena!" Mom said again. Like it was the only word her flummoxed brain could come up with.

Dad's mouth worked soundlessly. Behind him, Jackson and another cop stepped into view.

"Go." I folded my fingers around the Memo, hiding it. I pushed Kalan away. A wide, hopeful smile spread over his face.

He dashed down the hallway.

"STOP HIM!" Dad roared, flinging his hand after Kalan.

Dad, yelling in public? One point to me.

"Gunner, he's Populace, stop him!"

The two startled cops took a moment, then bolted. Even Jackson's catlike lope wouldn't catch him up to Kalan. Jackson's partner slowed before even reaching the stairs, giving up already.

Dad spluttered. I wanted to laugh with the triumph of the night. Until Dad turned to me. The fury in his taut neck muscles and narrowed eyes made a vise coil around my lungs. He wouldn't hurt me, he'd never hurt me. It was ridiculous to be afraid of my own father.

Mom shoved the bouquet of roses into Dad's arms. "Let's get home, Kierce. We'll talk about it there."

Crushing the flower stems, Dad marched down the stairs.

The squeezing bands around my chest released. "I need to change," I said, hoping to buy myself time away from Dad. "And tell Zahra—"

"Now, Genesis." Mom snapped her fingers and pointed down the stairs.

With shaky legs, I padded down the stairs after her. I shouldn't feel disappointed in myself for meekly following orders. Where would I go if I didn't go home? Cora waited at the exit, holding my shoulder bag. She'd known what the backlash from that dance would be. It was almost funny. Almost.

I snagged the bag. "Thanks…for the song."

She nodded, and her shoulders drooped. Like the emotion of the day had emptied her and that was the last effort she could make tonight. A tremor shuddered through me.

I had to get her Links back. Something whispered there wasn't much time.

The cool night air brushed my bare shoulders. I pulled my jacket from my bag and shoved my hands into the pockets. The edges of Kalan's unseen Memo bit into my sweaty hands. With any luck, Mom and Dad would banish me to my room the second we got home.

T-minus twenty minutes to the truth.

21

He put our lives so far apart
We cannot hear each other speak.

—Alfred, Lord Tennyson, *In Memoriam LXXXII*

I curled up on my bed, Kalan's Memo unfolded next to me. My banishment had happened almost like I'd expected. I'd had to endure a bit of shouting first. Then Dad stormed to his room to rant to Mom about their disobedient, disappointing children.

I picked up the Memo, staring again at the small menu. Two choices: INVESTIGATION and PERSONAL.

For the last hour, I'd devoured more than enough personal stuff from the Investigation memories. I wasn't ready for whatever truly private things existed in the Personal menu. A moment Kalan had shared from the hospital replayed in my mind.

I almost remember him, Valeria had said. *And almost is torture.*

I hated the image of her standing tall but somehow wilted. Living a life of almosts.

Kalan's whole existence lingered on the tip of my tongue. What had we been to each other? I'd never know, because my side of the story was in my own lost memory. I felt hollow. I felt almost.

But I had missed him all morning. Even before I knew he was gone. I couldn't remember him—but I hadn't completely forgotten him.

Another Memo moment flashed across my mind. My face, so close to Kalan's. His arms around me. The dark of the cliff wall, the light of the moon on my black hair. My hand touching his face, taking out the memory I'd stored in him. I could see it all, and I *hated* seeing it. Seeing was nothing. I wanted to feel it. I wanted everything that moment had been, not this secondhand version of looking back on it. Feelings in the moment and feelings looking back on the moment were never the same, and I'd never had to go without one of them before.

It wasn't that those remembered feelings were gone. They just weren't tied to the moment anymore. They floated, confusing me, making me guess where they were supposed to fit. The random wanting that coursed through me—that was likely tied to Kalan. The betrayal that pulsed like a sludge in my veins. That one, I could guess, belonged to Ren. But even when I knew where they should go, the feelings didn't knit themselves back to the memory.

Something niggled at me, a piece out of place. Ren had been in the business of stealing Links. She stole a Link from Cora, someone she'd known for ages. So why was she taking my memories piecemeal, through siphoning? I rubbed my eyes. My brain flipped through facts like pages of a book.

I rocked back as the domino effect hit me. Random memories collided in my brain.

My memory of Ren as the thief, still stored in Kalan's skin—something Ren would have come for if she'd taken my memory of giving it to him.

You! Dad's shout to Kalan after my dance. Recognition rang in his voice.

Kalan and I had thought someone was stealing my memories of our investigation. That wasn't it at all.

Someone was stealing my memories of Kalan.

Kalan was Populace. The last person in the world my parents wanted their perfect daughter associating with. It would be so easy to make me forget him. And if they had siphoned them away, those memories might still be here. Somewhere in this house where I wouldn't find them. Where I wasn't supposed to go.

Before I could think twice, I was out of bed. The voices from my parents' room were finally silent as my bare feet sped up the thin twirling staircase to Dad's study. I paused at the door, my hands hesitating in trained fear. I twisted the doorknob.

It was warmer and darker than the rest of the house. In fact, it didn't look like it belonged in our house at all. Wood framing jutted from the walls, waiting to be filled with drywall. Rough, unfinished floorboards scraped my feet. A low desk hunched in the center of the round room, bare except for a large, cloth-covered lump. An old wooden chair rested under the desk.

I slammed open desk drawers. They had to be here. Sequestered Links, a random knick-knack, anything. Every drawer was empty.

I whipped the fabric off the lump squatting on the corner of the desk. A bulky, electronic contraption—a Shared Link System. What was Dad doing with one of those? They were so tightly regulated you practically had to kiss the mayor's feet to get one. Houses didn't even have ports to connect to the grid.

The machine squeaked against the desk when I pulled it toward me. Two cords—a plug, and a thick, plastic-coated wire winding to a patched-up hole in the wall. We *did* have a grid port.

Which had to be totally illegal.

My eyes came back to the SLS. The complex hardware needed to process memory files made all of them large, but this one was bigger than Mr. Soto's standard-issue at school. Otherwise, it looked the same. The quartz port to store the memories before they were transferred to the network, a screen to navigate the system. I squinted below the screen. That was different. An infrared Share port. Useless. An SLS didn't share data with other wireless devices—it couldn't.

My fingers swept over the screen. This odd SLS had to have something to do with my missing memories. Maybe they'd been stored on the SLS network somewhere.

I flipped the on-switch. The screen glowed and a menu came up.

MEMORY IMPORT

MEMORY EXPORT

MEMORY FADE

I read it three times. My fingers clutched the edge of the desk. Were my memories here, stored inside the SLS? Or…what did *fade* mean?

"You're not supposed to be up here."

I didn't jump at Dad's voice, though I hadn't heard him climb the stairs. He sounded tired. For some reason, that completely pissed me off.

I turned. "What. Is. This.?"

"It's protection." He rubbed a hand over his eyes, pressing his fingers into the tear ducts. Mom stomped up behind him.

I ignored her and stared at my father. "You're the one who has been taking my memories."

"Gena!" Mom exclaimed. "What are you talking about?"

She didn't know. My throat tightened with gratitude that at least my mother hadn't betrayed me.

"How long, Daddy?" I whispered.

"Genesis—" Mom stopped when Dad held up a hand.

"I programmed it the night Cora lost her Link," he said. "You came home late, and you refused to talk to me about it. I needed to know why. After you fell asleep, I checked on you to see what had happened."

My stomach heaved. "Checked on me? You mean you *looked into my memories*?"

"Only a little." He sniffed. "All I saw was that Populace boy, he filled your whole mind. He was obviously the problem."

The problem. He took one brief glimpse into my life and saw what he defined as the problem. My anger cranked up a notch.

"And you made me forget him. Took away my memories. With this." I gestured to the SLS.

Mom's eyes fixed on the machine. "Kierce, what is that?"

"An SLS prototype."

"And you used it on me?" I said. "What did you do, steal it from Ascalon? What about all your we-don't-play-with-our-minds talk, and how dangerous it is to tamper with memory?"

"It's more dangerous to fraternize with a Populace boy who was on our side of town after dark." Dad pressed a button on the side of the machine. The SLS screen winked off. "You were terrified. I didn't want you traumatized by him."

"He didn't traumatize me, he helped me!" I wanted to throw something, but I had nothing to throw.

And oddly, it was Dad staying calm this time. "You were making poor choices. I was protecting you from the mistakes teenagers make."

I could barely breathe. "They were not mistakes. And if they were, they were mine to make. My choices, my *memories*."

Dad placed both hands on the desk and bowed his head. "Gena, honey, you're young. Ren is too. She made all the wrong decisions, and I didn't want that for you. This was a second chance for you to do things better."

"You don't know that I can't make the right decisions." I gripped my pajama pants so tight, my hands cramped up. "How can I possibly choose anything at all if you're making me forget everything?"

"I wasn't making you forget everything," Dad huffed. "I just faded out the memory of that boy, that one night. So you wouldn't have to worry about him. I didn't know he'd been following you."

Liar. "So why do I have days' worth of memories missing?" My throat felt raw, though I wasn't yelling.

Dad waved a hand. "You don't have days missing."

"I do! I went through them, and there are pieces gone."

"That's not possible. I haven't touched your memories since that…"

His sharp inhale pierced the momentary quiet.

"Your Link buds." His voice rose. "How many times have I told you not to sleep with them in!"

Sometimes I listened to music to help me fall asleep, like Mom. "What does that have to do with it?"

"It uses the Link buds to connect the SLS to your memories. Every time I turned it on and you had your Link buds in, the SLS followed its programming."

And stole any new memories of Kalan. Thin lines on Dad's face deepened into shadows. He wasn't lying. He didn't mean to hurt me.

Yes he did. That first time, he meant it.

"You had no right to make me forget anything at all."

He bristled. "If you had left that boy alone, you wouldn't have forgotten much."

Now he was going to blame this on me? "How did this tap into my memories through my Link buds? My connection wires weren't plugged in."

Dad rubbed his face again. "It's new technology. It uses signals similar to our brainwaves and nerve impulses. The same as how we move memories from Link to Link. I only had to sync your Link buds once."

I barely had the presence of mind to be impressed by this. A sound from Mom, half-gasp, half-sob, made me turn.

She stood, tall and pale, gaping at Dad. "How could you…?"

"It's not like we haven't done it before. It was your idea, that time."

Mom's face contorted. "Shut up. That was different. We had to."

We had to. The words echoed in my brain. They'd done it before. They'd taken memories from me, stolen my moments before now. Even my mom. How much of my life was real?

"What did you take?" I asked her.

"Nothing, I didn't know about this…"

"When did you do this *before*?"

Dad spoke. "You don't need to know. There's a reason we took it from you."

It. Only one memory. A few moments of my life that I'd never known were missing. But feelings would have remained. Unexplained emotions with no memory to attach to, unexplained fears that filled me with anxiety…

"Something scared me," I said. "So you took it away."

"You were so young, Gena." Mom lifted her hands, begging for me to understand. "Barely eight, you couldn't deal with it."

Barely eight. Memories clicked together. That was when we stopped seeing Grandma Piper. "It's about Grandma."

"You don't need to *know*," Dad said, his voice gruff.

"Do you have any idea what you did to me?" The heat of rage flooded my face. "You might have taken away the event, but you never took away the fear. I've lived with it for nine years, and it never went away because I didn't have the MEMORIES to tell me what it was for!"

"But you're not afraid, Gena," Mom pleaded. "You've grown up so well, you perform your dances without hardly getting nervous—"

"That's not what I'm afraid of. I'm afraid of *you*. Of punishment and pain. Of judgment." Even my own judgment. I wanted to take years' worth of that fear and shove it down their throats, to make them feel what they'd made me feel.

Mom stumbled into the wall. "We thought…we didn't want…"

"I don't care what you want. I want them back," I said. "All of them, any memories you ever took from me. I don't care if they're in other Links or in the SLS, they're mine. I'll go get my Link buds, and you can restore everything you took."

I headed for the door, careful to leave a wide berth between my parents and me.

"No, Gena, I can't." For the first time, a hint of guilt crept into Dad's voice. "Your memories of that boy aren't stored in the system."

I stopped, my foot slamming to the floor. "Where are they?"

"I used the fade setting. To make the memory dimmer, without taking it from your Links. Whatever hints you still have of that boy is all you'll ever have."

I turned slowly. "I don't have hints."

A flash of confusion crossed Dad's face.

My heart pounded in my throat. "I don't have dim anything. I have nothing." Only the un-Link-able, disconnected emotions. That wasn't enough.

Dad paled. "You have to have something. Dim images, the whisper of a voice. I set the fade on high, but you have to have something left."

"I have nothing." He was lying. He had taken them, he could give them back, turn them bright again… "*Give them back.*"

He spun to the SLS, slamming his hand against the button to turn it on. His fingers slashed and stabbed at the touch screen. I reminded myself that I knew how to breathe.

And then my always-appropriate father swore.

"They're gone." His hoarse voice scratched at me like a desert sandstorm.

"Memories are never gone."

"They're gone." His shoulders hunched. "The fade setting. Something went wrong. I didn't know, I just wanted you to be safe. The fade hasn't been tested that high, but I didn't know it would…it faded them to nothing. They aren't stored anywhere now."

The dry heat in the attic room sucked the moisture from my mouth. Gone.

Memories couldn't be gone.

Those things had happened, so the memories couldn't be gone. But they were.

And so was the me I had been in those moments.

Faded to black.

Unhappened.

"What about the other one? The first one?" I choked out. I wasn't sure I wanted the missing memory of Grandma. Maybe in the end, I'd rather keep the happy ones I had.

"It's been destroyed." He straightened and looked me in the eye. "Some things are best forgotten. I know the weight of abuse, and you'll never have to."

Abuse.

Grandma had spent her childhood getting hit by her own father. Being nearly killed by him. The Memor-X had fractured those memories until the pieces sliced at her with every internal movement. I'd seen the evidence in her short temper and angry outbursts. Dad had never said she'd abused him. But he'd never wanted us over there alone.

"I need to know," I whispered. "Please. So I can get past it."

Mom slid to the floor, her hands over her face. "She hit you, Gena."

"Hazel." Dad had the warning tone.

Mom ignored it. "Only once. But you were hysterical. You idolized her. We just wanted you to hold on to the happy memories. Not the hurt."

A ragged pain ripped through me in the place where my memory of Grandma had been torn. I had a glimmer of understanding. My parents had seen only my pain. They wanted to protect me. Wanted me happy and whole. I could almost forgive them for wanting to take that hurt away.

Except I'd borne the weight of it anyway. All they'd done was draw out the pain. Who would I have been without those years of irrational fear? Who would I be now if memories of Kalan filled my empty spaces?

I stared straight into my father's dark, defensive eyes. "You took more than memories from me. You killed me in little pieces. You destroyed the person I could have been. But you know what? I'm creating someone else in that girl's place, and you won't ever know who she is. Because I'm never going to let you."

Then I swung my leg up, flexible and strong, and kicked the Shared Link System to the floor. It landed hard with a shatter of electronic parts.

Dad cried out, reaching for me. I picked up the desk chair and smashed it into the machine. Splinters of wood grazed my face. Their pricks on my skin, piercing and real, released the pain inside me like a bursting dam. I screamed and slammed the broken chair pieces on the SLS again. The plastic case cracked. One more time, and pieces scattered across the floor.

"Gena!" Dad howled.

I opened my fingers. Splintered wood clattered to the floor. Let Dad grieve for his machine. I'd grieve for my lost moments. Elsewhere.

Before I stepped out the door, I knelt in front of my mother. "Mom."

She cried so hard she could barely talk. "…sorry…"

Until I heard the word, I didn't know how badly I'd wanted it.

I rested a hand on her cheek, touching her for the first time since that long-ago day on the swings. "Thank you. For the apology."

Her tears soaked through my glove, wetting my fingertips.

I pulled away and circled down the stairs. On my way out the front door, the cheerful *ding* of the security system bid me farewell.

22

With weary steps I loiter on…
My prospect and horizon gone.

—Alfred, Lord Tennyson, *In Memoriam XXXVIII*

I thought about going to Cora's, but our combined emotional instability had apocalyptic potential. Then I debated going to Kalan's. Except I chickened out. I couldn't handle a boy my heart claimed to know that my head didn't.

Which left Ren. Oh, the irony.

At least I knew she hadn't been stealing my memories. She wouldn't take them now, if she'd left me alone all along. Probably.

I knocked at her apartment and shivered in the night that had drained of warmth. Ren opened the door looking bedraggled and sleepless. And mad. I'd prepared a tirade on my walk over, but I was too tired for it now.

"I know you're the Link thief," I said, my eyes resting on her bare toes.

She squawked in outrage.

"I also know you weren't the one stealing my memories."

"What?" Now she sounded confused.

"It was Dad."

Her toes curled and she let me in. I sank onto her bed.

"Are you sure?" she asked, her voice as cold as the night. "You have a habit of creating facts out of assumptions."

"He admitted it."

A beat of silence. "That evil, evil…Why?"

"Kalan. The Populace boy." I was too emotionally exhausted to point out that she stole memories too, so she might want to reserve judgment. "Can I stay here tonight?"

She trudged to a closet and pulled out some extra blankets.

"Why did you do it, Ren?"

She threw the blankets at my head and burrowed into her covers, facing the wall.

I spent most of the night not sleeping on the floor by her bed.

We rose with the sun the next morning. Ren let me shower first. Numbness consumed me as I stood under the spray. I cupped my hands, letting them fill with water that overflowed and trickled over my fingertips.

Light lanced through the window, turning the falling drops into slivers of rainbow that pierced my open hands. I closed my eyes and let the streams fall on my face.

Grandma Piper. Funny, loving, temperamental Grandma Piper. Her temper had flared when I so much as dropped a cup. Apologies had always followed, but still. If something so small set her off, what happened when she got truly upset? My empty stomach roiled. She'd been the one I could always run to, the one I was certain would always love me no matter what.

Did she love me even while she was hitting me?

I wanted to rid myself of the contamination of her dark side. She'd had so much pain in her life, and I'd always known she had scars. It made sense, it totally made sense that she could never overcome her past.

What does making sense have to do with it? She hit you.

I clenched shaking fists and squeezed my eyes shut. I couldn't think about Grandma. Wouldn't think about her. Those memories tasted sour like lemon drops after all the sugar had been sucked away.

Dad had learned not to be violent like Grandma, but violence wasn't the only way to cause pain.

I trembled under the shower spray. The few memories he hadn't taken of Kalan twisted my heart. The honey of his eyes and the glint of his smile. The warmth of his hand sliding from mine. The bouncy ball. For a moment, I was back in the costume closet with that ball. Watching the swirling path of the glitter, remembering the agony in his face and realizing how well he knew me. A silent scream rose from my gut and clawed at my throat. My fingers convulsed over my Links.

I don't want it. If I can't have it all I don't want any. I don't want it don't want it don't want to lose it…

My knees gave way and thumped against the porcelain bottom of the tub. How could Dad say he loved me when he'd hurt me so much? The scream I'd tried to hold in came out as a half-sob, muffled by closed lips. I wanted to hate him. I *did* hate him. There was a power in it, an ability to tune out the hurt so I could hate instead, and I clung to that power. I gasped, inhaling water, coughing and gagging. A soft knock sounded from the door.

"You okay in there?" Ren asked from the other side.

I spit and wiped my wet arm across my mouth. "No. But I'm not drowning either."

Water pattered against the tub.

"Okay. I left some clothes by the door and made some coffee."

"Thanks."

I knelt in the tub until I could take normal, even breaths without having to force them. The invisible hand that wrenched my insides eased its grip. I needed the time-honored Mementi technique that was as close as we could come to forgetting—distraction. Coffee was distraction. Finding out why Ren stole lives was distraction.

I joined Ren in the kitchen-slash-living-room a few minutes later, wearing her jeans and gloves. She sat at the table nibbling buttered toast. A pre-filled mug waited for me on the table.

"You got another chair," I noted, remembering images of her apartment from Kalan's Memo.

She spun her coffee cup in circles. "A friend was moving. She gave it to me."

"I'm surprised Happenings doesn't pay well enough for two chairs."

"In their hierarchy, being Mementi means nothing. I don't have a college degree yet, so I'm only a lab assistant. And no, it doesn't exactly pay for luxuries."

Two chairs was a luxury? I swirled a sip of coffee around with my tongue, letting the warmth fill my entire mouth before I swallowed.

"So you're the Link thief."

She pressed her palms to her eyes. "Do we really have to do this?"

"At least I'm not yelling."

Her hands dropped to wrap around her coffee mug. "How did you find out?"

If I wanted honesty from her, I'd have to give some back. "I found the memory of what happened the night Cora lost her Link. I'd stored it in Kalan."

She choked and set her mug down. "You stored it in *Kalan*? In a person?"

"Well, I didn't have a lot of choices," I said. "Knowing it was you, I must have figured you'd come after that memory. Why didn't you?"

"I did," she admitted. "I ran home and watched you go inside. You weren't freaking out anymore, weren't even hurrying like you knew I'd be after you. It was obvious you didn't remember what you'd seen, so I traced your route, thinking you'd stored it some-where. I was right, I guess."

My lips twitched in a half-smile that faded. "Why, Ren?"

"Because Ascalon has gotten nowhere in the last fifty years on memory backups. We have to have live subjects. Happenings is the only place willing to go that far. And we need *that far*. We have nothing to protect our memories."

She scratched crumbs off the crust of her toast. "Rory, Trae, Blaire, and I all sent a project request to Liza, volunteering as live subjects so we could study how Mementi brains work. We decided I should stay on the outside, to have a Mementi mind working on the project." Ren snorted. "Not that I actually got to work on Liza's new pet project. I heard *she* even came into the lab after hours, as if she knew enough about the science to understand anything. I never met her, but I ended up as nothing more than her gofer."

"And that extended to stealing Links?"

"The experiment is only temporary," Ren growled. "It wasn't supposed to be like this. The three others told people stories about why they'd be gone, thinking it'd be enough to keep people off their trail for a few months. Trae was the Populace control subject, and it was easier for him—he just pretended he was transferring to a different branch. Everybody bought it. Except his fiancée, I guess."

Valeria. She would've seen through faked emails or whatever Liza had concocted.

"Blaire's mom didn't buy it, either," Ren continued. "She was the first one. She came to me to find out why she couldn't get a hold of Blaire, then started badgering Liza."

"And what, the CEO added to your job description? Steal Miranda's Links to shut her up? Not the most brilliant plan."

"Liza's not exactly a criminal mastermind. She panicked. She called me up one day and asked me to…keep Miranda's Links safe for a while."

"And you just said, 'sure, why not?'"

"You think it was that easy?" Ren snapped. "If I'd said no, Liza made it very clear I'd become another comatose test subject, and she'd have someone else take care of Miranda's memories. I was the only Mementi left on the outside of this. The only one who would actually keep Miranda's memories safe. Liza just wanted me because I had easy access to Miranda, but then the other families came asking questions. Liza said if I didn't take their Links too, she'd wipe my memory and turn me into the cops as the Link thief."

Her eyes shifted to her desk. I knew that if I opened one of those drawers, I'd find the missing lives of everyone in the hospital. I'd find Cora's missing two years.

"What about Jacie Moran?" I asked. "She was the first victim, not Miranda."

"I don't have hers." She shook her head. "Somebody else must have taken them. Maybe that's where Liza got the idea."

"What was the point of this project, anyway?"

"We wanted to understand how it works. How *we* work. Liza thought if she could induce a comatose state in a few of us, then

Link us into an SLS connected to monitoring equipment, she could study how we store and retrieve memories."

"Why a coma?" I asked. "Wouldn't it be more effective to do it when people are awake?"

"Wow. And here I thought you were all anti-Happenings."

"I don't condone the method. But the project sounds worthwhile."

"Finally willing to express an opinion, huh?"

I suppressed a growl. "Why a coma, Ren?"

"We did several weeks' worth of conscious studies too. But Liza wanted to see what happened when the brain was in a constant dream state. When it accessed the memories without any conscious purpose. She thought it would give us a better indication of how the neurons and peripheral nerves were connected. Maybe even see where the chain of command originated in the brain."

I couldn't help it. I was fascinated. "And did you figure it out?"

Ren hesitated. "I think so. But all the project files are confidential. I'm only a lab assistant, and the other scientists only give me basic updates to forward on to Liza. She just calls or texts me if she needs something, but she doesn't tell me much."

I pushed my mug away from me, the fascination fading. So much sacrifice for knowledge Ren didn't even have.

"And you kept doing her dirty work while she was too sick to get out of bed? That's what you were doing the night you stole Cora's Links, wasn't it."

Ren took her plate to the sink. "The project was almost over, okay? One other person had volunteered to go under. So Liza asked me to do another job, preemptive this time. I followed the guy out of the Low-G, and you and Cora came around and saw me."

"What happened to the guy? I never heard of any other thefts."

Ren's shoulders heaved, her back still to me. "I panicked and dropped the Links. I chased after you and Cora. To explain things. But Cora was so…Cora. When I caught up to her, I…"

"What?" I demanded. "Knocked her out and took the Link with her most recent memories?"

"I didn't want her to lose everything." Her voice sounded weak, pitiful. "Not Cora. And not you, either. I didn't think of siphoning, it would've made things easier on her—"

I slammed my coffee cup on the table. "Made things easier on her? Would you still have taken her memory—taken *my* memory— if you had to go back and do it again?"

Ren turned, her face crumpled. "That's not what I meant. I don't know what I meant. I didn't want things to go like this, I just wanted to help people. Help the Mementi grow."

She stared at her hands, clad in sheer red gloves, like she didn't recognize them as her own.

I sighed. "So what happened with the guy you were supposed to hit that night?"

"No idea. Probably just thought he'd passed out drunk. Liza was furious. Braxton still went under, though. He told his brother he was going on a business trip." She slumped against the counter. "I'm so tired of this."

"You know what you have to do," I said. "If you turn yourself in and explain all of this, the cops can arrest Liza." And Jackson, while they were at it.

"*Turn myself in*? Do you have any idea what they'd do to me?"

"Do you have any idea what you've done to those people you stole from?"

She closed her eyes. "It's only temporary. I can fix them."

"I don't know if they can be fixed. They've gone crazy, Ren, or they're going crazy. It's happening to Cora, even to me a little. Getting their Links back may not solve that."

Miranda's heartbroken face flickered in my mind. I second-guessed my opinion that Liza's project was worthwhile. Could the good that might come from it justify what had been done?

"We can't go to the police," Ren said.

"Why?"

"Because Liza fired me yesterday."

Oh, the horror. "So?"

"She emailed me digital 'evidence' memories she'd gathered that pinned everything on me if I exposed the project." Ren's nose twitched. "I've got no clue how she did it. Even with my memories as counter evidence, she's got a cop friend at the station. I'll go to jail and she'll keep experimenting. I've heard she's testing some kind of new SLS—"

"What?" A horrible churning started in my stomach.

"It's a rumor," Ren said. "But I bet she figured out how to do it after all her experiments on the Mementi."

A new SLS. Like Dad's. Using technology that mimicked brainwaves.

"Ren, that's how Dad did it," I whispered. "He didn't just siphon my memories away, he deleted them with an SLS. He said it was a prototype. I think he got it from work."

"He *deleted* them?" Ren said. "They're *gone?*"

I focused on the swirling wood grain of the tabletop.

"But how would Happenings get that SLS?" Ren said. "If Dad got it from Ascalon…you don't think…he stole it?"

I shrugged to hide the anger that tightened my shoulders. I didn't even know my father any more.

"But Dad hates Happenings. He'd never even talk to Liza, let alone sell company tech to her." She paused. "I take that back. I wouldn't put anything past Dad anymore."

I wouldn't put anything past Liza Woods with an all-powerful SLS. "If she has something like that, if she can erase memories from a distance…Ren, we have to stop her."

"Because that's going to be so easy."

Ren sank into her chair. In her face was the same regret I'd seen in Mom's eyes, but not in Dad's. Funny. I'd always thought she was more like Dad—always right, with no room for regrets.

The desk that held the missing Links hunkered against the wall. Maybe Ren was right. It's not like we could march in with blazing guns and take Liza down. If I wanted, I could quit now. I'd found who stole my memories, and who had stolen everyone else's. I'd never get mine back, but we could return the Links to Cora and the others. I could claim I'd finished what I started.

I could wimp out.

But other people could lose their memories the way I lost mine, without realizing it. Liza Woods had the tech to do it. I'd found the thief, now I had to stop the thief. Somehow.

My heart chided me gently. Someone else had been with me through everything. Kalan could help us. I hunched forward, trying to minimize the hole in my heart. I'd lost him three times, and I wasn't keen on going for round four. I didn't know him anymore. Despite the longing inside me, I wanted to keep it that way. Walking straight into Happenings sounded easier than talking to Kalan again.

Walking straight into Happenings…

"Ren," I said, "how many people know you were fired?"

23

Calm is the morn without a sound,
Calm as to suit a calmer grief…

—Alfred, Lord Tennyson, *In Memoriam XI*

Ren and I walked to Happenings through empty, quiet streets. Not the silence of a city still waking up. It was a tense, shifting kind of quiet, like a thief in the shadows. Goose bumps prickled my arms.

I stopped mid-step as we approached the square in front of Happenings. People had gathered already, both Populace and Mementi. They stood on opposite sides of the bedraggled grass, the pond in the middle acting as a dividing line.

No shouting today. No signs waving. The Mementi had their Link buds in and the Populace had their Cortexs or earphones on, listening for news. Angry eyes stayed trained on faces across the pond. The sun had begun to heat up the day, but the people's faces were cold. Police in black with large clear shields ringed the area.

This wasn't a protest. It was the precursor to a battle. The air hung thick and heavy as the crowd waited for the first gunshot.

Ren held her Link buds to her ears.

"News reports say the entire police force is out today. They arrested like twenty people last night." She snorted. "Most of them Populace. That's really going to tick people off. Drake Matthews is giving a press conference tonight. Probably another 'we're closer than ever' speech about memory backups."

She put the Link buds in her pocket. "Matthews is an idiot. He's been making the same vague promises forever, and nobody listens anymore. It's not going to calm anyone down. There's going to be another riot like at the Memoriam."

The Memoriam. Ren had told me about it burning. I couldn't think about it right now. No room for another pain.

"This is insane," I said.

"It wasn't supposed to be like this." Ren's hands fell to her sides. "This is my fault."

It kind of was. Except. "You didn't do *this*."

She looked away.

"You didn't do this," I said, stepping closer. "Whatever you did, these people are the ones who chose to come stare each other down like they're going to eat each other."

"I'm the one who did what they suspect each other of."

"Yes." I took a deep breath. "And I'm not going to lie, that's really horrible. But this isn't about the Link thief anymore. It's about revenge."

Ren let out a half-snort, half-laugh.

"Now come on," I said. "If we can get inside Happenings, you can help fix this before they turn the city into a warzone."

She followed me around the outskirts of the Mementi crowd. Nobody noticed us. Maybe this would stay a ridiculous all-day staring contest. And maybe Toben Roberts from Frankie and the Boy would climb in my bedroom window and declare passionate love for me.

We climbed the stairs to the Happenings entrance slowly. My anxiety built as I counted the hired security guards lining the top steps. I beat out a rhythm on my legs as I walked, not caring if I looked stupid. Everything was too still.

Ren's lab coat made the guards relax, and they parted a bit. "Serenity Lee, data lab assistant," she said, flashing a nametag.

We strolled right past them.

Ren exhaled. "I thought Liza might have told them not to let me in."

"She's sort of got bigger problems." Like the swelling, silent crowd.

"This is so not going to work." Ren paused outside the glass doors.

"You said most people aren't coming in anyway. Liza might not have announced that you left."

"Even if we get past the lobby, my DNA access is probably already revoked from the computers."

I peered through the doors, noting a figure behind the reception desk. "It's a big company, and there's a lot going on. We have to try."

Ren squeezed her hands together. She knocked on the glass of the revolving door. I counted the steps of the girl inside as she approached the doors. She squinted through the glass, and her face lit up when she saw Ren. With a soft click, the door unlocked.

"Ren!" she said. She gave a funny squeal—and gave my sister a hug.

"Samantha!" Ren returned the hug.

The bitterness in my heart surprised me. *Sorry, Gena, I know I hardly even smile at you anymore, but don't mind me while I hug this obnoxious Populace girl.*

Samantha pulled away. "This is nuts, I'm afraid they're going to set the place on fire or something." She shivered. "Anyway, what are you doing here? I thought you quit, there was a memo this morning."

Okay. Problem. I focused on not blinking or breathing too fast. Plan B.

Ren forced a smile that actually looked natural. She'd gotten good at acting. "Yeah, I did. I came to say goodbye and pick up some stuff I left."

"Ah, 'Renity, did you come to bid farewell to the bobbleheads?"

Ren laughed. "You know it."

Bobbleheads? Who the devil was this girl, and why did my sister hang out with her?

"Someone looks confused." Samantha tilted her head toward me. "Sister?"

"Yeah. She's going help me clear my stuff out."

"Well, little sister, we must introduce you to the company of the bobbleheads." With a forced laugh and her head turned firmly away from the crowd outside, she pranced toward the reception desk.

Ren followed without hesitation, but I had to grind my teeth to stop them from clicking. We had to hurry. Liza Woods could show up any second.

"Behold." Samantha made a grand flourish, gesturing to something on the desk.

She wasn't kidding. It was a lineup of actual bobblehead dolls. Some of them familiar. I leaned closer. "Is that Stephen Hawking?"

"Yup." Samantha laughed. "It's my bobblehead boyfriend collection."

Einstein. Carl Sagan. Jeremiah Lowton. Their oversized heads grinned up at me.

"He's my favorite," Samantha said, tapping Stephen Hawking and sending his head rattling.

Okay, maybe we could be friends. "Mine, too."

Ren cleared her throat. "Listen, Sam, I've got to get going before this mob does something crazy. Do you mind scanning me into the back?"

Samantha darted a look to a looming door flanked by a DNA scanner. Next to it, a sign stated, All Visitors Must Be Escorted Beyond This Point.

Above the sign was a large map of the building. To be safe, I committed an image of it to a metal Link.

"I can't let you back, Ren," Samantha said. "If they revoked your access already, I could get in trouble."

She had to let us in. She had to. If Ren tested the DNA lock, they'd know immediately she was here whether the door unlocked or not. This was our only option.

"Please, Sam." Ren's smile faltered. "I just need to grab some of the stuff I left at my desk."

"I can't. I could get fired, especially if your sister's there too." She brightened. "I could call someone to escort you back, though."

My pulse skyrocketed. Brilliant. Call in the cavalry to march us to jail.

Ren said, "I guess that works."

Uh, no. What? This wasn't the plan, we had to regroup, come up with something else before Liza Woods descended with fangs bared.

"Ren," I hissed under my breath.

She ignored me.

Chills prickled up my legs. Was I being betrayed by someone I loved again?

Samantha picked up the earpiece on her desk. Ren lunged for her.

I caught the edge of the desk. Ren clapped a hand to Samantha's face. For a brief moment, Samantha struggled. A smothered scream gurgled to silence, and she flopped into Ren's arms.

"What—" I gaped at Ren as she lowered Samantha to the floor.

She stuffed a piece of fabric in her pocket. "I'm not exactly strong enough to knock people out by hitting them."

A chemical. Something she used to knock out her victims. My pulse pounded, and I remembered my sister was the Link thief.

"She was your friend," I said.

"Which is exactly why I did that," she snapped. She turned, her eyes watery. Maybe even teary. "Now she won't get in trouble, and she won't get hurt."

"But they'll notice, the security…" A security camera sat tucked in the corner of the wood-lined ceiling.

"All security is patrolling the grounds, they have been for days." Ren picked up Samantha under the arms and dragged her toward the door by the desk. "The security feeds are unmanned most of the time lately."

Outside the glass doors of the entrance, the security had their backs to us. No one had seen a thing.

Samantha's head lolled to the side as Ren lifted her hand to touch the DNA scanner. A beep and click announced the door had unlocked.

"You can't hold the door open, it'll set off an alarm," Ren said. "Go through and open it for me when I knock. I've got to hide Sam."

The door closed behind me. An empty hallway stretched away from me, doors lining the sides. Thoughts of Samantha being crammed under her desk fled. My ears strained for the sound of a door opening, for angry words demanding why I was here.

A knock behind me nearly made me yelp. Shaking, I opened the door for Ren.

She pushed past me. "We've got to hurry. Sam's schedule said Liza's actually in today. I'd rather not get arrested."

I forced a grin in an attempt to not cry. "I'm all about having new experiences today."

She let out a strangled laugh. "Wow, Gen. You really did grow a backbone."

Our footsteps squeaked on the tile. The sound scratched at the inside of my chest like nails on a chalkboard.

Ren played with her gloves, tugging on the ends of each finger. "It's a lot quieter than I expected."

Agreed. Shouldn't there be someone to ask us questions? To wonder why Ren was here after she'd been fired? It almost would have made me feel better, instead of the waiting waiting waiting for confrontation that didn't seem to be there.

"Here." Ren turned into a room filled with long lab tables decorated with computers, tablets, and projection screens. It was as empty of people as it would have been on a weekend.

"What did you do, anyway?" I asked.

"In addition to fetching and carrying?" She snorted. "I was a data processing assistant. Basically, I ran computer simulations on all the information the head researcher, Dr. Lassen, discovered. Most boring job in the world."

She slid into a chair and picked up a tablet. "These are on a different security network than the door locks. Only a few guys in IT can change authorizations, and I don't know if they've been here today. Let's see how slow bureaucracy made them."

She swiped her thumb along a dark strip on the side. The tablet stayed blank. A tiny red light in the top left corner started blinking. My heart seized up. Red was bad. System failure, explosion imminent, security alerted—that's what red meant.

Ren dropped the tablet. "We've got to bolt."

She leaped up and spun, then stopped.

"Come on, Ren!"

She swore.

"What?" I jerked around to see who had found us. No one there, just an open door.

"That door isn't supposed to be open. It's an entrance to one of the higher-level labs." She tugged at the cuff of her glove. "This isn't right."

All the people gone. No security doors to stop us. No, it wasn't right.

"How long till security gets here?" I asked.

"Depends on how things are going outside."

We couldn't leave with nothing.

"Let's check it out, fast," I said. "If we are caught, we'll have all those lovely memories of yours to prove our story in a trial."

"Unless she erases them and throws us in the basement to be guinea pigs with the others."

Oh, lovely thought. "Why didn't Liza do that to you in the first place? Or instead of firing you?"

"I have too many family members who still talk to me for her to risk putting me under."

We approached the open door like a nightmare might be lurking beyond it. A faint electrical buzz sounded as we got closer. Ren and I paused on either side of the door. She nodded, and we stepped in together.

It was cooler inside, and emptier than the room we'd come from. No desks, no chairs, no people. Only an enormous machine in the middle of the tile floor, humming contentedly to itself. It came to my waist and was almost as long as I was tall. Several metal panels had been removed, showing a complicated maze of electronic parts. A large quartz stone and infrared Share port were embedded next to a touch screen.

"She did build an SLS," I said. "A giant one. What's she going to do with all that processing power?"

"Oh, Gena," came a voice from behind us. "I'd think your own experience would make that obvious."

Ren and I spun to find the ever-smiling Liza Woods crossing the lab.

24

When fill'd with tears that cannot fall,
I brim with sorrow drowning song.

—Alfred, Lord Tennyson, *In Memoriam XIX*

She'd trapped us. Behind us crouched the SLS, and Liza stood in the only doorway, blocking our exit.

Ren stared at Liza, her mouth open. "What—what *happened* to you?"

No kidding. Her media pics always painted the image of the stylish, approachable, youthful-but-mature CEO. Now, she slouched in her rumpled business suit. Her once-bobbed hair hung just over her forehead. Her bronze skin looked waxy, her face uneven and distorted, like a face-lift gone wrong.

Liza smoothed her suit jacket. "My health isn't the best, as you may recall. But it doesn't matter."

Ren's hands clenched and she gestured to the SLS. "What is this? What are you doing with it?"

Liza flounced into the room like a bad-postured model and patted Ren on the shoulder. "Dear Serenity. So intelligent. So eager. And always so many questions. Someday, you'll learn the value of silence. Someday soon, I should think."

Her sadistic smile focused on me. "And your sister. Genesis. So restrained and proper at first glance, and yet more like you than I'd realized."

How did she know so much about me? My voice shook. "You knew we were coming."

The smile showed more teeth. "Indeed. One of the many advantages of our dear SLS. We managed to, shall we say, *acquire* the sales data of those nice little Link buds you all wear. All we need is the serial number of a person's Link buds and a certain frequency, and we can wirelessly connect to your memories each time you put them in. It was very helpful for monitoring Ren after she left."

Ren had listened for news outside Happenings with her Link buds. I tried to count the number of times I'd worn my own. Too many. Plenty of opportunities for someone at Happenings to access my entire life. I squeezed my arms to my chest.

Liza crossed to the SLS. She caressed it with hands I would have expected to be decorated with fancy nails. Instead, the nails were cracked, the hands dry and frail.

"Of course, we have all the data on your SLS's, too. Makes it so easy to obtain every bit of information we could want. That's why this fellow had to be so big." She patted the machine, which gave a dull metallic ring. "So much data to process."

Data. Personal memories connected through Link buds. Medical records, police evidence, scientific discoveries. Anything stored on the SLS grid—or in Links connected to Link buds—was at her fingertips.

"It's really quite a wonderful piece of technology," she cooed. "In fact, there's something else it can do that I believe you're rather familiar with, Gena."

Dad's SLS prototype. "My dad's been working for you all along?"

"Yes. Well, not exactly working for *me*...but yes." She giggled, like a little girl with a secret. "He was quite distraught this morning, you know. The fade function was never meant for fully erasing memories. But now that we know it has that little side-effect, it seems it has its uses."

Dad. A spy for Happenings. Giving them Ascalon's research, sales data, who knew what else. No way. Not after his tirade against Ren working here, his constant Happenings insults, his adamant stance against human experimentation. Except that last bit had meant surprisingly little to him in the end. All the rest could be lies, too. Lies to me. To Ascalon. To all the Mementi.

I closed my eyes against the anger and tears. How could I hate him properly when I could never forget that I loved him too? It made his lies hurt so much more.

Liza tapped a rough fingernail on the control screen of the giant SLS. The sharp jab brought out a plea I nearly spoke out loud.

Don't make me forget again.

I edged toward the door.

"Guards," Liza called in a sing-song voice, lifting a hand to her mouth theatrically. What was wrong with her? Was this all some kind of show to her, some kind of twisted entertainment?

Two burly men came into the lab. Liza snatched Ren's wrist. Ren shouted and I raced forward, but Liza shoved Ren into the guards' arms.

"Please escort Ren to the lobby, and be sure to follow the new protocol." Her hand circled my bicep, cold and hard as steel. "I'll be along shortly with her sister."

She was letting Ren go? She couldn't possibly be letting her go. "Ren!"

"Gena!" she yelped. They hauled her away and shut the door.

I pushed Liza, trying to spin and twist out of her grasp. Her fingers bit into my arm.

"Stand here, please," she said pleasantly, shoving me at the wall at the end of the SLS.

"Where are you taking my sister?" I kicked at her. She staggered back against the enormous machine.

When she stood straight again I found myself staring down the barrel of a gun.

The cheerful lilt in her voice vanished, exposing a guttural undertone. "Against the wall, Gena. I'm not fond of shooting pretty girls."

I slapped my palms against the wall. She wasn't "fond" of shooting? But she would. Tendrils of fear snaked down my legs.

"It's only a tranq, of course," she said, the faked lilt returning. The show must go on. She tapped at the SLS screen. "And much as I'd love another Mementi test subject downstairs, you present an opportunity. A large-scale test of the machine's newly discovered feature."

Large equals worse. I didn't want to know about worse.

"You can make me forget whatever you want," I hissed. "But someone will find out what you're doing here."

Liza laughed. "Don't be silly, dear. I'm not going to make you forget anything at all."

All the tension, fear, and anger leeched from my body, replaced by a single word.

NO.

Liza tapped the screen one last time. "Ta da!"

She crossed to the door, holding it open for me to leave. "Let's see how well that worked, shall we?"

"You made everyone else forget." My voice echoed in the room.

"Yes, dear. You. Not a soul in town who's connected to their Link buds or an SLS will remember who you are. Nor will anyone who Links up as long as this machine is running." She sighed, tilting her head in contentment. "Such a convenient solution, isn't it? I don't even have to worry about killing you. Though I suppose in a way, I already have."

"I'll…I'll…" I took a gasping breath. "I'll go to the police. They'll still come, whether they remember me or not."

"You think so?" She rested a finger on her lips. "You'll tell them what you've found, and they'll Link up to take a report. Mementi reports are so easy to change. They're all just memories, stored in the SLS files. And the system is set to purge any memory of you completely. The moment they try to store you, they'll forget you. And everything you've told them."

She'd wiped me from this earth. The second someone put in a Link bud, I was gone.

"Let's do a little test. Go on." Liza gestured out the door.

I ran.

Ren was still being held here somewhere. She would remember me. She wouldn't put her Link buds in, not after what Liza had said. I slammed into a guard standing at the door to the lobby.

"She said I could go," I gasped. "Let me go."

The click of high heels sounded. Liza advanced in an awkward, hip-swaying slouch, like a kid trying to walk in her mom's shoes. I choked back a crazy, desperate laugh at this ridiculous woman with the power to steal my life.

"Relax, dear," she said. "I want you to meet someone before you leave."

Her fingers clawed into my arm again. She guided me past the guard and into the lobby.

Ren sat on a couch with a superior expression on her face.

"Ren," Liza said. "Thanks for coming in. I wanted to give you one last thing, personally."

Ren stood up, blinking in shock at Liza's face.

Liza reached her free hand into her pocket and gave Ren an envelope. "As a final thank you. A little bonus to tide you over."

Ren clutched the envelope, her lips pinching.

Look at me, Ren, look at me. Know me.

"Is that all?" she said to Liza.

"Yes." Liza beamed and stuck her hip out. "Oh, and have you met Gena? Stumbled in from outside, a bit scared by the protesters. She's leaving now."

Ren's eyes narrowed in what I knew was a suppressed eye-roll. "Nice to meet you."

Be sure to follow the new protocol, Liza had said to the guards. All it would have taken was a touch of a Link bud to Ren's head or neck.

I was wearing her gloves, her jeans. Didn't she notice that? We had the same dark hair, the same turned-up noses inherited from Mom. I tried to say her name. My voice stuck. Ren brushed back purple hair that hung in her face.

Ren. Don't turn around. *Look at me.*

She exited through the front doors. I thought of Kalan coming to my dance class. How I didn't remember him at all. It didn't matter how long Ren stared at me, she would never know me. I had been faded out of her life. Forgotten.

My knees weakened, Liza's tight grasp the only thing keeping me standing. She giggled. "Looks like it worked."

She dropped my arm. I tumbled to the floor.

"Come on, then. Home with you. Your help is *so* appreciated. And don't worry. I'll have you collected as soon as this experiment plays out."

Liza winked, a move that unbalanced her sickly face more, and left me collapsed on the ground. Alone except for my dull outline in the cold, shiny tile.

And I wasn't sure what was worse, forgetting or forgotten. Or if they were the same thing in the end.

Because either way, my life was unhappening all around me.

25

And come, whatever loves to weep,
And hear the ritual of the dead.

—Alfred, Lord Tennyson, *In Memoriam XVIII*

M y fingers trembled as I hit the buttons projected onto my palm.

Text from Genesis Lee to Cora Julieta Medina, TDS 9:43:07/5-11-2084
Where are you? Need to talk ASAP. Emergency.

I clutched the thin band of my Sidewinder with both hands, tapping it with gloved fingernails and counting the beats. Everybody couldn't have forgotten me completely. Cora might not have had her Link buds in.

My eyes shifted to the three other people in the tram. Sydney Little. Liria Soto, my teacher's oldest daughter. Jax Bennett. None of them had greeted me. They all focused on the news coming into their Link buds.

They had forgotten me.

I pressed the Sidewinder into my belly to suppress the nausea and turned to the window. We approached the city center. The skyline looked lonely without the silver Memoriam spiraling into the blue.

All the memories from those we loved had vanished in smoke. But we still had our own memories of them, so they lived in us. Not me. No one had memories of me. I was more dead than the dead. I'd never realized how much of myself was made up of the people around me.

Three buzzes in my hand; a new text.

Text from Cora Julieta Medina to Genesis Lee, TDS 9:45:23/5-11-2084
Sorry, you must have the wrong number.

The Sidewinder clattered to the floor.

Everything. Every second we'd spent together for the eight years we'd been friends was gone. How could she not notice she was missing such huge chunks of her life? With something so big, surely she'd *feel* I was gone. Surely she would miss me.

Maybe that wouldn't matter, since she didn't know it was me she was missing.

Maybe my friends and family would end up with the other patients in the hospital, crazy and losing themselves without understanding why.

Or maybe they'd feel a little sad for no reason they could see, and move on. Maybe I wouldn't leave much of a hole.

My hands pressed into the seat on either side of my legs. Each expansion of my lungs sparked an agony that closed my throat. Like my body knew I was dead and was trying to comply with the inevitable.

None of the passengers had reached down to pick up my Sidewinder and set it on a seat near me, a politeness I would have expected from other Mementi. It was like I wasn't sitting on this tram. To them, receiving a constant feed from their Link buds that erased me, I probably wasn't. I stumbled down the aisle to pick up my phone.

A voice chimed over the speaker. "Passengers are reminded that standing is not permitted on Havendale City Trams. Thank you."

I let out a shaky, heartbroken laugh. At least someone recognized I still existed.

When the tram announced my stop, I hurried down the steps to the street. To my surprise, Mr. Soto, my teacher, stood at the bottom of the stairs like a guard on patrol. My heart lifted. If he remembered me, he could help. He could tell everyone to keep their Link buds hidden away.

He adjusted his wide-brimmed panama hat and turned at the sound of my footsteps clanging on the metal steps. He wasn't usually a hat-wearer.

"Mr. Soto?" I said.

"Sorry, you'll have to wait for the next tram to take you out of here," he said, blocking my path. "No one's allowed down here but Mementi."

My foot hovered over the next step. "But I…" What would I say? He didn't know me.

"Come on, kid, back up the stairs." He adjusted his hat again. "Nothing against you. We're trying to keep everybody safe. Including you."

"Who's we?" I asked weakly.

"Some of us are trying to protect each other instead of hurt each other. Now—" His mouth hung open for a moment. "You've got a Link buzz."

My hand clutching the rail spasmed. A Link buzz, and him not recognizing me as Mementi…

"THIEF!" He lunged up the stairs.

I tripped on the stair behind me, falling hard on my butt. Adrenaline surged and I gasped. Run, before someone else comes, before they hurt me, before they rip away the Links they don't know are mine.

Mr. Soto reached for my shoulders.

Only one thing to do.

I ripped off a glove and reached for the only open skin he showed—his face. The moment our skin made contact, I focused as hard as I could on a memory. He froze as the touch allowed him to see what I could see in my mind. A normal day at school. Him at his desk, me among his students seated in the chairs around the room.

He jerked away, almost falling as he backed down the steps of the tramstop. "You're Mementi," he said hoarsely.

I climbed to my feet.

"You're a—a student of mine? You can't be. I don't know you."

I cleared my throat, trying to dislodge the lump there. "Someone erased your memories of me."

He tugged the high collar of his shirt. "No. Nobody would do that."

"Someone did it to me, too. Please, Mr. Soto, you have to let me pass. I just want to get home." My voice sounded small, like a child's.

"Who?" he demanded. "Who's doing this?"

If I mentioned Happenings, the word would spread. The mob there would explode. "I'm not exactly sure. But it's new. A new tech that uses our Link buds to remove memories."

"That's not possible."

"I didn't think so either. I watched it happen." A sudden panic gushed through me, shoving words out of my mouth. "You have to warn people. Tell them not to touch their Link buds, or an SLS."

The doubt on his face killed any hope. He wouldn't tell anyone if he didn't believe me.

And judging by his change in expression, doubt had turned to suspicion.

He stepped forward to block the stairs again. I leaped, skipping the last four steps and landing hard on the ground. Before he'd registered I was past him, I bolted down the street.

"Hey!" Mr. Soto's voice rang out behind me. "Stop!"

His footsteps slapped the pavement behind me. He couldn't keep up. He was too old, too fat. My house bounced in my vision. Couldn't go there. He'd know where I was, drag me out, take my Links, lock me away. My thoughts echoed the pounding of my feet.

Around. Go around the back of the house, pretend to weave down another street. Hide in the backyard.

I raced for the corner, sweeping past my front gate. I chanced a look behind me. Mr. Soto had fallen pretty far behind, but he was still chasing.

And still yelling. The streets were empty, but some of the locked-up houses would have people inside. If anybody else came running, I was toast. Burnt and crispy and memory-less toast.

Mr. Soto disappeared as I rounded the corner. My own low picket fence zipped past me.

Now. I grabbed the fence and vaulted over it in one leap. Trees. There were more of them at the center of the yard, near the gazebo. Far enough in he might not notice my Link buzz. I ran until cool shade fell over me. I dropped to the ground behind a spiny bush.

Grass tickled my nose, and I inhaled the scent of dirt. Had I jumped the fence in time? Had he seen me?

His footsteps clapped nearer. My blood rushed in my ears. I strained to hear the creak of the fence, the sound of him following me.

He cursed and kept running.

I buried my face in the grass and took whistling breaths through my nose. If I opened my mouth, I'd scream. No screaming. I thumped my hand on the grass over and over, beating back the choke of anxiety I still couldn't get away from. Get a grip, Gena. This wasn't over yet. There was one more chance for me, waiting inside the house.

Mom still had the night shift at work. She'd be home right now. Not plugged into an SLS, and with any luck, not plugged into Link buds either.

26

My own dim life should teach me this,
That life shall live for evermore…

—Alfred, Lord Tennyson, *In Memorium XXXIV*

I sagged in relief when the DNA scanner let me into the house. I'd been afraid it would reject me. Or worse, not react at all, like I was a ghost. But the lock clicked, and I entered to the sound of the security bell. The *plink plink plinkplink* of water dripped from the tap in the kitchen.

I eased open Mom's bedroom door. She slept on top of the comforter on a neatly-made bed. For a moment, I watched her breathe. We didn't look much alike. She'd only given me a few nondescript features, like my small upper lip and turned-up nose.

She'd given other things, though. Her love of astronomy. Dad had said I'd inherited her stubbornness too, and her determination to finish anything I started. I had things from her you couldn't see but rippled below the surface.

I tip-toed forward, hating to wake her, but needing her more than I'd ever needed anyone. I reached out to shake her shoulder. She would remember me. Even if no one else did, my mother would remember me. I needed to touch her, to feel that she was real. That I was real.

My fingers brushed the fabric of her shirt. Then they contracted, my hand clenching. Beneath her short blond hair, the tip of a Link bud hung from her ear.

An invisible hand punched my stomach. Air left me in a whoosh.

She had nothing of me. Nothing. Not even my birth. The only one who had that memory, that moment of bringing me into the world. I was no longer her daughter. I wasn't anyone's daughter.

She wouldn't remember teaching me how to find the North Star using the Big Dipper as a guide. She wouldn't remember the grueling reviews she gave me after school. Or letting me pierce my ears when we went shopping for my thirteenth birthday. Or watching my calories for me. I'd never missed her meddling so much.

I backed out of the room and bleakly surveyed the house. It was spotless, as always. No shoes by the door, like at Cora's house. No backpacks or basketballs like at Dom's. There was no sign *I* had ever been here.

My own room held signs, though. I opened my door and stood on the threshold. Neat and tidy and me. Dance shoes in the open closet. The silk Chinese fan on my dresser that had belonged to Grandpa Scott's mother. A holo-picture of me and Cora at the Beach, sticking out tongues colored red and purple by popsicles. Glow-in-the-dark stars in perfect constellations on the ceiling. Hades sunning himself under his heat lamp on my desk.

What would my parents think when someday they realized they weren't entirely sure what was in this room and opened the door? Would it scare them? Or be comforting, filling a void they hadn't realized was so deep?

I closed my door. The weight of forgotteness dragged me to my knees. I was nothing. I was no one. My family didn't know they were my family, and my heart screamed to have them back. I even clutched at my anger toward my dad, holding the pain as proof he was part of my life. I thumped my forehead against the carved Chinese cabinet in the corner.

A memory flowed into me. My mom's remembrance of a moment at their wedding, when my grandparents presented the antique cabinet of Grandpa Scott's as a gift.

I sat up, slapping my palm against the wood. Memories. My mother's favorite, most cherished memories stored in cabinets and knickknacks and priceless collectibles. I wrenched off my gloves and strode through the house, brushing my fingers against everything in sight.

And I was there.

I was in a small red rock on the mantle, hiking to Emerald Lake with my whole family, the only time we'd ever gone to the canyon together. I was in the glass ballet slippers on the side table, dancing in my first recital, complete with pink tutu. I was in a wooden wall hanging, helping my dad carve it when I went through an artistic phase.

The warmth of hope flooded my face. This was still my home. Mom and Dad and Ren were still my family. These memories kept part of me alive for them.

Through my bittersweet moment, a thought nudged into my head. What about everyone else?

Liza Woods was still carrying on with her experiments. Still stealing memories to hide that fact. And now she had a metal monster to spy on the Mementi and steal more memories. I was the only one who knew that.

I tapped my Sidewinder on. Only one person left in the world really knew me. I had no choice but to turn to him now.

Text from Genesis Lee to Kalan Daniel Fox, TDS 10:26:42/5-11-2084
Meet me at Havendale Canyon. I'm sorry for everything.

27

My spirit loved and loves him yet…

—Alfred, Lord Tennyson, *In Memoriam LX*

"Genesis Lee."

Kalan moved a tree branch out of the way and stepped forward. I dabbled my feet in the river, the chilly water a contrast to the sudden heat in my cheeks.

"How many times do I have to tell you not to be sorry?" he said.

"A lot, apparently. I've got a faulty memory." I rubbed a hand across the rock I sat on. Rough particles of weathered stone snagged on the fabric of my glove.

He sat on a rock next to me, resting an arm on his knee. His nearness made my mind yelp in protest, but I didn't move.

"What's wrong?" he asked. "You look…I don't know. Tired."

You'd think it would be freeing, or something. Nobody's former thoughts and opinions of you hanging around your neck.

But being almost the sole bearer of your own existence turned out to be exhausting.

If anyone understood the burden of being forgotten, Kalan did. It had to be the worst joke in the universe that the one person who remembered me was the one person I'd forgotten.

"It was you," I said.

"What was?"

The freezing river gurgled over my ankles and swirled around my toes. Like it wanted to comfort me. "You were the thing I was forgetting, not the Link thief. My dad didn't want me to remember you."

"Your *dad*?" Kalan rubbed his forehead. "He's never even met me."

"He saw you in my memories and took it upon himself to remove you from my life." I couldn't keep the bitterness out. Somehow, it hurt worse now that Dad didn't remember what he'd done.

"I don't..." His eyebrows twitched, gathering and dropping. A look between outrage and pain. "That's completely and totally the worst thing I've ever heard."

I had something else that could top it.

"So." Kalan paused. "Your dad didn't want you to know me. But you're here now, so...do you?"

I could feel the *yes* like a hunger inside me, ready to eat me alive if I parted from him. Was it as strong as my fear of losing him again?

"I need you," I finally said. "I watched the memories you gave me, and we were right. Liza Woods is the Link thief. I can't stop her without help."

By the time I'd explained everything, the sun had shifted into its early-afternoon burn, making our tree's shade irrelevant. I wiped sweat from my forehead. Tendons in Kalan's neck strained.

"I'm so sorry." He leaned toward me, then stopped.

My hand tingled. Touch. Not just any touch, Kalan's touch. I wanted it almost as much as I was afraid of it. I reached a gloved hand toward his. At the last second, I jerked my hand away.

Kalan pulled back, his shoulders dropping the tiniest bit. "It's okay, Gena."

My name sang in my ears and I remembered what it was to be known. All the grief inside me ignited in a sudden flame of rage.

"It doesn't make sense." I hurled a handful of rocks into the river. "Something is *wrong*. Liza shouldn't be able to use her SLS the way she does. Just erasing the memories, sure. But how is she accessing the info from the Link buds and the SLS grid? It's all Mementi memories. I don't even get why she wanted that in the first place. It's not like she's getting any money out of it."

"Sure she is," Kalan said. "She could have access to Ascalon's research, if your dad gave her the hookups. That gives her better stuff to sell. Plus, having Ren steal Links was a clumsy way to cover her tracks. If she can monitor everybody, then erase their memories, she can do basically anything she wants."

"But that can't be the first reason she wanted to create it. She didn't even know it could erase memories until Dad's attempt to fade you out screwed up. And why is my Dad working with her? How did he get involved with something like this?" I yanked at the scarf around my neck, and it pulled tight around my throat. "We still don't have all the pieces and I don't have a clue what to do next."

"We'll figure it out. I'm with you no matter what."

I could see why I liked this boy so much.

Behind us, tires skid across gravel. Someone pulling into the little-used parking lot—fast. Kalan and I spun.

"Stay here," he said, crouching. "It could be anyone."

I stood. The parking area was out of sight. "It's probably just—"

Kalan flung a hand out to stop me. "The town was ready to detonate when I left. They must have stopped the trams by now. It's probably people looking to get out of there, but I don't want to take chances."

He crept up the rocky bank. Then he shouted.

"Dad!"

His panicked tone set off springs in my legs. I bolted up the bank after him.

A nonautomatic car with sun-bleached paint glinted in the empty parking lot. A small group bunched next to it. I recognized Elijah's top bald, back-ponytail look from Kalan's Memo. There were two other semifamiliar faces—Anabel, looking tinier than she had in Kalan's memory, and Joss, who looked angrier.

And Kalan's sister, Rachelle. She slumped against the car, a streak of red smeared down her left arm.

"I'm fine," she protested to Kalan. I skidded up behind him, panting.

He held her arm, examining the gash near her shoulder. "What happened, Rachelle, who did this?"

"It was my fault." Elijah put an arm around Rachelle, on the verge of tears. She leaned into him. "It's for real this time, an actual riot. People are vandalizing trams, looting buildings, attacking each other. We only wanted to talk to our members who'd joined in. It's not the Lord's way, all this violence…"

He took a shaky breath. "We got out of the car to talk to Gabe, and Rachelle nearly got trampled by the crowd. The hospital's a nightmare. Since you said you were meeting Gena here, we thought it'd be our safest bet."

I eyed Joss and Anabel. Had they been among those Elijah had convinced away from the fighting?

"Don't even say it, Memental," Joss snapped. "I was trying to get Anabel out of town, and Elijah found us on the road."

Anabel peered at me from under a tangle of blonde hair. Her heavily lined eyes looked tired. "Hm, what's that I hear? Nothing? Nothing at all coming from Gena? Guess you should apologize, then, Joss. Especially for that nasty name-calling."

His sharp widow's peak angled down as he glared at Anabel. She smiled at him like an expectant child. After a moment, he muttered something unintelligible.

"Good as we're gonna get." Anabel fluttered over to me. "How've you been? Probably not so great, maybe I shouldn't ask."

"I'm…fine." It felt strange to be remembered by this girl. For a moment, I envied her the security of having memories stored in an untouchable place.

"She's not fine." Kalan glanced up from dabbing at Rachelle's bleeding arm with a handkerchief. She pushed him away, wincing. "Gena's lost her memories again, and now every Mementi in town have lost their memories of her. They don't even know she exists."

Rachelle gasped, her head lifting from her father's shoulder. Anabel's eyes rounded and she clapped her hands to her mouth. Joss crossed his arms, his hard expression fading.

"Oh, Gena," Elijah said, the grief in his eyes compounding.

Their pity was like a shot of gasoline to my anger. In a tight voice, I said, "Let's go to the pavilion. We should get out of the heat, and there's a vending machine if we want food."

We gathered under the shade of the wooden roof. Anabel tied Kalan's handkerchief around Rachelle's arm. It had finally stopped bleeding. The cut would probably scar without stitches, but physical scars couldn't compare to the mental ones Liza Woods could create.

Liza was still kicking back at Happenings, waiting to vanish memories like a song fading to silence. I had to bring her down.

And destroy the SLS. Preferably while inflicting as much pain as possible. I motioned Kalan aside.

"I've got to get back to town."

He nodded. "I'll see if we can borrow Dad's car."

"You don't have to come." *Please say you'll come.* "What about your sister?"

"She doesn't need me right now," Kalan said. "You do. I'm not letting you fight Liza alone."

"How do you know I plan on fighting?"

He laughed softly. "Because you always fight. Hiding your memories in me. Chasing down Jackson for clues when you knew what he could do to you. Showing up to meet me after you forgot me. Being here now after what happened this morning. That's you fighting. And that's why you need me, right? To fight with you."

My heart won out over my fractured memory. I reached toward him, brushing gloved fingertips against his knuckles. His hands opened, reaching for mine. My fingers drew back.

"Thank you for knowing me so well," I whispered. "I wish I could return the favor."

"Hey lovebirds," Rachelle called. "You going to eat with us or not?"

My face warmed. Kalan's sister grinned at us, holding her injured arm. Joss rolled his eyes, and Anabel waggled her eyebrows at me. Elijah, who had an armful of snacks from the vending machine, winked at his son.

A wink.

The domino effect hit me for the second time in two days. I gasped with the force of memories colliding.

Drake Matthews, winking at me before dinner with my parents, emphasizing his uneven cheekbones.

Liza Woods, winking at me after she stole my life, highlighting a face as unbalanced as Matthews'.

Liza's words about my father: *Well, not exactly working for me...but yes.*

Mom and Mrs. Harward, getting Chameleon treatments, their faces changing.

Faces changing.

"I don't believe it," I whispered.

"What?" Kalan said, alarmed.

"Have any of you had a Chameleon treatment done?" I demanded, marching toward the table. "Please tell me someone has."

Anabel raised her hand, wiggling her fingers. "Never had one done. God gave me the face He wanted me to have, you know? But I work at a spa. I'm being trained to give them."

"What do you know about them? Anything technical?"

"A little. I have to explain the details to customers." Her eyes closed, and she continued like she was reciting something. "It's an injection that uses a cocktail of protein enhancers and synthetic DNA to target different types of skin cells so they act younger. It doesn't take the place of your own DNA, it simply masks itself over certain portions so you look younger for a period of time."

"So it's a trick, basically," I said. "They trick the cell into interpreting the younger DNA and showing that on your face."

Anabel nodded. "It only lasts two to four weeks, though. When the cells die, they don't make new ones with the fake DNA."

"Makes sense. The synthetic DNA really is a mask, so when the cells go through mitosis, they're still using your real DNA."

"What are you talking about?" Joss asked. "What does this have to do with anything?"

I ignored him. "Kalan, it's *Drake Matthews*. The head memory researcher at Ascalon BioTech. He's pretending to be Liza Woods, using Chameleon treatments with her DNA to mask his features so he looks like her. He must've . . . done something to the real Liza Woods, so he could take her place and use the resources at Happenings for the live experiments."

Elijah paused in handing out the snacks. The rustling of packages stopped.

"How—what?" Kalan sank onto one of the picnic benches. "That's crazy."

Matthews' weird feminine motions at dinner. Liza's melodramatic, over-compensated girliness at the lab. All the awkwardness of her body and face. It was a charade, and Matthews was a crappy actor. He just had a decent costume.

"I knew something was off with that whole sickness ruse of Liza's," I said. "The Chameleon treatments are only skin deep, that's why she looks so weird. Why he had to spread around that she was sick."

"That's an interesting thought," Elijah said mildly, "but it's a little hard to swallow. Why would Mr. Matthews want to do that when he has his own lab at Ascalon?"

"Because it's *illegal,*" I said. "His own father helped make it illegal to directly study our brains or Links. It would be impossible to experiment on live subjects at Ascalon, they'd crucify him if he tried. But he's been working on making Mementi memory backups forever. It makes sense that he could only get so far without actually studying actual Mementi neurology. And when 'Liza' told me my Dad was working for her, but that he wasn't really working for *her*, it's true. My dad works at Ascalon with Matthews, who's using Chameleon treatments to pretend he's Liza Woods so he can use Happenings to do unsanctioned experiments without getting caught."

I drew a breath, almost dizzy from rambling out my revelations. And Dad. A tiny wave of relief licked at my heart. He wasn't a spy. He hadn't betrayed our whole Mementi world.

Just me.

"I don't see how he could be working as a CEO of one company and research head at another," Kalan said doubtfully.

"Liza's been 'sick,' remember? Ren said she's hardly been into the office except after hours. And I heard a report that Matthews has been missing days at his lab, too. He had easy access to Cham treatments at Ascalon, and he had perfect excuses for why he was never around."

"Okay, I guess I could sort of see that," Kalan said. "Except, where's the real Liza Woods, then?"

I swallowed.

"You think he *killed* her?" Anabel squeaked.

"I don't know. But I know that the Liza Woods I met at Happenings today is not the real one."

Kalan's forehead bore so many creases he looked like an old man. "How did you figure all this out?"

"I met him," I said. "Matthews, at my parent's house, last week. Liza used his same phrases, seemed to know things about me even though she'd never met me. And there's this thing that happens sometimes, in my head, where memories all link together and I can see the bigger—"

Kalan cocked his head.

"Forget it. The point is, Matthews kept winking at me all night. And Liza winked at me this morning. I can see the winks, side by side in my head. It emphasizes their facial structure, and both

Matthews and Liza have these weird uneven cheekbones. Under the skin, they're the same person. Literally."

The two faces flashed in my head as I spoke, my brain analyzing bone shapes and tiny muscle movements. Chameleon treatment couldn't touch bone. I could see Matthews in Liza Woods' face: the small forehead, the pointed nose, those cheekbones. Something filled out Matthews' face, though. Muscle tissue, maybe, or fat. He looked too much like Liza for it to just be a skin change.

"I swear, Kalan," I said. "If you could see it in my memories, you'd know what I mean."

He frowned. Joss shook his head. Rachelle had her head on the table, eyes closed. Anabel stroked her hair, humming slightly off-key. They wouldn't understand unless they could see my memory.

I dug into my bag, pulling out the second Memo Kalan had given me. The one of all our days together.

"How do I record onto this?" I asked.

"You want to put one of *your* memories on here?" Kalan gaped at me.

"You've got to see it."

He shook his head and pressed a button along the top of the Memo. A thin string, like fishing twine, slid out next to his finger.

"Hold this up to your tear duct and push this button again. It ejects nano-recorders along your optic nerve. You think of the memory you want and the recorders find it. They bring it back to the filament and save it as a digital copy."

"Are you kidding me? You inject things into your *brain*?"

"You can't feel it, they're microscopic. It's totally sterile, and the nano-recorders decompose if they accidentally get left."

Not a huge deal. I was only sharing a memory in the first place. Shooting little bee-bees into my head to record my private information. No worries. "Okay."

Kalan held out the string. "Will this work on you? I mean, your memories aren't in your brain."

"My brain is connected to my Links if I'm consciously re-membering things," I said. "It'll work."

Hopefully.

I grabbed the string and held it to my tear duct.

"Hold still," Kalan said. "Here goes."

I didn't feel a thing. "Did you push it?"

"Give it a minute. Think of those memories."

I called up the images again. Matthews and Liza, winking at me. I held them in all their photographic clarity: eyelids drop-ping, emphasizing those identical low left cheekbones. I clenched my teeth until my jaw ached.

There was a small beep. Kalan said, "Okay. All done. You can let go of the wire."

I opened my fingers. The wire zipped inside the Memo. "Play it."

Kalan motioned to his father and tapped the screen. The two of them huddled over the Memo for a few moments before Kalan lowered it.

"It could be, I guess," he said.

It could be? That's all I was going to get from him?

"It's hard for us to say," Elijah said. "Your brain makes quicker connections than ours. Granted, this doesn't look like Liza Woods. It doesn't really look like Drake Matthews, either."

"Isn't it obvious?" I snatched the Memo and watched it play. "The short forehead, the pronounced brow ridge, and here, their off-center cheekbones…"

I frowned at the Memo. Exhibit A why memory tech still couldn't hold its own with Links. It wasn't obvious, not on a screen. Something had gotten lost in the transfer. Even my quick-thinking brain had a hard time seeing what I could see in my own head.

I laid the Memo on the table. Joss snatched it.

"I promise, if you could see it the way I do, you'd understand."

Elijah closed his eyes, fingering a small cross around his neck.

Kalan's eyes caught mine. "I believe you, Gen."

I wanted to hug him. I took an instinctive step back.

Elijah cleared his throat. "The Lord looketh on the heart," he said. "And maybe He can see your mind, too. I'm going to trust you on this one."

Joss tossed the Memo to the table with a clatter, startling Rachelle. She glared at Joss before laying her head down again. Anabel glanced at the Memo, but made no move to pick it up.

"This is a total joke," Joss said. "What would we do with this, if it was true?"

"This could be huge," Kalan said. "If we can show everyone Matthews is impersonating Liza Woods, and that he's behind the Link thefts, it's all over. The thefts, maybe even the rioting."

"We don't know that Liza Woods is behind the Link thefts," Joss said.

"Actually, we do," I said. "Or at least I do. I have memories that can prove it."

Joss crossed his arms. "Even then, people aren't going to take a wink and some facial similarities as evidence this guy is cross-dressing."

I wanted to growl at him for being right. "We'll need real proof. A memory of him changing from one person to another."

"Memories aren't *real proof*," Joss said.

"They are in a Havendale court, if they come from a Mementi."

"Well, whoop-de-do, but that's not going to do it for the rest of the world. If he's using injections with Liza Woods' DNA, that's hard proof right there. That's what you really need."

I forced back a retort that what we really needed was him to stop being nasty. Joss was a pain. A smart pain with a tongue as sharp as his hairline.

"Fine. We need a syringe of the DNA too."

"So where do we start?" Kalan asked. "Matthews' house?"

"No," I said immediately. "He's getting them from Ascalon some-how, but I doubt he'd keep them there, either. Extras would be locked up somewhere really secure. He'd keep a few injections on him. That's what we need to aim for, but he's been at Happenings all day as Liza."

Kalan grinned. "Looks like we get to break into Happenings after all."

"What?" His words caught me off guard. "No way can we break into that place."

"Sure we can," he said. "You told me your friend had some kind of hack for the door locks. Happenings has everything we need. Matthews, the syringes, and that memory machine. The SLS. We have to take that out too, so it can't be used against you anymore."

"I *know*." I thumped my elbows on the table and gripped my scarf. "But it's not possible. Kinley's hack for the DNA locks only worked once. House locks are all connected to a city-wide sys-tem, and it's programmed to adapt. Happenings would have its own system outside the city-based one, but the best we could hope for is that the hack would get us into the building. We'd never get through any of the internal doors."

"Stupid plan anyway," Joss said. "We need simple."

Kalan and I both turned to Joss in surprise.

"What do you mean, 'we'?" Kalan asked.

"You two, taking on the entire town plus Liza-Woods-slash-Matthews alone?" Joss brushed a hand over the stubble on his head. "Like you said, we take down the thief, we stop the riots. Better than me smacking people's heads together until they wise up and stop hurting each other."

So. Beneath the rude exterior, Joss actually cared about people. In a weird, harsh sort of way.

"What's your simple plan, then?" I asked.

"Ambush Matthews outside Happenings, take one of his syringes, and go to the cops. That's all we really need."

"It's not all we need," I said. "Memories are key in a Mementi court. I have to get one of him switching to make sure he gets locked up for good."

Joss snorted. "A syringe full of somebody else's DNA in a Chameleon solution wouldn't be hard enough proof? Sounds like the Mementi justice system is a joke."

I opened my mouth.

"Okay, cool it, folks." Elijah held up a hand. "The point is, a syringe won't prove who the DNA was meant for. And it won't stop the riots, not soon enough. We need the shock value Gena's memory of Matthews can provide."

I nodded. "Especially if we pair it with my other memories that prove he's the Link thief."

"So what, we catch him in the shower?" Kalan said. "Not sure how I feel about that."

"He's been at Happenings all day as Liza," I said. "But my sister heard on the news that he's holding some sort of press conference. He's got to change from Liza to himself sometime before seven o'clock tonight."

"He could do it anywhere," Elijah said.

I rubbed my eyes with the heel of my hands. Happenings was the only place we knew for sure when and where Matthews would be. The only place we could stop both him and the SLS—and the riots. My fingers clenched at my forehead.

"Gena." Kalan sounded thoughtful. "Liza had her own private car, remember? With the trams down, it's the only way to get to Ascalon. Which means he'd have to get—"

My head jerked up. "To the parking garage."

A slow smile spread over his face. "It's the one place we know he'll be. If we can get inside, we ambush her—him—jeez, this is weird—anyway, we get everything we need. We use his Liza-self to get through the door locks and take out the SLS, inject Matthews with his own Chameleon treatment for Gena's memory, and then scram with a syringe that's got traces of Liza's DNA."

Joss opened his mouth like he wanted to protest, then shut it. Elijah rubbed the back of his neck.

A tingle of excitement set my fingers drumming on the table. "That's actually not bad. It could work."

He grinned. "I told you I'm pretty smart, even without that memorized encyclopedia." His high, happy eyebrows dipped for a moment. Like something had hurt him.

"Okay," Elijah said. "That's our plan then."

"Almost," said Joss. "This is gonna be dangerous. I don't think Gena should be going, or Kalan. They're just kids."

My smoldering temper flared, burning up any scrap of politeness I might have had left. "How old do you think I am? You're like two years older than me. We *need* a Mementi memory of Matthews transforming. I can upload it to a Memo for the Populace, but the Mementi won't go for it if it's from one of you. If I get to the SLS, I can use it to upload my memories directly to everyone who's plugged in."

My stomach turned in protest. It would be jarring. Violating, to force my memory into everyone's heads. But it was the only way to shock them enough to stop killing each other, and I could make sure it would never be done again. And even if I could never restore everyone's memories of me, at least I could make sure they wouldn't continue to forget me.

"I'm not a kid, either," Kalan added. "I'll stick close to Gena. She'll need a bodyguard."

Joss leaned back, hands behind his head. "Kal, I keep waiting for you to outgrow the arrogant twerp stage. You think me and Elijah couldn't protect her as well as you?"

"Hello?" I waved my hands in irritation. "Who says I need protection more than anyone else? I'm a lot stronger than I look." Ballet had that handy side-effect.

"Are you sure you want to do this?" Elijah said to me. "The worst they could do to any of us is lock us up. But you…"

If we got caught, Matthews could snatch my Links. Wipe me clean like a slate. A flutter of panic threatened to close my throat, and I tapped my toe against the floor.

I dug for my anger. Think of Liza's laughter as Ren left me behind at Happenings. Think of Drake Matthews sitting in my home mere days before he took it away from me.

My fingers rolled into fists. "I'm in."

28

To-night the winds begin to rise…

—Alfred, Lord Tennson, *In Memoriam XV*

Joss and Elijah rode up front in the car, Kalan and I in the back. Anabel stayed in the canyon with Rachelle.

We sped through the streets. Even in the deserted areas, the city seethed with wrath. The jagged edges of smashed windows bared teeth at us. Slashes of black spray-paint on a red front door cut the word FREAK into my brain. Scorch marks seared the white tower of Mr. and Mrs. Gibbs' lighthouse home.

The Gibbs. Among the last of the first generation. Lives already ravaged by trauma, only to be ravaged again. Hopefully they'd made it to the safety of the Arts Center next to Zahra's studio. Kalan was giving me updates from my Link buds, and he said a lot of Mementi had gathered there and set up guards at the doors.

Elijah slammed on the brakes for the fourth time. My head snapped forward and Joss swore.

A line of black-clothed, helmeted police marched down the street. A rush of Populace protesters surged away from the homes they were trashing. One man whipped a long metal pole forward. It careened toward the cops like a javelin. I gasped, about to call out a warning, but the pole clanged to the street. Narrow miss.

Crack. A flash of light and smoke erupted in front of the crowd. Smoke billowed, voices shrieked, bodies writhed, and hands flailed. Like hell was birthed beneath the hot sun. I clapped my hands to my ears.

"Go around, take a right," Joss said. The car screeched backward. We'd never get there in time, not with all the detours the riot was forcing on us.

I tapped the quick-time button on my Sidewinder and bit my lip. According to news reports, Drake Matthews would be unveiling "dramatic new technology" tonight. It couldn't be the SLS—that was at Happenings, and he wouldn't play that hand in public. But the only "dramatic" thing that would pull the Mementi away from these riots was the longed-for memory backup. The hope that sneaked into my heart terrified me. What would be the cost, if Matthews really had the backup? And would I be willing to pay it?

I'd know soon enough. Matthews was due at Ascalon BioTech headquarters within the hour.

But the people swarmed like termites, eating the city alive. I banged my head on the back of the car seat. *Go home! You have children to comfort and dinner to eat and plants to water. Go home and be human.* People flashed past the car window. A Populace man wielding a large hammer led a group the same direction we headed, toward the city center.

I told myself the glint of red on the hammer was my imagination.

The truth might not stop this. It wasn't about the Link thefts anymore. It was about what a few Populace had done to some Mementi, and what a few Mementi had done in retaliation. It was about the Memoriam crumbling to ash with the remains of our relatives, and the Populace old man who was beaten while walking his dog last night, and the twelve Mementi students hospitalized and the teacher killed when a group tried to destroy the SLS systems during school. How did we get so out of control?

Heat seared my veins. I wanted to sweep through town. Force them to look into each other's faces and see humanity. But even when you could share memories, you could never share the way you saw the world.

"We're almost there," Kalan said.

The ranks of rioters swelled around us again—Mementi, this time. I knew their faces, except I didn't know their faces. All I'd ever seen were masks of politeness, and they'd shed those. Was this twisting fury really who they were, or was it just another mask? A horror mask, one that would frighten them when they took it off and saw what they had become?

A shower of thunks and clinks thundered on the roof of the car. Outside, people picked up sticks and rocks from the desert landscapes of nearby houses, hurling them at us. No cops gathered to stop them.

As suddenly as it started, the hail of debris stopped. Which seemed oddly ominous. I craned my neck to see what caused the cease-fire.

Ahead of us, another car approached. Olive green, with dark tinted windows. A horde of people tailed it, racing after it and chucking rocks. Our own attackers abandoned us for fresh meat.

"Oh no." Kalan grabbed the seat in front of him. "Oh no, that's him."

"It can't be." My body went limp. "It can't be, we're so close."

"That's his car. Or maybe Liza's car, I don't know. We saw it at Happenings."

The other car sped up and passed us. Rioters converged on it, forcing it to slow again. Rocks crunched against metal. Red-headed Mrs. Downing picked up a metal shard that had fallen from a broken tram and beat at the windshield.

We were too late. Our targets—Matthews and the SLS—had separated. We couldn't get inside Happenings without him. Even if we did, without solid proof that Matthews was Liza, he could just rebuild what we destroyed. We might never stop him.

"Out, now!" I shoved Kalan toward the door.

"What?" The other two men turned to look at me.

"Matthews is the priority, we've got to beat him to Ascalon if we want a chance at him."

"They'll eat us alive out there!" Joss cried.

"We'll only get through this crowd before he does if we run," I said.

Kalan nodded. "We can use the chaos to blow right by them."

"Okay, then God help us," Elijah hollered. "Count of three, and we all go at once. One!"

Breathe in, breathe out. I slowed the rhythm, trying to control the shaking in my legs.

"Two!"

Elijah slammed the brakes. We all rocked forward.

"Three!"

The car doors flew open and we tumbled out. Shouts and sirens and bodies crunching together assaulted my ears. We sped past the car, headed the few blocks to Ascalon headquarters. In the frenzy over the other car, no one noticed us.

The glittering, steel-swathed glass globe of Ascalon BioTech rose ahead of us. Underground parking garage. Around the east side. We were so close.

A thrashing mass of Mementi protestors stood in our way, joining ranks with the riot police. I forced my legs forward. Maybe if we ran faster…

The rioters attacked.

Joss and Elijah struggled with the mob, lost in a blur of fists and shouts. Mementi, *hitting* people. The shock made me trip over my own feet. Kalan grabbed my hand, steadying me. We forced our way through the fighting crowd. A fist grazed my shoulder. I tucked my head down and ran. My blood raced, singing a song of urgency. Move, get out, run.

Someone bashed into Kalan, ripping his hand from mine. He rolled across the pavement. A figure jumped on top of him, fists flying toward Kalan's face. I did the last thing I ever expected of myself.

I punched the guy in the side of the head.

He pitched to the side, falling to his back. I cradled my throbbing fist.

"*Dom*?" I gasped.

He stumbled to his feet, his eyes empty of recognition. With a roar, he lunged at me.

Kalan reached for my hand. We darted into the crowd, weaving until Dom was out of sight.

Ascalon drew closer, the inner gardens that ringed each floor now visible. Outside, bushes circled the building, low enough not to detract from the view. Round the building, to the west. Ahead, bouncing in my vision, stood a line of police guarding the ramp to the garage entrance.

Should've thought of that.

"Gena, stop," Kalan shouted. He jerked me to a halt.

The guards eyed us, batons and shields blocking our path. Shouts behind us caught my attention. A mass of bodies barreled toward us—and the police line. Populace, this time.

"We have to go," I said.

"Wait, we need them a little closer."

Closer?

"Okay, go!"

We dashed toward the line of police with their thick shields and thicker black batons. Voices screeched in my ears. The ground thundered beneath me with the rush of so many feet. I counted it out like the pattern of a drum beat, trying to force back the panic swelling inside me.

The police rushed forward, batons swinging. The glancing blow of a baton on my shoulder sent sparks across my vision. I hunkered low, shoving through a narrow gap between bodies. A gunshot sounded. Let it be a rubber bullet. A familiar crack, and the spark of a smoke bomb. I gasped a breath and held it. A whiff of smoke tickled my nose.

I ducked. I ran. I whirled under outstretched arms and swayed around swinging sticks. My hand tore from Kalan's, then found him again. The cops rained their blows down, a cacophonous drum beat. It felt less like fighting and more like a mad dance of desperation.

We sped down the ramp and dived into the shade of a large bush by the garage entrance. Smoke and rage blinded the cops and the mob. We were either unnoticed or forgotten.

I collapsed, sandwiched between the building's concrete foundation and the bush. Dirt cooled my arms through my gloves. Branches poked at my heaving shoulders like woody fingers checking me for injuries. I adjusted the Links under my shirt, my fingers sliding along each bead. All intact.

"No one else?" I panted. "No one's coming?"

"Just us," Kalan said through heavy breaths. "I think."

"Where's your dad?" I wheezed. "And Joss?"

"Cops grabbed Dad. Joss tried to stop them. I didn't see what happened, but I'm sure they got him too."

Arrested, bad. Arrested by cops who weren't much better than mobbers themselves, terrifying. "What if they…"

"Dad wasn't fighting. I think they'll just haul him away. Hopefully Joss won't fight so hard that they'll hurt him." Kalan rubbed his nose. "They'll be okay. Are you okay?"

"Yeah," I said. "Good thinking. With the crowd."

He sat next to me, his lanky legs engulfed by the bush. "I figured if it worked once, it might work again."

"Worked once?" I sat up.

He paused. "You didn't watch all of the new Memo I gave you, did you?"

I rubbed the sore shoulder that had caught the police baton. "Not all of it," I whispered.

Another pause. "Right before we saw Liza in the parking garage at Happenings, we did something similar. I put it in the Personal memories, though. I didn't want . . . what happened after to upset you."

The guilt of cowardice shrunk my heart. It wasn't that I didn't want to know our history. I just couldn't take any more pain right now.

"I'm sorry."

"No sorries, Gen. I split up the memories on purpose."

He'd wanted me to have a choice. To decide what I wanted to remember about the relationship we'd built. I touched his face, smeared with blood and dirt from tumbling on the pavement.

A distant car engine hummed. The garage next to us screeched open. Drake Matthews had made it through the crowd.

"Okay." I rose to a crouch. "We don't know if he'll look like Liza or himself. Either way, we can swipe one of his Cham treatments and inject him right in the garage."

Anabel said the effects were almost immediate, but they left you weak for a period of time while your body adjusted to the change. We should have plenty of time to watch him morph and scram with an extra Chameleon treatment.

I'd seen Hades slough off layers of skin before. I had a feeling watching a human being do it would be un-enjoyable to the extreme.

Sunlight flashed on metal. The now-battered green car zipped into the garage.

"Go!" Kalan said.

We leaped over the bush. The garage door creaked down. I had to duck, but we made it through without much trouble.

Until a pair of hands grabbed me.

I screamed and tried to wrench myself away. My injured shoulder sent a shock of pain that curled my fingers. Hands tightened around my waist. Kalan wrestled with an Ascalon security guard a few feet away.

"What's going on?" a voice called.

My vision hazed red in fear. I knew that voice.

"Found two intruders," my guard called out.

"Gena, run!" Kalan's muffled voice rose from the pavement where the guard held him face down. "Forget his Cham injection, just run!"

For a split second, I wished the guard had gagged that big mouth.

Someone stepped out of the car.

"Why, Genesis Lee," Matthews crooned. "Fancy seeing you here."

He smiled, wide as Liza Woods, and winked at me.

29

O heart, how fares it with thee now,
That thou shouldst fail from thy desire…

—Alfred, Lord Tennyson, *In Memoriam IV*

"We are so stupid!" I hissed as we marched down a hallway in handcuffs. A holo-projection of a trendy, professional woman glided along the wall next to us, chirping about the many life-improving technologies Ascalon had to offer.

"Gena—" Kalan started.

"No, we were stupid! We should have known he'd have guards!"

I wrenched my arms in their handcuffs. The guard holding the cuff chain grunted as his finger twisted in it. Good. He deserved it for being such an idiot that he didn't know the man he worked for spent half his time masquerading as a Populace.

We'd rushed into the city, thrown ourselves into a brawl, and all we got for it was caught. And now Matthews knew that we knew who he was.

Because we were so *stupid*.

The guard shoved us into some kind of private lounge room and I got a look at him for the first time.

It was Detective Jackson.

Of course it was.

"We'll hold you in here for a bit. Matthews is doing the press conference now, but wants to question you afterward," Jackson said. His voice was softer than his motions, almost apologetic. The light of full recognition glinted in his eyes.

"You remember me?" I asked, startled.

He frowned. "Of course."

"But your Link bud…"

The tip of a Link bud poked from one of his ears. Proof that he was more than just a pawn.

My lips quivered in anger. "Your Link buds aren't connected to that SLS. You're in on the disappearances, the Link thefts. Everything."

"How do you know about the machine?" Jackson crouched the tiniest bit, his shoulders hunching like he was ready to spring. "Don't you say a word to anyone. That SLS is worth a few sacrifices. The things we can do with it…it means everything for our future."

"Worth a few sacrifices? Like me? He erased me, Jackson." I looked into his face that had so much presence in my Links. "He wiped out every memory of me from every mind in the city."

Jackson reeled back like I'd hit him. "He what? When?"

"Today."

He rubbed his forehead, then turned away. His uniform pulled over taut shoulders. "Gena, I—I'm so sorry, I didn't know.

I swear, I didn't, I would never…" He spun, stepping toward me. "This is insane, it's exactly why I'm involved. Matthews is the only one with the know-how to pull this off, but he's nuts, obsessed. I've got to make sure the SLS is used for the right things."

"So you get to decide the 'right thing' for everybody?"

"You don't understand this well enough to lecture me."

Now, where had I heard that before? No wonder he and my dad were best friends.

"That SLS is destroying lives," I said.

"That SLS is *saving* lives," he said. "It's the most important thing we've ever created. We still haven't managed to find a way to duplicate memories—"

I snorted.

Jackson glared. "It's not like hitting 'copy and paste.' But we've found a close substitute. With the research Drake has done, we'll be able to merge our memories without worrying about the taint of another person's mind. Backups, Gena. For people like Cora. Merge memories with others, then use the new SLS to trigger the brain to see it from our point of view. No danger, no side effects."

He clasped his hands, shaking them at me slightly. "There are so many applications. Wouldn't you give anything to be with your grandmother again?"

I blinked, sickened by the realization that I no longer knew if I wanted that. I wanted her as I remembered her, but she wasn't who I remembered. "What does that have to do with it? An SLS can't raise the dead."

He leaned forward, excitement lighting his face. "It can . . . sort of. We could take the memories of the dead and make them part of us. With us all the time."

"Merge memories with the *dead*?" I gaped at him. "Is that what you want out of this?"

I couldn't imagine anyone going for that idea. Just because I liked to visit the Memoriam didn't mean I wanted Grandma living inside my head. Especially now.

Except the Memoriam was gone, Grandma lost. If I had the chance, would I save her memories from the flames by taking them into me? My chest contracted with the pain of losing her again, and I didn't know. Whether or not her memories had burned, I'd lost her when I learned she wasn't who I thought she was.

I swallowed. It wasn't her fault. I couldn't blame her for it, it wasn't fair to her.

She wasn't fair to me.

I crushed the voice in my head. Not going to think about it.

"We can be truly connected to the ones we've lost." Jackson's arms drifted to his sides, fingers splayed like he could take an invisible hand. "We'd never have to say goodbye again. At least not really. We could learn from them even after they're gone, entwine their lives with ours. Think how much more we could grow. It's a kind of immortality, Gena, a kind only the Mementi can have. They could continue to live through us. And then we could live through others."

Bile scalded my throat. Grandma couldn't fix her past or build her future through memory. Memory might live on, but *she* was gone. As perfect as our memories were, they were only a remembrance of things we'd done, choices we'd made. This, now, was where I did the things I would remember. This, now, was what counted.

Jackson was like some kind of misguided memory necromancer. Who had he lost that hurt him enough to pursue something so revolting? My memories cobbled together conversations I'd heard over the years. His mother. One of the many first generation suicides when Jackson was eleven.

"You'll understand someday," he said. "When you've lost someone that matters to you."

I'd lost everyone that mattered to me. And they had lost me.

Jackson turned to leave.

"Hey, can we get the handcuffs off?" Kalan demanded, his intense look in place. "We're locked up in here anyway."

Jackson's nostrils flared, but he unlocked our handcuffs. I rubbed my wrists through my gloves and Jackson left. A DNA lock beeped.

I plunked myself into one of the high-backed chairs around a coffee table made from a giant, polished tree stump. Not the right kind of chair for lounging; it forced me to sit up straight. With a huff, I stood and paced. Pathways wound through actual gardens with thick, black dirt and leafy plants. Obnoxiously cheery holo-pictures of various scientists giving "thumbs up" next to their completed projects adorned the walls. Swooping steel beams outside created bars of shadows through the room. I pushed aside the branches of a small tree and peered outside. Tenth floor, and this was solid glass, not windows.

Kalan collapsed onto a yellow half-moon sofa surrounded by ferns. "If he keeps us locked in this room forever, I call the couch."

Despite the forced lightness in his tone, his face was locked in a worried position.

I shook my head. "He'll take us to Happenings. I'll become his newest comatose memory experiment, and you…"

I swallowed, wondering what had happened to the real Liza Woods. I had a feeling any Populace who got in Matthews' way would go the same way she did.

"I won't let them do that to you," Kalan growled. "I'll get us out of here."

I wouldn't let them do anything to him, either.

Kalan prowled the room, banging lightly on the thick glass and checking closets and cupboards. While he made his second futile circle, my brain clicked into action. Our phones had been taken. Elijah and Joss were in jail, with no idea we'd been captured. We had no one but ourselves. I pulled up a hundred memories a minute. Everything I knew about Matthews, everything Ren had told me, everything I knew about Happenings and Ascalon. There had to be a way out of this. If there wasn't, I'd make one.

"This could work," I murmured.

"Huh?" Kalan paused in his examination of the lofty, inaccessible ceiling.

"This could work, Kalan." I sat on the tree-stump table, leaning back on my arms. "Think about it. If Matthews takes us to Happenings, which I'm like 99 percent sure he will, we'll be exactly where we wanted to go in the first place."

"Yeah, but we planned on taking him prisoner, not entering as prisoners ourselves."

"But we'll at least be there. And we won't be able to get in through the front doors with all the rioters there."

"Happenings is equipped with a great number of back doors," Kalan said dryly.

Smart-aleck. "Exactly. They'll be employee entrances, with DNA-encrypted locks. He'll have to change to Liza to get through them." Unless he thought to use a drop of Chameleon treatment on the scanner.

Kalan leaned on the table next to me. "A memory of him changing won't do much good if we're comatose in the basement."

I dropped from the table. "So we just give up?"

"Jeez, Gena, I didn't mean that." He ran a hand through his hair. "We don't have many options if he takes us to Happenings."

The sound of the DNA lock made me turn. Matthews, smiling like a charming uncle, entered the room.

"Ah, right where I hoped to find you," he said. "There's someone I'd like you to meet."

A voice chattered excitedly from the hallway. "I can't believe it, Drake! It's not perfect, but using this new SLS to share memories, then merge them back to us as a copy . . . it's brilliant!"

My father entered the room, beaming like I'd never seen before. I momentarily forgot to breathe.

Kalan put a protective hand on my arm. Dad. He had taken my memories from me, my life. My relationship with Kalan. It served him right that he lost his own memories. I wanted to laugh in his face, but my eyes burned. It wasn't fair. Why did his punishment hurt me more than it did him?

Jackson stalked in and closed the door behind him.

"This is Kierce Lee, one of our esteemed directors," Matthews said. "Kierce, this is Gena and Kalan. They were hoping for a bit of a tour." He winked.

Dad smiled at us, still reveling in Matthews' grand reveal. "Bad day for a tour, I'm afraid. Normally I'd be happy to arrange one for you, but with everything . . . "

Kalan was right. We had to get out of here before Matthews dragged us to his lair. And Dad, whether he remembered me or not, might be our only shot.

I'd sworn I would never talk to him again. But Mementi were nothing if not great liars, even to ourselves.

"We don't want a tour," I said. "We're here against our will."

Dad coughed, his smile fading.

Matthews smoothed his hair, shaking a bit of dry skin onto his shoulders. As unconcerned as a cow in a pasture. Dad would forget this the moment he put in his Link buds.

Control play, then. Matthews was trying to prove how much power he had over me. But the dear mad scientist had overlooked something. Emotional memories had a habit of hanging around.

I stepped toward my father. "My name is Genesis Lee. My parents are Kierce and Hazel. But I'm afraid you've forgotten you have a daughter."

My voice broke on the last word. I'd basically told him in the attic I didn't want to be his daughter anymore. Now, to him, I wasn't. Why couldn't I just hate him and be done with it? Why did it have to hurt so much that my own words came true?

Dad gave a nervous laugh. "I do have a daughter, a few years older than you. I'm sorry, Drake, is she . . . ?"

Matthews smiled. "Oh, she's perfectly sane. A little pet of mine, very odd sense of humor."

Emotion. I had to appeal to his emotions. "You don't remember. Matthews has taken your memories of me. But I'm real, I'm your daughter." *Please, please don't let me cry in front of him.* "I love powdered donuts with raspberry filling, because you always bring them for me after my dance concerts. They're your favorite too."

Another cough. Behind him, Jackson shifted closer to him.

This wasn't fair. I needed to hurt him so he could help me, but despite what he'd done, I didn't want to.

Because it hurt me, too.

"You never understood the way I love the stars, like Mom does," I said. "But when I was thirteen and Mom was working a night shift, I almost slept through a meteor shower I wanted to see. You got up at three in the morning and woke me up. We watched it together in the backyard."

Those meteors flashed in my mind's eye, shooting bright pain through me. Anger couldn't hide the pain when I had to relive the moments where I loved him.

"Stop it," he whispered.

Jackson's neck muscles strained. This was his best friend. And Jackson knew I was telling the truth.

"Please, Dad," I choked out. "Matthews will take us away. He can't let us go now that we know what he's done, who he is. Please help me."

Jackson turned away. Dad's mouth opened and closed. Was he feeling anything? Would he trust that feeling?

He forced a smile. "Well. That's—that's . . . quite the story."

My hope collapsed. Dad wouldn't trust anything he felt if he didn't have memories to back it up. It didn't matter if he forgot me after this or not. He wasn't listening in the first place.

And Matthews knew that. Fury burned the tears from my eyes.

Matthews chuckled from behind me. "Dear Gena, I do believe you've upset the poor man. Tell you what, Kierce, we don't need a tour after all. You mind giving the news reports a listen and sending me an update on reactions to my announcement?"

Dad backed up, nearly bumping into Jackson. "Of course. Right. Nice to, uh, meet you both."

He took another step back, his eyes still fixed on me.

"Kierce," Jackson said quietly.

"Right." Dad left the room, slipping in his Link buds. I watched him go, more angry than sad.

But still a little bit sad.

Jackson flung a hand at the door. "Was that necessary?"

Matthews clucked his tongue. "It is always necessary to establish who is in charge." He nodded to me. "And it was a noble effort, dear, but a lost cause. Kierce is far too good at talking to people and far too busy to listen to them. A little like my own father, actually. Always too strict in his judgments. A bit bitter about his new talents, like so many of the first generation. Bitterness stunts progress, remember that, Gena."

Kalan slid his hand into mine and squeezed it.

Matthews clapped his hands together. "Well, my work here is done for the moment. I've finally given the people what we've been promising for years. Or at least the first stage of it. Now, would you care to join me in a little ride to see how Happenings is fairing?"

He opened the door.

"Cuffs again, please, Jackson." Matthews smiled. "I'll be taking these young people home."

The leer on his face when he said "home" made me shiver. My new home would be a basement lab at Happenings.

Kalan's would probably be a grave.

30

...Dragons of the prime,
That tare each other in their slime,
Were mellow music match'd with him.

—Alfred, Lord Tennson, *In Memoriam LVI*

Havendale looked like a ghost town through the car window. Debris and glass littered the empty sidewalks. Damaged trams leaned on their tracks. Broken chairs and tables decorated the gardens in front of the Low-G Club. Palm fronds waved in the breeze, tossing shadows over the destruction. As for the destructors themselves, they'd vanished.

"The department has cleared a lot of the streets." Jackson sat in the driver's seat with the car on auto-drive, addressing Matthews next to him. He tapped a touchscreen in the center console, his fingers flowing like he played a delicate instrument. A transparent police report lit up the windshield. "Arrested over thirty in the last few hours. Most areas report being calmer. The National Guard has been put on hold unless things heat back up."

"Finally," Matthews said. "This has been ridiculous. I never expected Mementi to fight." He sighed. "Even the backup announcement didn't bring people to their senses as much as I'd hoped."

I played with the Links around my neck. Insanity didn't require a response.

"They're reporting an estimated 30 percent of the Populace left the city, at least temporarily," Jackson said, still scanning the report on the windshield. "No solid count on that, though."

Matthews crossed his arms. "Good. We'll be free to pursue our continued development with less interference."

The car whipped around a corner, and my stomach lurched.

"Development." Kalan snorted. "At the expense of a few comatose lab rats locked up at Happenings."

Matthews turned to face us, annoyed. "Everything comes at the expense of something else. Some things are worth sacrificing for. Even I've had to make sacrifices to be myself as well as Liza." His fingers brushed his paper-thin cheeks.

Wait. Something was wrong. If he was impersonating a Populace... "How have you been hiding your Link buzz as Liza?"

"Ah, very nice attention to detail, Gena." He sounded pleased. "As myself, I keep some nonessential Linked memories in my pocket to create a buzz. Of course, I need my real memories at all times, even as Liza, so I had to find a new material. Something like skin that wouldn't give off a buzz, though without the emotional baggage. I found something similar."

Similar to skin?

"Bone." He lifted an arm so I could see it from the back seat. A white Link bracelet peeked from beneath his cuff.

I recoiled. It couldn't be human bone. He wasn't that depraved. Or maybe he was.

"But what does it do to your memories?" Testing new linking material was dangerous.

"It's similar to metal, actually. It separates physical memory from emotional memory." He shook his wrist. "Helps quite a bit with objectivity."

So that's why he acted so over-the-top. He may have started this plan because he cared about people, but he'd resorted to faking it for the crowd. His life had no more emotional connection. Sounded like a good path to ruthlessness.

"What did you do with her?" I asked. "The real Liza Woods, what happened to her?"

"She's of no concern." His tone was close to snapping. "I thought by working together in secret, combining our knowledge . . . but then she stole the Links from that first poor girl. Idiot woman, thinking she could learn anything from Links alone. She got justice."

"Seeing as you continued the Link thefts," I retorted, "what do you think you deserve?"

"My subjects were volunteers," he said, calm again. "The resulting Link thefts were unfortunate, but they're temporary."

My stolen memories—and the stolen memories of me—were not temporary.

Matthews continued, his tone dark. "I didn't destroy the Links, the way that woman did."

Destroyed Links. Oh, Jacie. She would never have her life back.

Ahead, the white walls of Happenings shone against a backdrop of red cliffs. The grass around it had been ripped apart; red dirt smeared the sidewalks. In the twilight, the shadows of rioters stretched, throwing contorted puppets on Happenings' walls.

People beat at the building, beat at each other, and beat at police. Hundreds of them, both Populace and Mementi.

The shadows twisted into screaming faces streaked with dirt, tears, and blood. They bolted toward us. A group of Populace converged on someone squirming on the ground. A Mementi cop raised her Taser in one hand and lashed out with her club. So much for calming the riots.

Matthews jerked forward in his seat. "What the . . . ?"

Jackson had already synced his Sidewinder to the car speakers. The call connected. "Who's stationed at Happenings?" Jackson asked. "It's a disaster over here."

"The mayor ordered we clear the streets," snapped a voice on the other end. "We had to pull most of the cops from Happenings to do it. Now the nutters are converging on Happenings again."

Jackson slammed a fist on the console. "So call the National Guard in!"

"We did. Won't be here for at least an hour."

"Then send the patrols back this way!"

"We're handling it, Jackson. This isn't your area. But if you can manage to spare a few precious moments, we could *possibly* use a bit more help."

The line went dead. Jackson let out a breath that sounded remarkably like a growl.

Outside, Kinley's youngest sister Rissa dodged around a palm tree. Blonde hair tangled over her terrified face. I raised my cuffed hands to the window. Behind her, a Populace man pulled his arm back, ready to throw.

"Rissa!" I screamed.

A rock hit her in the back. She arched, arms flinging out, and fell to the ground. The man behind her vanished into the crowd. Rissa pulled herself up, sobbing, and rushed away.

"She's okay," Kalan whispered in my ear, his hand on my arm.

"I thought you said the riots were over," Matthews yelled at Jackson. "We can't accomplish anything with this chaos."

"What do you want me to do, Drake?" Jackson barked as we sped around the rear of Happenings. "I'm only a detective, I can't command—"

Thump. I jumped. A woman banged on my window, battering it wildly with both fists. I slid closer to Kalan. People converged on the car, and Jackson was forced to slow down.

We edged through the crowd. Chanting roared around us. A rock crashed into my window. A rush of tingling panic jump-started my heart. They'd kill us before we even left the car. The tingling spread. The feet of a thousand ants, burrowing between layers of skin and muscle.

A vise squeezed my chest. Crushing. They'd crush us. Clubs cracking my bones and fingers gouging my eyeballs and rocks smashing my skull. Exactly what they did outside right now to each other. Sounds from a horror movie surrounded me. The dull thump of wood against flesh, the rolling crunch of someone thrown into the car, a muffled crack that could be a baton or a head splintering.

I scrambled away from the door. There was nowhere to go. There was only noise and noise and noise I couldn't get away from. It collapsed my lungs and rang in my head and—

Panic attack. Not again.

I knew now why the fear came. One small moment, one single time that someone I loved had terrified me. But knowing *about* that moment wasn't the same as remembering it. It didn't set me free. I hadn't been robbed of the pain—just of the healing. I'd be trapped forever, trapped with fists pounding on the glass, trapped with fear clawing at my neck. I gasped, rocking back and forth. Had to move, had to move.

"Gena?" Kalan's voice. Strained.

Another person struck the glass, struck at me, vibrations shaking me.

"Gena, you're hurting my hands."

I stared at Kalan's cuffed hands holding both of mine. When had that happened? I tried to let him go. My fingers only peeled back so far. Like I didn't have control. The fear always had control, and I wanted to scream because this was *her fault*. She'd paralyzed me with fear, taken my ability to make choices just like Dad.

I raised my head, stopping my rocking. Ready to tell someone. "She hit me."

Kalan sat up straight. "Who?"

Pounding on the glass. Matthews shouted something. I squeezed my eyes shut and started rocking again.

"Grandma. I don't remember. My parents took the memory."

Kalan was silent. His fingers twitched in mine.

"I want to hate her." It made me *so angry* that I couldn't hate her. That I had so many happy memories of her. That I never had a chance to make more memories with her. "I never had a chance to hate her and then find a way to love her again."

Kalan licked his lips. "Do you think you could have?"

I froze in my rocking. Sat up, slowly. Grandma had had a life of horror and trauma. She'd tried to move past it. Changed—but not enough. What if she'd had another chance? What if I could have worked through my fear and anger, and she could have, too? We could have changed, both of us together.

Grandma was gone, and so was any possibility of making new memories. That was the opportunity I'd had stolen from me. That was where the healing could have come. In changing our relationship again. In forgiveness.

"Yes," I whisper. "I could have."

Two thumps sounded on the window next to me. I ripped my hands from Kalan's and rammed my fists against the glass. A startled face outside the tinted window jerked back. He was just like Grandma. Just like all of us. Stuck in memories of the past, forgetting that memories can't change, but people can.

"Stop it!" I screamed. "You can stop this!"

The car inched forward, away from the stunned man outside. Matthews and Jackson argued and growled from the front seat, but I sat back and focused on the sound of my breathing. Steady. Even. For the first time, I hadn't just beaten back my fear. I had faced it. I had faced her with a truth I'd finally allowed myself to admit. Memories shaped who we had been, but we chose who we wanted to be now.

And I was taking that choice back.

Hesitantly, Kalan touched my gloved hand. "Are you all right?"

I curled my gloved fingers around his. "Yes."

Even if the panic came back another day, in this moment, I was okay.

"Get us in the garage," Matthews snarled to Jackson.

A line of armed private guards came into view ahead of us, patrolling the driveway to Happenings. The car sped up again as the mob fell behind. I sat forward, eyeing the building. One victory today wasn't enough. I didn't know if I could pull off another. But at least now I knew I had the strength to try.

"Where are the rest of those riot police?" Matthews swiveled his head around like he might be able to spot them on the march.

Jackson clicked a button. A transparent GPS map appeared on the windshield. "The first unit is two blocks out, the others are."

"Get the rest of Happenings security out there," Matthews said, thumbing at the line of guards as we passed them. "We've got a private force of fifty inside and outside. That ought to be enough to help keep these people off our grounds."

"They're not riot police, they're hired security. It could make things worse if—"

"Just do it." Matthews ruffled his hair in a Liza-like gesture, his face red and flustered.

Jackson called in the order as we screeched into the garage.

Matthews wasted no time. He yanked me out of the car. In my post-panic haze, I stumbled to the cement. Kalan was thrown out beside me. The garage door shut behind us, slicing off the fading daylight.

Jackson nudged us to our feet. He strolled behind us like we ambled through a park, but his calculated steps were the prowl of a predator protecting its catch. We approached the metal door leading to the building, and Matthews sighed. In the dim calm of the garage, he seemed to have regained his chipper attitude.

"Oh, dear. Give me a moment."

From the inside of his jacket, he pulled out a syringe. I spied three more tucked in his pocket. Liza Woods' DNA, fizzing inside a Chameleon treatment. Matthews rolled back his sleeve.

"Jackson, lock them together. I don't want them to run." He plunged the needle into his forearm and depressed the plunger.

The skin around the injection began to boil.

My handcuffs jangled and pulled at my wrists. Matthews braced himself against the concrete wall, his skin reddening and bubbling like lava. A fissure opened along his cheek and blood oozed out. Acid burned in my throat. Don't look away. My memory was evidence. If I could get it out of here.

So I focused on Matthews, my eyes watering at the slithery sound of flesh shifting and popping. He let out a strangled sound between a cough and a cry. He sank to the ground.

"A few more minutes, please," he said in a higher, throatier voice. Liza Woods now sat on the curb in Matthews' suit, blood trickling from the cut cheek to the white collar. "Still haven't got the vocal cords right. Have to have the fellows work on it some more. Some water, please, Jackson."

With a weak arm, he accepted a water bottle and sipped. No wonder he'd spread rumors about Liza being sick. The darker skin and brown eyes didn't cut it up close. Now that I knew, I could see him beneath her skin. He was too tall—that explained his slouch as Liza. The business suit emphasized his masculine shape.

Still, not a bad resemblance, all things considered. Matthews' words about vocal cords confirmed my suspicions that his version of Chameleon DNA changed muscle structure and cartilage. Completely disgusting.

Finally, Liza/Matthews stood. She—he—dabbed at his bleeding cheek with a handkerchief and frowned.

"I told you to cut back," Jackson said. "Your skin's getting too weak."

Matthews brushed at his neck with gloved hands, sending a puff of dust into the air. "Always better when I can have a quick rinse after a change. So much dead skin."

He removed a glove and pressed his Liza-DNA-imprinted hand to the lock next to the door. It beeped. Jackson separated my and Kalan's handcuffs, and we followed Matthews through a dark hallway. Another door, another beep. Matthews swept his Liza-hand in a grand gesture.

No way was I going in there willingly. My knees trembled, and I locked them, ready to bolt. There had to be a way out. Something that would take me anywhere but that room.

"Oh, come now, no need to be difficult. We're already past the point of no return." Matthews grabbed my arm and shoved me inside.

The door closed. Trapped. My fingers drummed my thigh until I wanted to laugh hysterically because finger drumming was going to do me a crap-load of good now.

"Always knew it would be the basement," Kalan said.

Get a grip, Gena. Focus on the facts to drown out the fear. My eyes swept the room. It didn't look anything like a basement. More like the lab Ren had taken me through upstairs. White tile from floor to ceiling, rows of computers and medical equipment, lab tables lining the walls. No windows. No doors except the one we'd just come through, which Jackson now guarded.

And four people in hospital beds at the center of the room.

I wanted to cringe away from them, but I knew my responsibility. I was a witness for these people, whether I got out of here or not.

Blaire. She looked so much like I remembered. And so different at the same time. She'd chopped her hair short, like Ren's. Had they done it together, friends going out for a spa night before one of them became an experiment and the other a thief?

A yellow tube ran into her nose. Small sections of brown hair had been shaved away, her head dotted with wireless electrodes. Machines pulsed around her. I wondered where the information from her brain was transmitted, and if the scientists working on it had any idea where it came from.

I took in each of the other victims. Rory, Trae, and Braxton. They looked eerily similar with their tubes and wires and pale blue blankets. Like variations on a cloned theme.

Matthews pulled off his gloves and laid them on a table, like he was coming home. He beamed at the limp bodies. "My faithful subjects. It's thanks to them that I discovered how our brains connect to our Links. It made the wireless SLS possible. Quite brave and amazing individuals, really." He turned that bright smile on me. "You're brave yourself, Gena. I think you'll fit in well."

I dragged my eyes from Trae, the only unknown face in the room. Valeria's lost fiancé.

Kalan's fists clenched in his handcuffs. "You let her go before. Why keep her now?"

"I'd always planned to bring her back," Matthews snapped. "Her Populace connections complicated matters."

Kalan snorted. "You people always underestimate us, don't you?"

"Not anymore." He smoothed his Liza-black hair out of his face. "You've provided me with a golden opportunity. The other Populace subject was simply a control. But now, with another of you…it's a chance to find out how Mementi went from *you*—to *us*."

Kalan's eyebrows contracted. For the first time, he looked afraid.

No. No way would he turn Kalan into a slug on a table. Or worse, a repetition of the first generation, of the Link theft victims. It was still a death sentence, just preceded by years of agony.

Plan A. Get Matthews talking so I could plot a way out of here.

"So that's what this is about?" I said. "Research?"

Kalan's eyes darted toward me. I brushed his shoulder with mine.

"Not research. The future." His voice droned as if delivering a memorized speech. "We've finally found a way to secure our memories, using the SLS merging. And the fade-out ramifications . . . do you know how important it is to forget things? To let time dull memory, so we don't have to bear the full weight of every moment? If we can keep detailed backups, but dim the memories we actually wear . . . there's so much mental and emotional damage we can prevent. That we can *heal*."

"How noble," Kalan said. "I'm sure it's also helpful that you can 'fade' any memories people might have of you murdering Liza Woods, and keeping four people as lab rats in your basement."

Matthews sighed. "Kalan, your mind is depressingly mundane. I'd have thought Gena would be discerning enough to choose her companions more wisely."

Jackson stood behind us with arms crossed behind his back. Blocking the only obvious exit. Maybe air ducts? Did that even work outside the movies? I needed more time.

"You're such a liar," I said. "This all started because you killed someone, and tried to cover your tracks."

I didn't see any air ducts, either.

"I had to protect the research," Matthews snapped. "That meant keeping it hidden. I did this for the Mementi."

"Liar."

Matthews paused, hands on the bed. His stare chilled me. Kalan lifted his bound hands to my shoulder.

Matthews reached into a cabinet on the wall, pulling out a vial. "Consider yourself lucky to be part of history."

He filled a syringe from the vial. No doubt something to knock us out. This was it. No way out. Kalan's hand squeezed my shoulder, his handcuffs bumping my shoulder blade.

Trembling shudders constricted my chest. I set my feet in a defensive stance and raised my hands as fists. Matthews paused, wary.

"Drake."

Jackson's voice startled me. He stepped past me and Kalan and spoke to Matthews in a low voice.

"I thought we were erasing their memories. You're not serious about putting them under?"

Matthews straightened into a commanding posture. "You know what we could learn from them. The boy, especially."

"He's Populace."

"Exactly. He could be the key to everything we don't understand about our origins."

Jackson hesitated. "You'll break his mind. Like the first generation."

Like my grandmother. Like his mother. I held my breath.

Matthews tapped the syringe. "You knew when we started this that your personal feelings have no bearing here."

"My personal feelings are the reason I agreed to help," Jackson said. "These two aren't volunteering. This is wrong."

Kalan tugged at my shirt. The door! Jackson had left the door unguarded. I dragged a foot backward along the tiled floor, easing toward the exit.

Matthews fingered the lapel of his jacket, stained with the blood from his cut cheek. "We do what we have to do. The project is too important."

Jackson clenched his fists by his sides. "No. This was not in the cards. They're kids."

Kalan and I backed closer to the door. Without warning, Matthews elbowed Jackson hard in the gut. Jackson doubled over and Matthews sprinted forward.

Kalan stepped in front of me, crouching. Syringe out, Matthews raced toward us.

I needed that syringe.

"Sorry," I whispered into Kalan's ear.

I grabbed his shirt and shoved him to the side. I twisted my cuffed hands as Matthews dove for me, trying to grab the syringe from the side. Matthews yanked it away, but I'd knocked his grip loose. The syringe went flying. A clink of glass on tile, somewhere behind Matthews.

His pleasant mask cracked, and he yelled. He grabbed my hands. I struggled, clawed, pushed. His fingers clutched my wrists, digging into my skin. I cried out.

We both rocketed to the side as Jackson barreled into us. Everyone fell to the floor. A shock of pain lanced through my arm as I landed on my sore shoulder. I screamed.

"Gena, run!" Kalan skidded across the floor and pummeled the downed Matthews with his handcuffed fists.

Matthews still had the use of both hands. He rolled to the side and swung a fist around, trying to hit Kalan off him. His knuckles split, and he howled. Jackson wrenched Matthews' arms back. Matthews bucked his body and kicked. His shoes squeaked on the tile floor.

No good, we needed complete incapacitation. Where was that injection?

Injection.

I scrambled for Matthews' jacket, searching for the inside pocket. The Chameleon injections. My fingers brushed plastic, and I yanked at it. Something snagged, then pulled out.

A pen. I threw it aside and wrenched his jacket open. Buttons pinged to the floor. Three syringes in the pocket. I tugged one out, threw off the plastic cap, and jabbed the syringe into Matthews' side.

With a gurgle, his body stiffened. His skin began to simmer, the color already lightening. Bingo. A double dose canceled out the Chameleon effects.

And had nasty side-effects, maybe from two injections so close together. Small clumps of hair fell from his head. Tiny cracks split his knuckles with each bubble of change. Matthews squealed in pain.

Kalan slid off Matthews, gasping, "Keys."

Jackson tossed a small key to Kalan. He unlocked my cuffs, and I unlocked his.

"Lock him up." Jackson jerked his head toward Matthews.

I blinked at him.

"The cuffs, Gena, lock him up."

"Jackson..." Matthews gurgled.

"I won't help you destroy an innocent kid's mind." Jackson fixed Matthews with an icy stare. "That's exactly the opposite of why I got into this."

He snatched the cuffs from me and chained the bleeding and still-bubbling man to a table. What about us? He'd saved us from horrific experimentation, but that didn't mean he'd just send us packing.

"Get out of here," he said over his shoulder. "Both of you."

Okay, maybe it did. Kalan helped me up. I clutched his hand to ease the shakiness in my own.

"We have to wake these people up." Kalan nodded to the sleeping test subjects.

"I'll get them out," Jackson said. "You two get lost. I don't want to see you again."

Ever, his tone said. He was going to disappear. My gaze flicked to Blaire and the others. I could get to the SLS now, share my memories. Stop Matthews for good. But...

"How do we know you won't just scram and leave them here?"

"I just took down the man who started this!"

"And you helped set him up, too," Kalan said. "We get these people out together."

Jackson turned and stomped to the first set of controls. His nimble fingers danced over the touchscreen on the life-support machines next to Blaire. I took his silence as assent.

"Kalan," I whispered, "stay with him. I've got to get to the SLS."

He leaned his head down to mine. "No way. We're not splitting up."

"All the guards are outside. It'll be cake to get into the lab. I can be done before you guys have those four out." I nodded toward the beds. "I have to stop the SLS from erasing me. And I have to upload my memories of Matthews before more people kill each other out there." I pinched my lips. "Then I'll destroy it."

Jackson unhooked the last of Blaire's wires, calling Kalan to help him wheel her bed out.

Kalan touched my shoulder. "Okay. I'll feel better with you out of here anyway. I'll tell Jackson you decided to scram."

I nodded.

Matthews reached out a shaking hand as I passed him. "Wait."

I knocked his hand to the side and grabbed the remaining two Chameleon injections. Liza's DNA inside them was as good as her hand on a door lock, and I had everything I needed. Evidence and keys. I dashed for the stairs, Kalan and Jackson wheeling Blaire down the corridor behind me. Matthews groaned and shifted on the lab floor while we began to undo the disaster he'd created.

31

The shadow sits and waits for me…

—Alfred, Lord Tennyson, *In Memoriam XXII*

My memory of the map in the Happenings lobby proved to be useful.

I sprinted up the stairs. This was the basement, northwest wing. I needed northeast. An image of the map lit up my brain, my pathway illuminated. Up one flight to the main floor, across the lobby, and to the lab.

I paused on the main floor landing. Two doors, one to the lobby and one to the south wing. I rushed for the lobby.

The door clicked open. Dim lights tossed murky shapes on the marble floor, and shadows lurked under ornate couches. The ferny leaves of a plant fluttered from a gust of air-conditioned wind. Faint screams sounded from the crowd outside. Goose bumps prickled my skin. Lovely. The haunted laboratory of an evil scientist. At least I was decently sure there was nobody crouched in a corner with a butcher knife.

A dull clunk echoed through the lobby. I jumped and peered around the corner of the small alcove I stood in. Three silhouettes clustered outside the main entrance. One of them reared back a shadowed hand. Something hit the door with a crunch, shooting thin cracks through the glass.

"Oh no," I whispered.

Across the lobby, a door clicked open. I pulled back to the stairwell as footsteps clacked across the tile. A guard. Didn't he have orders to be outside with the rest of them? I gnawed on my lip, counting the minutes that passed while his footsteps circled the lobby.

Another crunch sounded from the doors, and the footsteps paused. The guard shouted and ran. A door opened and shut.

More wary than before, I stepped into the alcove. I hesitated for longer than I should have, paranoid the guard would come rushing back with his buddies. Another splintering crack came from the main doors, but no guards. Time to go, before my time ran out. I bounced on my toes, building up a beat inside me to fuel me across the open floor. A shattering of glass splintered my rhythm.

I spun to find a jagged hole in the glass door. A canister spun on the marble, snaking smoke.

I scrambled for the stairwell door. Heat and noise blasted me like a giant, fiery push. The force slammed me to the floor, my head smacking hard tile. Lights flashed before plunging into darkness.

The throbbing of my sore shoulder woke me. Heat rolled over me in waves. I couldn't have been out long, but even that was too long. I sat up just as a mechanical wail split my eardrums and I clamped my hands over my ears.

Flames rippled over the rich rugs in the lobby and licked at the legs of the couches. Ceiling sprinklers didn't daunt the fire at all. I coughed, black smoke already growing thicker. Orange teeth chewed through the lobby upholstery, eating toward the wooden walls. I kicked the stairwell door closed against the caustic smoke.

I'd never get across that to the SLS.

"Gena!"

I jumped at Kalan's voice; I hadn't heard him come up the stairs through the fire alarm. He knelt next to me.

"What happened, are you okay?"

"A bomb," I shouted over the alarm. "Some kind of home-made bomb. Where's Jackson, and Blaire and—"

"Blaire's out," he yelled, helping me to my feet. "Jackson headed back to the lab the second we got her outside. I led a bunch of medics down to help get the rest of them, and Jackson and Matthews were gone. Then I heard the bomb go off..."

Something behind the door splintered and cracked in the fire. "We've got to bolt," Kalan yelled. "That fire's probably chemically fueled, it'll destroy this whole place."

Panic flared, hot as the flames in the lobby. "I can't, the fire control system will activate once we're out of the building. It'll stop the fire and the SLS will survive." I'd remain forgotten. The SLS would wait for a new evil to claim it.

"There's nothing we can do now."

There had to be, there *had* to be. There was always something. Another route from the Happenings map glowed in my head. Up to the second landing, across the atrium, down to the main floor of the northeast wing. Before the fire ate through to the second floor and destroyed the atrium.

"We can still get to the lab," I called over the shrieking alarm.

"No," Kalan said. A thin trail of smoke seeped under the lobby door. "I'm not letting you kill yourself."

I climbed to my feet. I wouldn't have time to upload my memories of Matthews to the SLS and send it out. The fire system would register someone was still in the building, and the airtight fire doors and oxygen removal wouldn't go into effect. The SLS might burn, but so would I. The longer I was here, the farther the fire would spread. I had to destroy the machine before the fire cut off my escape.

If I didn't make it through the fire, and my memories of Matthews didn't survive…

Wait.

"The Memo. Kalan, I still have your Memo from when I uploaded my memory in the canyon."

I pulled the smartplastic square from my pocket and released its nano-injecting tube. Not a great option. Like there were many of those left.

Kalan coughed in the gathering smoke and pulled me to the rear of the landing. "Gena, we have to *go*."

"Shh," I ordered.

Memories flowed through my mind and into the Memo. Images of Matthews morphing into Liza, proudly announcing himself as the Link thief, and pronouncing his justifications. Him next to four comatose subjects whose families didn't remember them, plotting my demise—and Kalan's. A few short moments of the theft victims in the hospital.

For good measure, I finished with an image of the streets of Havendale. Fists flying, people screaming, fires raging, homes looted and broken. So they could see how they'd helped fulfill a madman's desires.

It took only seconds. The collection of memories played in my mind like a movie, one I hoped would smack people out of stupidity.

Kalan would have to take it. I thrust the Memo and one of the Chameleon injections toward him. "Get this out there, make sure everyone knows what Matthews did. I have to destroy the SLS, or someone could still have control over every Mementi in town. Even me."

His face glistened in the heat. "I'm not going anywhere without you."

"You can't be everybody's hero, Kalan. We have to work together to win. I'm trusting you with this. Trust me, too."

He took my hand and kissed my palm. It scalded more than the ripples of heat coming from the lobby door. "I don't want to lose you again."

My heart skipped a beat. "If we hurry, you won't."

I wanted to say more, but my brain shut off my mouth. He laid my hand on his cheek. His eyes glowed with feelings I was half afraid of and half wished he'd put into words.

"I trust you," he said.

I brushed his cheek with my fingertips. He took the Memo and Cham treatment from my other hand.

It was harder than I'd expected to push him away. "Go. Hurry."

He backed toward the stairs. Then he whirled and sprinted down the steps. The alarm screamed louder in his absence. I took off in the opposite direction.

Deeper into the burning building. To the SLS lab.

32

But who shall so forecast the years
And find in loss a gain to match?

—Alfred, Lord Tennyson, *In Memoriam I*

I raced through the atrium above the lobby to the accompaniment of alarms and groaning floorboards. Cold ceiling-sprinkler rain drenched me, puddling the floor.

The floor creaked and buckled under my feet. I lurched, choking on a scream. A loud crack split the sound of the fire alarm, and the ground behind me broke. Thick smoke swelled through the gap. Heat seared my legs. I coughed, ripping my scarf from my head to cover my mouth. I saw myself tumbling in a shower of tile and wood, engulfed by the hungry heat below.

No thinking. Only running.

Ahead of me, a thick fire door rolled into motion. Crapcrapcrap. The sensors had malfunctioned. The door inched down to seal the room. Air would be sucked out until my lungs were as flat as deflated balloons.

My legs pounded forward. Tremors rattled the shattered atrium, quaking deep into my bones. I dove, rolling under the door.

The fire door clanged into place. I sat up and pushed wet hair from my cheeks. Alive. Not deflated. Bad way to go, that. If the fire had spread beyond the lobby, more fire doors would activate.

Oxygen deprivation wouldn't kill the SLS. I was the only one who could do that now.

I descended to the main floor and rushed down the hallway Ren and I had walked this morning. My running feet splashed and squeaked on the wet tile. Lab 3 loomed ahead on my left. Hours ago, I'd lost my life in that lab.

Someone stepped around the corner at the end of the hall. I yelped, skidding to a splashy stop. Detective Jackson, his blue uniform now nearly black from sprinkler water, strode forward.

"What are you doing here?" I said. "How did you—"

"The SLS," he yelled over the still-shrieking fire alarm. "I engaged the fire controls so it wouldn't be destroyed, but I don't know how far the fire has spread."

"Where's Matthews?"

"I let him go."

"You let him *go*?"

"We have to save the data." He waved frantic hands at the lab. "I don't have all of the updates on my personal backup, I have to sync up and save it."

"I'm not here to save it, I—" Argh, STUPID. My mouth was bigger than Kalan's.

The sudden wild look in Jackson's eyes reminded me how little I knew even of those I'd known my whole life.

Jackson crouched, his ferocity aimed at me. A panicked flutter brushed my ribs. I saw my chance drifting away. Saw myself knocked out, Jackson getting away with enough data to build his own SLS, leaving me to burn or choke.

Not going to happen.

I sped toward Jackson, ripping the plastic top off the Chameleon injection in my hand. He sprang like a jungle cat—leaping toward me, his hand swooping to the gun at his hip. Before he could unholster it, I plunged the needle into his neck.

He let out a strange mewl of pain. A creeping sensation brushed across my arm—his skin rippling against me. I jerked up, throwing the syringe at the wall. Jackson collapsed to the floor. His limp hands splashed in the sprinkler puddles.

The lab. I dashed inside, straight to the door that hid the SLS. Locked. Right. And my Cham injection was no more. I touched the DNA pad and it gave an angry red squawk.

DNA. There was a lot of random DNA floating around.

I rushed out and pulled a weakened Jackson by the arm. Weak, yes, but light, no. I grunted.

Liza Wood's features looked strange on a new face. They pulled differently over his longer forehead and wider nose, but I was right about the facial muscle structure changing too. He still kind of looked like Liza. In fact, he looked more like Liza than Matthews did. Maybe because he hadn't metamorphosed his skin until it became tissue paper.

Jackson moaned as I dragged him. I propped him next to the SLS door and slapped his hand against the DNA lock.

It dinged in welcome this time, and the door clicked open. I tugged Jackson into the room and took his gun. Wouldn't want him using that on me. The door shut behind me, cutting off the fire alarm.

And there it was, with metal panels removed to allow tweaking to its inner machinery. It hummed softly, like an audible twiddling of its thumbs. Idling away the time until it hacked apart people's memories. I shivered in my wet clothes and pulled the control screen toward me. It was set up similar to a tablet interface, with simple touch commands that led me through menus. I found RECENT COMMANDS.

I tapped it and a list popped up. New commands had been added, a few minutes after the one to forget me.

1. *Mention GENESIS LEE – fade maximum*
2. *Mention RORY HERNANDEZ – fade maximum*
3. *Mention TRAE WILLIAMS – fade maximum*
4. *Mention BLAIRE JACOBS – fade maximum*
5. *Mention BRAXTON SIMPSON – fade maximum*

A vein pulsed in my neck. So using their minds as his demented playground wasn't enough. He'd snatched their existence from every mind connected to the system. I wasn't alone in being forgotten.

My own horrible relief made me want to vomit.

Next to each name was a small X. The cancellation button. I had to make sure the commands weren't somehow left in force, or no one who used their Link buds would ever remember the five of us again. I stabbed the X's with my index finger, imagining myself poking Drake Matthews in the eye with each one. Stab, stab, stabstabstab. My wet gloves left tiny dots on the screen as each name vanished.

Something released inside me. I was free again, free to be remembered. If only a cancellation button could bring back all those erased memories to my family. My damp fingers streaked down the screen. I had one more thing to do.

Jackson squirmed on the floor. "What are you doing?" he rasped in a voice that wasn't his.

"Ending this."

I was no gun aficionado, but Jackson's weapon had bullets, a silencer, and a light weight. Easy enough. A safety button sat behind the trigger, and I clicked it off. Point and shoot. Shouldn't be that hard with the guts of the SLS wide open to me. I lifted the gun.

The screeching of the fire alarm battered my eardrums. I nearly dropped the gun as I spun at the sudden sound. Drake Matthews stood in the doorway, smiling. Blood dripped from his hands and water dripped from his remaining patches of hair.

"Did you know," he said, "that traces of old DNA still linger for a few minutes after a Chameleon injection? Not much, but enough for a DNA lock to read."

The alarm cut off as the door clanged shut. Matthews strolled forward with a laugh, but it came out weak and breathy. Still not a hundred percent.

I aimed the gun at the SLS.

With more power than I'd thought he had, Matthews lunged for me. In seconds, he had his arm around me, my back to his chest, and the gun pressed to my temple.

He was going to shoot me. Shoot me through the brain, through the temporal lobe, plaster pieces of me on the wall. My body shivered with the cold of that tiny bit of metal on my skin. And I realized, remembered or forgotten, my life had still been real.

Blood rushed through my body. Tingling fingers and flushed cheeks and pounding heart. All of it one twitch of a finger from a standstill.

"Drake." A weak voice warbled through the room. "Don't, Drake. She's Kierce's daughter. Don't."

My eyes met Jackson's—the eyes that weren't his. He pulled himself to his feet, shaking. A single step was all he could manage before his knees gave out.

He couldn't save me this time.

"I don't care who she belongs to." Matthews' grip on me tightened.

His calm words echoed. Not in the room, but in my mind. He didn't care. He might have once, when he started this. Now he only cared about himself.

My face burned with sudden heat, melting the ice of fear. *You bested him in handcuffs, and this is how it ends?*

The gun nudged my head, trembling in his hands. Hands that ripped as easily as paper. Praying he wouldn't notice, I slipped my glove off. My fingers crooked like claws and I clenched my muscles. I swung my arm up and raked my nails over his hand.

He cried out and the gun clattered to the floor.

Twirling from his grip, I stamped down as hard as my ballet-strong legs could, right on his toes.

He howled, crunching forward in pain. The gun lay at his feet, inches from him. I sprang for it, half surprised when my hand closed around the metal. His fingers snatched my hair. With a cry, I jerked upright. I swung my arm out and cracked him across the head with the butt of the gun. His skin split. Spurting blood, he sank to the floor with a grunt.

I turned in time to see Jackson creeping toward me, leaning on the SLS for support. In a flash, I brought the gun up. My gaze followed the barrel straight to his chest.

Jackson froze, eyeing the gun. "We both know you're not the kind of girl to shoot somebody."

I glanced at Matthews, who wavered with dizziness as he tried to sit up.

"Maybe not. But I have no reservations about shooting this thing." I stepped to the open panels in the center of the SLS, aiming the gun at the machine's innards.

"No, wait!" Matthews raised a hand to his bleeding head. "Gena, the backups! That SLS is the only way they're possible. I can use it to return your memories. Your family's, too."

The gun suddenly weighed down my arm. "You erased them. Faded them out of people's Links and didn't store them anywhere else."

He put a hand in the air, palm out. "I know. But there's that remnant left, that bit of emotional memory in your brain. We don't understand it, not yet, but we're using the SLS to strengthen it. Sync parts of other people's memories with your emotional memory. That's how the backups work. It triggers your brain to view shared events from your point of view. Make the memory your own again."

If it was true. If it was possible. There was a chance I could live again, that I could have Kalan back, that my family could regain what they'd lost. A chance full of coulds and maybes. But still a chance.

"They'll go crazy, Gena," Matthews said. "The ones closest to you are the ones who lost the most. It doesn't have to be like that. It's why we created the machine in the first place. So we can be better than we are, so we can protect ourselves, save ourselves from tragedies like this."

The gun felt cool in my hands. The SLS, the monster that had destroyed my life, could heal the very hurt it had caused. It was the memory security Mementi had hoped for since our very beginning. But it was also the method by which our memories could be stolen in secret.

Ren had said some risks were acceptable. Dad had insisted that memories shouldn't be tampered with, and had proven it with his own tampering.

Maybe there was a balance. A way to straddle the line.

"Please, Gena." Jackson inched toward me, hunched like an old man. "It just has to go into the right hands."

The gun dropped several inches. Maybe Jackson had the right idea after all.

"I panicked," Matthews said from the opposite end of the SLS. He pulled himself up, hanging on the SLS touchscreen. "I shouldn't have done what I did to you, to the Link theft victims. There are people out there, our people, who could gain so much from the SLS. I just wanted to help people. Let me help fix this."

My eyes flickered to him, and I saw the lie. He had injected emotion into his voice like he'd injected Liza's DNA into his skin. Memories flashed in my mind of all the people he didn't care about. Cora's exhausted eyes. Miranda's wails over a daughter she didn't know she had. Kalan's anguished face.

My family. Years of their lives removed in chunks, leaving them wounded and waiting for the infection of untethered emotions. If I destroyed the SLS, they'd lose any possibility, no matter how remote, of being whole again. But whole for how long? Until someone tapped in and stole something else?

A hand reached into the corner of my vision. Matthews, going for the gun. I threw my elbow out, catching him in the nose. He reared back with a cry of pain.

Sometimes there's only one right thing to do. Even if it required a sacrifice I shouldn't have the power to make.

I swung the gun back to the SLS and squeezed the trigger. The gun kicked back and the shot exploded in my ears. Through the ringing that followed, Jackson moaned and slid to the floor.

Matthews fell across the SLS, scrambling for the quartz port. If he touched it long enough, he could transfer the data I was trying to destroy into his Links. His palm flattened over the quartz.

No way, Mr. Mad Scientist.

I fired at the machine again. Ren's face, empty of recognition, passed through my mind. Another shot. Dad's confused smile when I told him I was his daughter. I squeezed again. Mom curled into bed, a Link bud dangling from her ear.

I blew holes into the enormous SLS. Hole after hole into the justifications people would create to use it. Hole after hole into the possible restoration of my life and other people's sanity. Fireworks burst from the machine, parts flying with each gun blast. Sparks arced through the SLS, electrifying its metal casing. Matthews was zapped away from the quartz port.

Clickclickclick. The gun was empty.

Hands grabbed my knees, clutching at my jeans. "You didn't. You didn't," Jackson gasped.

I twisted away from him, my ears still ringing.

Matthews lay crumpled next to the SLS, his hand out like it was reaching for the data I'd destroyed. Blood streamed from his head wound. He didn't move. Not a twitch. For a horrible moment I wondered if that spark of electricity had killed him.

A guttural groan rose from him. He looked around him in confusion and tried to speak.

"Mmmuuuuunng."

His arms thrashed, uncontrolled and wild. He let out a shriek of terror, and I scrambled back. Had he cracked for real now?

"Uhhhhh." His mouth worked frantically, but he only made disjointed sounds.

"What the devil just happened?" I said.

Jackson sat up, rolling slowly upward. Matthews jerked his head back, staring at Jackson. His eyes were blank. Unrecognizing. Then I noticed his white bone Links, shattered and smoking, scattered around him.

His memories had been destroyed.

Jackson's eyes went to the smoking SLS. "It must have been the power surge. He was touching the metal and the shock destroyed his memories."

Matthews moaned again. His legs kicked and jerked, as uncoordinated as a newborn.

"His procedural memories," Jackson said softly. "I think the shock destroyed them, too."

His memories of how to walk. Talk. Ride a bike. Swing a baseball bat. They were still stored in our brains, but even that hadn't escaped the destruction of the SLS.

I wasn't sure if I should feel as satisfied about that as I did.

Jackson's hand nudged an electronic part sizzling on the floor. He sagged. "The backups. The memory merges. The data on them. You destroyed it all."

"It could have destroyed all of us," I shot back. But I couldn't help the tendrils of remorse I felt for him. For all of us. "The city will know, Jackson. They'll know what you did to create this thing."

He picked up the tiny piece of hot metal, his back to me. "Not all of them will condemn me."

Which was terrible, and probably true.

I wrenched open the door, welcoming the cooling sprinkler water and deafening alarm. Had Kalan gotten out and shared my memories with the city?

I ran. Through the raining hallways and out a side door. Around the building, toward the front of Happenings. I staggered to a stop on the grass, halted by the scene in front of me.

Smoke bloomed into the night-dimmed sky. Firemen sprayed torrents of water into the building, quenching the few flames that still fought. Above me, a National Guard helicopter whooped through the air, spotlights sweeping the ground. Flakes of ash drifted like snow.

It was too silent for the size of the mob on the huge lawn. Some stared at the charred Happenings wallscreen. A news report played the recording of my memory through a film of smoke and water.

Several people had fallen to their knees. At the fringes of the crowd, others still fought, but most stood still. Shocked.

I trudged toward the parking garage where Kalan should have come out. A flurry of activity, including several ambulances, filled the area. The test subjects in the basement—Jackson had helped save them. Did that make him the good guy or the bad guy?

Even good people could do bad things. Even people like me. When my choice came out—when people learned I had sacrificed a potential cure to kill the disease—would they see me as the good guy or the bad guy? At the moment, I didn't know how I saw myself. No one ever told me that right choices could have consequences too.

Faces from the crowd stood out to me. The ache of loneliness crept in. Mrs. Harward stared at the ash gathering on her shoes, like she wanted it to pile up and cover her. Only a few days since

I'd last seen her, but the ten years her Chameleon treatment had removed had come back quickly. I shouldn't talk to her. It would only prove how alone I was.

Hope makes us do terrible things.

"Mrs. Harward?" I asked. "Are you alright?"

Her head rose as slowly as the sun. She stared at me without recognition, then shuffled away.

Others followed her, leaving the Happenings grounds. Face after face. Keilani Wellington, sophomore class vice president. Len Nori, star tennis player at Havendale U. Magdalena Sanchez, three-time winner of the annual yard beautification award. Other faces came to mind, ones that thankfully weren't here. Zahra and Cora and Ren and Mom and Dad.

None of them knew me anymore. And in the end, that was partially by my own hand.

I'd won today and still lost everything. The unfairness scraped at my insides until I wanted to run through the crowd, begging someone to tell me my name. People poured past me. No one asked if I was alright. No one said they'd help me home. In the middle of this crowd, I had never been more alone.

"Gena."

Kalan strode through falling ash, his curls matted with water and soot. He knew me, but that thought didn't bring me much hope. I ached with that peculiar homesickness, missing him though he stood right in front of me. Despite the new memories we'd made, the hours of struggle and trust we'd gone through, he was a stranger.

He reached out to take my hand, but I kept my arms at my sides. Touching him felt like lying. Like I was pretending something I had dreamed of but didn't exist.

"The Memo," I said. "You did it."

"So did you."

Sirens wailed and helicopters chopped the air. "It didn't fix everything."

"I didn't think it would." He dropped his hand. "I wish there was a way to make everything how it was."

The next thing that came out of my mouth was not what I meant to say.

"I'm alone, Kalan."

People pushed past us to go home and deal with what they'd done. Kalan stepped closer.

"But you're still strong," he said.

I wasn't strong. I was cracked, broken.

"You don't have to be strong alone." His eyes pleaded with me through his damp, tangled curls.

"I don't know you." The words came out harsh.

"But you *can* know me."

My lips parted and I took in the smoky air. Hope lifted me like a life preserver. I had already started building new memories with him. I could do the same with my family. The past was gone, but there was still the future.

I lifted a gloved hand to touch his cheek. He placed his hand over mine. He was filthy, sweat and water dripping through soot streaks on his forehead, the left side of his face mangled from our rush toward Ascalon. But for a moment, I saw through that and glimpsed who he really was. A boy who had stayed with me. Fought with me. Reminded me again and again who I was. He deserved more than harsh words. He deserved another chance.

He held out the Memo to me, the one with his private memories of us. I pushed it back to him.

"Will you hang onto this for me?"

The barest hint of sadness flickered in his face, but he took it. "Too much right now?"

"It's more than that. I don't want to start something based on memories that aren't mine. I want whatever I create with you to come from me."

I pulled off my one remaining glove and dropped it. I took his hand, skin-to-skin, unafraid. His fingers wrapped around mine.

It was more real than anything I'd ever known. I felt the callouses and creases in his palm, the heat and pressure of pulsing life. It flushed through me, setting my nerve endings tingling, convincing my brain to believe my heart. It was power. It was trust. It was a moment I never wanted to forget.

"Don't lose that." I nodded to the Memo in his other hand. "I still want to know how we started, once we've had time to start again."

"That sounds like a fantastic idea, Genesis Lee."

He leaned his head toward mine. His lips brushed mine, softly, and my hands curled around his neck. Arms encircled me. His kiss reminded me I was alive. The warmth of him overwhelmed me until the darkness inside me burst with stars, and I was no longer in the shadows alone.

We pulled apart, still breathing the same air.

"There's something else I have to do now," I said.

He smiled, the kind that said he knew me and knew what I had to do. I smiled back, then slipped my hand from his neck and ran through the crowd.

33

O, yet we trust that somehow good
Will be the final goal of ill,
To pangs of nature, sins of will,
Defects of doubt, and taints of blood...

—Alfred, Lord Tennyson, *In Memoriam LIV*

I knocked on Ren's door for the sixth time, but she didn't answer. I'd heard the TV on when I'd first knocked, blaring words from my memory as Matthews declared his treachery. She'd shut it off, though. I couldn't blame her for not opening the door. With a sigh, I reached into the dirt of a potted cactus for her hidden key.

"Ren," I called. "I'm not going to hurt you, I swear."

I pushed the door open and switched on the light. She crouched behind the kitchen table wearing frog pajama pants and holding a pot, ready to swing.

"I'm not going to hurt you," I said again.

"What do you want?" she demanded.

I smiled a little. Same Ren. Same greeting she'd have given even if she remembered me.

"My name is Genesis Lee. I'm your sister."

The pot clanged to the ground.

"You have something I need to return to a friend."

* * *

By the time I got to Cora's, distant sirens and the sounds of fighting still rang out occasionally. But for the most part, Havendale was quiet. Contemplating its disaster.

Ren hadn't remembered being the Link thief. Matthews' commands to forget the other Link victims had wiped her own actions from her mind. When I'd searched her desk and found the Links, she'd rushed to the bathroom and hidden for a full five minutes.

I held Cora's single Link in a gloved hand. After Ren had promised to take the other Links to the hospital, she'd given me a clean pair of gloves. I didn't want to touch Cora's Link with my skin. These were her memories. As I walked, I studied the bead in the light of burning buildings. It was red, its glitter deepened in the orangey firelight.

This Link held memories of me. For two years, at least, Cora would remember me. I closed my fist around it. Returning the memories wouldn't cure her like I'd hoped. Not with more memories missing. But I would be beside her. I would help her heal, help my family heal, the way Kalan had helped me.

It was near midnight when I knocked. She probably wouldn't answer. A shuffle sounded behind the door, and my heart leaped. I held the Link up to the peep hole.

The door flung open. Cora looked clean and frightened. She hadn't been fighting in the streets tonight.

"I think this is yours." I held out the Link.

Cora gasped, reaching for it. I dropped it into her hands. She moved to take off her gloves, but her fingers froze. Afraid. Of the memories on the Links? Of what would happen if they all came rushing back at once? She closed a gloved hand around the bead.

It was better that she waited, no matter what I'd wanted. Better that she not have the confusion of remembering me while I stood in front of her.

"How did you—how did you—" Her eyes were wide, thankful. Unrecognizing.

The blankness in her face shattered me again. I didn't know I could splinter into so many pieces, so many times.

"Just keeping a promise." The chill of a tear cooled my cheek. "I'll see you around."

I walked down the steps.

"Wait," she called. "Do I know you?"

I turned, hopeful. "Do you?"

She studied me. "I don't recognize you. But I feel like I should."

Maybe like me with Kalan, her heart remembered me when her mind didn't. A few pieces of my soul knit together.

"You will know me."

She put one hand on her hip and cocked her head, her confused stance. As the door closed, she turned and cried, "Mom!"

The walk to my own house was short. And long. Distance does funny things to your head when you're tired. My hand rested on the white front gate when I finally stood outside my home. It still felt like mine. It was mine.

"Gena?" A soft, accented voice from behind me knew my name.

I whirled to see Zahra rushing toward me. She put her hands on my shoulders, familiar and frightened. A whimper escaped my throat.

"Gena, where have you *been*?" she cried. "Cora said your parents took you from the concert, but I haven't heard from you, and your parents, I called them, but they did not even remember your name! The police, all your neighbors, they have forgotten you. How can they not—"

I threw my arms around her neck and buried my face in her hijab. "You remember me!"

"Gena, what is going on?"

Zahra didn't have Link buds. With her old-fashioned attitude from growing up outside tech-crazy Havendale, she'd never bought them.

I wanted to hug her forever. I wanted to be with someone I knew who knew me too. Take moments to talk, to heal, to reminisce. With a sigh, I pulled myself away.

"It's a long story, Zahra, and I have to see my family right now. But I'll tell it to you tomorrow. Okay?" The last word came out pleading.

Zahra's smooth face wrinkled with concern. "All right, *ma chouchoute*. But tomorrow for sure. You scared the heebie-jeebies out of me."

I smiled at her bungled phrase.

"You are okay?" she asked.

"I will be."

She squeezed my shoulder. I watched her walk until she disappeared in the darkness. One more person who remembered. That was enough.

I stepped to my front door and hesitated. It would scare their hair off if I walked in. This was a new beginning, and I wanted it to start right. I smoothed my ash-streaked, blood-stained, water-logged clothes and laughed. I was going to scare their hair off no matter what.

I counted my breaths. One-two-in, out-three-four. As I reached up to ring the bell, the door opened. They must have heard me laugh. Dad stood in the door frame, his face twisted and terrified.

"You!" he cried. "You! You're in my house. *How are you in my house?*"

I opened my mouth to say I wasn't in the house yet when I remembered. Mom's memories. They'd found the fragments of me that Mom had scattered into her precious objects. I was, quite literally, *in* the house.

Dad's forehead glistened with sweat in the porch light. Funny, him scared of me now. Twenty-four hours ago, he hadn't batted an eye while I yelled at him for stealing my memories. Now he backed away from me. The ghost who haunted his home and teased his subconscious. He had no idea how he still tortured mine.

Behind him, Mom came into view. She leaned toward me, almost reaching out. "It's you," she whispered.

The joy in her voice wrapped around me. She had forgotten me, but she hadn't forgotten her love for me. I could bask in that tiny glory for years.

"It's me," I said. "Can I come in?"

Dad stumbled away from the door, but Mom moved forward. With a gesture she hadn't used since that day on the swings, she took my hand. I stepped inside my home.

And I felt a new life happening all around me.

ACKNOWLEDGMENTS

A book doesn't begin with the first words on a page. This one began decades before that, which means there are an awful lot of people who helped out. In no particular order, thanks go to these people.

To my team: My agent Hannah Bowman, for being a ninja wizard of editing and the warrior who championed the book. My editor Kristin Kulsavage, for loving the story and being so dedicated to getting the best version possible out to the world. Everyone at Sky Pony who worked behind the scenes, even when I didn't see you there.

To my teachers: Mr. Richard Soto, who taught me in sixth grade never to use the word "can't." Miss Sharon Bodily of AP English fame, who showed me that my true love really was literature. Mr. Neil Newel, who taught me what a story truly is—thank you, thank you, Master Newel. Brandon Sanderson and Dan Wells, who gave me the tools to take the next step.

To my critique group: Chersti Nieveen, Rachel Giddings, Kevin Smith, Joel Smith, and Karen Krueger, for finding me, welcoming me, strengthening me, amusing me, improving me—and for Doctor Who. Michelle Merrill, for rooting for the book from draft one to the end. And to Chersti one more time, for always, always being there.

To the WrAHM girls: Who listened to me gripe and squee, made me actually LOL, and gave me enough gifs of Tom Hiddleston and Benedict Cumberbatch to keep me motivated. Keep WrAHMpaging on!

To my beta readers and fact checkers: Teralyn Pilgrim, Melanie Fowler, Lily Herrmann, Tanya Reimer, LaChelle and Darren Hansen, Madeline Bartos, Kami McArthur, Jessie Humphries, Nancy Heiss, Jeni Tolley, and Liesl Shurtliff. Thanks for taking the time to help make this book more than it was.

To my grandmothers: Delores Tanner, Evelyn Cutler, Opal Rowley, and Rose Mower, who all made little appearances in this book, for the shaping experiences that made me a better person and a better writer.

To the author who inspired me: Lois Lowry, for the book that changed and disturbed and inspired me, and showed me, even as a child, that I not only wanted to read great books—I wanted to write them.

To the family I grew up with: Mom, for being my perpetual cheerleader, and Dad, for being my first ever critique partner. Kylee, for not killing me for exercising my privilege as big sister to turn playtime into a chance to act out my stories. Camri, for helping me keep my French (and creativity) sharp. Preston, for loving my previous book so much I had to write another one.

To the family I created: Danny, for your patience and love and faith—you are the reason I made it this far. Asher, for keeping me laughing and always assuring me that you like me. Amaya, for your smooshy kisses and squeezy hugs that remind me I'm more than just a writer.

To the God who gave me everything: All I can say is thank you, even though it will never feel like enough.

Just as a book doesn't begin at the first word, it doesn't end at the printing press. So thank you to all you readers for giving this book a chance and making it your own. You are why I do this.

Shallee McArthur has a degree in English from Brigham Young University. When she's not writing young-adult science fiction and fantasy, she's attempting to raise her son and daughters as proper sci-fi and fantasy geeks. A little part of her heart is devoted to Africa after volunteering twice in Ghana. This is her first book. McArthur lives in southern Utah with her husband and three children.

1. Gena's memories, like all our memories, help shape who she is. How do Gena's memories—and her lack of memories when she forgets—shape her character? How are we all shaped by our experiences and memories? What other things besides memory shape our characters?

2. Because of the perfect memory storage of her Links, Gena is afraid of forgetting (and with good reason). But she also learns that some form of forgetting can be helpful. What are the pros and cons of forgetting? Are you afraid of forgetting, or do you think it's a necessary part of the human existence?

3. Gena's anxiety makes her afraid to trust herself and her own feelings. Do you agree with Kalan that sometimes our feelings tell us truths we can't see with our heads? Why do you think Gena was able to learn to trust herself and her feelings in the end, even though her anxiety was still a struggle for her?

4. Why do you think the Mementi in Gena's town were able to overcome their differences to create their Mementi community? Why was it so difficult for them to overcome other differences with the Populace and include them in their community? Discuss parallels to our modern world with diverse groups who struggle or succeed in working together.

5. Gena's family relationships are complicated, but they are important to her—even when she learns her family has hurt her. Why do you think she was willing to fight so hard for those relationships? Do you think forgiveness and healing is a possibility even after betrayal? What changes

need to be made in Gena's family for them to continue with better relationships?

6. Kalan says that "nice doesn't mean a thing." How are politeness and outward expressions of being nice different than being truly kind? Does that mean being polite has no worth at all?

7. Gena says that "even good choices can have consequences." Do you think Gena made the right choice in destroying the SLS machine because of the harm it could cause, when it could also have possibly done some good? Are there times, as Gena says, when there is "only one right thing to do?" How do you determine what choices are good or bad? What would you have chosen in Gena's place?

8. Many of the technologies in Gena's world have both positive and negative consequences—the Memor-X gene therapy, the SLS devices, the Chameleon injections, etc. Many characters (Gena, Ren, their father, Detective Jackson, and Drake Matthews) have different views on how far technology should be allowed to go. Is technology always worth the risk, to continue to improve lives? How do we determine the line where technology has gone too far and needs to be stopped?

9. The real Liza Woods (not Drake Matthews impersonating her) did some terrible things, including stealing the first set of Links. But she also donated Memos to help people with diseases that affected their memories. Gena says she "didn't want evil Liza Woods to do good things." What do you think she meant by that? Why do you think people who make wrong or hurtful decisions can also choose to help and do good? How do we define someone as "good" or "bad?"

10. Different people in the book view their memories, their ability to share them, their inability to forget, and the vulnerability of their memories in different ways. If you were Mementi, how would you feel about the way your memories work? In what ways would it be an advantage or disadvantage in your own life? How would you live as a Mementi?

11. When the Populace and Mementi begin to fight, Gena says they were "eaten up by fear until they'd forgotten who they were." Especially in the Mementi who cannot forget, what do you think Gena meant? How are fear and violence connected?

12. Gena tells Ren that even though she was guilty of stealing Links, she wasn't to blame for the townspeople turning on each other. Do you think that's true, or does Ren still bear part of the blame? Which side was more to blame for the violence—the Mementi or the Populace? How do we determine who is at fault in any conflict—and is it necessary to do so?

13. Each of the chapters is headed by a quote from Alfred, Lord Tennyson's In Memoriam. Pick a quote/chapter. How do the quotes relate to the events, themes, or characters in that chapter?

14. The ending of the book was not wrapped up in a "happily ever after." Do you find the ending tragic, hopeful, frustrating, etc.? Why do you think the author chose to end the book this way? What impact does it have on the story as a whole?